Texas Reckless

Also by Gerry Bartlett

Texas Lightning
Texas Trouble

The Texas Heat Series
Texas Heat
Texas Fire
Texas Pride

Texas Reckless

Gerry Bartlett

LYRICAL PRESS
Kensington Publishing Corp.
www.kensingtonbooks.com

LYRICAL PRESS BOOKS are published by

Kensington Publishing Corp.
119 West 40th Street
New York, NY 10018

All Kensington titles, imprints, and distributed lines are available at special quantity discounts for bulk purchases for sales promotion, premiums, fund-raising, educational, or institutional use.

Special book excerpts or customized printings can also be created to fit specific needs. For details, write or phone the office of the Kensington Sales Manager: Kensington Publishing Corp., 119 West 40th Street, New York, NY 10018. Attn. Sales Department. Phone: 1-800-221-2647.

Lyrical Press and Lyrical Press logo Reg. US Pat. & TM Off.

First Electronic Edition: December 2019
eISBN-13: 978-1-5161-0717-9
eISBN-10: 1-5161-0717-9

First Print Edition: December 2019
ISBN-13: 978-1-5161-0720-9
ISBN-10: 1-5161-0720-9

Printed in the United States of America

Chapter One

Rhett Hall was driving too fast and he knew it. Like he was running away. *Oh, hell no.* He eased off the accelerator. He'd been ready to leave Austin anyway. See more of Texas. So he'd taken off down the first side road he'd come to. Now he was lost and he didn't give a good goddamn. Not after what had happened with the hot tattoo artist he'd left behind. Dumped. For the first time in his sorry-ass life.

He glanced at the speedometer. He was pushing ninety again. Lucky for him Texas had generous speed limits. He was on the open road, enjoying the powerful engine in the rented Corvette.

The blur of something crossing in front of him came out of nowhere. He slammed on the brakes but not soon enough. Whatever it was crashed into the car. He fought to keep out of a creek bed coming up on his right and steered left toward a gravel drive. By the time he rocked to a stop, steam poured from the smashed front end of the car. Busted radiator.

Rhett turned off the engine and climbed out to see what he'd hit. A deer lay in the road. Shit. He'd killed Bambi. His sister Scarlett would be crying. He felt pretty bad about it himself. He looked both ways, then hurried over to make sure it was dead. Yep. Dead as a doornail, his dad would say. He grabbed its front legs and dragged it out of the road before it caused another wreck. Then he walked back to the once beautiful car. It might as well have joined the deer in heaven.

He picked up his cell from the front seat. No signal. And not another car in sight. Where the hell was he? The only thing he remembered about that little town with the obscenely low speed limit was that it had one of the biggest Chevy dealerships he'd ever seen, mostly stocked with pickups.

He'd left it about ten minutes ago. At the speed he'd been traveling as soon as he'd blown past the city limits, that was way too far to walk.

At least he'd crashed in front of an impressive stone entrance surrounding an iron gate. There was a call button. He punched it and waited. No answer. Of course not. This was not his day, his week or even his month. The fence on either side of the gate was topped with barbed wire so he'd leave that alone. He had no choice but to climb over the gate. Eight feet. No big deal for a man who worked out.

Well, usually. Since he'd been in Texas most of his workouts had been with Casey—bike riding, hiking and activities of the horizontal variety. Damn, he didn't need to think about how great that had been. As it was he'd never be able to forget her, thanks to the tattoo circling his left bicep. He'd been a sucker for l—lust, not love. He wouldn't admit to that. Not when he'd been kicked to the curb.

He pocketed his keys and his cell phone and took a running jump at the gate. When he got a good hold of the top rung, he swung a leg over, cursing when he heard a rip. Of course he had on the wrong pants for gymnastics. Now he'd be showing his jewels when he got to wherever this driveway led. He dropped down on the other side and brushed his stinging hands on his thighs.

The gravel drive was long with a gentle rise. He couldn't see what he assumed would be a ranch house at the end of it. Brown-and-white cattle grazed on either side of him, held back by more barbed wire. In the distance, buzzards flew over something. Wouldn't be long before they discovered Bambi. He didn't want to think about that.

There were trees scattered around, and most of the cows clustered under their shade. It was hot for May and he was already feeling it. In the distance, oil wells pumped. Perfect Texas scene. He pulled out his phone to remember this with a picture. He'd just stepped on a rock next to the fence for a better angle when he heard hoofbeats. A horse thundered toward him down the drive, its rider wearing a cowboy hat.

Rhett stayed where he was. He was a trespasser and didn't know how this rancher would feel about it. He kept his hands out by his sides and a smile on his face, then started to step down from the rock. He figured he'd say something stupid like "I come in peace."

"Don't move!" The rider pulled out a rifle and aimed it at him.

"Hey!" Rhett froze. Move? Holy crap. Was he going to be killed for jumping onto private property? He waved his phone. "I was just taking a picture. Instagram?" He eased his foot off the rock.

"I said don't move!"

The rifle shot was so loud and close, Rhett fell back. Dirt and rock kicked up inches from his right foot and instinct made him grab the wire fencing with both hands. Shit. The metal barbs bit into his palms.

"All right. Now jump off the rock and come toward me. Fast. In case that thing has friends." The rider slid off the horse, gun still aimed in his direction.

"Thing?" Rhett peeled his wounded hands off the wire and jumped, staggering a little before he hurried in her direction. Yeah, he could see now. The shooter was a woman. She took off her straw cowboy hat and wiped her brow with her sleeve, holding her rifle easily in her other hand.

"Look at what you almost stepped on." She gestured with the gun.

"God." It was a snake. Or what was left of one. She'd blown its head off.

"Rattler. Might be a nest of them under there. They like to sleep under rocks like that during the heat of the day." She frowned at him. "What were you doing climbing over my gate?"

Rhett's heart pounded and he had to take a minute. "Uh, car trouble. Tried the call button but nobody answered."

"Saw you on the camera. You didn't wait very long before you went into business for yourself." She nodded toward the phone Rhett had dropped when he'd grabbed the wire. "Did you call for help?"

"Couldn't get cell service." He knew he should go after his phone, but then if the snake had a family over there...

"There's a dead zone outside the gate. Reception's a problem around here." To his shame she didn't hesitate, just walked over, limping slightly in her well-worn cowboy boots. She carefully skirted the rock then plucked the phone out of the grass. Quick-stepping toward him, she wiped it on her jeans.

"For a minute there, I thought *I* was in a dead zone." Rhett forced a laugh. At least he hadn't wet his pants, but it had been a near thing. Tough guy. Easy to fake in the pages of the fiction he wrote. Facing a rifle? He swallowed, sure he was still pale.

"Sorry if I scared you, shooting like that. You okay?" She handed the phone to him with a smile.

"Now that I know you weren't shooting at me..." Rhett gingerly stuffed the phone in his pocket, then found a smile for her, too. "Rhett Hall." He offered his hand.

She looked at it and frowned. "You're bleeding. I'll help you take care of that back at the house. My fault. I scared you into grabbing that wire. I really am sorry." She touched her fingers to his sleeve. "Sierra MacKenzie.

What kind of car trouble? You need gas? A tire changed? We can handle that here."

"It's worse than that. I hit a deer. It ran right in front of me. I killed it and it killed the front end of my car." He shook his head, fascinated by this woman who could shoot like that and had an air of femininity that he couldn't miss. Her flowered shirt tucked into those worn jeans showed off a nice figure. She had blue eyes that looked him over from head to toe. It made him aware of how he didn't fit in here. Not yet, anyway.

She started to say something when there was a honk from the other side of the gate. "Company." She glanced at her watch. "You're obviously blocking my gate." She pulled out a device clipped to her waistband then hit a button, and the gate slowly opened. "We'll have to do something about that."

Rhett followed her as she led the horse out of the way and dropped the reins. He hadn't thought about blocking anything when he'd come to a stop, just happy to avoid that creek bed. Now a van sat on the shoulder of the road, motor running. Half a dozen kids hung out of the windows, staring at his car.

"Oh, you really did a number on it." She left the horse, which stayed obediently while she walked up to the van driver. The man was out of his vehicle, looking over the Corvette. "What do you think, Dale?"

"Needs a tow. Call Will. He'll be careful pulling her in." The man stared at Rhett.

"Will?" Rhett introduced himself. He showed his bloody palms when Dale extended his hand.

"What happened?" Dale frowned at Rhett's wounded hands.

"Never mind that." Sierra turned to Rhett. "Put the car in neutral. Will it hurt too much if you steer while Dale and I push this thing out of the way? Inside the fence."

"I think I can manage. Who's Will?" Rhett opened the car door.

"Will's the owner of the Chevy dealership in town. If you drove through Muellerville, you saw it." Dale took up a position behind the car. "He loves Corvettes. He'll treat it right."

"I saw that dealership. Couldn't miss it." Rhett didn't like the idea of Sierra pushing while he didn't do much more than steer, but he was in no position to argue. His hands were killing him. It was torture enough gripping the steering wheel carefully with his fingertips. Soon she and Dale had the car inside the gate and out of the way.

"Dale, mind taking Rhett up to the house with the kids? He can use the house phone to call Will." Sierra stepped up to the van door. "Now I wonder who is going to ride with me up to the barn. Any volunteers?"

There was a chorus of "me," but she finally picked a skinny little girl who looked like a brisk wind would blow her away. Sierra quickly put her up in front of her on the horse and they rode away.

"Guess you're stuck with me." Rhett settled in behind the driver next to a quiet little boy. He had dark circles under his eyes, like he had allergies or a sleep problem. His foot never stopped jiggling. It made Rhett wonder about this van loaded with kids. It had a school district logo on the side. Did they have special needs or was she doing charity work? He smiled at the boy. "You excited about riding?"

"It's okay." The boy stared solemnly out the window. A buzzard had moved in and was picking at the snake carcass. "What's that?" He pointed at it.

"Sierra shot that snake. She said it was a rattlesnake. I stood on a rock to take a picture then almost stepped on it." Rhett shook his head. "I come from a city back east. Boston. This is all new to me. What about you?"

"I grew up around here. I know better than to mess with a rattlesnake." He frowned at Rhett. "Sierra's a good shot, then."

"Yes. She scared the, uh, stuffing out of me." Rhett saw a low-slung ranch house straight ahead. It was nice, well kept, with a gleaming pool next to it. There were several outbuildings, including a big barn and a corral with horses in it. Sierra came toward them with the little girl holding her hand. The woman was still limping. Had she hurt herself recently or was it a permanent limp? She slapped her hat against her thigh, her cotton shirt pulling against full breasts. She wore her blond hair short, framing a face dominated by those big blue eyes. She stopped to say something to the girl then looked up at him. Whatever she said made the child giggle. Making fun of the Yankee? Wouldn't be the first time since he'd arrived in Texas. He could take it.

* * * *

"You telling her how you scared the, hmm, stuffing out of me when you shot that snake?"

"Stuffing? That's one word for it." Sierra *had* just described the scene to Cindy. She shouldn't laugh. But he'd turned so pale when he'd grabbed that barbed wire, not even flinching when it had cut into his palms. She owed him another apology, she really did.

"Very funny." He shook his head. "I'm grateful, but a little warning would have been nice."

"You're lucky I settled for shooting the snake. You did climb over my front gate. How was I to know what you were after? In fact, I still don't know if it was smart letting you stay here." It aggravated Sierra that she had to be suspicious of strangers, but things had been happening lately that had made her cautious. "We have security for a reason."

"You saw my car. You think I killed Bambi on purpose?" He held out his hands as if they were proof of his innocence. "You want me to go stand in the heat next to my car and wait for a tow? I can take my bleeding hands right on down the road. Might be hard to climb back over that gate, but I can probably make it." He stared down at his palms. "I wonder if my tetanus shot is up to date. But what do you care? I might be dangerous."

Sierra could swear he was hiding a smile as he looked at her through some damned long lashes. What color were his eyes? Green? Hazel?

"Yes, you might be. Of course, I'm armed. Are you?" She looked him up and down. Bad idea. He was tall and built. Exactly her type. No, she wasn't supposed to be noticing that.

"You want to frisk me?" His arms were out again. "It would be my pleasure. Go ahead. Check me for hidden weapons." This time he didn't hide his smile.

"I think I'll take the kids on down to the barn." Dale the van driver looked back and forth between them. "Sierra, I'll see you down there when you're ready to ride." He herded the children ahead of him. "I talked to Darrel. He said there's a new calf and a foal. Let's go see the baby horse, kids! I wonder if it looks like its mama." That got a cheer from the crowd and they hurried away.

"You might as well come inside. You need to clean and disinfect your hands. Barbed wire can be dangerous. You may need a tetanus shot if you haven't had one lately." Sierra didn't like the fact that she sounded surly. All she needed was a lawsuit from this city slicker in loafers and no socks.

"It hurts like hell, too. But, don't worry, I just remembered—I've had my shots. I won't be suing you." He grinned at her like she should be charmed. He reminded her of one of her brother's friends in Houston, the kind Mason kept trying to set her up with for a date. Definitely the city-guy type—tall, toned and neatly pressed in something he'd probably picked up at Neiman's. He looked like he was ready for a cookout at the ranch. *Spare me.*

"Gee, thanks. I'm sure you would have a strong case. Seeing as how you were trespassing at the time." Sierra shook her head. "Look. I'm sorry

I scared you, but it was a shoot first, talk later situation. You'd be in a world of hurt if I'd let that rattler strike." Sierra pushed into the kitchen. "Sit down. I'll get the first aid kit."

"I'm sorry about the deer. It was a beautiful animal. I tried to stop, but I was going too fast and it came out of nowhere." He settled at the kitchen island, his bloody hands out in front of him, palms up.

"It happens. Deer are fast. Nothing you can do when they take a notion to run in front of you." She liked the fact that he'd appreciated the deer's beauty. Points for him. "The car's front end looked bad. That'll take a while to repair." She soaked a cotton ball in hydrogen peroxide and started dabbing at the mess on his palms. He hissed at the pain. "Sorry."

"That's okay. I can take it. Keep going." He hissed again. "Distract me. Tell me about this ranch. Is it yours?"

"Yep. It was my family's ranch. My dad left it to my brothers, mother and me. They insisted on signing it over to me after he died. So I run it now. It used to be our vacation home but now it's my permanent one." She finished cleaning the left hand and started on the right. Why had she told him all of that? None of his business. But he kept listening and it had just spilled out.

"Big responsibility."

"For a woman?" She looked at him suspiciously. Was he like the majority of men she met around here? The type who thought she needed someone to lean on, to take over for her?

"I wouldn't dare say that. I have a mama who taught me better. The way you rode up toting that gun? I'd say you can handle anything life throws at you." He grinned at her.

"You'd better believe it." She didn't want to like him, but she did. He had strong hands. He must play a sport or do some sort of workout that kept him in shape. She caught him staring at her. Time for her to ask the questions.

"What are you doing in Texas? Your accent says you're not from around here."

"And I try so hard to fit in." He jerked when she began to dab on antibiotic ointment. It was messy, especially since she used it liberally. She planned to wrap his hands in bandages.

"So where's home?" She kept dabbing until both palms were covered. Then she reached for some gauze.

"Boston. My sister moved to Austin for work last fall and I came to visit. She had some trouble, but when that finally got settled I decided to stay and see more of Texas. I'm a writer, doing research for my next book." He seemed fascinated by the way she held his hand as she wound the gauze around and around then taped the thing together. "Neat job."

"Thanks. What do you write?" Sierra started on the other palm. When she looked up, she caught him staring, interested, at the way she dealt with his wounds. That explained things. He was taking mental notes. He'd seen her limping. How long would it take for him to ask the inevitable question? She knew what had happened but not why. If she did, she'd feel a lot better about settling for her life the way it was now—how she walked with what her dad had called a hitch in her giddyap.

"Mysteries. Thrillers. I like to solve puzzles. Sometimes I find a little local story gets my juices flowing." He grinned when Sierra dropped his hand. "You know what I mean. My creative juices."

"Sure. You drove through Muellerville, judging by the direction your car was facing when you landed in my driveway." Sierra began gathering her supplies and stuffing them into the battered first aid tin. "Did that place look like a hotbed of mystery?"

"You never know." He stood when she got up to put the tin away in the pantry. "Tell me, Sierra MacKenzie, do you have any secrets? Any mysteries you'd like solved? I feel like I owe you. You did save my life today."

Sierra felt him close behind her. He was masculine, good looking and so sure of himself that she wanted to scare him again, just for the hell of it. Secrets? She had plenty. And, yes, there was a mystery here, and she almost wept at the offer on the table. Help. From an outsider who might actually see things she'd missed. No one had ever taken her suspicions seriously. An accident. Of course they all said it had been an accident that left her stumping around like Peg Leg Pete. But she'd never been satisfied with that answer. Never.

She turned and faced him, startled that he was so close. In her space. He'd quit smiling, clearly feeling like he was onto something. So he had instincts. Good to know.

"I have kids waiting for me in the barn. The phone is right there on the counter. Will's Big State Chevy Dealership is your best bet, or call Triple A if that's your preference. You can always check Information for those numbers. I'll be back in an hour or you can find me out there. The barn is big and brown; you can't miss it."

He just kept staring at her, so damned close. "About that mystery."

She forced a smile. "Take care of your car. Right now, I can't let those kids down. They have enough problems without my disappointing them." She took off like her tail was on fire. He was looking at her with such intensity, she couldn't handle it. But she made herself stop at the back door and turn around.

"Oh, Rhett, there's a sewing kit next to the first aid tin in the pantry. You might want to use it while I'm gone." She looked him up and down, stopping at his zipper. "Not a good day to go commando, bud." With that she turned on her heel and headed out, biting back a grin. The look on his face!

Men. She wasn't good with them. They always got the better of her. What had she been thinking even inviting him up to the house? She had a satellite phone and could have called Will on the spot for a tow for this handsome stranger. But, no, she'd pulled Rhett in and now she was thinking... Stupid. How could she possibly get answers after all these years? But she had to try. Because the questions just wouldn't go away, damn it.

Step one. Call someone who could help.

Chapter Two

Rhett stared after Sierra as the back door slammed. Really? She'd noticed that rip in his pants but had never said a word until her parting shot. He bet she did have a few secrets. The idea of prying them out of her made him smile.

"You want to shuck those pants and let me sew them up? Or will you do it?" An amused voice behind him made him wheel around.

The woman who stood in the kitchen doorway grinned like she couldn't wait to see him bare assed. She was probably in her sixties, though her dark hair didn't have a hint of gray. She picked up a wooden spoon as if she might use it on him if he made a run for it or at her. His mama had taught him early that one used right could hurt like hell. But the twinkle in her eyes made him stop. Oh, hell, he was flashing her.

"Uh, excuse me?"

"Did you really think Sierra would leave you alone in her house? A perfect stranger? I'm Rachel Devine, her housekeeper." She laughed when he moved his hands protectively over his crotch. "Look at your hands! That girl does love her gauze. She called me from the barn and told me what happened to your car. Of course I heard what she just said, too." Another husky laugh. "You'll have a heck of a time stitching wrapped like that. Go on in the bathroom and hand out those pants. I'll sew 'em up quick as a wink. You can pull on a towel if you feel like coming out and joining me for a cup of coffee."

"Thanks, Ms. Devine. Coffee sounds good after the morning I just had. I was wondering how I could even thread a needle with my hands mummified." Rhett tried to wiggle his fingers. No luck. "I can sew a little.

My mama believed men should be self-sufficient. Though I never did get the hang of making gravy."

"I think I'd like your mama. Call me Rachel; everyone does." She pulled another tin box out of the pantry. "This won't take but a minute. There's a towel in the closet in there."

"Be right out." In the bathroom, Rhett struggled to shuck his pants then pulled out the biggest towel he could find. The steaming cup of coffee was on the table when he came out with his pants under his arm. Rachel stitched while he found out that Sierra was teaching the kids out in the barn to ride because they had been referred by their teachers.

"She's an expert on what they call horse therapy. My own grandson is one of them kids. Breaks my heart that he needs something like that." She bit off the thread and shook out his pants. "All done."

"That was quick. Thanks." Rhett's curiosity kept him pinned in his seat. "Horse therapy. How does that work?"

"Beats me. Some of the kids need to calm down, like my Billy. That boy just can't sit still in class. Drives his parents crazy, teachers too. Then there's his temper. Flies off the handle at the drop of a hat. Working with horses seems to soothe him. Of course if you asked him, he'd say he only comes out here to see me. Which I'm fine with. His daddy and I don't get along. Man can be an asshole. But my daughter loves him for some reason, has since right after high school." She sighed and picked up her own coffee cup. "Other young'uns out there are too quiet. Some have a bad history. Sierra's got a world of patience. She seems to know just how to handle them. I sure couldn't do it."

"That's a real talent." Rhett sipped his coffee, wanting to hear more.

Rachel leaned in. "It is. You should see her with them. Of course the horses are real gentle. Caring for them, riding them, seems to make the kids forget their cares." Rachel pulled a tissue from her apron pocket. "Danged if I can figure out what Billy's cares are or why he's so angry all the time. He's got everything a little boy could want. Except a daddy who knows how to hold his own temper. Could be Billy just takes after Will. Nothing we can do about that."

"I'm no expert on kids. Maybe the boy will find a different role model. Someone who can help him learn to control his temper. Like Sierra and this therapy she's doing." Rhett leaned back. "I was a handful when I was growing up. Had a sister and was out to prove I was all boy. Know what I mean?" Rhett saw her eyes fill. She was a sturdy-looking woman who seemed to have her act together. Obviously, though, her grandson was a big concern. It reminded him of how his own grandmother had fussed over him decades ago.

He patted her hand. "Hey, my mama sent me to summer camp as a last resort when I was twelve. She was sure I'd end up arrested if I didn't get away from the crowd I was running with." He smiled. "I came back ready to take school seriously. The worst of my friends had found other pals and didn't like my new attitude. I ended up going to college and am able to make a decent living doing something I love."

Rachel stared at him. "Summer camp. Will could afford it, one with horses, but he'd never consider it coming from me. I'll put the idea to my girl, Billy's mama, and see what she thinks about it."

"Worth a try. I fell in love with horses that summer. Maybe what Sierra is doing will be enough to show Billy his attitude needs adjusting. Like mine did." Horse therapy. It sounded interesting. Might fit into a book...

"That's what I keep hoping. That he'll outgrow whatever is bothering him." She sniffed. "I don't know why I'm spilling my guts to you, a stranger. You're a good listener."

"So are you. I don't tell just anyone about my wild youth." Rhett was relieved when she got up to put that sewing kit away. A woman's tears undid him every time.

"Well, thanks for telling me about it. You give me hope. Where are you from? You talk more like a Yankee than a Texan." She stared at him.

"Boston. My sister moved to Austin and I came here to visit. Now I'm seeing the rest of Texas." He got up. "I'd better see about the car."

"Texas is a big place. It'll take you a while. And you'll need a good car. A reliable one." She picked up the house phone. "While you put on your pants, I'll call the Chevy dealership for you. Will owns the place. He may not like me, but he'll probably want to run this tow in himself. Sierra said you drive a Corvette, and Will does love Corvettes. There isn't much call for them out here. They aren't practical for ranch country."

"You're probably right. Maybe I should think about that. The Corvette is a rental. Thanks, I'd appreciate the call. Tell him I'll call the rental company myself and make sure it's okay." Rhett stood, careful to keep his towel in place. By the time he was dressed and in the kitchen again, Rachel was pulling things out of the refrigerator.

"It'll be a while. Saturday is a busy day at the dealership. I was right, Will wants to handle your car himself. You might as well stay for lunch. We roast hot dogs out by the pool for the kids before they leave. I don't think Sierra will object if you join in."

"Sounds good. What if I go out to the barn and watch the therapy session?" Rhett was really curious.

"Don't get too close to the kids. Some of them are mighty skittish." Rachel looked him over. "Mind your shoes. She keeps a clean barn, but you never know what you might step in close to the corrals."

"Right. When I left Austin this morning, I had no idea I'd end up on a working ranch or I would have worn boots and jeans." Rhett took his empty cup to the sink. "Thanks for the coffee. See you at lunch." Boots and jeans. He had the jeans but needed to buy boots while he was in Texas. It was on his list of things to do here. He headed for the barn. Big and brown. It *was* impossible to miss.

* * * *

Sierra had been afraid this would happen ever since they'd started work today. Billy had been in a mood, sullen and looking for a fight. Cindy had been happy and eager to get going. The other children were further along in their therapy, so after they'd worked with the horses for a while she could hand them off to the two men she had trained to help her. José and Brian had settled the kids on their mounts and walked their own horses alongside them toward the pond. It was at the end of one of their favorite trails, where they could watch the ducks. She had no trouble getting Cindy mounted and ready to ride.

Then it was Billy's turn. He knew his grandmother was working in the house. He clearly wanted to go inside and sit with her. First he'd fussed about his helmet, complaining that the chin strap was too tight. Now he refused to get on his horse.

Sierra wasn't going to put up with that. He liked to ride, but he was trying to take control of the situation. Was he still brooding over the fact that she'd picked Cindy to ride with her earlier instead of him? Sierra stayed calm, determined to be patient. She'd dealt with kids like Billy before.

"Billy, you are wasting time when we could be on our way to see the ducks. I have corn in my saddlebags. Don't you want to help feed them?"

"I don't give a shit about those nasty ducks." He kicked dirt at Sierra.

"Language!" She took a breath. He had just missed her bad leg. If he hit her, all bets were off. "One more outburst like that and you won't get lunch with the rest of us. Your grandma will be so disappointed if you have to stay in the barn, mucking out stalls, while the rest of us enjoy the pool and hot dogs."

"Come on, Billy. I'm ready to go." Cindy spoke up, unusual for her.

Sierra watched Billy's face turn red. He swung a fist and hit Cindy's foot in her stirrup, which made her horse shy away from him. Sierra was holding the reins, so the horse couldn't bolt, but the sudden movement and the hit terrified the fragile child. Her scream pierced the air.

"What's going on?" Rhett ran into the barn just as Billy pulled back his arm to take another swing.

"Billy, no!" Sierra put herself between the boy and Cindy.

"Stop right there." Rhett grabbed the boy with both hands, pulling him off his feet. "Who were you going to hit? A little girl? Miss Sierra? Or the horse?" He walked a kicking and screaming Billy back toward the barn door.

"Let me go. Put me down, you bastard." Billy kept kicking, trying to connect with Rhett's shins with his boot heels while digging at the man's arms with both hands. His hard helmet was doing a number on Rhett's chest as he banged his head into it. That had to hurt.

"Watch that potty mouth. Your grandmother would be so ashamed. I just met that nice lady. Bet she has a bar of soap up there with your name on it, Billy." Rhett just held on, seemingly impervious to the beating he was taking. Gripping the struggling youngster had to hurt his bandaged hands. "Now calm down and I'll set you on your feet. I won't let you go, though, until I'm sure you're not going to hit anyone else." He looked at Sierra, who had a sobbing Cindy in her arms. "How's the little girl?"

"Upset. But she'll be fine once we get to the duck pond, won't you, Cindy?" Sierra brushed the girl's fine blond hair back from her face.

Cindy finally quit crying. "Maybe. Can we go now? Leave Billy here. He's mean! I hate him!"

"No, Billy needs to come with us. Don't you, Billy?" Sierra gave the boy a hard look. "If you don't, I will have to discontinue these visits, permanently. Is that what you want?" She saw him struggle against Rhett's hold, his furious look finally disappearing in favor of a thoughtful one. She knew he looked forward to these Saturdays. His father worked every weekend and his mother? Well, Sally Ann spent more time shopping than mothering Billy. He did like to ride, she knew it. And to come here to see Rachel.

"All right, I'll get on the stupid horse. Let me go." He quit trying to pry himself loose and raised his hands. "Please."

"Now that's more like it. What if I ride with you? Is that allowed?" Rhett smiled at Sierra. "I may look like a city slicker, but I took riding lessons as a kid. I enjoyed it. Can I saddle a mount?" He looked around the barn. "I see some extra horses still in their stalls."

"What about your hands? Think you can handle the reins like that?" Sierra nodded at where she'd gone nuts with the gauze. *Nerves.* He'd been staring at her, checking her out while she'd worked on him.

"I think so." To her shock, he ripped off the tape and unwrapped his hands. He showed her his palms. "Look. No bleeding. I won't claim they don't hurt, but I'll live." He rolled up the gauze and stuck it in his pocket. "Might as well give it a shot."

"Tough guy, huh?"

"You'd better believe it." He winked. "Now, what do you think? Going to trust me on one of your horses to ride alongside this kid?"

"All right. But don't expect sympathy if you start bleeding again. Or more hand-holding." Sierra gestured to one of her men who'd been standing by, watching the show. She'd talk to him about that later. He should have stepped in when Billy got physical instead of letting Rhett, a stranger, handle it.

"Darrel, please saddle up Blanco for the gentleman. Cindy, let's go into the bathroom and wash your face." She led the girl to the washroom and helped her scrub the tears from her cheeks.

Soon they were mounted again. This time Billy got on without a hassle and with a hand from Rhett. Then Rhett checked the saddle, girth and stirrups on his mount like he knew what he was doing, something she approved of. She tossed him an extra hat they kept on a rack in the barn.

"It's hot out there. Best keep your head covered. Sunstroke would just add to your misery." She had to smile at the way he was holding his reins gingerly. Acting tough wasn't easy. His palms had to hurt.

"Thank you, ma'am." He just shoved the battered hat on his head. He should have looked ridiculous. Instead, he grinned and she realized the old Stetson made him seem to fit in.

"Sierra, before you go?" Darrel, the ranch hand, stood close to her horse. "I need to warn you, found two more dead this morning. Not far from that pasture you were worried about."

Sierra glanced at the children. "I saw the buzzards. We'll talk about this later. Call the vet. We need to figure out the cause."

"Yes, ma'am. If he can from what's left." Darrel flushed at her meaningful glance at Cindy. "I mean, sure. I'll drive a truck out there and pick up the, uh, remains right now. Already called Doc Cibrowski."

"Thanks, Darrel." Luckily Cindy didn't seem to be listening. She was too worried about keeping her horse under control. But Sierra could see that Rhett hadn't missed a thing. He'd be full of questions; she didn't doubt that. She had some of her own. Who or what was killing her cattle? She'd lost a half dozen head in the last two weeks, now two more. She suspected poison. But where were the cattle picking up anything poisonous? Time for her to pay for an autopsy. Which wouldn't be cheap. She'd also call the sheriff again. Sheriff Myra Watkins needed to take her seriously.

The children were waiting and the horses were getting restless. She urged Ranger forward, Rhett and Billy falling in behind. She glanced back. Blanco was a big, steady horse and she was relieved to see Rhett handling him with ease. Rhett Hall was way too charming. Because otherwise she'd never have let a stranger ride out with her children. She would watch him every minute. Parents trusted her with these troubled kids. If he made one wrong move...

She almost turned back then and there. It would be the responsible thing to do. But for some of these children this outing was the one bright spot in their week. Thank goodness she'd gotten a phone call back while they'd been saddling up. Her contact had done a quick check on this guy. He really was a famous author. Clean record. So at least he wasn't a pedophile in disguise. She shuddered. The very idea that someone like that could have climbed her gate made her glance over her shoulder again.

"So where are we going?" Rhett called.

"We have a pond in a pasture not far from here where a family of ducks makes their home. The kids like to feed them." Sierra reached out to touch Cindy's leg when she saw her trembling. "Cindy, are you okay? What's the matter?"

"Billy's gonna hit me again. I don't like him. Who is that man? I don't know him." Tears filled her big blue eyes.

"Now Cindy, I won't let anyone touch you. I swear it. That man is Mr. Rhett. He helped with Billy, didn't he? You don't need to be scared of him." Sierra sensed Rhett listening to every word. She knew Cindy had been abused by her father, who was no longer in the picture. "But Mr. Rhett will stay far away from you if that's what you want." She gave Rhett a warning look.

"Yes, please," Cindy said in a very small voice as she knuckled the tears from her cheeks.

* * * *

Rhett pulled back on the reins to make even more space between them and the girl and Sierra.

"You don't have to worry, Cindy. Billy and I will stay away from you since that's what you want. Won't we, Billy?" Rhett turned to the boy. Billy just stared at Sierra and Cindy, his face unreadable. "What do you say?"

"Whatever."

Rhett wasn't happy with that answer but decided to let it go. "You ride very well, Billy. I'm feeling muscles I forgot I had. It's been a long time since I sat on a horse."

"I don't need a babysitter." Billy tried to move his horse closer to Cindy's mount.

Rhett reached out and grabbed Billy's reins, pulling his horse to a stop. Damn, that hurt. Maybe taking off the gauze had been stupid. "What's your problem? Are you determined to start trouble? You heard what Cindy just said. We're staying back. She doesn't want me close and she sure doesn't want anything to do with you."

"What do I care what she wants?" Billy snatched at his reins. "My problem is you. Who are you, anyway? I never saw you around here before."

"That's a fair question. You saw my car, didn't you? I had a wreck outside Miss Sierra's gate. Hit a deer. She let me come in while I wait for a tow truck." Rhett really wanted to smack some sense into the kid. But he knew better. Sierra had shown tremendous restraint when the brat hit the little girl.

"I didn't notice. Had a game on my phone. What kind of car was it?" Billy looked him over.

Rhett told him.

"Aw man, my dad will be all over that. He loves Corvettes." Billy suddenly looked worried. "He's not coming out here to get it himself, is he?"

"Your dad is Will, right? Owns the Chevy dealership?" Rhett saw Billy's face go pale before he nodded. "Your grandma said he'll be here as soon as he can."

Billy's shoulders sagged. "Of course he'll come. He thinks nobody can handle a Vette but him." He jerked at the reins. "Can we ride on now? I'll stay away from that stupid girl."

"You promise? No more hitting. I can see Miss Sierra has a bad leg. You almost got a piece of it before." Rhett didn't know what he'd said, but the anger seemed to have gone out of the kid. Billy just nodded so he let him go. Sierra and Cindy were pretty far ahead now and he could always catch up if he needed to. Rachel's grandson clearly had issues. The kid was what? Nine? He was acting out with violence and was big for his age. When he got to be a teenager, he could turn into a bully and become a real problem. Rhett hoped whatever this therapy was supposed to do worked, or young Billy here was headed for trouble.

"She doesn't like me," Billy mumbled, but Rhett heard him.

"Who? The little girl?" Rhett leaned closer.

"Miss Sierra. She chose Cindy over me." Billy frowned as he kept his horse moving.

"She could have picked anyone. Cindy was lucky this time. Maybe next time it'll be you." Rhett didn't know a damn thing about kids. Billy just glared at him like he was a moron. "Hey, I met your grandma. She's cool."

"Yeah. I come out here to see her. Otherwise, I'd be home playing games on my computer."

"Oh? What do you like?" Rhett knew a few video games, and the boy began telling him about his favorites, all of them pretty violent. Soon they came to the pond. It was a nice spot surrounded by trees, and sure enough, a family of ducks called it home. When the ducks saw the horses and the kids, they swam to shore, eager for what apparently was a ritual.

"You like feeding the ducks?" Rhett pulled up close to a cluster of trees, away from Cindy and Sierra. He wasn't taking a chance that Billy would blow up again.

"It's okay. We each get a bag of corn to feed them. Wait and see what they do. It's pretty funny." He laughed when Rhett staggered as soon as he hit the ground. "You really are out of shape."

"Told you. I haven't ridden a horse in years." He held out his arms. "I'll help you down."

"Back off. I can do it." To prove it, the boy flung over his leg and leaped off the horse, almost knocking Rhett down. It was a stupid move, and Billy yelped when he landed funny.

"You all right?" Rhett tried to help him up from where he'd fallen.

"Back off, I said. I'm fine." He got to his feet, limping as he headed to where Sierra was handing out small paper bags she pulled from her saddlebags. "Leave me alone."

Rhett followed at a safe distance. He was determined not to limp, but it took a moment for his thigh muscles to quit shaking. Of course his palms screamed. Man! He'd forgotten how much of a workout riding could be. Billy had taken his place in line, waiting his turn for a bag of corn. Each bag had a name written on it in marker.

Sierra smiled at Rhett. "See the names on the bags? We can't have littering. Any one of them leaves a bag, it means cleaning out a horse stall before he or she eats lunch."

"Wow. You're tough." Rhett shook his head when she offered him some corn.

"You have no idea." She moved closer to where the kids had scattered, chattering as they threw corn at the excited ducks. There were some new yellow ducklings guarded by a big mama duck. Billy approached her and squatted down, holding out his hand to show her his corn. To Rhett's amazement, she took it from him, then waddled away. The boy sat back on the grass and watched, not saying a word to the other children.

"He looks sad, doesn't he?" Sierra said quietly to Rhett.

"Yeah. Don't know if that's better than mad or not." He turned and bumped into her. She smelled like fresh air, sunshine and horse. It was surprisingly pleasant and womanly. She didn't back off and he stayed where he was, his arm brushing hers. "You having trouble with your cattle?"

"I can't talk about that now."

She nodded at Billy. "Billy's a complicated kid. I don't know if I'm helping him or not. I guess all I can do is try." She limped over to the other children, stopping to talk to each one.

Rhett admired her shapely behind in her jeans before he walked to the edge of the pond. Watching kids feed ducks. Not exactly the excitement he'd been looking for when he'd left Austin, but it was okay. He was relaxing; that was something. And the place was pretty. This was a side of Texas he hadn't seen before. He'd like to learn more about the ranch. Dead cattle. Sabotage? Disease? If he could stay here a while and pick Sierra's brain, there might be a story in it. He saw cows in the distance and could hear the steady chug of those oil wells pumping. Lots of things to study here.

He noticed Billy had gotten up and had moved closer to the rest of the kids, including Cindy. Was that a good idea? The little girl stood next to the water. If that boy thought he could push her in, he was going to be very sorry. Rhett moved quickly, ready to intervene if needed. But to Rhett's surprise, Billy just handed Cindy the rest of his corn. A peace offering. Maybe there was hope for the boy yet. Or was it a ploy? A way to lull her into trusting him until he could do something hurtful again?

Rhett decided to keep an eye on him. He stayed close to the group until Sierra announced it was time to head back for lunch. She'd made each child feel special and now stopped and praised Billy for sharing with Cindy. Oops. The boy frowned, not happy that his moment of weakness had been exposed. Rhett decided that was his cue to get involved.

"Billy, let's see if we can beat everyone back to the barn. What do you say? Can you show me the way? I'm not sure I remember."

"Yeah, let's go. We'll leave these suckers in our dust." Billy made a gesture that had Sierra frowning before he limped over to their horses. He didn't object when Rhett helped him mount this time. Sierra's frown deepened. Did she think Billy's limp mocked her? She probably hadn't seen him fall off the horse. Rhett would explain it over hot dogs. The boy was already on her shit list for things he'd done deliberately.

"Wait for me. I told you, I'm not sure of the way."

"Yeah? Then you'd better hurry, old man." Billy laughed and wheeled his horse while Rhett was still finding his stirrup.

Well, hell. The brat was leaving him in his dust as well. But old Blanco knew his way back to the barn. Rhett nudged his horse faster while he cursed under his breath. Did he really want to learn more about Texas ranches? So far he'd been bested by a kid, had aches and pains in strange places, and a woman had made him feel like a fool when she'd almost shot off his foot. Not exactly stuff he could use as book material. But, then again, he had questions, lots of them. He sure didn't want to move on until he got some answers.

Chapter Three

Sierra was furious as she watched Rhett take off after Billy. The man had no idea how she ran the therapy group and, galloping away in some kind of imaginary race wasn't part of it. At least she was sure Billy had mastered his seat on a horse. But he had so many emotional issues, she didn't like the idea of his being unsupervised anywhere on the ranch. Hopefully Rhett had figured that out.

By the time she got the rest of the children on their mounts and everyone paired up, too much time had elapsed. She dreaded what she'd find when she got to the barn. Caring properly for the horses was an important part of the therapy. If Billy had just left Charley standing after that run, she knew one of her men would see to him, but she'd have to make an example of the boy or the other kids would notice and get ideas. They were already restless, talking about going faster, testing each other. Not a good idea when some of them, like Cindy, were just getting comfortable in the saddle. Sierra breathed a sigh of relief when the barn came in sight.

Inside, she had to take a moment to adjust to the dim interior. She heard Rhett's voice before she spotted him. He was working on Blanco, showing Billy how he'd been taught to brush out his mane. The boy was imitating him, and they seemed to have progressed to the point where the horses were cooled down and ready to be led into their stalls. She saw that the saddles and bridles had been put away.

"Gentlemen." Sierra walked up to Billy. "Billy, you know I don't approve of taking off like you did." No answer.

"I'm sorry, Sierra. My idea." Rhett nodded toward the boy. "I was showing Billy what I remember from my summer camp days. We always put our horses away properly after cooling them down, making sure they were groomed and watered." Rhett shook his head when Billy just kept brushing his horse and didn't say anything.

"Charley does seem to be enjoying your attentions, Billy." She was careful not to touch him. He didn't like it, and that was too bad. If ever there was a child who needed a hug, it was this troubled boy.

Rhett filled in the silence. "You think Billy can go see his grandma now? Maybe he can help her in the kitchen. Get lunch going." Rhett winked at her. "I'll put Charley and Blanco away."

"Can I, Miss Sierra?" Billy whirled around, suddenly coming to life. "Granny can't haul all that stuff out to the pool without help."

"Sure, Billy. Go ahead. Mr. Rhett can put Charley away for you." Sierra laughed when Billy raced past her. But he was running awkwardly. "What's with the limp? Did he hurt himself?"

"Yeah. I think he twisted his ankle jumping off his horse. He was showing off and wouldn't let me help him down. Nothing serious. I looked at it and didn't find any swelling. I told him to let his grandmother see it." Rhett glanced at the other kids, who were busy working with their own horses. "I really am sorry about that racing thing. I was afraid he was going to go after Cindy again. What I know about kids wouldn't fill one of those paper bags you use for corn." Rhett patted his horse. "Forgive me?"

"You shouldn't have taken off like that. All the other students were hot to race after you." Sierra looked away from the appeal in his eyes. When was the last time a man had tried to charm her? Too long. She was letting him get to her. She stepped back. "No harm done. Darrel will show you where to put those horses. I've got to help the other kids. I'll see you out by the pool."

She walked away, very conscious of his eyes on her. If only she didn't look so damned awkward when she walked. But there was no help for it. Four surgeries and she'd called it quits. If it had been up to her daddy, she'd have gone on, trying specialist after specialist until even the doctors would have had to admit she was a lost cause. She had learned to live with it, stuck with a limp that reminded her of one of the worst days of her life.

She got the group organized and the horses put away. She was very aware that Rhett hadn't gone on to the pool but was helping some of the other boys with their horses. It was good to have the help. She'd had to cut back on labor recently, and now they didn't have one-on-one therapy like she wanted. Her family had offered her money to continue some of her special projects like this. She should probably accept it. Helping children filled a hole in her heart.

"Miss Sierra, can we go see the new foal again before lunch?" Cindy had just put her horse in its stall.

"Sure, let's check on it. We need to name him. Think about that." Sierra led the group to the back of the barn where the mare and her baby were kept.

"You have a lot of horses here," Rhett said as they walked.

"Yes, I'm part of a horse rescue organization. What can I say? I can't bear to see a horse abused. If a horse needs a home, no matter what shape it's in, I take it." It was another expense she couldn't afford. But some of the horses were so pitiful...

"Are you crying?" Rhett stood very close.

"Of course not. Hay allergy. It's a real problem when you run a ranch." Sierra backed away from the stall once they got there so the kids could see the foal.

"I don't know. Looks like tears to me." He surprised her by handing her his wad of gauze. "Use this. Very absorbent. I know from experience." He patted her back.

"Yuck." But she looked it over and saw no sign of blood, so she did dab her cheeks with it. "You don't know how rough this mare had it before we rescued her. She came in so malnourished it was a miracle the baby survived to term. Now look at the foal, standing there next to its mama on spindly legs, such a sweet sight. I—I can't stand the way some folks mistreat animals. It makes me so damned mad."

"Language, Miss Sierra." Cindy looked up at her wide-eyed. "I have a name for the baby horse."

"What's that, Cindy?" Sierra sniffed. She had to get hold of herself.

"It's a boy. So it had better fit him."

"I think it fits a boy." Her forehead wrinkled. "Miracle. You always say it's a miracle he lived to be borned. That any of your special horses live. What do you think?"

"It's perfect." Sierra bent down to hug the little girl. "Miracle it is. Thank you, Cindy. Now I think I smell hot dogs grilling. Let's go to the pool." She was ready to go but Darrel stopped her. The vet was here.

"Rhett, would you mind taking the children outside? I'll be there in a few minutes. Ranch business." She hoped her face didn't show her concern. She'd seen the battered ranch truck outside with a tarp covering what had to be the mangled cattle. What would the vet say? The more important question was, who or what might be poisoning her herd? She'd lost eight head in the last two weeks.

"Everything all right?" Rhett touched her hand. "Anything I can do?"

"All right? Not really. You can help by getting the kids to the pool. Please?" She didn't know this man, but she already trusted him.

"You got it." He turned to the five children who stood gazing at the mare and her foal. "I'm hungry. How about you guys? Miss Sierra says we need to go to the pool for lunch. Davy, will you lead the way?" He got them organized and on the move, still careful to give Cindy her space.

"Miss Sierra?" Cindy held back.

"Run along, Cindy, I'll be there in a minute. I have some business with Dr. Cibrowski, the vet. It's important. Save a hot dog for me. Okay?" Sierra made scooting motions with her hands, and the child followed the rest of the group, her shoulders slumping.

"He's out behind the barn. I moved the pickup there. Didn't want the kids to see him with them dead cows." Darrel led the way. "They were torn up bad. Had to yell to get the buzzards off. Pew-ee! Like to tossed my cookies!"

"Thanks, Darrel. Be sure to stop by the pool and pick up some lunch. There's plenty. If you feel like eating after what you had to deal with." Sierra stepped into the bright sunlight. She was glad for her hat but wouldn't have minded a pair of sunglasses. The stench stopped her several feet from the truck.

"Shoot, I can always eat, Miss Sierra. Nothing messes up my appetite." Darrel stayed beside her. "You want me to stick around for this?"

"No, you've done enough. I may have to ask you to bury the carcasses later. Take a break now. Eat lunch. I'll let you know when I need you again." Sierra braced herself as he hurried away, going through the barn, a shortcut to the pool area. She didn't blame him for hurrying. The stink made her want to heave. The vet, Ted Cibrowski, had thrown back the tarp and was examining the remains. He had some plastic bags and a cell phone in his hand, taking pictures before he used a tool to put samples into the bags.

"What do you think, Ted?" He'd actually become a friend, taking her out for coffee a few times. He was fortyish, nice looking and, of course, well educated. But there were no sparks. So when he'd asked her out for dinner, she'd made excuses. He'd gotten the message. Sometimes Sierra wondered if she should have given him more of a chance. Too late. He was engaged now to a teacher at the local high school.

"Darrel said you suspected poison. You're right. Come up here if you can stomach the stench. There's foam around the mouths. These cows ingested something toxic. I need to go out to the site where the bodies were found. Look around. See what they got into. You walk your pastures? Check for dogbane and nightshade? If a cow or horse gets into either of those, they'll die. Just like these did." He looked very serious and upset.

"We inspect our fields regularly. Treat any plants that might spring up that could be toxic to livestock with a safe herbicide." Sierra knew she sounded defensive, but she'd never leave something as dangerous as those plants in a field where cattle or horses grazed. The idea that she would be negligent...

"Calm down. I didn't say it had to be your field or your fault. It could be something else. A poison introduced another way. You have water tanks in the fields where the animals graze? We'll check those. The salt licks too." He helped her up into the bed of the truck. "Easy now, this isn't a pretty sight."

Sierra studied the poor dead animals. The buzzards had done a number on them, yes, but it was also obvious that they'd died from something they'd eaten. That foam. She was determined to stand there and not gag, but it wasn't easy. Finally she jumped down to the ground, glad that Ted followed her, holding her steady with a hand on her elbow when she wobbled.

"Easy now. I'll go out to the field with your hand Darrel. You go on to the pool with the children. Darrel will show me what I need to see. If I run across something suspicious that the sheriff needs to hear about, I'll let you and her know. Okay?" Ted removed his hand, his eyes kind as he put his samples away in the black metal suitcase he used like a doctor's bag.

"You're right. The children are waiting for me to join them. I'll send Darrel to get you. He can take you out there in another truck. Should he go ahead and bury these bodies?" She waved at the carcasses.

"Not yet. I may want the sheriff to see them. Darrel and I can go in my truck." Ted smiled. "I looked in on that foal. Glad to see it's doing well."

"Yes. That's one bright spot around here. We just named him Miracle." Sierra wanted to cry. She really couldn't afford to keep losing cattle. She counted on their sale to support this place.

"Hey, we'll figure this out. Can you think of anyone who would deliberately go after your herd?" Ted frowned at the dead cows. "That is, if this wasn't an accident."

"I have a few ideas. Developers have been after me to sell the place. But this seems extreme." Sierra sighed. "I don't know. Maybe I was careless. Or got so caught up in rescuing my horses, I left pasture maintenance to hands who didn't know a weed from healthy grass."

"Well, wait on my investigation before you jump to that kind of conclusion, okay?" Ted set his case in the back of his truck. "Tell Darrel I'll meet him in front of the house."

"Will do." Sierra thanked him and walked back through the barn. She'd get a bill for this. Another worry. For another day. She heard childish laughter coming from the pool.

Put on a smile. It wasn't easy. At least she had the excuse of going into the house to change into her suit before she had to face anyone. She couldn't linger, though. Responsibilities. They never went away.

* * * *

Rhett stayed next to the pool while Sierra splashed in the shallow end with the kids after dining on hot dogs, chips and ice cream. He'd been offered a pair of swim trunks but had decided to wait in a lounge chair for the tow truck. Besides, he was enjoying the view. Sierra had come out of the house in a one-piece bathing suit that was conservative but still sexy the way it hugged her figure. She supervised the kids, seemingly unaware of the way the suit rode up when she bent over to help a timid Cindy float on her back. Rhett caught Rachel's eyes on him and got a wink. Yeah, he was a dog, thinking what he was thinking.

He stared at the road map of scars on Sierra's left leg. The woman had suffered; that was clear. No wonder she limped. Whatever had happened to her had been serious and painful. She climbed out of the pool and watched the children splashing each other. Then she grabbed a towel and wrapped it around her waist.

"They love this part of the day. Some of them never get a chance to use a pool. It's certainly hot enough for a swim today." She took a bottle of water from Rachel and settled in a chair next to Rhett. "Tow truck should be here soon."

"Guess so." Rhett couldn't take his eyes off her. The sun had given her a healthy glow and she had pushed her wet hair back behind her ears. Her unconscious beauty fascinated him. That and the way she cared so much about the children and her horses.

When her ancient dog ambled up, she ran her hands through his fur.

"You seem to have a soft spot for all animals, except rattlesnakes." Rhett smiled. "Thanks again for saving me earlier. And for letting me go along on the ride. My legs are letting me know it's been too long since I've been on a horse."

"You did well." She leaned back on the lounger, clearly tired. "Thanks for handling Billy. He gave you a good beating with his helmet too." She nodded toward the boy, who was never far from his grandmother's side. He hadn't gone into the water, instead talking nonstop to Rachel.

"I just jumped in. Probably screwed things up. Sorry about that."

"No, you had good instincts."

"Thanks. You know, I'm setting my next book in Texas. This ranch is giving me lots of ideas." Rhett leaned toward her. Okay, time for his pitch. She'd probably shoot him down but what the hell. "The first thing I do when I start a book is research, to get a feel for the place. Sometimes my plot comes from things I find out as I explore the sights and meet people."

"Sounds interesting. But you said you write thrillers. Mysteries. Life is pretty dull around here. Or at least we hope it is." Sierra turned away when one of the kids shouted for her to watch as he did a cannonball off the side of the pool. They both were sprinkled with water when he did the dive. "Good job!"

"The action thriller part comes from here." Rhett tapped his forehead. "Though I'll admit my life got pretty exciting when you almost shot off my foot."

"Did not!" She laughed. "I hit what I aim for."

"I believe that." He leaned closer. Man, did he like her laugh. "Let's just say I have a vivid imagination. But I've been taking in what you've got here. It's fascinating—the horses, oil wells pumping in the background. I want to learn more about it." He thought about taking her hand, but something told him that would be pushing it. He picked up his water bottle, satisfied that she was really listening to him, her eyes on his.

"Really." She watched him drink then licked her lips. It gave him ideas he didn't need to dwell on right now. He was selling a proposition.

"Yes, really. I don't suppose you'd consider letting me stay on for a while. I'd be happy to pay room and board." He put down the bottle then held out his hand, which still stung from his encounter with the barbed wire. "Strictly a business arrangement, you understand."

"Of course." She looked from that wounded hand back into his eyes again, as if reading his earlier thoughts about how she'd look without that stretchy bathing suit. He caught her glancing down to where Rachel had stitched up his pants. Was she remembering what she'd seen? A smile tilted her lips when there was a horn honk.

The driver had returned with the van. Sierra didn't say a thing before she got up and turned to the kids. She announced that playtime was over. There was a scramble for towels and clothes as the children got ready for their ride back to town. Apparently the van would take them to school where their parents would pick them up.

The roar of a tow truck coming up the drive got Rhett out of his lounge chair. What now? Did he just leave and never come back? Sierra hadn't turned him down. But she hadn't said yes either. Was she thinking about it? He was surprised at how reluctant he was to let this go, to say goodbye and forget Sierra MacKenzie.

The tow truck pulled up in front of the house, in the circular drive, and a big man got out. He was in his thirties, about Rhett's age. He wore a polo shirt in black with a red Chevy logo on the pocket and pressed khakis. When he noticed the kids clustered around Sierra, he frowned, then started toward them.

"What the fuck is my kid doing here?" He glanced at the school district van. "Billy! Did you come here with that bunch of—"

"Will Jackson, don't you dare say one more word." Sierra was in his face so fast, Rhett couldn't believe it.

"I didn't give permission for my son to have dealings with your so-called therapy, Sierra MacKenzie." He reached out and grabbed Billy's arm. "In the truck. Now!"

"Daddy, please. Let me stay. Granny will bring me home later." Billy didn't cry, but his face was red. He held on to his grandmother's hand. "Mama signed the papers so I could come."

"Your mama's not in charge in our house. Clearly your grandma was in on this too. Keeping secrets from me. I won't have it! Now shut up and get in the truck!" He snatched the boy from Rachel and shoved him toward the tow truck.

"Will, calm down. You got a customer here. Did you forget that? I can take Billy home later, no problem at all." Rachel moved next to Sierra. "Sierra, the children are getting upset. Why don't you get them loaded into the van?"

"The driver can do that. I need to set Will straight." Sierra stood toe to toe with the big man, who loomed over her, twice her size. She didn't seem intimidated, just mad as she raised her chin but kept her voice low so the children couldn't hear her. "Will, you can't come onto my place and start yelling at me. Your son doesn't need to be handled rough like that either."

"Now, Sierra. You know I like you, always have." The man ran his fingers over her bare shoulder. She flung off his hand. "I'll handle my boy any way I please. Billy is not one of your crazy kids. I won't have him labeled like them. Hear me?" He stepped closer but Sierra held her ground.

"Don't be a jackass, Will. All we're doing is giving these kids riding lessons and a chance for some fun. What could it hurt to let Billy come out once a week for that? See his grandmother at the same time. The only one labeling these children is you." Sierra's fists were clenched and she was almost vibrating with anger.

"Then why do you have to have permission slips? Put them in one of those short buses?" He pointed to where the other children were ready for the ride back to school.

Rhett noticed that Cindy was crying. Loud voices had set her off. Damn this jackass. He wanted to wade into the fray but had a feeling Sierra could hold her own.

"What are you afraid of, Will? That someone will think you're not a good father?" Sierra challenged him.

Will just laughed. "You always were pretty when you were riled up, Sierra." He brushed her pink cheek with the back of his hand, and she recoiled. "You want to play with other people's kids, fine. Leave mine the hell alone." He stomped over to where Billy was clinging to his grandmother again. "I said get in the truck, boy!" Will jerked him away from Rachel and walked him to the truck, shoving him inside. The boy was crying quietly.

"No need to get excited here." Rhett stepped up. "I'm your customer, Rhett Hall. You hit that boy and I'll call another tow truck even if it has to come from Austin." He stood next to Sierra. "Are we clear?"

"Hey now. No reason to get excited, as you put it. That was family business. I saw your vehicle next to the gate. Beautiful Corvette like that? No one will handle it better than me, I assure you, mister." Will's face was red now.

"It's a rental. I don't give a shit about it. You want my business, you treat Ms. MacKenzie with respect." Rhett had kept his voice low, sure the children couldn't hear him. "Are we clear?"

"Crystal. You're going to need another rental. I can fix you up. The Vette will have to be hauled to Austin for repairs. That where it came from?"

"Yep. Papers are in the glove compartment." Rhett turned to Sierra. "Are you okay? Should I go with this asshole? Is there another choice for a tow?"

Sierra glanced at the van that had its engine running. "Will's the only game in town. Better take the tow and get another rental."

"Then I guess this is goodbye." Rhett didn't like the man. But what choice did he have? Was this going to be the last time he saw Sierra? Did she want him to drive away and let that be the end of it? "Thanks for taking me in, Sierra. Rachel, nice to meet you." He held out his hand.

"Come back. Once you have wheels." Sierra looked surprised that she'd said it. She was clearly still in shock over what had just happened. "I mean, I would like to talk to you. About your, um, idea for research."

"Sure. I'll be back as soon as I can." Rhett took her hand. She barely squeezed it, careful of his injuries. Rachel just waved to him, her eyes on Billy in the truck.

Will smirked. "Then looks like it's a date. Let's get going. Got to get the car moved. We're busy at the dealership. I need to get back."

"Right." Rhett climbed into the tow truck where Billy sat, sullen and knuckling away his tears. The school van pulled out first, the children waving to Sierra, some of them calling Rhett's name as well. Hmm. Guess he'd made an impression. It didn't take long to get the car up on the flatbed. Once at the dealership, it was clear that he was going to be driving a Tahoe or some other big SUV or maybe a truck. Well, why not? When in Rome and all that.

He had to smile at the sign over Will Jackson's office. "Need financing? Where there's Will, there's a way." The man ordered people around, fussing at the salesmen who brought him deals he claimed weren't good enough and the teenager who fetched the big shiny Tahoe he was renting to Rhett.

"That had better be vacuumed, Dickie." Will strode around the SUV, inspecting it. "Get a rag, I see a spot on that rearview mirror."

"Yes, sir." The boy jumped and ran for a rag. Rhett could imagine Billy stuck with that kind of job when he was old enough.

"Looks fine to me." Rhett could tell this man was a bully. Billy had been put on a chair in the office and ordered not to move. His foot was jiggling again, like it had been in the bus earlier. When a shiny black Corvette screeched into the parking lot, everyone showed an interest.

"Look out, the shit's about to hit the fan," one of the salesmen murmured.

"Don't you got somewhere to be, O'Dell?" Will glared at him. When a woman slammed the Corvette's door and stomped up to him, Will put on a smile. "Baby doll, what's got you in a lather? You got no call to mistreat a fine car like that."

"Don't I? I see Billy sitting on a hard chair with tear tracks on his face because you jerked him away from his grandma."

"You let our son go out there with those crazy kids. I won't have him labeled like that. You hear me?" Will seemed to forget his audience. "Take him out there to see his grandma some other time. Hell, go now. Move out there and stay. Be fine with me."

"You sure? Mama called and said you had your hands all over Sierra MacKenzie. You got something going with her, Will? Didn't want Billy out there to catch you with your pants down?" She was a pretty woman, with dark hair that fell past her shoulders. Her tight jeans were belted with a rhinestone longhorn buckle. Animal-print high heels let her hit maybe five foot two. She was a small package that made a big impact.

He couldn't help comparing her to Sierra. To his surprise, the rancher's subtler beauty made this woman's heavy makeup and blatant sexuality seem contrived.

"Baby, you're letting your imagination go wild again." Will grabbed her fist then pulled her to him before he finally looked around and remembered he had a customer and a parking lot full of interested bystanders watching the show. He shrugged as if he didn't mind. "Why would I need to put my boots under some gimpy broad's bed when I've got my hot little prom queen right here?"

"I know about your appetites, Will Jackson, and you sure as hell ain't getting any at home." She glanced around, biting a lip painted a hot pink that matched cheeks flushed with anger, or was it excitement?

Rhett was taking mental notes. This was pure small-town Texas, all of it—from the way these two moved to the words they used. He itched for his computer so he could write some of this down.

"Sally Ann, you know how hard I work. I got lots of irons in the fire. Big business deals that will make us more money than even you can spend, sweet pea, if you can just be patient." Will ran his hand over her butt. "But I'll take care of you tonight. Why don't you get Billy on home, call a sitter and we'll go out as soon as I close up here? We'll have a nice steak dinner at the Wagon Wheel, then I'll show you how much I appreciate you. Okay, baby?" He leaned down to nibble her neck, just missing her large silver earring.

She jerked away from him when he tried to kiss her. "Don't mess up my lipstick. Billy! Come here!" She stared into Will's eyes. "I'm taking him back to my mama. If I see that slut Sierra, she's going to hear a thing or two, I tell you that."

"And I'm telling you, I'm not doing her."

"So you say." Sally Ann looked down at Billy when he bumped against her hip. She spit on her thumb and wiped his cheeks. "Don't you cry, sugar. Mama's here. I'm taking you back to Granny's. You're going to spend the night. Because I'm making a reservation at a hotel on the River Walk in San Antonio for Daddy and me."

"The hell you say. I don't have time for that. I got people to see. Deals working. I told you that." Will put a hand on her shoulder to stop her when she turned away.

"Make time." She stomped one high heel. "This dealership is closed on Sunday. So we're going to spend the night in a honeymoon suite and you're going to prove you're still my man or else."

"Or else what, honeybunch?" He narrowed his gaze on her. "I don't take kindly to threats."

"You don't want to know, Will Jackson. You aren't the only one with deals in the works." She punctuated that with a stab into his polo shirt; then she grabbed Billy's hand and stomped off. It wasn't long before the Corvette roared out of the parking lot.

"All talk, no follow-through. You can quote me on that." Will turned to Rhett. "If you ain't married, stay single. As if I'll let a woman tell me what to do." He stomped off toward his office muttering about paperwork.

"He'll go." The salesman, O'Dell, chuckled. "Sally Ann rules that roost, make no mistake about it. She's a nutcracker and a firecracker. You play, you pay, with that woman."

Rhett had nothing to say to that. He was busy thinking about his book. Characters. He was getting plenty of those. Now all he needed was the mystery.

He headed for Sierra's ranch. It was almost dark when he punched the button on the gate, wondering if she might have changed her mind and would refuse to let him back in. But the gate opened almost immediately. Apparently she'd recognized him on the camera. He drove toward the house. What was in store for him this time? Then he spotted the sheriff's car coming down the drive. Maybe the mystery was closer than he thought.

Chapter Four

"What's taking so long? I thought you'd have that land tied up by now."
The voice sounded calm but there was steel there.

"I have a plan. Tonight things are moving forward. If this doesn't get
her to accept your offer, then nothing will."

"Nothing is not an option. Make it happen. There's a lot of money on
the table. Fuck this up and I'm not the one who will be hurting. Am I
making myself clear?"

"Crystal."

"Just so you know, I've got eyes on you and on the situation down there.
I expect results."

"Tell your people who are watching to pay attention. Tonight will be
big. What happens should scare the shit out of her. I bet she'll be calling
begging for that contract before the end of the week."

"Then that's your deadline." Dial tone.

Great. Someone was watching. Who? A quick look around didn't help.
Everyone nearby looked innocent *and* guilty. A quick call. The dumbass
hired to do the job wanted to back out. The fool liked Sierra MacKenzie.
Well, too damn bad. That bitch had to go. She never should have settled
in this county in the first place.

Another phone call and the alibi for tonight was airtight. Sending Sierra
running back to Houston would be a pure pleasure. And long overdue.

Chapter Five

"I passed a sheriff's car coming out of your place as I came in."

Sierra wasn't going to get into her frustration with Sheriff Myra Watkins with a man who was a virtual stranger. "She was here investigating some cattle I lost yesterday. I don't think it was an accident. She didn't seem too worried about it." She led the way into the den. "Sit down, let's talk about you staying here for a while. If you were serious about it."

"I am. I just spent a couple of hours at Will Jackson's Chevy dealership. I'm itching to write down the things I saw and heard there. Lots of ideas for my book are buzzing around in my brain." Rhett sat across from her, in the leather chair that had been her dad's favorite.

"If you ran into Sally Ann, Will's wife, then I'm sure you did meet a character. She's Rachel's daughter and is what folks around here call a 'pistol.'" Sierra rubbed her knee. *Stop it.* "So you're serious. You really want to stay."

"Definitely. But tell me about the cattle problem. Lost? As in dead or strayed?" He leaned forward, elbows on his knees. He had that intent gaze again, like he really wanted to know every detail.

"Dead. Poisoned, we think. The sheriff would like to blame me for not paying attention to my pastures. I'm not careless." Yes, she sounded defensive, but she was sick of how these locals treated her—as if she didn't have a clue how to run a ranch. She'd been at it for years now, but she'd forever be 'that girl from Houston' to people like the sheriff.

"I'd hope not. What are you supposed to do? Check for weeds in every pasture?" He clearly didn't know a thing about ranching.

"Something like that. We ride them regularly. The poisonous ones are easy to spot and eradicate. I know that and take care of the problem." She'd said as much to the sheriff, not that she'd listened.

"What do you think happened?" Rhett leaned back, obviously ready to listen to her concerns, and Sierra found herself pouring out all of her pent-up frustrations.

"I think someone is trying to get me to sell out. There have been some offers. Supposedly Muellerville is perfect for one of those big senior citizen retirement villages. Sections of land are being purchased by an outfit from Dallas called Oxcart Development. They've approached me more than once but I told them I wasn't interested. Then the trouble started." Sierra couldn't sit still. "It's cocktail hour. Join me in a glass of wine?"

"Sure." Rhett followed her across the room. He raised an eyebrow when she hit the button next to the deer head mounted on the wall and a door slid open in the paneling. "A hidden bar!"

"Surprised you, didn't it? My dad had it put in. He liked his cocktails. Red or white?" Sierra could go either way after the day she'd had.

"Whatever you like." Rhett reached for the opener and two glasses while she dug into the wine fridge and pulled out a bottle of her favorite white. "This is quite a setup. Slick."

"Daddy designed it himself." She handed him the bottle, watching him expertly pull out the cork. "Did you think all ranchers drank Lone Star or sipped bourbon?"

"I try not to think in stereotypes. But I do like this hidden option." Rhett filled the glasses.

"There's another button that hides our gun safe." She smiled. "I'll show you where that is when I know you better." That had him examining the room like he was looking for it.

He stopped next to the deer head. "Who shot the deer?"

"Dad. None of us kids are much for hunting. I have two brothers. Both are too busy working to have time for it and never caught the bug. Brother Mason is CEO of Texas Star Oil; that's the family business. My brother Dylan is a lawyer." She clinked her glass against Rhett's. "Cheers."

Rhett smiled. "Yes, indeed. Cheers. I have one sister, the one in Austin. Scarlett." He held up his hand when Sierra started to speak. "If you're going to say something about *Gone with the Wind*, spare me. My mom is addicted and was originally from Atlanta. My dad claimed he had to get a vasectomy or he'd have had a Melanie and an Ashley after us."

Sierra spewed wine. She grabbed a towel and mopped her shirtfront. God, it was good to laugh.

Rhett shook his head. "Hey, it's not that funny." He laughed. "Well, maybe it is. I'm used to it. But you can see why I use a pen name. For my novels."

"R.B. Hall. I had you investigated. Since I'm thinking of letting you stay here." Sierra used the towel to wipe her cheeks. She was a mess.

Her resource had done a deep dive on Rhett Hall after she'd called the detective back and told him she was thinking about letting him use her place like a bed-and-breakfast. Leroy Hobbs worked for her lawyer brother and was excellent. She now knew that Rhett a.k.a. R.B. Hall was a best-selling author who could well afford to pay a generous rent. He came from Boston and his story about a sister in Austin was true. Scarlett had suffered this past year, but her troubles seemed to be over.

"Investigating a stranger you were thinking of letting stay with you was the smart thing to do. I have nothing to hide. Well, I did get a ticket on the way out of Muellerville a little while ago. Damned speed trap. It took me a while to get used to the Tahoe I rented." He nodded toward the couch. "Sit. Let's talk terms."

Sierra was glad he wasn't offended. "I'm sorry about the ticket. Muellerville is bad about that. It's a major source of revenue." She sat, surprised when he sat beside her, knee to knee. This close she could smell him. It had been a long day for both of them, but he had that masculine scent that made her realize it had been way too long since she'd been close to someone like Rhett. He smiled, and she found herself smiling back for no reason except that he had that certain something. Charisma, charm, whatever you wanted to call it. He was easy to talk to and he was different, new.

She cleared her throat. "Honestly? I could use the money and the company." She sipped her wine for something to do with her hands. She realized she wanted to touch him. His thighs were close, and looked firm beneath his jeans.

Oh, girl, you've been way too long without a man.

Rhett kept smiling, his knee brushing hers. "I could use the experience on a ranch. For a book. If someone is poisoning your cattle, I'd like to look into it. Find out if it was an accident or not. If this company is trying to run you off your place, that's a damned ugly way to go about it. Why not offer you more money?"

"Oh, they've jacked up the price a couple of times. It didn't work with me. I don't need money." Sierra could see she'd confused him. "Okay, I know I said I could use your rent. So I'm not making sense. I have oil money. You saw the wells pumping. The offers the Dallas developers ran by me were generous, and even let me keep some of the property, but their plans would cut up the land. Oxcart wants access to that highway from Muellerville you came down earlier. That would make it hard to work with my horses. Of course they agreed to leave me the mineral rights. That was clever, but they overlooked one thing—I don't like to be pushed." She sighed and took a drink.

"They won't take no for an answer? Look for another way to get to the highway?" Rhett leaned in, his knee firmly against hers now.

"I guess there isn't another way. Not that's direct. I don't want to ruin this deal for the community. I've heard plenty from some of the locals about it." Sierra set down her glass. "Honestly, I just want to be left alone to enjoy my place that I've loved since I was a kid. The company can throw money at me all they want; it doesn't mean that much to me. This place does."

"Most people would take the money and find another place. It's an option." He was solemn, making a reasonable point.

"Did the company send you here to argue their case?" She stood. "Have I let a rattlesnake into my house?"

"No. I have no idea who is behind this land grab." He stood in front of her. "Hell, I've never even been to Dallas except to change planes once. No, take that back. I did a book signing. In and out in one day. No time to work up a conspiracy."

"This is serious, Rhett."

"I see that." He didn't smile. "I didn't mean to come across as anything but sympathetic. Your land, your decision. No one should be allowed to push you around."

Sierra took a deep breath. She was being paranoid. He'd only suggested what several people, including her hairdresser in town, had told her she should do. For most people a big buyout would be a godsend. She sat.

"Sorry. I'm a little sensitive on the subject. Let me explain."

"Please. If you don't mind." He glanced at the bar. "You want a refill?"

"Why not?" She waited for him to top off her glass, then took a sip before she explained. "You see, my family is rich. I could get help from them to support this ranch if I asked. But I don't want to ask. When Daddy died, I took this place as my inheritance rather than my share of Texas Star. My mom and brothers got the rest in company stock. They've insisted all along that the deal wasn't equitable, especially since the price of oil has come up. I disagree. All I wanted was a place for my horses. But I need to make this place self-supporting. It's a matter of pride." Sierra shut up. Why was she telling this perfect stranger her business? No one knew this much about why she had dug in her heels on this ranch.

"I get it. When I started writing, I had a tough time. You think I sold my first book? Or even my third?" Rhett put his hand on her knee. "Dad offered to let me live at home, be the starving artist on his dime. He's a literature prof at Harvard, brilliant guy. But he always dreamed of writing his own novels. Never did it." He shook his head. "Anyway, I couldn't take him up on it. I left home, took crappy jobs that paid enough to get my own place and just wrote, hours a day. Went through the mill submitting and getting rejected. It took years for me to even get an agent."

"It paid off. I saw that one of your books is being made into a movie." Sierra covered his hand with hers for a moment. "That's so cool."

"I'm not holding my breath. It could still fall through. But it *would* be cool." Rhett smiled. "Bottom line? I know what it's like to want to make it on your own. Refusing to let your family bail you out."

"Thanks. But if I keep losing cattle, I may have to either give up some of the horse rescues or sell off part of the place. When you put a pencil to what I'm doing here, it's more of a hobby than a profitable business. So says my accountant."

"You'll figure it out. My rent will help give you time." Rhett pulled her to her feet. "Are you hungry? I heard there's a good steak place in town. The Wagon Wheel. If I'm really allowed to stay, why don't I shower and we head over there for dinner?"

"I'd love that." Sierra really wanted to hug him but stepped back instead. "A shower. Yes. Let me show you to your room. There's a bedroom with its own bathroom this way. You can bring in your stuff." She named a price that was just slightly exorbitant and Rhett agreed to it. "I'll call and make a reservation. The Wagon Wheel has great food and is popular on a Saturday night. Eight sound good?"

"Perfect." Rhett put his arm around her shoulder. "Thanks for agreeing to let me stay here, Sierra. I promise I'll use my 'company manners,' as my mother calls them. If I do anything you don't like, you just call me out. Okay?"

"I appreciate that, Rhett. We can set some ground rules over dinner." Sierra felt like all of this was moving too fast. But then she'd been stuck in a rut way too long, letting things happen and then reacting. Was this another example of that? Had she been bulldozed into taking Rhett on? He had a strong personality. But then her father and her two brothers had take-charge attitudes, and she'd always held her own.

Where was her tough MacKenzie spirit? It was past time for her to reach out and take what she wanted. What if some fun with a hot guy was just what the doctor ordered? Sierra grinned as she limped toward her wing of the house. Rhett had wasted no time bringing in his stuff, and she could hear him singing in the shower. What was that tune? Rhett Hall had obviously been listening to the local country music station.

"If it's meant to be..." he sang.

If only.

* * * *

The Wagon Wheel was packed. The full parking lot made it clear this was a popular place. Rhett could feel all eyes following them as they headed for their corner table. Sierra stopped and spoke to several people before the hostess finally got them seated.

"Something smells good." He inhaled and felt his taste buds do a happy dance. Somewhere nearby, steaks were on a grill.

Sierra smiled. "You're smelling mesquite wood on the fire. It can make my eyes burn if it gets too strong, but it makes a steak taste good." She pointed to the menu, which was heavy on grass-fed beef. "I'd recommend the ribeye."

"Sounds good. Medium rare for me." He smiled at her across the candlelit table. She had put on makeup, a subtle amount that suited her. She wore a clingy top that dipped low enough for him to appreciate her feminine curves. The bright red looked perfect with her blond hair and tan.

"Let me order some of the sides they're famous for—jalapeno creamed corn and au gratin potatoes. You'll love them." She smiled at the waitress who brought them a basket of yeast rolls. "Marty, hi. I hoped we'd get your table. How's Buddy?"

"Fine. Working himself to death." The waitress was a pretty brunette in a green-checked shirt and jeans.

"Marty, this is Rhett Hall. He'll be staying with me for a while."

"Oh, really? Good for you, girl. About time." Marty winked. "What can I get you to drink? We've got a fine selection of Texas wines."

"What do you say, Rhett? You want to try one?" Sierra grinned at him, clearly in her element here.

"I'll bring you a cabernet from Caldwell that's supposed to be really good with steak. You are having steak, aren't you?"

"Of course. Nice to meet you, Marty. I'd like to try a Texas wine." Rhett picked up Sierra's hand. He didn't mind being linked with Sierra. Why not play along? She didn't jerk her hand away.

As soon as Marty left, he picked up a roll and buttered it. Of course Sierra was staring a hole in him. "What?"

"Hand-holding? Are you going to pretend to be my boyfriend while you're here instead of admitting you're a writer doing research?"

"Would you go along with that?" He offered her half the roll. "I didn't see you deny Marty's assumption."

She took the roll and bit into it. When butter glistened on her lips, it was all he could do not to lean forward and add another element to this show. Yes, he'd like to lick that away, take it deeper, experience the taste of her. She must have seen his thoughts in his eyes, because she finished the roll, then wiped her mouth thoroughly with her cloth napkin.

"I don't need to tell the world my business. Let them think what they want. You and I know the truth. You're paying for the privilege to stay with me. Period. No bedroom access included." She picked up her water glass and drank deeply.

"If people thought I was your significant other, it might make it easier for me to ask around, get information." Rhett smiled at her raised eyebrow.

"I told you, I'm an outsider here. Being connected to me won't buy you any access." She looked up as Marty approached with the wine bottle and showed Rhett the label. "Trust me on that."

Rhett ignored her, getting into the act of approving the wine selection, watching Marty open the bottle and sniffing the cork. "Seems good." He tasted the sample. "Nice. Should go well with steak." He held out his glass to Sierra. "What do you think, honey?"

She rolled her eyes but took the glass and tasted. "Good, Marty. Pour it."

They ordered, then sat back to watch the crowd. It was a full house and people were dressed up. A small Texas town didn't go for suits and ties, though a few men wore them.

"Sierra MacKenzie, you have a nerve, showing up here." A man in a jacket over his jeans slapped a cowboy hat against his thigh as he knocked against the table, making their glasses rattle.

"Randy, you're drunk. Go home and sober up." Marty grabbed his arm and tried to pull him away. "Sorry, Sierra."

"I'm not going anywhere. Not until I've had my say." He bumped the table again and this time their wine bottle swayed and would have hit the floor if Rhett hadn't caught it.

"You'd do well to listen to the lady. Take off." He stood and faced the man. They were about the same height, and he could smell the beer on the man's breath. "You're making a scene."

"Who the fuck are you?" The guy pushed Rhett with a beefy hand on his chest.

"Big mistake, bud." Rhett handed Marty the bottle and gripped the man's hand, twisting it until it was behind the bozo's back. He had the element of surprise and sobriety. Before the guy could wind up and make a fist, he'd walked him fast toward the front door. "Say one more word, Randy, and we can finish this outside."

"The hell you say." Apparently Randy had the idea that he was going to prove he was a badass. Rhett just shoved him out the door and onto the gravel parking lot, where he landed facedown.

"Get up and I'll be happy to give you a lesson in how to speak to a lady." Rhett watched the man roll over.

"Lady? The bitch is holding us all hostage. Making us wait while she—" He fumbled at his waist.

Rhett knew that move and stepped on the other man's wrist before Randy could pull out his gun. Open carry. Texas was nothing if not gun friendly.

"Ow! Shit! Get off my arm!" Randy struggled to get his hand free.

"No way in hell." Rhett leaned harder, his foot firmly on the forearm. "You want a broken wrist?"

"I called the police. They should be here any minute." Marty hovered behind him. "I'm real sorry about this. Randy and his pals in the chamber of commerce have a lot riding on that senior citizen land deal. You know about that?" She looked up when a sheriff's car with lights and siren pulled into the parking lot. Small town, quick service.

"A little." Rhett nodded at the deputy, who took one look at the man on the ground and got out his handcuffs.

"Sierra needs to reconsider selling. A lot of people want that deal to go through. The town is dying otherwise. Just saying." She turned and told the deputy that Randy had made a drunken fool of himself. Apparently it wasn't the first time. The deputy disarmed the man on the ground then took a brief statement from Rhett before he let him return to the dining room.

Sierra still sat where he'd left her. She'd made good progress on that bottle of wine.

"Randy is on his way to jail." Rhett sat back in his chair and picked up his own glass of wine. "He can sober up there. Are you okay?"

"Am *I*?" She looked up at him with stricken eyes. "How about you? He shoved you. Then the way you handled him…" She took a drink. "I can't believe I just sat here. Frozen. I should have jumped up, confronted him. Defended myself. Not let you do it."

"Hey, I got to pull out my man card. Show you I'm not just a writer but a doer. Were you impressed?" He was determined to lighten the mood. Sierra MacKenzie took way too much on herself. He'd already figured that out. And why the hell should she be blamed for the problems of a dying town? Let them figure out their own solutions.

"Very impressed." She finally smiled. "I'm really sorry about that. Randy Cox owns the local Quik Stop. He's one of several small-business owners who would benefit if we had that senior living deal go through." She looked him over. "You didn't answer me. Are you okay? That move you made looked like you'd had law enforcement training or something. I didn't see that in your background."

"Did you worry about me?" Rhett smiled. "You can see that I'm fine. Didn't even break a sweat. I took a course in self-defense as research for one of my books. Did a ride-along with cops in Boston as well. It comes in handy when I have to write a fight scene. I've had to use it in every book." He glanced around the room. "Anyone else here going to attack us?"

"Maybe. I hope not." She drained her glass, then waited while Rhett gave her a refill. At this rate they might need another bottle. "Let me explain why Muellerville is getting this attention all of a sudden. Why the development company isn't likely to give up. This town has a unique geographic location. It's why my dad bought the ranch so many years ago."

"What do you mean?" Rhett leaned in. He wished he could bring out his cell and record this conversation. But he'd remember. He was finding anything this woman said memorable.

"We're exactly ninety miles from Houston, ninety from San Antonio and the same from Austin." She put down her glass. "Three major cities and each only an hour and a half away. The roads are good, speed limits are high, and people don't seem to think anything of driving that far for a weekend getaway or a good meal these days. Not in Texas anyway." She looked around. "I bet there are people from Austin here right now for a Saturday night out."

"You're probably right. There's a huge population of aging baby boomers from all three cities who might be interested in a retirement community here. That's genius, actually. Especially if you add some amenities that the demographic might like." Rhett's mind was clicking on all cylinders. Hey, he'd even like to invest in a project like that. Though he sure wouldn't tell Sierra that.

"I know! Trust me, I've heard the sales pitch." She drained her glass again.

"You could benefit from being in close proximity to such a project, Sierra. Forget the cattle and expand into a kind of bed-and-breakfast thing for visitors to the seniors. Or rent out the horses. Offer rides to the grandkids who'll come to visit." Rhett couldn't contain himself. Then he saw her face. Bad move.

"Would you quit being so damned logical?" She threw down her napkin. "I'm going to the ladies' room. I'm sure our steaks will come while I'm gone." She stormed off in the direction of the restroom sign on the far wall.

"Well, hell." Rhett refilled his own glass.

"Steaks will be out in a moment. Another bottle of wine?" Marty arrived when he flagged her down. "Sierra didn't look happy."

"She's not. I talked to her about that senior living project. She won't sell. She loves her place." Rhett stopped Marty with a hand on her arm after he ordered a second bottle. "How do you feel about this proposed project?"

"I'm for it." Marty bit her lip. "Sierra does love her place and her horses and makes sure everyone knows it. But do you have any idea what a big deal this would be? How many jobs it would bring to a town that has a pitiful few?"

"I'd have to look into it." Which Rhett planned to do as soon as he got back to his laptop.

"My husband has an auto repair shop. His only competition is the Chevy dealership. Imagine hundreds of seniors living in the area. Many of them drive foreign cars. Buddy can work on Hondas, Toyotas, you name it." She laughed. "Hell, I'd be able to quit this gig and stay home for a change. I can see it now."

"You're right. It would be a boon. But years away from completion, Marty." Rhett could imagine what Sierra would face if she was the spike in the road.

"I could wait if I knew something good was coming. Besides, the construction workers would be here in the meantime, doing business with all of us." She leaned in. "I love Sierra, but if she fucks this up?" She looked around. "She won't have a friend in this town. And that's the truth." She hurried off when she saw Sierra coming out of the restroom.

Rhett stood when Sierra approached the table. Damn. This put a new light on her problem. She had to live in this town, and what she wanted might just make her public enemy number one. He had some research to do. That was obvious.

Marty approached carrying a tray loaded with their plates and two bowls of side dishes. The smell was enough to lighten his mood. At least temporarily. But not for long. Not even some of the best food he'd ever eaten could take his mind off the trouble Sierra might have ahead of her. He was definitely staying. How could he get lost in a fictional tale when the real one around him was so damned interesting?

Chapter Six

When they got to her gate, Sierra gave him the code without hesitation. Probably not smart but she *had* agreed to let him stay. Besides, she was just tipsy enough that she didn't dare walk around the SUV to put in the code herself. At the house he parked his rental where she told him to, then helped her out of the car.

"Thank you for dinner; you didn't have to do that." Sierra gave him her hand then let him keep it as he walked her across the gravel drive to the back door.

"I have to thank *you*. The Wagon Wheel had great food and more Texas characters." He stood aside while she tried to unlock the door. "You need help with that?"

"Here." Sierra had to admit the wine had gotten the better of her. "You unlock it. I'll get you your own key tomorrow. I hate that I have to lock up at all. We didn't used to do it, but with the cows dying and fence problems, I got paranoid." She leaned against the porch post. "My brother put in the security system at the gate and everywhere else he thought I needed it. We've got alarms all over the place." When she gestured she lost her balance and fell into Rhett, gripping his muscular arm.

"Hey, careful." He grinned down at her as he steadied her then flung the door open. "Same code here?" The whine of the alarm in the house started as soon as the door opened. His smile in the light next to the back door was part amused, part interested. Good for her ego.

"Sure. See if you remember it." All that wine. No wonder Rhett was looking good to her.

"Got it."

She smiled up at him when the alarm beeped then went silent. "Maybe I should be more suspicious of you, showing up like you did."

"I'm innocent, I swear it." He left her propped against the kitchen island then turned and threw the dead bolt. "Scratch that. Not exactly innocent, but I'm not here to work on you to sell this place." He took her purse from her hand and set it on the counter. "This ranch suits you. You want to keep it? You should."

"Thanks, Rhett. I wish everyone agreed with you." Sierra leaned against the hard stone and gazed up at him. She couldn't let herself be a fool for a good-looking man.

Now that she thought about it, this coincidence was a little too good to be true. Hot guy landing on her doorstep. Yes, she'd had him checked out, but clever people faked that stuff all the time. The internet could be manipulated. She'd seen it happen on a TV show, that one about...

"Your eyes are closing." He laughed and gently steered her down the hall toward her bedroom. "I think you've had a long day."

"I have." She was tired. Through the haze of good wine and good food, she felt a bone-deep exhaustion. He was taking care of her. Nice.

He found her bedroom at the end of the hall, helped her kick off her shoes—had he noticed she'd tortured herself with heels?—and brought her a glass of water from her bathroom.

"Drink. It'll help the inevitable hangover tomorrow." He pulled back her comforter, and she sat on the side of the bed. "Want me to stay?" He put on a hopeful look, but she somehow knew he was teasing.

"No, thanks." Sierra gulped down water. "I'll be fine. Just...need sleep. See you in the morning." She waited until he left, shutting the door behind him. She had to get out of her tight skirt. Managed that. Pulled on boxers and a T-shirt, then slid under clean sheets. Bless Rachel for that. The housekeeper wouldn't be here tomorrow. Sunday. Darrel would do morning chores. Sierra's day off too. She drifted into sleep thinking about a man who had been a gentleman. Maybe too much of one.

A screeching siren jerked Sierra out of a deep sleep. Pounding nearby before her bedroom door burst open.

"Your barn is on fire!" Rhett shouted, tossing a robe at her.

"My horses!" Sierra jumped to her feet, pushing past him as she ran for the back door. Boots. Her barn boots sat next to the door, and she thrust her bare feet into them. Then she was outside, shoving her arms into the robe but not bothering to tie it. She could smell the smoke now, hear the terrified screams of her horses. *God.* Flames lit the night sky. She realized Rhett ran next to her.

"I called 9-1-1. Hit the remote to open the gate by the highway." He shouted that in her ear as they ran. The doors were open and Darrel met them, pulling two of the horses out of the barn. The whites of the horses' eyes were showing as they cried out and tugged at the leads.

"What happened? What started this?" Sierra's eyes stung as she grabbed the leads while Darrel opened the corral gate. "Darrel!"

"I don't know. Fire alarm went off and woke me up. I came running. Back wall is on fire. Give me those leads." Her ranch hand, the only one to live in the bunkhouse, snatched the lead and pulled Charley into the corral.

Sierra led Rex, her favorite mount, inside, then took a moment to lean against him. No, she didn't have time for this, though she felt his trembling and heard his labored breathing. A final pat and she hurried back toward the barn. It took everything in her to face the heat and smoke.

"Fire's too much for a watering hose. Horses come first." Coughing and gasping for breath, Darrel wiped off his filthy face then grabbed a couple of empty feed sacks from a stack inside the barn door. He sprayed them with the hose he must have turned on when he first heard the fire alarm. Then he turned the hose on himself. "Going back in."

"Right behind you. We have to hurry." Sierra swallowed nausea, thrust the hose into the horse trough, then picked up sacks and wet them before she ran inside. God, the horses' screams. She'd hear them forever in her nightmares. There were still six more geldings and a stallion in there, but the mare and her foal were in the stall closest to the dangerous back wall. She had to get to them first. The heat and a wall of smoke hit her as soon as she got inside. She stumbled to a halt. The frantic kicks of horses trapped in their stalls went straight to her heart. They would die if she didn't move fast. No time for her to doubt if she could do it.

"Stay back, I'll go." Rhett had sacks in his hand and tried to shoulder past her.

"My horses, my problem. Get Blanco. He's right there and he knows you." She shoved Rhett toward the stall where the big horse was throwing himself at the slats. She desperately worked to stay calm as she fumbled with halters and covered the eyes of frantic horses, then passed them on to Darrel.

It was getting harder and harder to see in the heavy smoke, her eyes watering. Flames licked up the doorway to the tack room, way too close to where the mare shrieked in fright. Sierra stumbled closer, the wet feed sack heavy in her hands as heat hit her and made it almost impossible to catch her breath. She grabbed the halter then threw open the stall door, talking soothingly to the mare.

"There now, Sunshine. Let's get you out of here." Her voice trembled on the verge of a sob. She was terrified that she couldn't do this. The mare fought her, out of her mind as she kicked and lunged. It was hard to even get the wet sack over her face. Finally Sierra managed it and the mare settled. At last, halter and lead line on, it was time to worry about the trembling foal. No halter for the baby. She'd have to pray it would follow its mama.

"Okay, baby. You're a miracle. Prove it." Sierra's throat closed as the smoke and flames roared. *Too close. Stay low.* That's what she knew was the right thing to do. She heard Rhett and Darrel calling her name. Good thing, since it was impossible to see. She grabbed the mare's lead line and started down what had been the center aisle of the barn. A crash behind her made her jerk the reins.

"Whoa, Sunshine." She reached back. Thank God the baby was with them, huddled near its mother.

"Sierra!"

She couldn't answer, just stayed as low as she could while she kept walking. It was hard. Her leg hurt and the horse was fighting her. Embers fell from the roof. The flames had spread. Finally, finally, she felt hands reach for her. Rhett. Darrel took the lead line.

Fresh air. Or what passed for it. She staggered forward and found a fence post. She leaned against it, taking a clean wet cloth that Rhett handed her to wipe her face.

"Are you all right?" He stood close.

"I'll live. Let me see about my horses." She wiped her eyes and checked the corral. Sierra did a quick count. "My God! Where's Chief?"

"I'm on it." Before she could stop him, Rhett ran back into the barn. The flames were higher now and obviously the fire had spread beyond the tack room.

Sierra grabbed more wet bags and ran into the barn. Did Rhett even know that Chief, a stallion, was in a box stall on the left side of the barn? How could he find him in the heavy smoke? The screams, of course. No one could miss them. Then she saw Rhett with a halter in his hand, talking as he eased open the gate.

"Careful! Cover his eyes first if you can." She could hear Chief kicking from where she stood. She bent over, the smoke almost too much for her. How was Rhett managing?

The kicking stopped. Rhett emerged from the stall with the horse and ran toward her. Both he and the stud were being hit by falling embers, the roar of the fire all around them. Timbers crashed at the back of the barn, and it seemed like the barn itself would collapse if they didn't get out of there soon.

Sierra seized the lead line while Rhett kept a wet sack over Chief's eyes so they could get outside. A few steps more and Darrel took the lead and hurried the horse into the corral. Then Rhett leaned over, gasping for air. Sierra pulled at his arm. They were still too close to the inferno that was engulfing the barn. Her barn. Everything she'd worked for since college.

At least now all of the horses had made it out safely. But what next? She couldn't keep all her horses in the corral. She glanced at the nearby pasture. No, she didn't trust it. Someone could have thrown poisonous weeds in there. Like she believed they'd done to kill her cattle. Her hay was in the barn, going up in flames fast. Damn it, how was she going to feed them? Not now. She'd think about it after the fire devouring her property was brought under control. She wiped her eyes and picked up the water hose. It was worse than useless, making mud but doing nothing to put out the flames that had reached the door.

"Let me. Go check your horses." Rhett took the hose and aimed it higher. At least he kept the sparks from igniting the fence nearby.

"Thanks." Sierra walked over to the corral. Darrel had disappeared. Maybe he'd gone to call the fire department again. Whatever. She stepped inside and began to look over each horse. Poor babies were restless and still upset. No wonder. The air was heavy with smoke. At least a light breeze blew most of it away from the corral, but the roar of the fire was loud. Each crash of falling timbers startled the horses and kept them on edge.

It didn't help that the wet feed sacks had been flung aside into a messy stack next to the gate. Sierra tossed them over the fence since the horses were giving them a wide berth. Now that she thought about it, it was funny that the sacks had been handy by the barn doors. They were usually stacked in the tack room. She'd ask Darrel about that when he came back from wherever he'd gone.

Horses first. Sierra did her best to soothe each one as she made a methodical visual inspection that assured her all of them, even Chief, seemed to have fared okay. The stallion had a few raw spots she'd want the vet to take a look at, but he was breathing normally. Sunshine, the mare, stayed close to her foal, guarding him from the other horses. That was a good thing. They should be separated from the rest. Sierra was making sure the trough was full of water when she finally heard sirens approaching. The town had a volunteer fire department so this response was fairly quick for them. In addition to Rhett's call, the new alarm system must have alerted them as soon as the first smoke detector went off.

The fire truck drew up in front of the barn, which was now fully engulfed in flames. The main engine was followed by a pair of pickup trucks. A dozen men piled out and went to work, setting up efficiently as they arranged their hoses and began to spray the fire. Once the fire seemed under control, the fire chief came over to talk to her. Sierra knew before he spoke that the barn was a total loss.

"Get all the horses out?" Jim Weber wiped the soot off his face and pulled off his heavy gloves. He nodded toward the corral.

"Yes, thank God." Sierra shook his hand. "I appreciate the quick arrival."

"We were already at the firehouse. Had a grass fire earlier and had just gotten back. It was lucky for you or this might have spread to your other outbuildings, maybe the house, before we got here." He frowned at the structure when a portion of the roof caved in. "Hell of a thing. You'd better move back. Keep an eye on your corral. It's a little close to the fire."

"I already figured that out. I've been watching for sparks." Sierra felt a sob trying to work itself up from her chest, and she swallowed. "It's clear I'm going to have to farm the horses out to neighbors until I can get a barn up again." She rubbed her stinging eyes and took a breath that ended in a cough. Where was Rhett? He'd disappeared when the firemen had arrived.

When she could speak, she asked the question that had been on her mind since she'd first seen the barn in flames. "Any idea what started this?"

Jim cleared his throat. "You have a visitor, some guy named Hall? He told one of my men he thought he smelled gasoline near the back wall. You don't have any vehicles back there that could have leaked fresh gas so that's suspicious. Hall made a point of passing that word on to me. It's a blessing your propane tank is near the house or we'd have had an explosion."

"Gasoline. Like someone set the fire?" Sierra started walking. Her limp was worse, of course. This late it would be, especially when she was tired. She skirted the dying fire, which put her in rough terrain. Her chest hurt and breathing was painful. Add in depression and worry and she just wanted to go back to the house and crawl into bed. She'd like to resume the dream she'd had going before that alarm had gone off a lifetime ago.

Shoulders sagging, Sierra finally arrived at the spot where Darrel and the vet had parked their trucks earlier. Darrel's was gone, of course. He parked next to the bunkhouse at night. Still no sign of her ranch hand. Rhett was there, talking to a fireman. The chief had followed her.

"Can one of you show me where you smelled gasoline?" She sniffed the air but all she got was burned wood and, damn it, leather. The tack room had been full of saddles, thousands of dollars' worth of equipment burned to a crisp.

"Here, Sierra." Rhett gestured to a spot next to the back door. It led to the tack room where she kept all the gear necessary to ride and take care of the horses. "Mark Chen was showing me where they think the fire started. You get right up on it and you can catch a whiff of gasoline. I've done research on arson and this looks like a classic case of it to me."

"I'll take your word for it." Sierra didn't think she could smell anything but smoke at the moment. He should let the professionals do their job. Except, wait a minute, these weren't pros. Mark was the local pharmacist and Jim, the fire chief, was the high school principal. What they knew about arson they got off the internet and from a few extension courses if they had time to take them. Like Rhett did, no doubt. He came to her side. "Are you okay?" He held her arm as if to support her.

Had she wobbled, shown a sign of weakness? She wanted to jerk away from him. Scream at him that, no, she was not all right. Her barn was a smoldering mess and her horses were scared. She hadn't even had time to feed them or tend to them properly. God, she should get the vet out here again right away.

More money going out and none coming in. She had insurance, but a deductible equal to the cost of a small car. Before she knew it, she couldn't see. Her eyes had filled with tears. Oh, great. Turning into a weak female.

The firemen got busy looking for embers that needed more water. Rhett moved closer and pulled her into a hug. Damn it, that felt good. She shoved him away and took a breath, which sounded like a wheeze.

The fire chief heard her. "How about some oxygen over here? Mark? Call for the first aid truck. Tell them to move it as close as is safe." The chief gestured to a spot well away from the smoldering barn. "Sir, are you a friend of Sierra's? Relative?"

"Sorry, Rhett Hall. I'm visiting Sierra." He held out his hand and they shook, like this was a meet and greet.

Sierra wanted to admit he was a virtual stranger. She couldn't get the words out because she was having trouble catching her breath. Rhett kept his arm around her, studying her with a frown.

"Sierra, come sit down on the back of this truck. Take some oxygen. That'll help you breathe. You're clearly suffering from smoke inhalation." Rhett eased her toward a truck that had pulled in. It was equipped with emergency first aid equipment, including oxygen tanks and a cooler. One man handed her a mask and was obviously the designated paramedic on the crew.

Sierra coughed, then did what he said. Her lungs were straining, and she needed a minute to take in this disaster. The horses had *seemed* to be okay. One day at a time. That was all she could handle right now. When she finally felt like she could speak without hacking up a lung, she pulled off the mask.

"Your voice sounds hoarse. You could use some oxygen too, Rhett."

"I'll get some in a minute. You need more." Rhett nodded at the oxygen mask.

"Talk to me while I do it. Tell me about this supposed arson." She took another breath of the cool, clean oxygen and almost moaned. Yes, she'd needed it. What would a horse do if she tried to give it a breathing treatment? She remembered how close to the fire Sunshine and the foal had been. They'd inhaled a lot of smoke. And Rex. He'd been shuddering with fright and wasn't a young fellow. Could a horse have a heart attack? She'd have to ask the vet about that. She inhaled again and waited for Rhett to start talking. He was exchanging looks with the fire chief.

"This is just my opinion, you understand. Based on research for a book I did a while back." Rhett went on to explain his occupation to the chief, which got some attention from the other men nearby, and they were all ears as he started to explain what he knew about arson.

"Back to my barn, Rhett?" Sierra knew she sounded testy but she wasn't feeling so well. A little hungover and a lot depressed. When one of the men offered her a cold bottle of water, she smiled gratefully.

"I smelled gasoline, and the path the fire took makes me think the gas might have been splashed around the base of the walls there on the inside." Rhett walked close to the still-hot embers and was admonished by the chief. "Sorry. Anyway, I don't think there was any effort made to hide the cause of the fire. Whoever did it wasn't bold enough to leave the gas can, but they made it pretty obvious to anyone who paid attention."

Rhett stared at Sierra. "Look how your saddles burned. What a shame." He was pushed aside by the fire chief who studied the scene. "Someone wanted Sierra to know that the fire was started deliberately. Maybe to scare her, hurt her horses, or as a warning."

"Now that's a stretch. You sure you're not putting your storytelling to work here?" Jim, the chief, frowned and took a second look at the place where Rhett had claimed the fire started. "Usual reason for arson around here is when you get rid of a useless ranch hand and he takes it hard. This nonsense about scaring her doesn't make sense." Jim walked back to face Sierra. "Why would anyone want to scare you, Sierra? As far as I know you're well liked in town. You and your family have made generous donations to the fire department and your horse therapy has helped some troubled kids. I can attest to that."

"Thanks, Jim. I had to lay off a couple of hands because of budget concerns recently, but we parted ways amicably and they both already have other jobs." Sierra ignored Rhett's concerned stare. "There are other things going on you may not know about."

"Like what?" Jim picked up a loose board and poked at the ruins of the tack room. The embers flared into fire. Sierra got off the tailgate, reluctant to leave the oxygen but determined to make the fire department take this charge of arson seriously. "This isn't the first problem I've had recently. Talk to the sheriff about that. Fences damaged, cattle poisoned. Bad things started happening when that outfit from Dallas made an offer to buy my land and I turned them down flat."

"From Dallas?" Jim tossed the board aside.

"Where have you been, Jim?" Mark Chen moved closer. "They want to build a senior citizen development near here. Haven't you heard about it?"

"Oh, that. Yeah. Didn't know Sierra was involved. The senior living project would be a boon to the economy, of course, but I can't see it affecting the schools so I didn't pay attention to the gossip. I did wonder why they haven't broken ground yet." Jim glanced at the other men raking the ground around the barn to build a fire break. "Give this some more water. We're staying until we're sure there's no chance it will flame again." He walked to Sierra's side. "You really refused to sell to them?"

"Sure did. I need my land. For the horses and cattle. And I've got wells with good production on part of it. I have no interest in letting some company come in here and tear my place apart for a cookie-cutter subdivision. I grew up in Houston, which is full of them." Sierra realized every fireman was listening intently. "Can you blame me? I've been coming here since I was a kid to get away from that rat race. I love the country. It was my dream to run my own horse ranch. Why would I sell out now?"

Mark handed his hose to the man next to him, then stomped closer to her. "I don't know, Sierra. For the money? The town? Because you can raise horses anywhere and this is the chance of a lifetime?" He looked around and got nods from the other firemen. "Muellerville is dying. That senior living proposal will bring us back to life. You have any idea what senior citizens and their needs would do for a pharmacy?"

"I get it, Mark." Sierra didn't like the animosity coming off him. "But can't you see my side? They need to go somewhere else."

"If they could, they would." Mark shook his head. "Jesus, Sierra, you've got to see reason. If you're the one holding up the development, no wonder someone saw an opportunity to try to push you out of here."

"That's enough, Mark." Jim grabbed his shoulders and pushed him away from her. "Go see about the crew at the front. What Sierra does with her land is her business. Would you sell out your drugstore just because someone made an offer and thought you should go?"

"If the offer was right." Mark scowled. "I get what you're saying. I love our little town and have deep roots here. I'd hate to just pack up and go. But Sierra's from Houston and everyone knows it." He gave Sierra one last look. With that he strode off toward the front of the barn. His departure was punctuated by a crash as a wall fell in with a shower of sparks.

"Was this a warning?" Sierra sat on the tailgate next to Rhett, who was inhaling oxygen. "Could Mark be right?"

"You heard that drunk last night. He agreed with Mark."

"Randy." She stared at the barn, which would soon be nothing but the steel frame. She picked up a rock by her foot and threw it at the remains, barely missing one of the firemen.

"Hey!" He looked shocked.

"Sorry. I'm just so damned mad." She felt Rhett's hand on her arm. "Whoever did this could have killed my horses. You, me, Darrel! All for a fucking land deal?"

"Settle down. You don't know that." He handed her the oxygen mask. "Take another hit of oxygen. You still sound like a bullfrog with a bad cold."

Sierra nodded. Yeah, the cool air helped her throat but did nothing to cool off her temper.

"I won't be scared off." She threw the mask next to the tank.

"Maybe that's not why your barn was torched. Have you made anyone else mad lately?" Rhett shook his head at the paramedic. "I think we're done with the oxygen. Thanks." The man began packing up his equipment.

"Yes, thanks, Ronnie." Sierra realized she'd been rude to the man, who was a neighbor. "The oxygen helped."

"No problem, Sierra. Sorry about the barn. You need a place for a horse or two, call me. I'll come with my trailer." He jumped down from the back of the truck. "I hope we catch the fucker who did this. Burning barns with horses inside. That's pure evil." He nodded. "I'd better see if anyone needs me up front."

"Evil. You've got that right. Yes, I'll take you up on that tomorrow. Appreciate it." Sierra moved out of the way so the man could move the truck. "You see? Not everyone around here hates me."

"Good to know." Rhett frowned. "Have you thought of anyone else who does?"

"You were a witness yesterday. Clearly Will Jackson is pissed at me for putting his son into my therapy group." Sierra realized it would be a long time before she'd get to work with her kids again. Another reason to be furious and sick to her stomach.

"He's just enough of an asshole to want to make you pay." Rhett glanced over at the ruins. "First, you need to call the sheriff and get her out here. Since we all agree this was arson. I don't know how volunteer fire departments work, if they have their own arson investigator."

"In a small town like Muellerville? It'll be the sheriff's job. I hope this time she takes me seriously. Surely she won't think I burned down my own barn." Sierra's eyes stung. God, the smoke had done a number on her.

"The fire looks about done. Why don't we go into the house? You can call her and anyone else you think needs to know about this." Rhett guided her around where the firemen were still watching the smoldering barn.

The ground was muddy, and Sierra slipped. She landed awkwardly and fell into his arms. For a moment she stayed where she was, cheek against his bare chest. His nice broad chest, now covered with dark streaks of soot, felt good, warm, under her face and hands. She leaned back and touched the colorful tattoo circling his bicep.

"Flames? Really? Can't say that does it for me right now." She traced the red, yellow and orange tattoo with a fingertip.

"My first best-seller was *Firestorm*. That's the one that made me do a deep dive on arson. I recently dated a tattoo artist. Getting this seemed like a good idea at the time." Rhett held her by the shoulders.

"It's beautiful." Sierra smiled up at him. "Thanks for pitching in and risking your life to save my horses, especially the last one. You definitely played the man card there. You even helped the firemen find the source of the fire. Is there anything you can't do, Rhett Hall?"

"Plenty, but I hope you never find out what those things are." He brushed a finger across her cheek. "I'm sorry about your barn, Sierra. I had to man up when you were taking off into a burning building like the guardian angel for all those horses." He smiled, his hand warm on her skin. "I admire the hell out of you."

"Uh, thanks." Sierra blinked back the tears that had been close to falling since she'd first looked at those poor horses in the corral.

"You're covered in grime. You didn't get burned anywhere, did you?" Rhett ran his hands down her arms.

"No, I'm fine. Just mad as hell." Sierra grabbed his hands and held on. "I swear to God, Rhett, we'd better find the bastard who started that fire and bring him to justice."

"Damn right. Call the sheriff. If we're lucky, she'll find some evidence to identify your firebug." Rhett turned her toward the house and gently helped her over the rough ground.

Did he think she was an invalid? Feel sorry for her because of the limp? At this point, bone tired and sad, Sierra found it impossible to care. It was clear that if someone was determined to force her off her ranch, she needed help. Rhett was obviously willing, but he was a stranger. Family would be better, people she'd known all her life, guaranteed to want what she wanted. Her brother was a lawyer and knew people, like the investigator who'd looked up Rhett's background. Yep, she was calling in favors. She didn't like depending on anyone, but desperate times...

They reached the front of the house just as the sun rose in the east. A car rolled up at the same time. The sheriff. Apparently Jim had decided the arson claim had enough merit to call her right away. Good.

Sheriff Myra Watkins climbed out of her car, took one look at Sierra, then at the firefighters loitering nearby and taking their time rolling up their hoses. Myra frowned and shook her head.

"What?" Sierra didn't understand her reaction.

Rhett scrubbed a hand over his face, looked down at her, then cleared his throat. "Uh, now that the sun is up, you might want to go inside and change clothes. Or at least pull your robe together before you talk to her."

"I've been working a fire. So I'm a little dirty. And wet." She'd been sprayed a few times. A hazard when you're standing near the firefighters. She hadn't given a thought to how she looked since she'd jumped out of bed.

Rhett fought a smile. "Look down at yourself, Sierra."

She did. Well, there it was. The white T-shirt she'd slept in was filthy, of course. And wet. So her boobs were on display for all to see—nipples prominent and tight in the chill morning air. She blew out a *humph* of disgust with men that sent her into a coughing jag. That made the firefighters stare and nudge each other. Well, let the little boys gawk all they wanted; she had important things on her mind. She turned on her heel and headed into the house. While she was there, she'd shower. Sierra grabbed her cell phone and called her brother while she walked. Yes, important things. Like figuring out who had almost cost her every horse she owned, not to mention her barn and tack.

Chapter Seven

By the time Sierra got back to the living room, Rhett realized he and the sheriff had reached an impasse. The sheriff had started off suspicious of anyone "not from around here." That Rhett had shown up on Sierra's doorstep the day before the fire made him even more of a suspect. He had the opportunity, staying just steps away from the barn and all. Seemed to the sheriff that this was an open-and-shut case. Who else could get past the security at the gate and throw gasoline around, then get clean away without leaving a trail?

Rhett knew he should be worried but instead was taking mental notes like crazy. Sheriff in a small Texas town, Myra Watkins was the widow of the former sheriff. She'd taken over when her husband had died on the job. Oh, he hadn't been gunned down in a shoot-out. Heart attack. She made it clear that she might have been elected on a sympathy vote but had kept the office because she was hard on crime. She'd met her late husband while at a law enforcement seminar put on by the FBI. She looked Rhett right in the eye and dared him to try to treat her like anything but a cop determined to do her duty.

"Yes, ma'am. Ask me anything." He knew better than to come across as defensive as he fielded her questions. She could probably throw him in the local jail just for *looking* guilty. Sheriff Watkins frowned through Rhett's explanation of how he happened to be staying with Sierra.

"I tell you, Sheriff, I've spent exactly one day in Dallas. Flew in, signed a few books at a bookstore, then flew back to Austin, where I was staying with my sister."

"Am I supposed to be impressed that you're a big shot author? My cousin wrote a book. If I found her at the site of a suspicious fire, I'd treat her just like I'm treating you." She made a note in her spiral-bound book. "Give me details of that trip. You sure you didn't connect with that outfit trying to buy Sierra's land?"

Rhett told her everything he knew about the store where he'd signed, the people he'd met and the date he'd been there. He had to rein in his rising temper. She was being thorough. Which was a good thing. But this was a waste of time. The sheriff should be out looking at the evidence, checking video if Sierra's security system had that capability. He mentioned that.

"Good idea." Myra stood when Rhett got up and headed for the kitchen. "Where are you going?"

"My throat's dry. I inhaled a lot of smoke. I need water. Would you like a bottle?" Rhett opened the refrigerator and grabbed a bottle. He wished like hell he could shower, like Sierra had obviously decided to do before facing off with the law.

"No, thanks. Sierra's been trying to convince me that developer is behind why her cows are dying and her fence was pulled down." The sheriff had followed him into the kitchen. "Where's Rachel? I sure could use a cup of coffee."

"It's her day off." Sierra came into the kitchen looking clean and fresh, yet exhausted. "I'll make us a pot. Sit at the table, Myra. How about some breakfast? I can scramble some eggs, make toast. Rhett?" Her smile looked forced.

Rhett touched her shoulder. "Show me to the skillet. Eggs are one thing I can throw together." He turned on the faucet and scrubbed his hands. Didn't help much since he wore soot and smoke from head to toe, but it made him feel better. "Start the coffee, then sit. The sheriff and I were just wondering if your security system includes video."

"We have cameras recording at the gate, others but not behind the barn." Sierra filled the coffeemaker and punched the button.

"That's too bad. Hall, if you're going to cook, put on a shirt first." The sheriff pulled out a chair. "Sierra may like staring at your manly chest but I've seen enough of it. Kind of puts me off my food, if you want to know the truth."

Sierra rolled her eyes. "Sorry, Myra. Maybe we should let Rhett shower instead of cook."

"No, sit there and rest, Sierra." Rhett set the pan on the stove. "Be right back. You take it easy." He heard Myra express her sympathy for the lost barn as he strode toward his room. He wiped off his chest with a washcloth, then put on a clean T-shirt. He still stunk of smoke but it couldn't be helped. As he stepped back into the kitchen he heard the sheriff talking.

"Bastard who started that fire is going down. Hard. I promise you that."

"Thanks, Myra." Sierra was breaking eggs into a bowl.

"I've got that. Sit. Drink your coffee. It's ready." Rhett poured them cups then pulled the milk and butter out of the fridge.

"You really don't have to cook for us." But Sierra collapsed into a chair, her face pale. "I'm just so tired."

"I know." Rhett knew shock when he saw it. He went through the process of fixing breakfast, his stomach waking up to the fact that he was starving.

"Start at the beginning, Sierra. Where were you when you noticed the barn was on fire?" Sheriff Myra fired questions at Sierra while Rhett made toast and dished out three plates before he carried them to the table. He refilled their cups and poured coffee for himself.

"Cream? Sugar?" He felt like a waiter.

"Black is fine. But I could use a fork." Myra smirked, like she wasn't surprised that Rhett had forgotten one of the essentials.

"Sure." Rhett started to turn away when Sierra grabbed his hand.

"This looks delicious. Thanks." She smiled at him. "Now sit down. I'll get utensils and napkins." She stood and wrapped her arms around his waist. "And thanks for last night. If I forgot to say it earlier." She looked up and wrinkled her nose. "We should have let you shower before breakfast."

"Sorry if my reek offends you." Rhett smiled to show he didn't mean it. "We saved your horses. That's all that matters."

"Eggs are getting cold. And I wouldn't mind some jelly for this toast, while you're up, Sierra." Myra was deep into her coffee.

"Right away." Sierra put her back to the sheriff and gave Rhett's waist a final squeeze. "Got to keep the law happy."

Rhett watched her wearily pull out a drawer, then open the refrigerator again. He sat down across from the sheriff. "Go easy on her. This has been a rough night. Can't you see how exhausted Sierra is?"

"I've got a job to do, Hall. She wants this arsonist caught, so don't tell me what to do or not to do." Myra took the fork and knife Sierra handed her. "Isn't that right, honey? You're not too tired to help me figure out who might have done this, are you?" She twisted the top off a jar of strawberry preserves and spread plenty on her toast.

"No, I'm not. But that won't rebuild my barn. Or get my horses settled." She sat down and poked a fork into her eggs. "One of my brothers is on his way. He's a lawyer. He'll act as a liaison with your office. And with the insurance company. They'll probably send their own arson investigator."

"Good. You're right. You need a trained arson investigator on this." Rhett put down his coffee. "When can we expect your brother?" He didn't know how long he'd be welcome here with family arriving, but he was glad Sierra was getting the support.

"Liaison? To my mind that's another word for interfering outsider. It'll be bad enough having someone from a big insurance outfit digging around here." Myra shook her head. "Call your brother off."

"No. I want him here, and it's none of your business who I ask to stay with me." She turned to Rhett. "Dylan will be here later today. He just had to tie up a few loose ends at his office so he can stay awhile."

"Am I in the way? Do you want me to leave?" It took everything in him to make that offer. Leave without finding out if it *had* been arson? And, if so, who'd set the fire and why? He needed to know how a story ended. Especially because Sierra looked haunted, vulnerable. She certainly wasn't the full-of-fire woman she'd been just hours earlier.

"After how you stepped up last night, I think you've earned the right to stay and continue your research. I'm sure this kind of"—she swallowed—"action is interesting to you." She still hadn't eaten a bite, but she finally sipped some coffee.

"Not just interesting, Sierra." Rhett hated that she thought he was that objective, using this situation for his own purposes. Though she wasn't so far off base. His damned writer's mind wouldn't be still. Of course he itched to write down his impressions of the sights, sounds and smells of what had happened last night.

"Let's talk about last night." Myra had polished off her breakfast and got up to refill her cup, making herself at home. "I need a timeline. See how this played out exactly. Your houseguest here claims he woke up when the fire alarm went off. Is that how you remember it, Sierra?" She looked her over with an eyebrow raised, as if implying they'd shared a bed.

Sierra stabbed her eggs with her fork so hard it screeched against the plate. "I have no idea when he woke up. I was asleep in my own bed at the other end of the house." She stared at the sheriff. "I heard the fire alarm about the same time Rhett banged on my bedroom door."

"Alarm company puts that at 3:48 this morning." Myra's notebook was on the table now, next to her empty plate.

"I was too busy to look at a clock." Sierra scooped up more egg. "My horses were screaming!" Tears filled her eyes. "You ever heard a horse scream in terror? Imagine ten of them crying and kicking and—" She jumped up and flung her plate into the sink, where it broke. Then she stood there, facing the window above it. Her shoulders shook as she cried silently.

Rhett jumped up and pulled her into his arms. No, he didn't really know her, but he couldn't let her cry like that, covering her face with a worn dish towel. He held her against him, his eyes meeting the sheriff's over her shoulders. "Can't you do this later, Sheriff? Sierra's obviously reached her limit."

"Fine." She got up, chair scraping across the floor. "I'm going out to talk to the fire chief again. Maybe he's found something in the wreckage, a clue to help us track down the perp. We'll talk later." The door shut quietly as she left.

Rhett just stood there, Sierra's hair brushing his chin, breathing in her clean womanly scent. The way she kept that cloth over her face killed him. As if she had to hide her misery. He tried to tug it away but she held firm as she kept crying.

"Sierra, come on now. You'll make yourself sick. Why don't you lie down for a while? Until your brother gets here. I need to shower and change clothes; then I could make some calls for you. You have a list? Maybe names of those neighbors who could take a horse or two until you get a new barn built?"

She pushed back so suddenly and with such force that Rhett rocked back on his heels. "Get a barn built? Just like that? And how long would it stand before whoever wants me gone burns it down too? Maybe they'd get smart this time and cut the phone line first so the alarm didn't go off. Killing a few of my horses as a consequence. That would sure send a message. 'Get the hell out of here, Sierra. Sell out and give us your land.'" She wiped her damp cheeks with her palms and stomped around the kitchen table.

Before Rhett knew what she planned, she picked up his plate and aimed it at the sink. *Crash,* it joined hers in pieces. The sheriff's was next. Apparently destroying pottery was her way of dealing with anger. Coffee cups were next. Hey, she wasn't totally out of control. Every piece went right into the sink. No extra mess to clean up. Rhett just stayed out of the line of fire. When she turned to eye the counter, he put his hand over hers.

"Please spare the coffeepot. I need a cup to wake up every morning." He held out his hands. "Feel better?"

"Of course not!" She shook her head.

"Want to hit me? Would that help?" He offered his chin. He knew better than to smile when she actually made a fist.

"Only if you were the one to start the fire." She glared at him. "Were you?"

Rhett froze. "Seriously? You're asking me that after I ran into that fucking fire to save your horses?" His temper stirred. "What in the hell would be my motive? Oh, I forgot, I'm a stranger. Maybe this is an elaborate setup arranged by that evil Dallas developer." He stared into her eyes. "Someone who I have never even met. But don't let the facts confuse the issue."

"Facts? The fact is you conveniently landed on my doorstep, then all hell broke loose." Sierra had her chin up, fire in her eyes. "I'd be stupid not to be suspicious of you."

"Fine. I'll pack my bags." He stomped out of the kitchen and toward his bedroom.

"Rhett, wait!" She stopped him with a hand on his back. "I'm sorry. Honestly? I—I don't know what to think right now."

He turned around, and Sierra's hand landed on his chest. She had to feel his heart pounding. The thought of leaving here pissed him off. He wanted to stay. And not just for the story. Hell, he wanted to know where this chemistry that thrummed between them might go.

"I do remember how you helped save my horses. I'll be forever grateful for that." She backed up. "Can you give me time to think about what happened?"

"Sure. And I understand your suspicions. If the word of a stranger isn't enough for you, I'll gladly take a lie detector test, if that's what you need to believe me." He was a decent guy. Loved horses. He'd never... Well, forget that. "I stink. I'm taking a shower. You look beat. Maybe you'll decide I'm on your side after you've had a nap." With that he turned on his heel and walked away. Good thing, because he'd had the stupid urge to kiss her. To pull her in and show her that he was not only on her side but could comfort her until she was boneless.

Down, boy. She was still in shock over the fire. And he sure as hell didn't need to touch her when he reeked of smoke and horse. He stripped and stepped into the shower. He could wash away the stench of what he'd been through, but he'd never forget the sound of those terrified horses trapped in the blazing building. Their screams had pulled him in when his better judgment had urged him to stay safely outside. He was no hero, but he'd never let an animal suffer if he could prevent it.

Thank God he'd managed to get out again. His lungs burned when he tried to inhale deeply, and he bent over, coughing until he almost strangled. *Shit.* Not since his college days, when he'd thought it cool to pull all-nighters in smoke-clouded rooms, had he had such a weight on his chest. He hoped the steam from a hot shower would soak away some of that heaviness and the fresh country air of Sierra's ranch would take care of the rest. He just hoped she let him stay and her brother didn't try to run him off. He'd had the urge when he'd found his sister shacked up with a stranger. Of course, his feisty sister wouldn't allow him to run her life. Would Sierra stand up to her brother? Or would she decide Rhett couldn't be trusted? Damn it, he didn't deserve her suspicions.

When he finally got to the living room, Rhett felt human again. Then he saw Sierra asleep on the leather couch, a pad of paper and pen on her chest. She'd been exhausted. Seeing her like that, his anger seeped out of him. The paper was a list of names and phone numbers. These must be the neighbors she hoped would take in her horses until she had a place to keep them. If he called them for her, it might help prove he was on her side. He walked quietly into the kitchen and picked up the house phone.

It soon became obvious that small towns had busy networks. Call it gossip or just a grapevine, but most of the ranchers he called had already heard about Sierra's fire and were more than willing to take a horse or two. They accepted the fact that he was calling for her and claimed they were already hitching horse trailers to their heavy-duty trucks. By the time Rhett got to the bottom of her list, he was sure all of the horses would have safe places to stay.

"Who the hell are you?" The voice came from the back door. The man wore jeans and a white dress shirt. He carried a suitcase in one hand and had a garment bag slung over his shoulder.

"Rhett Hall. Sierra's houseguest." He stood and extended his hand. "You must be her brother Dylan."

"Yes, I am. Houseguest?" Dylan frowned and looked him over. "That some kind of euphemism for boyfriend?"

"No. I'll explain—" Rhett didn't have a chance to say more before Sierra ran into the room and straight into her brother's arms.

"Dylan!" She gave him a hug then stepped back. "Rhett's just a new friend. Not a boyfriend. Quit giving him the evil eye."

"It's my duty as your big brother." He held her at arm's length and looked her over. "I'm sorry as hell about the barn. I saw it. Looks like a total loss. Clearly you've been through the wringer. What do you need for me to do?"

Sierra held his hand. "Help us find the bastards who did this and shut them down. So I can get back to my life here without looking over my shoulder all the time. Think you can handle that?"

"We'll see." He picked up his gear from where it had hit the floor. "This bozo using my room? Or yours?"

"Um, I did give him your room." Sierra flushed. "We can move things around."

"Not necessary. I'll take Mason's room. That puts me right between you two." Dylan grinned. "As for solving your problems, I'll need a hell of a lot more information than you've given me so far, sis. Pull out all the papers you've received from this Oxcart group. You know how I love paperwork." He headed down the hall.

Rhett handed Sierra the list he'd left by the house phone. "So, this bozo made some calls for you while you napped. The checks are next to the names of neighbors who will be here soon with horse trailers."

"Really?" She took the paper. "Thanks. I guess I owe you an apology for earlier. Accusing you... I wasn't myself." She touched Rhett's arm. "I think everything that happened got to me. Throwing dishes!" She frowned at the mess in the kitchen sink. "What was I thinking? Rachel will kill me."

"You were upset. Sometimes you just have to vent." Rhett moved closer. "I'll clean it up."

"No, I did it. I'll deal with it." She groaned. "I've never lost control like that before."

"You were provoked." Rhett moved behind her and rested his hands on her shoulders as she plucked a broken cup out by the handle. "You sure you never lose control? Not even..."

"I thought you two were just friends." That voice again. "What the hell happened to the crockery, Sierra?"

"I had a temper fit." Sierra turned in Rhett's arms so they were chest to chest. "Um, we are becoming friends." She wiggled away from him to get the trash can.

"You look cozier than friends." Dylan stepped closer.

"Back off, Dylan. This man helped pull my horses out of the barn when it was burning. He was almost killed doing it!" Sierra swatted her brother with a washcloth. "I owe Rhett and I haven't been fair to him."

"You're forgiven." Rhett smiled. He knew better than to say more. "As long as I can stay like we arranged."

"Of course." Sierra smiled back.

"Cozy. I don't like it. But we can discuss this later." Dylan walked to the door and opened it. "Sounds like you have company. Pulling horse trailers."

"The neighbors. So soon!" She rushed to look outside.

"You'd better supervise them, Sierra. I'll clean up the mess here." Rhett dragged the trash can next to the sink.

"Thanks, Rhett." She walked over and kissed his cheek, then walked outside, the screen door slamming behind her.

Rhett heard her call a greeting to the new arrival.

"Watch yourself, Hall. She's vulnerable." Dylan moved to follow her. "I'm onto your tricks. Playing the hero, are you? Stop it. And stay out of her bed."

Rhett kept his smile hidden. Brotherly bluster. He'd tried it a time or two himself. It wasn't worth spit. Sierra would do what she wanted, when she wanted.

"Right now, your sister is tearing her heart out over deciding where each horse is going to spend the next few months while she builds a new barn. Can we shelve this discussion? Get out there and help her." Rhett followed him. Then he looked down at Dylan's loafers. "You might want to change shoes. Even I have learned that boots work best here."

"You son of a bitch. Those are my boots you're wearing." Dylan had noticed.

"Yeah. Thanks for the loan. Lucky we wear the same size. I'll gladly pay for them. There are two more pair in that closet."

"You have on custom-made Lucchese ostrich. Dumbass. You don't wear those to muck out stalls. You wear the worn leather ones." Dylan clenched his fists. "I'm running a background check on you, Yankee. First thing."

"Don't bother. Sierra already did. Give your sister credit. She's sharp and not as trusting as you seem to think she is." Rhett frowned. "Ostrich? Sorry about that. Obviously I need to learn more about boots. Thanks for the tip." He glanced outside. Eight trucks were lined up, each with a horse trailer, some of them doubles. Sierra was talking to the men and women who had driven them. She obviously had special considerations when deciding who got which horse. The stallion was the hardest to handle and there was some discussion about who would take him.

*   *   *   *

"Don't worry about him, Sierra. My boy Miguel is good with even the toughest stud. Let him see what he can do." A large man with a swarthy face nodded toward a young man sitting on the fence near the stallion. He was talking quietly to the animal.

"Thanks, Mr. Rodriguez. If Miguel can get him into the trailer quietly, I'll be amazed. We had a heck of a time getting him here after he was rescued. The abuse he suffered… No wonder he's a handful. Believe it or not, he's settled down since we got him. I know you'll be kind to him." Sierra turned when Rhett joined her. "Everyone came. I'm so grateful." Her blue eyes sparkled in the sunlight.

"I know this is hard for you." Rhett saw his mount being led into a trailer. "There goes Blanco. I guess I won't be riding for a while."

"Neither will I. And forget the therapy group." Sierra's shoulders drooped. "Whoever did this has no idea how many people this affected."

"Maybe they did." The sheriff walked up. "Not everyone liked that therapy group you ran. I hear you had words with one of the parents about it just yesterday."

"True. But I can't imagine..." Sierra shook her head. "Will Jackson didn't want his son in therapy, but he'd never burn down a barn. Would he?"

"He's not a rancher, so he sure might. You'd better believe I'll be talking to him. I don't care how many Chevys he sells the town at a discount." Myra glanced at Rhett. "I consider everyone a suspect until I personally clear them."

"Good to hear." Dylan walked out of the house in his own leather boots. "How are you doing, Sheriff Myra?"

"Dylan, good to see you. Not that you need to worry yourself about this investigation. I'm handling it." The sheriff nodded. "I'd best be going. Got plenty to do."

"I'll be by your office later. Just to hear about your progress." Dylan smiled.

"All righty then." The sheriff walked away toward her police car.

"She doesn't want anyone looking over her shoulder." Rhett saw that Sierra was too involved with the horses to have noticed that last exchange. Her ranch hand Darrel had appeared and was helping her.

"She'll have to deal with it. She's got too many deep ties in this town to be objective. I'm getting a top-notch arson investigator up here if I have to hire one myself." Dylan walked over to his sister and put his arm around her.

Rhett liked that, and decided he liked Sierra's brother. Too bad Dylan might try to get in the way of whatever might develop with Sierra. Rhett had jumped over obstacles before. He could do it again.

Chapter Eight

Sierra had just seen the last horse into its trailer when her cell phone rang. She knew this number and braced herself. Damn her brother for looping in the rest of her family.

"Hi, Mama."

"Baby, are you all right? Dylan told me you ran into your burning barn to rescue horses." Great cell service. Her mother's voice was so clear Sierra would swear she could hear the catch as Mama fought tears. "What were you thinking?"

"I saved every last one of them. Thanks to some help. Darrel and a new friend." Oh, hell.

"New friend?"

"I'm real busy here, Mama. Can I call you back later?"

"No, you can't, young lady. I want to hear about this new friend. Right after you tell me how your barn caught fire." Mama sobbed. "My God, I don't know what I'd do if I lost you."

"You didn't lose me. I'm fine. I inhaled a little smoke, but you wouldn't believe how professional the volunteer firefighters were. They gave me oxygen and insisted I be looked over by the local doctor." Sierra didn't admit that the only doctor she'd let look at her had been the vet. Dr. Cibrowski had frowned but finally listened to her lungs with his own stethoscope and declared them clear. That had been after he'd checked her horses. He still wanted her to make an appointment soon with her own physician.

"Oxygen! That doesn't sound good. I'm coming home on the next flight."

"Don't you dare. You and Harvey are on your honeymoon. I won't have you interrupting that for me." It was bad enough her mother had made her man wait years before she'd agreed to tie the knot. "Promise me you'll stay put."

"Harvey will understand. I made it clear when I finally agreed to marry him that my family would always come first." Her mother had that stubborn edge in her voice.

"There's nothing you can do here. You'll just get in the way." Sierra looked around to be sure no one else was within earshot. "I'm just getting to know this new friend. He's a famous author. You'd like him. He ran into that burning barn and pulled Chief out, risking his own life to save him."

"So this *is* a new boyfriend." Now her mother was really listening. "I get it. You're sure you aren't hurt? That you don't need me to take care of you?"

"I'm sure. Dylan is here. He's helping me with the insurance stuff." God, she hoped he hadn't mentioned arson to Mama. The fact that her mother hadn't brought it up made her think he'd kept his mouth shut about that.

"You need a good man by your side on that ranch. You think he's interested in settling down?"

"It's early days to start that conversation, Mama." When had she become such a glib liar?

"I like that he saved your horse for you. Tell me more about him."

"I really don't have time now. The horses have to board at the neighbors' while I see about building a new barn. It's a logistical nightmare. Can I call you tomorrow? Will you tell Mason and Cassidy about this and make sure they know I'm fine? I really have enough help right now. I promise you." It took another ten minutes, but Sierra finally got her mother off the phone with a promise to call daily with updates.

One last look around, and she was glad to see that things were settled. The firemen were gone. Dylan, with Tramp at his feet, was talking to Darrel, who'd finally appeared to help with the horses. Her insurance agent had shown up and stood frowning next to both of them. Fred Meadows said something that made Dylan raise his voice and a fist. Sierra turned her back on them. If there was a problem with the insurance, she didn't want to hear it. Not right now, when she was already overwhelmed.

Rhett smiled at her from across the pool, where he had stripped off his shirt and was using a hose to wash off his face and hands. *Oh, my.* What a pretty sight. He caught her staring, so she waved at him then gestured toward the house. It was sunset and she was exhausted. She started walking and didn't look back.

Inside, she collapsed on the couch, smiling when Rhett followed her into the living room. He'd put his shirt back on, darn it.

"I'm glad you finally came in. You look worn out." He sat beside her. "What did the vet say?"

"He assured me that the horses had only minor burns. Chief got the worst of it." She took the bottle of water Rhett handed her. "He's lucky to be alive, thanks to you. Doc said Miguel is great with him. Held his head and soothed him while Doc managed to put ointment on the places that needed it."

"Good. Now drink. The fire chief's orders. I know my throat is still raw from inhaling all that smoke."

"Thanks." She twisted off the cap, and the water did feel good going down. "How are your hands?" She picked up one of them. His palm was red. It had to hurt. "I should put more antiseptic on them."

"Torture me again? No thanks. They're sore but I'll live." He smiled. "Just drink."

"Fine. Be brave, macho man." She dropped his hand. For a few moments they just sat there, side by side, drinking quietly. Rhett finally set his empty bottle on the table in front of them and looked at her.

"I know it was hard to watch all the horses leave."

She couldn't stand his sympathy right now; the tears she'd been desperately holding back might finally fall. She nodded and stared at her water bottle.

"They'll be fine. You know that, don't you?"

Who was this man? Where had he come from? And why did she trust him? But she did. He'd never been far from her side all through the hellish day, and when she'd watched her rescued horses being taken away in trailers. Damn it, she had nursed some of them back from the brink of death. Would she ever see them again? She set down her empty bottle then covered her eyes. Now she was being ridiculous. She could drive over right now and check out the places where each of them was being boarded.

"Hey, look who's here." Rhett squeezed her knee. "Rachel, where did you come from? Isn't it your day off?"

"Oh, honey, when I heard what happened..." The housekeeper rushed into the room. "Sierra, are you all right?"

Sierra didn't have to answer because she was pulled up into Rachel's motherly embrace. It was comforting and kept her from crying. Good thing. She was sick of feeling sorry for herself.

"Hey, I'm okay. My horses are okay. My barn is a total loss but I have good insurance, I think." She pushed back. "Thanks for coming."

"How could I stay away?" Rachel wiped her eyes with a tissue from her pocket. "Now that I'm here, I'm fixing you all a good dinner. Rhett,

I hear you were a real help with the horses. And I saw Dylan outside! It's been too long since that boy visited."

"Yes, it has. Is the insurance agent still here?" Sierra wondered if she needed to pull out her policy.

"No, Fred Meadows took off. Insurance. Seems like you have to have it, but make a claim and they'll figure out how to screw you every time." Rachel sniffed. "Don't listen to me. Dylan will handle all that." She tied on her apron. "Now I know you must be hungry. I'm fixing your brother's favorite, chicken-fried steak. Any word on the rest of your family, Sierra?"

"They're all in London. Negotiating a big deal. Well, Mason and his wife are negotiating. Mama is there honeymooning and giving Mason her opinion as a major stockholder in Texas Star." Sierra was glad to have something to talk about besides the fire. She turned to Rhett. "My other brother is head of the family oil company and his wife is CEO of Calhoun Petroleum. They're working together now. Quite the power couple."

"Wow! I've heard of both companies. Who hasn't?" Rhett smiled at Rachel. "Chicken-fried steak. Can't wait to try the Texas version, Rachel."

"It'll be better than Boston's." She smiled. "You two just sit and relax. Dinner will be ready in about an hour."

"I appreciate your coming in today, Rachel." Sierra sighed. "Truly. I was just trying to decide if I had the energy to nuke some leftovers."

"I don't guess it's easy to call for a pizza delivery out here in the country." Rhett pulled out his phone. "That's my go-to in town."

"Oh, they'll deliver, but it'll be cold. Just relax. I take care of my people." Rachel collected their empty water bottles. "You want beer or wine before dinner?"

"Just water. We're staying hydrated after inhaling so much smoke." Sierra started to get up.

"I can get it." Rhett jumped to his feet.

"Sit back down. Both of you." Rachel said it so sharply he dropped instantly. "Sorry, but I want to wait on you. When I saw that barn in ruins..." Her eyes filled with tears. "Well, just relax. I got this." She hurried out of the room, her tissue out again.

"I'm scared to move." Rhett smiled at Sierra." You're lucky to have her."

"I know. Rachel has worked for our family since I was a little girl. You heard her—Dylan is still a boy to her. We came to the ranch weekends and most of the summers, because I was horse mad. She was here when I had my accident." Sierra gestured at her bad leg, which she had propped on the coffee table. It throbbed from all the exercise she'd gotten running with the horses and staying on her feet all day.

"Your accident." Rhett was clearly fishing for her story.

Why not? "It happened when I was barrel racing."

"Are you kidding? Explain." He leaned forward so he could look into her eyes. Rhett curious was intense. And flattering.

"We're timed as we race around barrels set in a cloverleaf pattern. It takes a special kind of horse to do it, one trained to respond to the rider's commands. I had an amazing horse, Destiny. She was so responsive. When we competed, it was as if she could read my mind." Sierra's sigh turned into a cough. "I was sixteen and at the top of my game. I ruled at the local rodeo here. Won first place at every event that last summer. No one could beat me." She smiled at Rhett. "Of course, you know teenagers. I was full of myself. Obnoxious."

"I can relate. I played sports in high school. When you're winning, your ego can be as big as Boston." He grinned. Obviously he had some memories of his own.

"I begged my daddy to let me enter the Houston rodeo, which is held every February. He wasn't eager for me to do that. It's more professional than the local events and the competition is fierce. Around here, the other racers are just the girls from town and neighboring counties. But I set out to prove I was ready for the big time. I entered every local competition I could." She rubbed her thigh. "And won."

"Obviously you and Destiny were amazing." Rhett picked up her hand. "So what happened?"

"We went to the Austin rodeo as a warm-up for Houston. The competition was a little stiffer. Daddy even let me cut school to prepare. I had a room full of trophies by then."

"I'd like to have seen you ride around those barrels."

"It goes really fast. Seconds. Destiny could hug those barrels, get close without knocking one down." Sierra leaned forward, reliving those races in her head. She could almost feel the rush of riding hell-for-leather into the arena, racing toward the first turn. God, how she missed it, even after all these years.

"You're flushed just talking about it." He squeezed her hand. "What happened, Sierra?"

"I was always careful with my tack, I swear it. Maybe I was too excited that day and it made me careless, I don't know. There is no way what happened should have happened. One minute I was tearing around the barrels, making great time. Then—" She shuddered and looked away. "I flew through the air. My saddle slipped and I was under my horse. Destiny stumbled, hit a barrel and landed on top of me."

"God, Sierra. You could have been killed!"

"Yeah. Believe me, when a thousand pounds of horse falls on you, it hurts." She was gripping Rhett's hand again. "Poor Destiny struggled to get up, of course. She didn't mean to step on me but I was tangled up in the reins, the saddle. Shit! I have no idea why the whole thing was such a mess." Sierra leaned back and closed her eyes. "Everything after I fell is still a blur."

"I guess so." Rhett stayed quiet while she pulled herself together.

"Destiny was okay, thank God. I wasn't. They took me in an ambulance to the nearest hospital. Did what they could there while Daddy flew in the best orthopedic specialists in the country. He spared no expense and the surgeries began. Oil money does have its uses." She opened her eyes and met Rhett's concerned gaze.

"After the accident and college, I decided this was where I wanted to be." Sierra looked around the room, so full of memories. There was Daddy's secret bar, the stuffed trophies and Mama's books on a shelf. Down the hall was another room with her own trophies of a different kind. She used it as her office now. This was her home. And people wanted her to just leave it? For money? She shook her head.

"That had to be painful. All those surgeries." Rhett obviously was still thinking more about her fall. Storyteller. He wanted to know how it ended.

"Yes. There were a lot of them. Until I called a halt." She slapped her aching thigh. "This is as good as it's going to get." Keep it light. It was the only way she could deal with it.

"What happened to your horse? I didn't meet Destiny in your barn."

"Good question." Sierra liked that he cared about her horse. "Daddy went haywire after the accident. By the time I was aware enough to know what had happened, he'd sold Destiny to a family back east. I didn't speak to him for a long time over that. I loved that horse, and I never even got to say goodbye." Oh, shit. Her voice broke. After all this time. But that had hurt.

"I'm sorry, Sierra. I know how you are about your horses." Rhett's warm hand on hers was comforting.

"Don't get me wrong. It took me a while, but I realized Daddy did the right thing. Destiny loved to race and I had to come to terms with the fact that I'd never race again. The family who bought her had a daughter who barrel raced. I checked. She won a lot of races with Destiny."

"You could never race again?" He looked into her eyes. "Are you sure?"

"Oh, yeah. Barrel racers are athletes. I got sick of going under the knife, but I'm not stupid. It was clear to me that I was never going to be the same. No matter how many surgeries I had or how much therapy I went through, my leg was not going to be right again. Daddy would have never quit calling in specialists so that I could walk 'normally' again." Sierra made her "screw it" face. "I decided it wasn't worth it. Mama backed me up."

"You do fine." He leaned forward and kissed her softly on the mouth. "More than fine."

Sierra took a beat to just breathe. Oh, but she'd needed to hear that. Then she eased back and looked away. "Thanks, but I can't run worth a damn. You saw that last night." Deep breath. "Here's the deal, Rhett." She focused on him, this man who seemed determined to be her ally, to help her. Well, maybe he could. "What I can't forget is the way my saddle fell off Destiny that day. What the hell happened? I'd run dozens of successful races before and I swear I checked my gear carefully that day, just like I always did. It was automatic with me. You know what I mean?"

"Yes, I do. Some things, safety concerns, do become automatic. Like when I get in my car I scan for gas, oil light, simple things like that. I'd imagine that when you're doing a dangerous ride like you were preparing for, you'd be extra careful to make sure your saddle is secure. Check and double-check everything before you get on your horse."

"Exactly!" Sierra found herself leaning closer. He looked tired and had a sexy five-o'clock shadow. Neither of them had stopped after breakfast, and now it was dinnertime. Above all he had those kind, kind eyes. "Thanks for understanding. I don't share this with just anyone. But I have always wanted to find out the truth about that day. Trouble is, it's been so long now. Twelve years. Most of the day itself is a blur to me. I was unconscious after being slammed against a barrel and trampled by a horse."

"One thing I'm good at is research, Sierra. Give me some details about that day—the date, the name of the event, as much as you can remember about who was there—and I'll see what I can find out. Leave it to me." He leaned back.

"And to me." Dylan stood in the doorway with two bottles of water in his hands. "Damn it, sis, you never told me you suspected foul play back then."

"What good would it have done?" Sierra grabbed the bottle he handed her and took a deep drink. She'd needed it. Her throat was raw, and she'd felt like she about to cough the whole time she'd been speaking.

"What *good*?" Dylan frowned as he gave Rhett the other bottle. "If some maniac sabotaged your gear on that horse before you raced, then that's attempted murder."

"Maniac? Or someone who wanted to win the race herself?" Rhett had his phone out, already looking at a website about barrel racing.

"Calm down now, both of you. I said I had a suspicion. No solid evidence. I don't even know what happened to my saddle and the rest of the tack I used that day."

"I know." Dylan paced the floor in front of them. "I was there, in law school at UT Austin. I've never seen Daddy so upset. It was all we could do to keep him from shooting Destiny on the spot. He blamed the horse. Mama talked him down from that."

"God! He couldn't!" Sierra gasped when something bumped her knee. It was Tramp, who had run in from the kitchen. He had obviously been outside then fed recently. He reeked of wood smoke and dog food. She rubbed his head then gently pushed him away. He trotted over to Dylan. Her whole family loved animals. For her father to have talked about killing a healthy horse... Well, thank God that hadn't happened.

"Dylan, what about the saddle, all of my barrel racing gear? If we could look at that, we might be able to see if it was tampered with." Sierra shook her head, as if she could shake off the past.

"You were in terrible pain. Daddy blamed himself. He was a lawyer, logical most of the time, but when it came to his kids, he could get, well, emotional." Dylan ran a hand through his hair.

"What did he do, Dylan?" Sierra recognized the gesture. All of the men in her family did it when they were stressed.

"Burned it all. Made a real big bonfire. Mama was so mad at him. Said he should have donated it to someone who needed it, like Rachel's girl Sally Ann. Daddy wouldn't hear of it. Claimed that Sally Ann might get hurt too. Told Rachel she'd be smart to forbid her daughter to race again. Then he lit that pile of very expensive leather and watched it go up in smoke."

"I remember that." Rachel stood in the doorway. "Never saw your daddy in such a state before. We all cried happy tears when they managed to save your leg, Sierra." She had the tissue out again. "I told my girl that I wasn't spending one more dime on barrel racing. She had to quit riding that summer. Entry fees were too high for her to pay without my help."

"I'm sorry for that. Sally Ann was good. She had a decent horse too. Came in second to me many times." Sierra stood and stretched. She'd finished her water. "This talk is depressing. Besides, something smells really good. I don't remember eating lunch."

"Yes, it does smell good." Rhett was up beside her. "And we did skip lunch. No wonder I'm hungry. Is it ready, Rachel?"

"Sure is. Come on into the kitchen. Or I can set you up in the dining room."

"Kitchen's fine." Sierra was glad to leave talk of the past behind as she followed Rachel. She sat at the table and finally relaxed. She'd like to leave this to Rhett and her brother. Rhett had certainly proved himself last night. Working as hard as she had to save her horses. And now he was willing to look into the event that had shaped her adult life. Even if he didn't find anything, it was a relief to hand it over to someone who took her seriously. She'd voiced her concerns to her parents in the hospital as soon as she was lucid. But they'd been too shocked, too worried about her leg, to listen. Then there had been her headaches from the head injury. Had she really told them anything? Much of that time after the accident was a haze of pain and doctors. Maybe she'd dreamed the scene where she'd told them her suspicions.

Enough. She let the delicious smell of Rachel's home cooking wash over her. After the stench of her burning barn, it was a welcome relief. But she couldn't forget that the fire was no accident. Who had set the blaze? Was this just another attempt to get her to sell out and leave? She suddenly lost her appetite as the other three filled their plates. Was she a fool for risking her horses and maybe her life for a piece of property?

"You'd better eat, sis. Rachel has outdone herself. Mashed potatoes, creamed corn and sweet peas from the garden." Dylan dropped a piece of steak on Sierra's plate. "Don't insult the cook by just sitting there. Dig in."

Sierra grabbed his arm and squeezed. "Thanks for coming. Did I say that?" Oh, hell. Her eyes filled with tears.

"You don't have to say it. I wouldn't be anywhere else." He plopped a spoonful of potatoes on her plate next. "You cry and I'll make you eat two pieces of steak." He added corn and peas. "You hear me?" His eyes were shiny. "Anyone wants to hurt you has to come through me."

Rhett smiled, his mouth full. But he nodded. Like he was agreeing.

"Okay then. Maybe I could eat." Sierra reached for the gravy boat. "Rhett, you need to try this gravy."

He swallowed and wiped his mouth with a napkin. "I have a confession to make."

Sierra stopped, her hand trembling. Oh, no, surely he wasn't—

"Don't look at me like that. I didn't burn down your barn."

She carefully set the small pitcher on the table. "Guess my nerves are more shot than I realized. Go ahead, Rhett. What are you confessing?"

"Remember I told you that my mama is from Atlanta. She cooks a great chicken-fried steak. With a dynamite gravy, Rachel. So going in, I was reserving judgment. It takes a lot to beat my mama's steak and gravy." He smiled.

"Well, what's the verdict?" Sierra's heart finally was beating normally again.

"If you ever meet my mama, don't tell her, but, Rachel, this beats my mama's chicken-fried steak all to hell." He cut another piece of it and waved the chunk with a perfect golden crust in the air. "Sorry if I freaked you out, Sierra."

"That's okay. It's my fault. I need to eat, I guess. This looks great, Rachel." She attempted a bite of Rachel's rightfully famous creamed corn. Sweet. Delicious.

"Dylan, tell me about your law practice." Rhett winked at her.

Sierra ate slowly as the conversation moved on to Houston and her brother's successful practice. Wow. She'd had no idea she was so on edge that one little statement could send her into a potential meltdown. She couldn't begin to finish her meal, but she ate enough to satisfy Dylan and a watchful Rachel. The housekeeper shooed them all out of the kitchen after they declared themselves full. She offered coffee and pie.

"Couldn't possibly. I'm ready for bed." Sierra had hit a wall and didn't pretend she hadn't.

"And I need a shower and bed myself. In the morning we can sit down and get those details about your accident. That okay?" Rhett hovered near her.

Dylan had his laptop out on a desk against one wall of the den. "I have work to do. See you both in the morning." He watched them.

"Good night." Sierra put her arms around Rhett. It would serve her nosy brother right if she laid a big kiss on Rhett. Too bad she didn't have the energy for it. "Thanks for today. And last night. You don't know me yet you risked your life to save my horses."

"Glad to help." He hugged her then stepped back. "See you in the morning." He looked down at his shirt. "I reek. I doubt these clothes are worth saving."

"Put them in the hamper in the hall bathroom and I'll see if I can wash the smell and stains out." Rachel stood in the doorway. "I'll do that tomorrow. Right now I'm heading out as soon as the kitchen's clean. I'll get here early and fix you all a good breakfast. But not too early. No horses to feed. You can sleep a little later. Right, Sierra?"

"Right." She thanked Rachel again then headed down the hall. Exhaustion overwhelmed her, but her mind wouldn't quit. By the time she was in bed, she figured she'd just lie there staring at the ceiling, wondering about the fire and who'd started it. But exhaustion won and she was out like a light.

Chapter Nine

"I want to hear more about how you ended up staying in my sister's house." Dylan shut his laptop then followed Rhett to the kitchen. He'd obviously risen early and been waiting for Rhett to leave his bedroom.

"Be glad to answer any questions right after I get my coffee." Rhett smiled at Rachel. "Something smells good." He took the mug she handed him. "Can we wait for Sierra to wake up? Unless she's already outside."

"No, she's still in bed." Rachel glanced at the clock. "It will do her good to sleep past seven for a change. You two go sit in the den and get acquainted while I finish this batch of cinnamon rolls. I'm sure the smell will wake her up. Surprised the bacon didn't do the trick." She turned back to the counter and a bowl. Tramp sat at her feet, hoping for bacon.

Dylan hugged the housekeeper. "Your cinnamon rolls are one of the reasons I come here." He refilled his own coffee. "Can't wait."

"Don't worry. I'll call you as soon as they're done." She slapped his hand when he reached for the raisins. "Go on now. Scram! Dog, go with them."

Dylan laughed and headed back to the recliner where he always sat. Rhett followed him. Tramp found his spot in front of the fireplace.

"You afraid I'm here with nefarious intent?" Rhett settled on the couch. He wished Sierra were there beside him, her firm thigh pressed against his. At least she was getting some sleep. He'd never seen anyone work as hard as she'd done yesterday. Her limp had been worse by the time they'd finished dinner, and there had been dark circles under her eyes. If her brother hadn't been watching last night, he would have carried her to her bedroom. Not to try anything, just to make it easier for her.

"'Nefarious intent.' Showing off your vocabulary, writer?" Dylan set his mug on the side table next to him. "I had my investigator send me a copy of the report he did for Sierra. I'm glad she had sense enough to have him run the background check."

"Sierra is certainly a sensible woman. She's been through a lot recently, though, and I'm glad I was here." Rhett leaned forward, elbows on his knees. "I'll be honest with you, MacKenzie."

"Please do." The recliner snapped down. Dylan looked ready for a cross-examination.

"I had no intention of staying on a ranch when I crashed in front of this place the other day. Sometimes things happen, and I've learned to pay attention when they do." He saw Dylan smirk. "You think that's funny? Some kind of metaphysical bullshit?"

"You talking about fate?" Dylan rolled his eyes. "Give me a break. I'm more inclined to think this is a setup. I told my guy to do a deeper dive on you. Check bank records. Make sure you don't have a backdoor deal with that outfit from Dallas. Seems a little too convenient that you land here one day and the barn is ablaze that same night."

"Go ahead and dig all you want. You won't find any dirt. Besides, if I had set the fire, would I still be here, waiting for breakfast?"

"It would be a clever way to cover your tracks." No smile on that intent lawyerly face.

Rhett understood Dylan's skepticism. Hell, hadn't he worried about his own sister's new man recently?

"Trust me, I'm not bluffing about that investigation." Dylan picked up his phone from the table.

"Fine. I just thank God I was here. You have no idea how close your sister came to dying yesterday, man." Rhett saw the phone drop to Dylan's lap. "Sierra was determined to save her horses. Her ranch hand stepped in, but he just grabbed the ones nearest the barn door, leaving the horses closest to the flames to your sister. She risked her life pulling out the last of them. Believe me, it took all three of us to get them to safety."

Dylan looked away, obviously fighting emotion. "You have no idea what Sierra has been through. Shit, if she'd died..." He swallowed. "Hell, I believe you. She'd do anything to save a horse." Dylan picked up his coffee and stared at Rhett over the rim. "She told me you were a big hero, saving Chief. She's crazy about that stallion. He came here in really bad shape and she nursed him back to health."

"I admire how she rescues abused horses." Rhett looked away from Dylan's probing gaze. The lawyer was probably good in court, getting confessions from guilty people.

"Who wouldn't admire her? Pretty gutsy to run into a burning barn, though." Dylan sipped his coffee. "Why'd you risk it, Hall? Just because you love horses? Or to impress Sierra? Unless..." He examined Rhett like he would a witness on the stand. "Oxcart sent you. Make your pitch yet? Don't bother to answer that. I'll ask Sierra when she gets out here."

"Ask her about the other problems she's had. The poisoned cattle and the threats. If I did tell her selling out might be the smart play, counselor, it's because I'm thinking she shouldn't dismiss the barn fire as an isolated incident. It appears that Sierra is the only one standing in the way of future prosperity for Muellerville. If that's so, you think the barn fire is the last move whoever is behind this will make to get her to give up and sell?"

"Shit. You're making sense. What other threats? Letters? Phone calls?" Dylan glanced toward his sister's bedroom.

"You'll have to ask her. Like I said, I landed here by accident. But your family needs to pay attention to this mess Sierra is in. She needs help. While you're talking to your investigator, have him do a deep dive on Oxcart. Do they always put pressure on reluctant landowners to sell? What are their methods?" Rhett drained his cup and stood. "I smell cinnamon rolls, and I think I heard the shower running a few minutes ago."

"Yeah, I heard it too." Dylan stood. "For now, let's call a truce. Unless my guy finds out you've been lying to me and to my sister. Then all bets are off." He held out his hand.

"Truce. But I've said it to the sheriff and I'll say it to you. Go easy on Sierra. This fire has hit her hard. And she's tired of people telling her what to do. She almost took my head off when I suggested she give up just a part of this place." Rhett shook Dylan's hand. "It would help if you could figure out a decent solution for her. One that lets her keep her ranch and still make the citizens of Muellerville happy."

"A solution. I like the sound of that. What I don't like the sound of is your bullshit about fate." Dylan dropped his hand. "That sounds like an excuse to make a run at my sister. If she's as vulnerable as you say she is, she sure doesn't need some random guy making moves on her now."

"I know how to treat a woman with respect." Rhett smiled. "And how to comfort one."

"You son of a—" Dylan raised a fist.

* * * *

"Stop right there!" Sierra ran down the hall. "Am I really going to have to throw myself between you two?" She stepped in front of Dylan. "What's going on here?"

"Just setting this Yankee straight." Dylan kissed her cheek. "How are you this morning?"

Sierra looked from him to Rhett. "I'm fine. Rested. Don't mess up my day by starting a ruckus."

"We won't. In fact, we just called a truce." Rhett grinned at her. "Your brother is just being protective. Which is how I am with my sister Scarlett." Dylan started laughing. "Seriously? Scarlett and Rhett? What is this, some kind of *Gone with the Wind* joke?"

"Stop it, Dylan." Sierra grabbed his hand, then Rhett's and stood between them. "I smell Rachel's cinnamon rolls. Let's eat. I'm starving."

"Relax, Sierra. I'm used to that reaction. Yes, Dylan, my mother is a big fan of the book and movie. She's from Atlanta where the movie was filmed." Rhett smiled showing all his teeth. "You want to make fun of my mother now?"

"Boys, play nice." She didn't wait to see what they'd do, just dragged them both toward the kitchen. The trash talk stopped at the sight of good food. Breakfast was reasonably cheerful, with only a few barbed comments from her brother. He still thought he had to protect her from any man who showed an interest. Nice that Rhett was definitely interested. She dreaded going outside to face that black stain on her land that used to be her barn. Instead she lingered over her coffee until Rachel went outside to feed her chickens.

"We need to talk about this deal with the developer, Sierra." Dylan had on his stern lawyer face. "Rhett filled me in."

"Thanks, Rhett." Sierra debated getting up for more coffee. "What do you have to say, Dylan?"

"I need that paperwork. I don't like what's going on here, but maybe you should consider their offer. If the entire town is for it." Her brother pushed back from the table. "The evidence suggests that."

"Evidence. A few disgruntled business owners want the trade the senior citizens would bring them. Am I to give up my dream of running this ranch to make them happy?" Sierra stood and glared at both men. Rhett got up immediately, playing the gentleman. "I'll get you the paperwork. But, remember, I own this property. I'll let you consult as my lawyer, brother dear, but I can always hire a different one. Someone who will take my side."

"I'm always on your side, Sierra." Dylan followed her. "Damn it, I didn't say you had to sell. I just want the facts."

She marched into the den and found the folder where she'd stuffed all the correspondence from the development company. There was a lot of it. For the last two weeks, she'd gotten letters daily. And then there had been the phone calls.... She almost threw it at Dylan, then stomped off toward her bedroom.

"Sierra!" Rhett was right behind her. "What are your plans today?" She turned around and bumped into him. "I don't know. First, I'd like to drive over to the neighbors and check out the places where my horses are staying, arrange to pay for their feed. Then I'm going to see if the sheriff has any news for me." Sierra looked past him. "Shoot! I need to ask Dylan about the insurance. He said he'd handle that."

"I'll tell him." Rhett held her shoulders. "Mind if I go with you? See these other ranches?"

"More research, Rhett?" She had to admit she wouldn't mind the company. He looked good this morning. He'd shaved and had on fresh jeans and a white shirt that showed off his tan. She glanced down. He still wore Dylan's boots. She'd gotten an earful about those boots over breakfast.

"Research, and to offer you some moral support. If you want it." He noticed where she was looking. "Maybe we could stop in town. I hope there's a place where I can buy my own boots. Give the town some trade and get Dylan off my back. Apparently I'm wearing some very expensive boots for walking around a ranch. I planned to pay for them, but your brother would rather have them back. Custom-made, he said."

"Yes, all the men in my family have a thing about their boots and hats being made to order." She smiled at him. "Sure, come with me. I'd like your support, and it would be a nice gesture of goodwill to take you into the Trading Post so you can spread some money around." She laid a hand on his chest, warm, solid. "You should pick up a few western shirts too. The kind with the snaps."

"Like you have on your shirt." He touched the top snap with the pearl cover. "I'd love to hear the sound of those snaps popping open."

"I'll just bet you would." She turned away from his grin, her heart fluttering. His flirting gave her interesting ideas. When she got to her bedroom door she looked back. He still stood where she'd left him. "This train is leaving the station in five minutes. Be sure to tell Dylan about that insurance policy."

"Yes, ma'am." He winked and turned away.

Sierra smiled all the way into her bathroom. A little touch-up on her lipstick, a brush through her hair and boots on her own feet and she was ready to go. She liked Rhett, maybe a little too much. It was easy to forget that she hadn't known him more than a day or two. How long did it take, though, before you knew if the chemistry was right? It wasn't as if she was looking for something long-term. With all that had happened, wouldn't it be nice to have someone to hold her close for a change? *Oh, God, yes.* With that thought she left the bedroom and headed for the truck. It was in her garage, behind the house. Good thing the fire hadn't spread to that and the bunkhouse. Rhett was waiting for her.

"Your brother said to tell you he'll be meeting with your insurance agent and an adjuster out here sometime today. You're not to worry about it; he'll handle it." Rhett opened the driver's door for her.

"Oh, maybe I should stick around then. I am the property owner. I saw him talking to Fred Meadows yesterday and Dylan looked upset." Sierra didn't climb into the truck.

"Let the lawyer throw his weight around. I could tell he wants to. You need to see about your horses." Rhett looked around the large garage. "Would have been a shame if this had burned down."

"Yes. I've got another building with a tractor, hay baling equipment and other expensive ranching supplies. That didn't burn either, thanks to the firemen. They obviously hosed the roof down as soon as they got there. It's right behind the barn." Sierra climbed into the driver's seat. "I use those four-wheelers to check the pastures. The extra truck is handy for taking hay out to the cattle in the winter." She waited until Rhett was buckled in then backed out. "This is my town truck. I bought it last year after my brothers gave me a hard time about being seen in the other one."

"I can see why. That other truck is more rust than metal. What hit the tailgate?"

"Bull got it. After that I decided to sell the big monster. It's easier to buy heifers that are already pregnant than to deal with a bull. Truth be told, I'd like to quit raising cattle and concentrate on the horses, but that doesn't bring any extra income." She drove through a rut that sent the truck bouncing and made Rhett hit his head on the headliner. "Sorry. The fire trucks and their water hoses tore up my driveway last night. I'll need to grade it again." She grinned at him. "You can quit clutching the armrest. I'm an excellent driver."

"Obviously." He rubbed his head then kept teasing her about her driving as she headed down the driveway and hit the remote for the gate.

Four hours later, all teasing had stopped. Sierra had visited all but one of the ranches where her horses would be spending the next several months. Some of the accommodations were great, even better than she could provide. But the last ranch they'd visited had her worried. She had been tactful, careful not to let her disappointment show as she talked to Mr. Hawkins, but his barn had been in poor repair and not very clean. On top of that, the horses had been crowded into small stalls.

"You thinking about the place we just left?" Rhett spoke as they turned into the gate at the last place on her list.

"Yes. Charley looked okay, but he won't get much exercise there. Fred Hawkins is overworked and understaffed." Sierra made a decision. "I've got to find a tactful way to get Charley out of there."

"I'm sure you'll think of something." Rhett was out of the truck as soon as she stopped next to the round pen. He'd been doing that all morning, helping her out of the truck. She hoped he was just being a gentleman and it wasn't because he thought she was frail. She took his hand and stepped into the muddy yard. It had rained while they'd been out, and while that was good for the pastures, it made a mess in the pens.

"Looks like Blanco is having a good time." She walked over to lean against the fence. "Hey, Mary, how's it going?"

"This bad boy is having way too much fun." The woman had a lead line in her hand. She looked over her shoulder and grinned. "He rolled in the mud and now look at him. It's time to put him up and he's not having it." She was suddenly pushed from behind and screamed as she tumbled into the mud face-first.

"Oh, boy." Rhett started to open the gate.

"Stay here. I've got this." Sierra ran inside. "Close the gate behind me, Rhett." She reached down to help the sputtering woman to her feet. "You okay?"

"I should know better than to turn my back on a frisky horse." She laughed and wiped mud off her face. "Can you believe this?" She picked up a water hose that she had left running into a trough and ran it over her hands.

"Give me that lead." Sierra took it and approached Blanco. "You big bad boy. What are you thinking?" The horse kicked up his heels, having fun and obviously happy to hear her voice. He tried to nose her into the mud too, but she was used to his tricks. She quickly snapped the lead onto his halter then pulled him over to the trough. "Think you're smart, don't you?" She took the hose from Mary and gave him a good washing. It wasn't easy to keep the mud from hitting her, but she managed it. She patted Blanco's shoulder when she was sure he was clean enough to be put away, then gestured for Rhett to open the gate.

"Thanks, Sierra. I'll be the first to admit that Blanco's a little too much horse for me to handle. I've got a hand out in the pasture who might have to do it." Mary walked beside her. "He's a fine boy, though. Sweet as can be when he's not playing with me."

"I've got a smaller horse, just right for you. Charley is over at the Hawkins place and it's a little crowded there. What if I bring him over here instead?" Sierra put Blanco up where Mary indicated. She liked the look of this barn with its sand floors and fresh hay in bags in each stall.

"That would probably be better. But where will this big guy go?" Mary leaned against the stall and watched Blanco grab a mouthful of hay.

"Miguel Rodriguez would probably enjoy exercising him, don't you think, Sierra?" Rhett had followed them into the barn. He introduced himself to Mary. "I'm not sure we got to meet yesterday."

"That's a good idea, Rhett. Mr. Rodriguez has plenty of room and I can slip Miguel some extra money. He's saving to go to college. I'm sure he'd be happy to have the cash." Sierra smiled up at him. "Sounds like a plan. Thanks."

"Well, I'm glad you figured that out. We all want to help you, Sierra. I hope they catch whoever burned down your barn. You find out anything yet?" Mary's eyes were kind but curious.

"Definitely arson, that's all we know for sure. I suspect the outfit from Dallas that wants to buy my land." Sierra sighed. That nugget would fly around the rumor mill at top speed. "I sure won't sell because I'm scared."

"Damn, that's ugly, if it's true." Mary gripped Sierra's hand. "Like blackmail, isn't it? Don't give in to it. Unless…" She glanced at the horse, then around her own barn. "Well, you have to weigh the risks. Texas is a big place. Lots of land where you could settle. The Morgan place is for sale. Last I heard it's not in line for development by the Dallas group. Something to think about."

"Didn't know that." Sierra knew that ranch and didn't think much of it. The pastures were rocky and water access was a problem. The widow who was selling out had let her outbuildings get run-down, too. Sierra kept her opinion to herself. Rhett stood near her, hovering. Did he want to say something? She glanced at him but he was looking around the barn, studying it.

"Anyway, be careful, Sierra. Wish I could board your horse for free, but you know how it is." Mary shrugged.

"Yes, I do. They don't say 'eats like a horse' for nothing. I've got it all arranged at the feed store. I called Max this morning and gave him your name." Sierra gave Blanco one last pat. "You're doing me a huge favor, Mary. Call if you need anything."

"Rhett, do you know horses?" Mary walked with them back to the truck.

"I rode as a kid and love horses. Hoped to do more riding until Sierra lost her barn." He smiled at Mary, then put his hand on Sierra's elbow. "Farming out the horses was a hard day for her."

Sierra noticed that Mary's shirt was clinging, making it obvious the woman didn't bother with a bra. Surprisingly, Rhett hadn't lowered his eyes from Mary's face before he walked around to help Sierra into the truck after he said goodbye. Amazing. He'd also been logical, and had obviously paid attention during their long morning when he had suggested the Blanco move. She usually resented a man who tried to solve problems for her, but how could she argue with a good idea? Okay, so he was scoring points all the way around.

She realized as she drove the short distance to town that she wasn't as depressed as she'd expected to be after seeing her horses settled at her neighbors' ranches. Having Rhett by her side had made the day bearable.

Chapter Ten

Sierra parked in front of the Trading Post and turned to him. "How about lunch before boot shopping? The City Café has great burgers or a chicken pot pie that's right up there with Rachel's."

"You read my mind." He gestured toward the café down the sidewalk. "Let's go."

"I already called Rachel and told her we wouldn't be back for lunch at the ranch." Sierra pulled her buzzing phone out of her pocket. "Damn. I recognize this area code. Dallas."

"Don't answer it. If they need to talk to you, they'll leave a voicemail." He took her phone and turned it off. "Whatever they have to say might ruin your appetite. I'm thinking burger. I'm a beef man."

"As a cattle rancher, I'm glad to hear that." Sierra took back the phone and turned it on again. "The insurance agent or Dylan might call. I can't afford to keep this off." She heard the beep that signaled a voicemail.

She saw a man coming toward them.

"Hi, Eddie." He was the local blacksmith and she gave him plenty of business.

"Sierra." He doffed his hat. "Sorry about your barn. Horses come out all right?"

"Yes, thank God, but it was a close one. This is Rhett Hall, my houseguest. Rhett, Eddie Franz, best blacksmith in town."

"Only blacksmith in town." Eddie held out his hand. "Mr. Hall."

"Call me Rhett. Blacksmith. That sounds like an interesting job. You go to school to learn that trade?" Rhett was in his usual research mode.

"You can. I happen to be a third-generation blacksmith and farrier. My grandpa started the business here then handed it down to Dad. I'm doing

most of the work now that Dad's trying to retire. Sierra's a good customer."
Eddie hit his hat on his thigh. "I think I'm one of the few people around
here who's not all for this senior citizen community they've been talking
about. Won't help my business."

"Have you been approached by anyone from the company trying to
buy your property?" Sierra dropped Rhett's hand. How had she ended up
holding it, anyway?

"No, I'm on the other side of the highway. Focus seems to be on your
side." He looked up when a truck with a horse trailer drove past. "There's
my next customer. I sure hope that outfit didn't think burning you out
would get you to sell. Don't do it, Sierra. If that's the way they do business,
we sure don't want their kind in our neck of the woods." He patted her
shoulder then took off down the sidewalk.

"He has a point." Rhett stared after him.

"He certainly does." Sierra headed into the café just ahead of them.
It had a late lunch crowd of chattering patrons. It seemed like everyone
looked up when they entered and the talking stopped. Moments later, as
they stood in the doorway and waited to be noticed by a busy waitress, the
conversations started again. Could someone here, calmly scarfing down a
burger, have torched her barn? The thought sent chills through her. Maybe
she wasn't hungry after all.

"Hey, Sierra. Glad you see you out and about. Let me get you a table." A
woman came from behind the counter with two menus. "How's the barn?"

"Total loss, Ellie. Thanks for asking." Sierra followed her to a corner
table in the back. "I guess Mark told you about it." The firemen must have
spread the word as fast as a brush fire. Eddie had heard about it, and the
ranchers who'd called to take in her horses certainly knew about it. Small
town, big gossips.

Right now she could feel dozens of eyes on her, tracking her progress
across the room. Some were probably resentful, wondering if that blaze
had done the trick and she was going to cave in and do the right thing
for the town. Her shoulders slumped. What if a horse or horses had been
killed? Was her dream worth it?

"The boys in the fire department had a rough weekend. Then Mark had
to open the pharmacy this morning." She smiled and held out her hand to
Rhett. "Ellie Chen. This is my café. You must be the Yankee Mark was
yammering about. My husband worked the fire at Sierra's barn. He met
you out there."

"Sure did." Rhett shook her hand. "He's a busy man."

"You don't know the half of it." She laughed. "What are you drinking?"

"Iced tea." He sat across from Sierra.

"The same. Thanks." Sierra saw Rhett watching the shapely brunette walk behind the counter to the kitchen. "Bet you never would have put those two together."

"I like her. Mark was tired and angry when I met him. She's friendly and full of energy." Rhett smiled across at her. "Good characters."

"You and your research. I hate to think of the notes you're taking about me." Sierra picked up her menu, though she always ordered the same thing here, the killer pot pie. Hopefully she'd manage to ignore the stares she was getting and choke it down.

"If you think I'm studying you, tell me to back off." He glanced at the menu then dropped it on the table. "I would need to get much closer, though, to make it a real in-depth research project." He had that glint in his hazel eyes that made *her* want to lean closer.

"Closer. How close?" She licked her lips.

"Here are your drinks." In a case of bad timing, Ellie was back. "You decided on your lunch?"

Sierra looked up and gave her order. Rhett went for the burger and fries. As soon as Ellie left, Sierra's phone rang again. Well, hell. Of course it was the Dallas number again.

"Want me to show you how to block it?" Rhett reached for her phone.

"No, I'm answering it this time. Might as well. I want to settle this." She answered. "This is Sierra MacKenzie."

"We've been trying to reach you, Ms. MacKenzie. How are you today?"

"I'm fine, just fine."

"Good to hear. I wanted to let you know that I am prepared to raise our offer on your property by twenty percent."

"Why that's very interesting, Mr. Greenbacks. This is Mr. Greenbacks, isn't it? Lots of money on the table every time you call me."

"Ha, ha. Actually, Ms. MacKenzie, that's Brubaker. Alfred Brubaker. But you can call me anything you please as long as you will seriously consider my offer. So many citizens there are behind this. People call me daily wanting to know when we'll start breaking ground. I hate to tell them that you are holding up progress." He paused to let that sink in. Was it a threat? "Any more delays and we will move the project to another, more accessible site. East Texas looks promising. Something closer to Dallas." Another pause, and it was definitely a threat.

"Surely that would cost your company too much. After you've invested in the land here." Sierra knew they'd bought several ranches already.

"Contracts can be broken, Ms. MacKenzie. Our lawyers know how to write in contingencies. I assure you, we can pull out of Muellerville without much pain at all. I hope I make myself clear. Without access to that highway, we will. So here's the deal: we really need to hear from you in the next twenty-four hours. Otherwise? We'll pull the plug on the entire venture."

"It seems to me you've been toying with the local investors, Alfred. No pain for you, but will the people here be made whole?" Sierra waited for an answer and didn't get one. Shit. This sounded like blackmail, and she wasn't caving in to it. "Listen to me. Twenty-four hours won't be necessary, I assure you. I have already made up my mind."

"Really? Are you accepting our terms?" He was almost giddy. She could hear it in his voice.

"Not exactly. You see, I had a little problem the other night. My barn burned down."

"I'm sorry to hear that." He oozed sympathy. "I assure you, that doesn't decrease the value for us. We aren't interested in your buildings. Just the land."

"Oh, I'm very aware of that." Sierra gripped the phone. "Unfortunately, the barn wasn't empty when it went up in flames. Thank God I was able to get every one of my horses out safely."

"Good, good. Was anyone hurt?" He was saying all the right things.

"No. But it was quite an ordeal. I inhaled a lot of smoke while I was saving my livestock." Sierra faked a cough. "With the barn a total loss, I was left with no place to keep my horses."

"Oh, my. That *is* a real problem. Of course I would be happy to assist you in locating a new place for your dear animals. I'm connected to a real estate firm here in Dallas that could find you a prime piece of land with a nice barn that would suit your needs. At a good price of course. Right after you accept our offer. We'll be demolishing your outbuildings anyway to build that new road into the senior living facility. Having your barn gone would just speed up the project."

"I appreciate that, Alfred." Sierra took a steadying breath. Rhett's hand landed on hers, as if he could see it was all she could do to hold on to her temper. "Now let me tell you what I'm thinking. I'm thinking that it's probably not an accident that someone torched my barn. And I somehow doubt that it's a coincidence that you call me within forty-eight hours of that disaster offering to buy me out. Again."

"I've been calling you for weeks, Ms. MacKenzie. The timing isn't unusual. I have to admit I find your tone disturbing. What are you suggesting?" The voice was no longer calm or persuasive.

"I'm not suggesting, I'm saying this plainly. I think your company tried to burn me out so I'd have no choice but to sell." Oh, shit, she was about to cry. Couldn't do it. She sucked in a breath. "Sorry, but your plan didn't work. I'm more determined than ever to stay put. My arson investigator will prove that your people were behind that fire. When they get through, you or your minions will probably be looking at a grand jury indictment. Of course that's what my brother, a high-powered lawyer, says. I'm more inclined to come to Dallas with my shotgun." She ended the call and threw the phone on the table, where it bounced once then hit the floor.

Rhett handed her a pile of paper napkins.

"Sorry about that." Sierra mopped at her wet cheeks. "Those people. They make me so damned mad. It's like he was ready to dance on my grave." She shook her head. "Wrong metaphor. You're a writer. Can't you come up with something better?"

"Wouldn't dare. You were brilliant." He just stared at her. "And sexy as hell."

Two plates were slammed onto the table in front of them.

"I can't believe you just turned them down again. Everyone in here heard you." Ellie stood next to Sierra. She wiped her hands on her apron, her cheeks flushed. "Mark said your barn was a total loss. A friend told me you moved your horses to other ranches. What's it going to take, Sierra, to make you see that you are holding us all hostage with your stubborn 'no sale' attitude?"

"You too, Ellie?" Sierra pushed back her chair and stood. "I thought we were friends."

"Business is business. I'd think that was a lesson you would have learned at your daddy's knee. Or don't rich kids bother?" She turned on her heel and marched back toward the kitchen.

Sierra looked around the room, which had become very quiet, and slowly sat again. Yes, there was a lunch crowd, but now that she paid attention, she noticed the place was only half-full. Ellie worked hard and kept the place open early for breakfast, then all day until nine at night, seven days a week. She had twins at home. Balancing work and family would be a challenge. Her husband had his own business and did firefighting too, so he wasn't a help at home. No wonder they both were looking forward to the boon of a new development nearby. Hadn't she heard the same thing at the Wagon Wheel?

"More tea?" The young waitress refilled their glasses. "I'm sorry if Ellie said things that upset you. She works too hard and has a lot on her mind. Those twins of hers are so danged smart they're gonna graduate from high school early. Now both of them seem set on becoming doctors. Can you imagine?"

"They can't be that old." Sierra couldn't remember the waitress's name but knew she was a local.

"Mia and Max are ten now but everyone expects they'll be headed to college at sixteen. Ellie is determined to get them through college, med school, all of it, without burdening them with student loans. Can you imagine what that'll cost? That's why we're open such long hours here. Why Mark does the firefighting, too." She shook her head, then turned when a customer waved his empty tea glass. "I'm not supposed to be gossiping but I just admire Ellie so much. She works all the time but business is down. I don't see how she's gonna pay for two kids and all that education." She shrugged. "I shouldn't have bothered you. I know you don't care about her family drama or Muellerville, Ms. MacKenzie. Enjoy your lunch." She sauntered over to the next table to fill that tea glass.

"Whoa. I hope not everyone thinks that way about you, Sierra." Rhett spoke as he picked up a french fry.

"Me too." Sierra wondered if she'd been wrong, digging in her heels all this time. Her throat was closing over a lump the size of a boulder in her north pasture. *Had* she been selfish, putting her own needs ahead of this small town's future?

"Damn it, I do care about this town." She used one of the rumpled paper napkins to wipe her cheeks again.

"You don't need to decide anything now. Or prove anything to anyone here." Rhett looked around the room then touched her hand. "Eat. The food looks delicious."

"And the pot pie has a sealed crust." Sierra stabbed it with her fork and watched the steam leak out. "So Ellie didn't have time to slip in any poison."

Rhett grinned. "Good point." He lifted his bun and checked out the burger inside. "I'm taking my life in my hands, but I believe this is okay too. What do you think?"

"I think we need to leave a big tip." Sierra blew on her bite then began to eat. "And eat fast." She still felt eyes on her and none of them were friendly. Maybe it was time to move on. But could she let her own dream go that easily?

Chapter Eleven

"I just got reamed out because she turned down another offer from Dallas. Which means you fucked up."

"No, I didn't. That barn went up quick. Total loss."

"Yeah? Then how come all the horses got out? The woman's still there, dug in and swearing to stay forever."

"I weren't going to kill no horses. Not for what you paid me."

"Don't give me attitude. I expected to hear she was packing her bags and taking the deal. Instead, there's an arson investigator coming. You know he'll be going over that barn with a fine-tooth comb. You leave evidence? Any way this can come back to me?"

"Relax. It went real smooth. Well, except for Miss Sierra's new boyfriend. First, he drags those horses out through the flames likes he's Superman, then he starts poking around. Says the fire was suspicious. Acts like he's a detective or somethin'."

"Is he? Where'd he come from? I want a name."

"Hall. That's all I know. A writer, not a cop. He don't know jack about ranchin'. Looks to me like he has the hots for Miss Sierra. He was just trying to impress her. I'm thinkin' if I was to arrange a little accident for him or her that might do the trick. Finally blast her out of here."

"I don't pay you to think."

"I ain't stupid. They can call it arson but nobody has a clue it was me behind it. I knocked down some more fence, which they'll notice before too long. Especially when some cattle go missing. They'll think that's how whoever set the fire got in."

"I thought she put in some fancy security system."

"Not on the fences. Now listen to me. Miss Sierra's already a gimp. A little accident now would put her down for quite a while. Her brother just got here. Next, her mama will probably show up. Wouldn't be surprised if the family drags her back to Houston. The new boyfriend is a Yankee, a city guy. He might go caveman and take her away himself."

"You don't know a damn thing about women, do you?" The voice hardened. "You really think she'll leave because her family or a boyfriend says so?"

"She was already struggling to make this place work. She's been keeping that a secret, but I know things. Her family's rich but she don't take money from them. If insurance don't pay her claim right away, she won't have her horses back for a long time. But they're still eating on her dime." He chuckled.

"Puts her in a tight spot, that's for sure. No money for a new barn. Horses staying elsewhere and feed bills mounting up while insurance takes its sweet time investigating. Cattle have been dying on top of that."

"She was real shook up about letting those horses go, I tell you. Said there's no point in building a new barn until they catch whoever set the fire in the first place. But we know that's not going to happen."

"Don't get too full of yourself. That leads to mistakes."

"I tell you, I'm onto something. Miss Sierra is right on the edge of giving up. One more bad thing happens and she'll be happy to sell and move on. I guarantee it."

"You can't guarantee spit. You don't make a move without my say-so, you hear me?"

"Loud and clear. Now you hear me. I expect ten thousand dollars in my special bank account by tomorrow or I'm liable to drop a hint to the sheriff that she needs to look at some of the investors behind that senior place."

"You threatening me?"

"No, just laying my cards on the table. I took all the risk here. You want to keep your part a secret, pay up." Darrel ended the call and looked around, pleased that he'd thought of that. *Not paid to think.* By damn, he was smarter than anyone gave him credit for, always had been. He wanted enough money to get out of this one-stoplight town.

Maybe he'd go ahead with his own plan. Sometimes the big shots forgot what worked.

Yeah, he could arrange a little accident for Ms. Sierra MacKenzie. Not a real bad one. She'd always treated him fair. Of course the job didn't pay enough to keep him in new boots. Couldn't even afford a brake job for his pickup. If she'd just let him drive her truck, he wouldn't care. But no, she kept reminding him about that old DUI on his record. Well, he'd show her. A little accident. He had just the thing. Putting the truck in gear, he headed out. No one would know he was behind it because they underestimated him. Always had. He'd show 'em who had the smarts around here. Then he'd take off for greener pastures. He pumped the brakes when one of Sierra's cows strolled into the road through the broken fence and he almost hit her. He sat there for a moment until it wandered over to the other side and into a ditch with fresh clover. Perfect. Oh, yeah. This was going to be good. For him. Not so hot for the boss lady.

Chapter Twelve

"They think I started the fire myself?" Sierra slammed her fist into her palm. "You've got to be kidding me."

"Calm down, sis. It's a knee-jerk reaction. What all insurance companies go for first when arson is suspected." Dylan tried to take her into his arms. Sierra wasn't having it.

"You told them about my horses, didn't you? How they were trapped? What they mean to me?" She turned to Rhett. "You were a witness. They can interview both of us about that night. Darrel too."

Dylan paced and ran a hand through his hair. "I know. Believe me, the agent and investigator got an earful from me. By the time I got through with them, they were backing off. Even the firemen could verify that you and Hall had smoke inhalation issues after saving the horses." He nodded at Rhett. "The insurance people will want statements from both of you. Don't go anywhere, Hall."

"I wasn't planning on it. Not unless Sierra kicks me out. Right now I doubt she has the strength for it. She had a rough day." He gestured toward the hidden bar. "How about a glass of wine, Sierra? I wouldn't mind a drink myself."

Rhett knew she was hanging on by a thread. They'd gotten a pretty cold shoulder in the store where they'd gone after lunch. The man running the Trading Post had been happy to see Rhett's credit card but not so happy to see Sierra. He was another store owner who was all for the new development. When Rhett had gone into a dressing room to try on some new jeans and shirts, apparently the guy had unloaded on her. Rhett had come out to find her almost in tears. She wouldn't talk about it but he'd decided to wait before buying boots. He'd be damned if he'd spend any more money than necessary with the asshole who had put that look on her face.

"Wine? Yes, I'll have white. Dylan?"

"I'm going to pass for now." He studied his sister's face. "Rough day? What happened?"

"More of the usual. It seems everybody in town wants me to sell. I'm not feeling the love." She sat on the couch and put her leg on the coffee table, her sock hitting so hard she winced.

Rhett recognized that move and obviously so did her brother.

Dylan frowned. "Nobody's going to push you out of here. You have my word on that, kid."

"Thanks. So it's war. That should be fun." Sierra smiled and rubbed her calf. "Now tell us what you've found out."

"I got a report back from my investigator on that Dallas company. I don't like what was in it." Dylan picked up a sheaf of papers from the desk. "I've got copies for you both. Since the Yankee here came up clean, I'm figuring he's on our side in this."

"Hey, thanks." Rhett pushed the button for the hidden bar. That raised Dylan's eyebrows but didn't stop him from handing over a stack of printouts.

"It looks like Oxcart Development is into some shady practices. Burning down your barn isn't typical, but applying pressure on landowners is." Dylan dropped the papers in Sierra's lap. "Let me explain."

"I can read." Sierra's voice sounded surly as she started looking through the stack.

Rhett opened the bottle of wine he'd pulled out of the minifridge. He recognized the attitude. His own sister would be just as resistant to her big brother trying to take charge. He poured Sierra a generous glass then splashed bourbon into a tumbler for himself.

"Sierra, I'm sure it would be easier if we let your lawyer here explain what he found out. I for one don't relish reading a bunch of legal mumbo jumbo." Rhett handed her the wine and sat beside her. "You are going to make this simple, aren't you, Dylan?"

"Sure." Dylan actually smiled. "This company likes to swoop into small towns like Muellerville and allow the locals to buy a small stake in the development. They've already done it in New Mexico and Arizona. Then they start buying up land for the senior living projects. I found out that these deals can be real moneymakers, especially if run right. Unfortunately, Oxcart isn't known for follow-through. They put up cheap housing and never finish all the amenities promised in their brochures. The city councils in the little towns give them big tax breaks to get them to come in the first place, but unless a new investor is found to complete the project, it's usually a failure."

"So I'd be smart not to give in to this pressure to sell." Sierra sat up from where she'd slumped against the cushions.

"Maybe, maybe not." Dylan walked over to the bar and fixed himself a drink. "I've been thinking. Muellerville really is perfectly situated geographically for this kind of project."

"Not you too!" Sierra threw the papers on the coffee table.

"Well, it is. The triangle of Houston, San Antonio and Austin with this town in the middle of it? I'm surprised no one has taken advantage of it before." He stepped closer. "Come on, you know it too. But we sure as hell can't let a group like Oxcart take it on." He sipped his drink and smiled. "Daddy sure knew his bourbon."

"Stick to the subject." Sierra stared at him.

"I'm going to Dallas. I want a face-to-face with these people. It'll be hard to prove that anyone there arranged your barn fire, but it sure looks like something they might do." Dylan finished his drink then crunched the ice cube. "Let me see what I can arrange. I promise you I will not let you lose your ranch. Okay?"

"How can you promise that? Have you looked at my books? If the insurance won't pay for my barn..." Sierra gulped her wine. "Well, I won't let the family bail me out. Keep that in mind."

"Don't worry. We've had years to get used to your stubborn, independent spirit." Dylan set his empty glass on the bar. "Here's my plan: There's a plane leaving Houston for Dallas in three hours and I'm going to be on it. If anyone from Oxcart calls you, don't answer. I want to surprise them."

"No problem. I've already told them what I think." Sierra finished her wine then walked over and hugged her brother. "Thanks for jumping in on this. Be careful. I already didn't like those people, and what you just shared doesn't make me feel any better about them."

"Then we're on the same page. I will be careful." Dylan locked eyes with Rhett, who stood behind Sierra. "You. Watch my sister. She already had one close call. Too many people feel like she's standing in the way of prosperity around here. I don't like it one damned bit."

"Neither do I. Don't worry, I'm not letting her out of my sight." Rhett extended his hand.

"I didn't say go that far." Dylan's handshake became a contest of strength.

Sierra gave her brother a hip bump. "Leave him alone. I've got my guns and know how to use them. If I want Rhett here, he's staying. On your way or you'll miss your flight. Let me know what you find out."

"I certainly will. Be careful yourself. I don't like this talk of guns or letting a stranger stay here." Dylan gave Rhett one more warning look before he stalked off toward his bedroom. He returned in minutes with his hanging bag. With a wave, he was gone.

"He loves this kind of challenge." Sierra pulled her buzzing phone out of her pocket. "This had better not be... Oh, it's Darrel. What's up?" She pressed the phone to her ear. "Not again! I'll be right there. North or south? Four-wheeler? Sure. Give me a few minutes." She ended the call.

"What is it?" Rhett finished his own drink and set down his glass. "Sierra?"

"Fence is down and some cattle got out. I knew we should have stopped at the sheriff's office in town. Darrel said it was probably the way whoever torched my barn got onto the property. I wonder if Myra knew about that fence?" She walked toward the kitchen where she'd left her boots. "I have to meet Darrel at the fence line. He's trying to herd all the loose cattle back inside the opening." She ran a hand over her face. "God knows if he'll find all of them. Damn it, I didn't need this right now!"

"How can I help?" Rhett sat down to put on his boots. He wasn't about to let her go alone.

"I'm taking one of the four-wheelers out there with the fencing supplies. You know anything about fencing?" She stomped her foot into her second boot.

"I know enough not to grab barbed wire bare-handed." He tried to coax a smile out of her. It worked.

"I'm sure you won't forget that lesson." She laughed. "Come along then. Four-wheelers are easy to drive. I assume you can figure out how."

"What about the ranch truck?" Rhett was on her heels as she pulled on a denim jacket that hung next to the back door. It was probably going to get chilly out, so he grabbed one that probably belonged to Dylan. Lucky for him they were the same size in jackets as well as boots.

"The four-wheeler is already loaded with what I'll need to repair the fence. Remember, this has happened recently, a couple of times." She stepped on a rock and staggered, brushing off Rhett's attempt to help steady her. "Damn it, I wonder how many head escaped before Darrel noticed that?"

Rhett gave her space. Clearly Sierra was on a roll, intent on the problem ahead of her. She didn't want him acting the gentleman. "The bigger question is who tore down your fence, Sierra. Is Darrel right? Could it have been whoever set your barn on fire? We need to check with the sheriff before you tamper with the evidence of a break-in." Rhett looked around. Rachel had already left for the day and it was getting dark. "Maybe this should wait until morning. The sun's going down."

"I can't afford to wait. More cattle could get loose. I sure don't have time to call the sheriff. Honestly, Rhett, this is an emergency. If you think you can manage the four-wheeler, I'd appreciate the help. They have headlights and I know where I'm going. Follow me. The keys are in the ignition." Sierra didn't slow down, punching in a code before the large garage door rolled up automatically. She immediately began to check the gear in the back of her vehicle.

"I can drive one. It looks like a golf cart on steroids. Remember, I write thrillers. I'd be a pretty poor researcher if I hadn't driven at least a few of the vehicles I put in my books." He got into the driver's seat of the other four-wheeler and turned the key just enough to see what the dash looked like. No surprises there.

"Good." She nodded. "Check your gas gauge. We sure don't want to run out in the middle of a pasture."

"Already did. Tank is full." Rhett made the call to the sheriff's office. He knew enough about crime scenes to figure this new information about the fence was important.

"Mr. Hall, no more problems out there, I hope." Sheriff Watkins had answered the phone herself.

"Just something to report. Sierra and I are on our way to fix a downed fence on her property. Did you know there was one?"

"Happens all the time. Especially to Sierra these days. What's your point?"

"I think whoever started her fire could have come in through that break." Rhett didn't think the sheriff was taking him seriously.

"Maybe. Does Sierra know exactly when the fence went down?"

"Sierra, when was the last time you checked that fence?" Rhett caught her as she got behind the wheel.

"We check it every few days. I don't know. Darrel usually does that section."

"Where is it?" The sheriff had obviously heard her answer.

"Where are we going? What part of the ranch?" Rhett was encouraged that the sheriff had asked the question.

"We're going toward the highway. Southeast side. Hang up, Rhett. We're losing daylight."

"You'd better do what she says. One of my men reported that break the day of the fire. I've got it in my notes. Might be a possible access to the barn so we checked for prints. Found a couple belonging to Darrel Lockhart.

He's in our system because of a bar fight a few years ago. I questioned him but of course fixing Sierra's fences is part of his job. Not a good lead, in my opinion. Tell Sierra she's cleared to take care of her fence again."

"Thanks, I will." Rhett had to wonder about Darrel. Arrested in a bar fight. It didn't seem to worry the sheriff. He'd only met the ranch hand a couple of times and under stressful circumstances. He seemed like a decent guy and he'd certainly stepped up, running into the burning barn to help save the horses.

"Mr. Hall? I talked to the insurance agent today. Tell Sierra I backed her up on the arson claim. People around here may be aggravated that she's holding up progress, but no one would ever think she'd set fire to a barn with horses inside." The sheriff said that emphatically. "I had to investigate it properly, but I knew from the get-go Sierra wouldn't risk her animals."

"I appreciate that, Sheriff. I'll pass that along." Rhett hung up when he realized the line had gone dead. He told Sierra what the sheriff had said.

"That's something, anyway." She gave him a brief smile. "Now let's go." She drove out of the garage.

Rhett's four-wheeler started easily and he quickly fell in behind Sierra. It was already hard to see in the deepening darkness. He turned on the headlights. Sierra was obviously counting on him to stay close as she drove quickly down the driveway, apparently unconcerned that each bump made his teeth snap together.

Before they got to the gate that led to the highway, Sierra stopped and jumped off to open a gate into a pasture. She waved Rhett through, drove on herself, then hurried back to close the gate securely. Then it was a long, uneven ride across a pasture where cattle grazed. They dodged a few trees and at one point skirted an oil well that pumped steadily.

Rhett was glad Sierra knew where she was going because it was fully dark now. The lights near the house had disappeared. Luckily they must be close to the highway, because he saw headlights flash by from time to time. He had no choice but to follow her red taillights.

Finally she slowed, then stopped. Were they there? No, she got off again and opened yet another gate.

"Drive through. I'll close it after I'm on the other side."

"I can close it this time." Rhett was determined to pull his weight.

"Do you know how?" Her voice was teasing. She had a flashlight, and the beam hit him squarely in the face.

"I'd be an idiot if I can't figure it out." He drove past her then hopped off. He was back to the gate as fast as he could manage. Which wasn't fast since he had no idea what he might be stepping in. The air was pungent with cow patties. Then he thought about rattlesnakes. Shit. Did they come out at night?

She sat on her vehicle, waiting until he was finished. When she revved her engine, Rhett hurried then regretted it. The ground was uneven and he almost took a header.

"Don't leave me here," Rhett called out as she moved forward.

"Wouldn't dare." She grinned and shined her light under her chin, making a face like a ghoul in a fun house.

"Very funny. Make the city guy sweat." He looked around. He'd have a hell of a time finding the house if she did abandon him here. He wasn't a coward, but he couldn't forget that someone wanted Sierra gone. Why hadn't he brought his gun? Had Sierra brought her rifle? He hadn't noticed. Stupid.

He saw movement nearby and froze. Then he realized it was yet another cow, chewing grass. Noises filled the air—the pump of the oil rig, the lowing of another cow and a suspicious rattle. Not that he could have really heard it over the nearby idling engines. His writer's imagination was going wild. He had to calm the hell down and get on with it. He got back on his ride and followed Sierra again. Ahead he saw twin headlights cutting through the darkness. Hopefully it was Darrel waiting for them.

"Hiya!" The sound meant someone was driving cattle. Rhett had learned that already. Sure enough, a moving light, probably a flashlight, came toward them.

"Sierra? Got about six head here. Turn off your engine and lights, I've got them turned toward where I want them. Your lights will confuse them." Darrel was giving orders.

"You think you got them all?" Sierra turned off her engine.

Rhett followed suit but wondered why the truck's headlights stayed on.

"Not sure. I'll come out here in the morning when I've got daylight and double-check. Who's that with you? Dylan?"

"No, it's me, Rhett." Rhett climbed off. Did he have a flashlight? He dug around between the seats, no luck. Going by feel, he found a glove compartment and hit pay dirt. He didn't care what the cattle wanted; he needed light. Good thing, because what he saw ahead of them made him lunge for Sierra.

"Watch out! There's a ditch right in front of you." Rhett caught her elbow just before she stepped into it.

"Where did that come from?" Sierra clung to his arm. "Darrel, what's going on here?"

"Don't ask me. I'm busy with these danged cows. I think one is about to drop a calf. You hear her?" Darrel moved in front of them then screamed. "Shit. I think I done broke my leg."

"Don't move." Sierra shined her flashlight down into what looked like a freshly dug gash in the earth. Darrel lay in the bottom of it, his face a mask of pain. "You need help getting up?"

"Yeah. I really think it's broke." The ranch hand struggled to sit up but couldn't manage it. He was sweating and his face was pale. His leg stuck out at an awkward angle. "Son of a bitch!"

"I'll get you." Rhett moved his own flashlight to see what he was up against. "Where did this hole come from?" He made his way carefully down the side of a steep ditch. Fresh dirt fell as he slid to the bottom.

"Utility work maybe." Darrel pointed a shaky hand toward light poles running along the side of the road several feet away.

"On the wrong side of the fence?" Rhett shined his flashlight around the area. This didn't make sense.

"What's going on down there? Rhett? Darrel?" Sierra stood near the edge of the hole.

"Stay back. I'll help him move across to where I see the ground levels out. Meet us by his truck, Sierra. Be careful where you step!" Rhett finally found a spot where the earth hadn't been disturbed and aimed his light toward it. "We're going this way. Look at where my light is shining."

"I see it!" She began to move parallel to them.

"Get me out of here. This hurts like hell." Darrel was struggling to stand. "I can't believe I did that."

"Grab my arm and I'll help you." Rhett managed to get Darrel to his feet, but it was obviously extremely painful for the man.

"Take him to his truck, Rhett. Keep moving toward the headlights." Sierra was making her way slowly in that direction, using her flashlight to help them find the way. "I'll meet you there."

"We're coming, but it'll be slow going." Rhett helped a cursing Darrel move along until they were on flat land. Sierra was waiting for them there. The truck faced the ragged hole in the fence. Darrel had effectively blocked the cattle in with the pickup after he'd driven them inside.

"I need a hospital." Darrel moaned when Rhett carefully edged past barbed wire to heave him inside the truck cab. "Call 9-1-1."

"I can't get a signal." Rhett had already checked.

"I have one." Sierra made the call. "We need an ambulance on the county road that runs by my place, Connie." She gave the number. "My hand Darrel had a fall. He thinks he broke his leg. Yes, you can get to him. It's next to the fence line. Thanks." She patted Darrel's shoulder. "They'll be right here. You know they'll have to take you to Austin if it's a complicated fracture."

"I can't afford that." He gripped the dashboard. "I mean, I've got good health insurance, thanks to you, but the time! You need me."

"I'll manage. Take care of yourself, Darrel. We'll get your truck back to the house for you. Don't worry about it. And we'll see to the cattle." Sierra glanced at the pasture. "You really think one of the heifers is about to drop her calf?"

"Hell, I don't know. Could be I was imagining it. Fix the fence before you lose any more of your herd. This is not... Oh, shit, I hurt like hell." He leaned back and closed his eyes. "How long before they get here?"

"Volunteer paramedics, you know. Fifteen minutes if you're lucky. The doc in town will X-ray you; then we'll see how it goes." Sierra glanced at Rhett. "We do need to get that fence repaired. Let's go."

"In the dark? You want to break your leg, too?" Rhett didn't relish stepping into the dark himself.

"We know about the hazard now. It'll be easy." Sierra walked to the front of the truck.

But it wasn't easy. The job was to hold the wire taut while Sierra hammered in special nails to secure it to the fence posts. Doing that in the dark to Sierra's exacting standards convinced Rhett that what some people thought was a glamorous life on a Texas ranch was a fantasy. Reality was a hell of a lot of hard work. He was sweating and threw off the jacket halfway through the job.

While they were finishing, the ambulance showed up. Luckily there was an extra paramedic on board who offered to drive Darrel's truck back to the bunkhouse. That left Sierra and Rhett in the dark and inside the fence with six cows and two things that Rhett was beginning to think of as clown cars. When one cow began bawling and kicking, he had a feeling his night wasn't over.

"Damn it, that heifer *is* giving birth. Shine your light over here, Rhett." Sierra approached an enormous cow standing alone next to a tree.

"Is it smart to get near her? Can't you see she's upset? Look at those teeth." Rhett had no choice but to pursue Sierra, who was determined to see to the distressed cow.

"There she goes. She's dropped over to her side. That means she must be close to delivering." Sierra was obviously excited.

"Watch out! She's trying to kick you!" Rhett grabbed Sierra's arm, but she jerked away and grabbed the cow's tail. "What are you doing?"

"Lifting her tail. Look! Here it comes. I see the hooves. That's a good sign; the calf's in the right position."

"You're kidding. We're delivering a calf right here in the middle of a field in the dead of night with nothing to help the mother and certainly no vet." Rhett could hear himself babbling but holy shit! The poor cow was making a terrific noise, bawling and carrying on like she was dying. All the other cattle were smart enough to move away and give her a wide berth. Birth.

Not the time to think about wordplay. He should be paying attention. Taking a picture. Except it was about to get disgusting. He was pretty sure of that. Still, this could go in a book.

"Come on, Mama. You can do it. Push that baby out now." Sierra murmured more encouragement and moved behind the heifer so she was out of danger from the thrashing hooves. She reached over to stroke the cow's massive stomach. With a mighty heave and some pretty awful sounds, the cow got serious and her calf slid into the world. Sierra's face lit with pure joy.

Rhett just stared. Not at the cow or the calf. No, at Sierra. Fascinating, strong. None of the mess bothered her, and there was a hell of a mess. No, she was delighted. She oohed and ahhed over the calf as if it were the most beautiful creature on God's earth.

"It's a boy!" She looked up at Rhett with a grin on her face that made him wish he *had* pulled out his phone. Sierra glowed. "He's perfect. I'm so glad we were here for that. Aren't you?" Sierra stood and wobbled a bit, putting out a hand to brace herself against the tree trunk.

Rhett couldn't say a word, only nod. He grabbed Sierra's arm to steady her.

She hugged him, obviously high on the whole experience. "We might as well go. Mama's cleaning him up. She doesn't seem to need us."

Rhett walked her back to the four-wheelers. His flashlight flickered and he stopped. Had he ever thought being out in nature under a million stars would be romantic? Hell, he just hoped he got them both back safely to those vehicles without falling into a hole, stepping in shit or getting bit by a rattlesnake. Sierra seemed unconcerned. She walked by his side, leaning on him a little as if she was tired from their day and night, but not worried at all. Sure, she limped, but it was part of her, more proof that nothing could hold her back or get her down.

"You're honestly just going to leave them out here?" Rhett finally said as he heard the cow moo again.

"I'll check on them tomorrow. If there's a problem with either of them then, I'll call the vet. But they both look good to me." She squeezed Rhett's arm. "Thanks for coming. This would have been a disaster without your help."

"It *was* a disaster. Darrel broke his leg falling into a hole that shouldn't have been there. He was your only ranch hand. What are you going to do now?" He helped her into her driver's seat then just stood there looking down at her. He really wanted to kiss her. But he also really wanted an answer.

She turned on her headlights. It was easy to see the cattle then. There were five large ones, calmly standing in a bunch. Then there was the one who had stood to let her baby take her first meal. Sierra ran a hand over her face.

"I'm thinking I want to sell my cattle, all of them."

"What? Why?" Rhett leaned against the steel roll bar.

"You just saw how much trouble they are, and the time is right. The market price is up a little right now. The truth is I don't enjoy this part of my business as much as the horses." She nodded toward the pasture. "Think, Rhett. That precious life that just came into being is destined for a dinner table." She gripped the steering wheel. "*That* doesn't exactly bring me joy."

He touched her shoulder. "No, I guess it wouldn't. You have to be tough to be part of the beef industry."

"I can be tough. I've proved that. But if I can just work with horses, it would make me a lot happier. Without the cattle, I wouldn't need a ranch hand either, now would I?" She turned on her engine. "Let's go back the way we came. Stay close. When we get to a gate, I'll stop and flash my lights. Then I think I'll let you open and close all the gates this time, if you don't mind."

"It would be my pleasure." Rhett leaned in and kissed her as he'd been wanting to do. She slid her fingers into his hair and held on while they both lingered, learning each other's taste and texture. Finally Rhett eased away and stepped back. "That was my pleasure too."

Chapter Thirteen

By the time they got back to the house, it was late. Sierra was tired, yet exhilarated. Watching a new life come into the world always did that to her. Then there had been that kiss. Her blood was still singing from the connection she'd felt when she and Rhett had finally come together. She had a lot to think about, good and bad. Yes, bad. Poor Darrel and another downed fence.

Her phone rang before she could do more than park and take Rhett's hand when he held it out to help her from the driver's seat. The number was unfamiliar but the area code was local, not Dallas.

"Hello?" She smiled up at Rhett. He wasn't letting go.

"This is a nurse at St. David's Hospital in Austin. Darrel Lockhart asked me to call you."

"Oh, yes, Darrel. I'm his employer. How is he?" Sierra leaned against the dirty vehicle behind her.

"He's about to go into surgery. I'm sure he'll be fine but it's a complex fracture. We expect to keep him here a few days." The nurse cleared her throat. "He asked me to tell you he's sorry."

"Sorry?" Sierra looked up at Rhett. "I guess he means because he's leaving me without help. I'll try to get up there to see him soon. Thanks for calling."

"He said not to come. He's arranging for a buddy to collect his truck. Then he's going to,"—she seemed to be studying notes—"an aunt's house in Tyler to recuperate. Anyway, he thanked you for the good insurance coverage but didn't want you to bother visiting him. He said he'll be in touch." She sighed. "I'm just the messenger. He was in pain, being prepped for surgery. I hope that message makes sense to you."

"Sure, thank you." Sierra hung up. "That's too bad about the surgery." "I heard most of it. I guess Darrel is one of those men who doesn't like to be seen when he's down." Rhett smiled at her. "Ready to head for the house?"

"More than ready." She loved his warm, strong hand in hers. "I didn't know he had relatives in east Texas. Or any relatives. But then he didn't talk much."

"Can we forget Darrel for now?" Rhett pulled her out of the garage. "You do lock up this garage, don't you?"

"Sure. See the keypad? Same code as the back door and the gate. There's a camera out here now too." She hit the button by the large door and it came screeching down. "You in a hurry to go inside, Mr. Hall?" She stopped and faced him. He'd changed into one of his new shirts after dinner. Now it was streaked with mud from pulling Darrel out of that hole.

"Are you hungry? That meat loaf wore off a while ago." They'd eaten their meal early at Dylan's insistence. After he'd told them about Oxcart and heading to Dallas, she knew why.

"I'm hungry all right, but not for food. I bet you're exhausted, though." He stared down at her. "Is this day typical for you? Fixing fences, cattle drama?"

"Not exactly typical. I didn't get a ride in." She flushed when he grinned. But it was enough for her to do the unthinkable. She pulled open some of those snaps on his shirt. "What do you think? Are you too tired from all this unaccustomed activity to try something else tonight?"

"You're kidding me." He scooped her up in his arms. "Too tired for what I think you're suggesting? That's the kind of challenge a man just has to rise to." He carried her to the screen door then reached down to pull it open. "Bet you didn't even bother to set the alarm in here when we left."

"No, we were in a hurry." She ran her hand up the smooth column of his throat. "You started this, you know. With that kiss in the pasture."

"I couldn't help myself. You were so damned sexy out there. I'm crazy about strong women." He leaned down and kissed her, the screen door slapping him in the back.

Sierra held on and breathed him in. There was something about this man. She couldn't get enough of him. She *had* been tired, and she did ache from too much walking over rough ground. But she also yearned for the closeness Rhett could give her. He made her feel desirable. Which was crazy considering where they'd been and the filth on her shirt and jeans. His mouth on hers was fire and thirst and a craving for all the things she'd needed for so long. Too long.

"Inside." He growled it as he turned the doorknob and got them into the kitchen. "I'm locking up and setting the damned alarm right now. If it goes off, it had better be Armageddon."

"You've got that right." She tossed her phone on the counter. "Wait. Leave the muddy boots by the door." She wrinkled her nose. "Dylan is going to kill you. You definitely stepped in something."

Rhett set her on the kitchen island. "Woman, don't slow me down with shit I couldn't care less about right now." He made quick work of her boots, dropping them by the door. He sat for a minute to get rid of his own and handled them carefully. "You're right. He's going to be unhappy. We'd better order him a new pair."

"I can do that." Sierra reached for Rhett. "Tomorrow." She hadn't finished with his snaps. Now she got the rest of them open and ran her hands over his chest. Firm, warm and strong. She wanted all of him.

"That feels good. Keep going." He reached for her snaps.

"I hate to say this, but I'm sure I smell like the back end of that heifer." She stepped back.

"I didn't notice." He reached for her again.

She stopped him with a straight-arm to his chest. "I did. Meet me back here in ten minutes. After showers. I promise to make it worth your while." She winked, then hurried as fast as her bum leg would allow toward her bedroom. Maybe she was giving herself a little time to calm down. Or him time to reconsider. Honestly, where had all this lust come from? But she couldn't deny it seemed to be on both sides. It didn't take her long to get clean and even shampoo her hair. Smelling like roses was a vast improvement. She donned underwear and her typical jeans and shirt. Yes, she was going to make him work for this. If he met her like he'd promised, there were going to be fireworks.

He was there, sitting at the kitchen table looking scrubbed and hungry, but not for leftover meat loaf. He bounded to his feet as soon as she appeared.

"Now why did I think you'd be in a slinky robe and nothing else? I should have known better." He moved in and slipped his arms around her waist. "Not that I object to this. It's you. A lady rancher who can pull a calf into the world without blinking an eye."

"I didn't have to pull it. He slid out on his own. All I did was watch in case mama needed my help." Sierra leaned against him. "Now where were we before I took a whiff and decided I wanted to do this right?"

"Here." He picked her up and almost ran down the hall toward her bedroom. When he stopped by the side of her bed, she expected him to drop her on it. Instead, he laid her down gently then ripped off his shirt.

"Stop." She gazed up at him. "Let's get something straight, Rhett."

"Planning on it." His grin was wolfish.

"I'm serious. Why are you being so careful with me? Is it my leg?" She leaned up on her elbows.

"I don't want to hurt you." He sat beside her. He popped open her snaps and leaned forward. He was about to kiss the dip between her bra cups when she stopped him with her palm on his forehead.

"Stop. I mean it." She left her shirt open. She wasn't stupid. This was going to happen. She was so turned on she was melting in all the right places. But this had to be said.

"What's the matter? I didn't plan to rush this. But *you* started it this time. God, I love snaps." He held his hands out by his sides. "Is this some kind of game?"

"Not at all. But listen to me." She ran her hands over his chest again. She just couldn't get enough of it, him. She wanted to open his belt and see what else he had to offer. *Not yet.*

"I'm listening." As ordered, he wasn't touching her, but he gripped the bedspread. "You're killing me. You know how pretty you look in that pink bra? I can see your nipples pressing against the lace. Turned on, aren't you?" He didn't wait for an answer. "I can see that they're a slightly darker pink than that lace. Do they ache as they rise and fall with every breath you take?" He was using his writer's skills to paint a picture, his eyes narrowed as he studied her.

"There's a pulse pounding in your neck. I got your heart rate up even though all I did was talk. What would happen, I wonder, if I touched your nipple? Pulled that sweet bud into my mouth and drew on it. Hmm? You're breathing faster now. And you just *had* to lick your lips." He took a breath and licked *his* lips. "Jesus, Sierra, you're killing me. Am I allowed to kiss you before you tell me whatever the hell you've got on your mind?" He leaned forward as if he was going to do it regardless of her answer.

"No. Stop trying to distract me, Rhett." Sierra knew his words had worked too well. She had to concentrate to remember why this was so important. She tried to slow her breathing. Not possible. His gaze burned her everywhere it touched. He moved closer so his hip pressed against hers. But he was still being careful. If he would just throw his leg across her and take her as hungrily as she wanted...

"Are you distracted?" He did lean down and breathe against the lace of her bra, torturing her and making her shiver with delight and longing.

Oh, God, but she was on fire. "Let me get this out!" She knew she sounded desperate. Yes, desperate enough that he raised his head and looked at her.

"What is it?"

"I am not going to break, Rhett. My leg will not shatter again. Yes, I limp when I'm tired. Okay, I limp all the time. And my leg hurts when it's about to rain or if I overdo things. But I am not fragile. Throw me down, make serious love to me. Treat me as you would any woman." She gave in and slid her hand into his jeans. Oh, yeah, he was hard and ready and his whole body jerked when she squeezed him. "I want you. And I plan to have you every which way there is. Are you up for it?"

"Shit, lady, I am yours." He threw himself on top of her, using his elbows to keep from crushing her, then took her mouth hungrily. There was no more talking. One of his hands worked open her bra. He grasped her breast in his hand then rolled her aching nipple between his fingers. Suddenly his mouth took over.

Sierra groaned her pleasure before she got busy opening his belt buckle. She ripped the belt out of the loops then tossed it aside. His jeans were next. Of course he'd gone for the button style. Stupid. Zippers were so much easier. But she got them all open and found him hot and heavy in her hand again.

He rolled her so that she sat on top of him. Her blouse and bra went sailing. "Beautiful." He went right to work on her jeans. She reached down to help him. Of course she could tell him over and over again that he couldn't hurt her, but he was still being careful. It would take time and proof that she wasn't going to break before he believed it. By the time his hand slipped over her bottom, taking her panties and jeans with it, she was beside herself with need.

"I have a condom in my pocket." He looked around like a wild man. "Where the hell?"

Sierra laughed and kicked away her jeans then found his on the floor. After that they managed what needed to be done. She didn't tell him that she wasn't comfortable on her knees but he seemed to figure it out. He was above her when he finally pushed inside.

"Oh, God!" She gripped his shoulders, the feel of his strength outside and inside more than she could have imagined. Her breath stalled until he moved and took her with him. They fit perfectly. A chant of "More, more, more!" seemed to build inside her. Had she ever been this filled, this completely connected? No more thinking, as waves of pleasure took over and he kissed her endlessly. When Sierra thought she'd found ecstasy, he pushed her even further.

He whispered things in her ear no man had ever said to her. Poetry that praised her body, her moves, her very essence as she gave and gave and then took from him. He had a way with words, seductive words, this man who wrote for a living.

The room blurred, pain that never seemed far away suddenly vanished. Sierra breathed through a rush of such pleasure she thought she might drown in it. Never had she let herself go like this. Floating down to earth took a while. It wasn't a journey she was eager to take. Earth was where bad things happened. Earth was where people didn't love her.

Not that this had been about love. No, this had been about pure pleasure. She'd take it. She lay staring at the ceiling, too wired to fall asleep. Rhett kept his arm around her, heavy but reassuring. She wasn't alone. He clearly cared about her. It was a good feeling. She was glad to let the world go away for a while and just float.

Of course, that wasn't the Sierra MacKenzie way. She was responsible, wary, and for good reason. She'd never told Rhett the details about her accident. Tomorrow she would. She'd seen no signs that he felt pity for her, but that was always in the back of her mind. He hadn't flinched when he'd seen her scars, either. But he seemed good at hiding his thoughts.

She didn't really know him. Had she made a big mistake, taking this stranger in and allowing him to steal a piece of her heart? His hand moved over her breast, and she turned to see him watching her. Mistake or not, she wasn't about to shove him out of bed and lose the best lover she'd ever had.

"Round two?" She smiled when she felt something nudge her hip.

"Round two."

* * * *

Sierra had just come out of the shower with a towel around her when there was a knock on her door. She glanced at the clock on her nightstand. Was it really almost nine?

"Sierra? Your phone has been ringing for a while now," Rachel called. "Everything all right in there?"

Wonderful, fantastic. A masculine arm snaked around her middle, under her towel. "Fine. I'll be out in a bit." Sierra stuck her hand out through a narrow crack in the door. "I'm, uh, not alone. Can you save us some breakfast? For when we're ready for it?"

Rachel dropped her phone into her hand. "Well, sure. Sorry I bothered you. Ignore the phone. I can be outside for a while with the chickens. Then I'll work in my garden. Reckon I can put two plates in the oven and you can fetch them yourselves. When you're ready." The housekeeper chuckled then went whistling down the hall.

"Was that awkward? Should I have skulked down the hall to my room before she arrived?" Rhett hadn't bothered with a towel. His warm, damp body pressed close.

"I'm an adult. I can entertain men in my room anytime I want." Sierra turned and kissed him. "Umm. I guess I should care who called me so early." She let him whip off her towel. "But I really don't."

"I feel used. But I can take it, insatiable woman." He tugged her toward the bed. "Have your way with me."

"I do believe I will." She laughed and set the phone aside. She could deal with the calls later. She had no intention of letting reality ruin her day just yet. She threw herself at Rhett and they tumbled to the bed. Fun and pleasure, something she'd been missing for too long. Maybe she was insatiable because she'd needed this. Had denied herself in her determination to prove how damned independent she could be. Suddenly that just felt lonely. *Enough thinking.* It was definitely overrated when there was a clever man touching her, kissing her and setting her on fire. By the time she heard her phone ringing again, she'd found yet another reason to spend the day in bed. Why wouldn't people leave her alone?

"You'd better see who it is. Your brother might be trying to reach you." Rhett looked completely relaxed and self-satisfied. He should. "I need time to recuperate anyway. If you have more in store for me."

"I'm hungry. I thought I smelled biscuits when I opened the door. Sausage too." Sierra reached for the phone.

That earned her a light slap on her bottom. "And you kept me in bed?" Rhett reached for his jeans. "I'm going after those plates. Breakfast in bed. One of my favorite things." He bolted out of the room, not even bothering to close the door behind him.

Sierra pulled up the sheet in case Rachel changed her mind and came down the hall in search of laundry. Then she scrolled down her missed calls. Of course that last caller had given up. Not her brother, but the Dallas area code. She knew better than to call back, but she listened to the voicemail. Not all of it. Brubaker again with a sales pitch. No way. Delete. There were the usual spam calls, then one from Sally Ann, Rachel's daughter.

Now that did get her attention. They hadn't really been friends since the summer of her accident. Oh, they saw each other, it was unavoidable with Rachel working here, but what had bonded them had been their love of barrel racing. After the accident, Sierra had been out of it and Rachel had quit paying for Sally Ann to enter competitions. Her daughter had been given a choice, ride for fun or prepare to go to college.

Sally Ann had defied her mother and wound up marrying young and foolishly before she graduated from high school. When that marriage had ended, she'd come home and gone to work at the Trading Post. It proved a good place to meet men. Lucky for her she'd connected with Will Jackson, who'd been from a rich family, something she'd always claimed was a requirement in her next husband. Her marriage to Will had seemed to stick. Too bad her husband was an obnoxious bully. He was still rich, though. Could he be part of the Oxcart group?

Curiosity made Sierra call Sally Ann back while she waited for breakfast. The phone was answered right away.

"Thanks for calling me back, Sierra." She could hear what sounded like wind noise around Sally Ann.

"Is this a bad time? Are you driving?" Sierra took the cup of coffee Rhett handed her with a smile. He set his on the nightstand on the other side of the bed, then left the room again.

"I am, but this is hands-free. Will always sets me up with the latest Corvette. You should see it. Pretty sweet. Hang on. I've got the top down and it's damned noisy." There was a whirring sound. "I'm pulling over and putting up the top."

"Sally Ann? Call me back when you're ready." Sierra hung up and took the tray Rhett handed her. "Where did you find the trays?"

"Rachel had set them out. She obviously was encouraging us to make a morning of it. I really like that woman." He grinned. "Anyway, now we're all set." He settled in beside her. Sierra picked up her phone when it rang. "This must be Sally Ann again. She was putting the top up on her Corvette."

"I saw it. Nice car." Rhett continued eating right after he reached over and pulled down the sheet that had been covering Sierra's breasts. "Carry on."

"I will." Sierra smiled. "Eat." She jerked up the sheet again. "Hi, Sally Ann." She would not look at Rhett. He loved to play with words and with her. "What's on your mind?"

"I've been hearing a lot of talk in town about that senior living project someone wants to build around here. Some pretty nasty things have been said about you, Sierra. It's got me worried, hon. Will heard someone burned down your barn out of spite. Cause you won't sell to that Dallas group. Is that true?"

"Why, thanks for your concern, Sally Ann." Sierra picked up her coffee. "I appreciate that. It's true they're calling it arson. We can only guess who did it or why. If Will knows something, he should tell the sheriff. You're right. I've been getting a lot of pressure from the folks in town. I'd think Will would be one of them who wants that development here."

"I'm sure he wouldn't mind it, but he has plenty of business already at the dealership. Instead he keeps carrying on about another big deal he has in the works." Sally Ann sighed. "Fast food! Can you believe it? He went to one of those franchise fairs in Houston and now that's all he can talk about. As if he doesn't already work six days a week, fourteen hours a day."

"That's too bad. Makes it hard on a marriage, I'm sure. So you don't think he's in on this senior development deal?" Sierra glanced at Rhett.

"I have no idea. But Will is a business owner. You have to know that in a place like Muellerville any new development that'll bring in lots of people will help the existing businesses. That's why so many of the folks in town are counting on the senior living project to pump up their bottom lines, honey. You've got a lot of townspeople against you for holding it up. Have you thought about how it will be to live here if you ruin this thing? What if the feed store won't deliver to you? If Ellie won't serve you in the café or Bill down at the John Deere outlet won't service your tractors?"

"All of those people are invested in the Oxcart deal?" Sierra realized Rhett had stopped eating. Sally Ann was loud and he could no doubt hear all of this.

"Oxcart. Yes, that's the name of the company. Stupid name, if you ask me. What does it mean?" Sally Ann was tapping something. Her nails on the steering wheel? She'd been vain about her fingernails, even when she'd been barrel racing. "Listen, I've always considered myself your friend, Sierra. You know what I mean? Ever since we rode together in those contests."

"Sure, we were friends." Had they been? They didn't ride together; they were competitors. Sally Ann had wanted to win but had never managed it. Her temper fits when she lost were legendary.

"I'm just trying to give you a heads-up. You should hear them down at the Twist and Curl. Annie is threatening to turn you away the next time you need a haircut. What are you going to do then? Go all the way to Houston for your trim?" Sally Ann swore. "Would you look at this? That bitch sheriff is stopping to see why I'm on the side of the road talking on my phone. As if this isn't a free country." She slapped something, probably her dashboard. "Aw shit. I'm still in a school zone. I just dropped off the kid. Now she's getting out her ticket book. I cannot have one more ticket. Insurance is already sky-high. Will is gonna blow his top."

"You'd better deal with this, Sally Ann. It's against the law to talk on a cell phone in a school zone."

"Hands-free? I don't think so. If that bitch sheriff wants to be reelected next spring, she'd better cut me a break. But think about why I called, Sierra.

Why not sell a little slice of your land and make everyone here happy? It would sure make your life easier in the long run. Take care, girlfriend." Sally Ann ended the call.

Sierra dropped her phone on the bed. Girlfriend? "Well, that was interesting."

"You got some friendly advice. Better than the threats you've been getting." Rhett attacked his plate again, right after he pulled down her sheet. "She's not wrong. Living in this town will be hell if you make all of those people lose money or business when the deal goes south."

"Unfortunately, that's true. It's something to think about." Sierra picked up her biscuit. Then she turned to face him. He was eating steadily but caught her movement and stopped with the fork halfway to his mouth.

"What?"

"You buttered my biscuit." God, she might just fall in love with him.

"Of course I did." He smiled and leaned over to kiss her. He tasted of grape jelly, sweet and then sexy as his tongue touched the corner of her lip. "Mmm. Sausage crumb. You are one very special lady. Can we spend the day in bed?"

"I wish." She really did. Too bad she was practical and had responsibilities. But, oh, did Rhett Hall make her heart sing. He kissed a lingering path down her neck to her breast, taking a moment at her nipple. "I do need to eat, Rhett. Things to do today besides you."

"I appreciate that." He sat back, never losing his grip on his fork and the sausage link poised on the end of it. "I also appreciate the fact that I was first on your agenda."

"I know how to prioritize." Sierra dropped a kiss on his bare shoulder. She'd never been playful before with any man. This felt right. No, perfect.

Except bad thoughts kept niggling at her. Sally Ann calling out of the blue like that. Why? Had Rachel asked her daughter to step in? Of course the housekeeper was worried about her. With Sierra's mother moving on to a new life, Rachel clearly thought of herself as Sierra's mother figure. Rachel knew everyone in town too. So she'd probably heard all of the threats as well and no doubt had been asked to pass them on to her boss. She hadn't said a word, loyal and not about to upset Sierra.

But what about Sally Ann? Had they ever been friends? The sad truth was that Sierra had few real friends here. She was working all the time, seeing to her horses, her cattle and trying to make ends meet. She had good friends in Houston and in the horse rescue group. She'd thought there were some friends in town, but they had been quick to turn on her with this Oxcart venture in the picture. Ellie and Marty had lunched with her occasionally. Even her hairdresser had been friendly. Not friendly enough, apparently.

Her family filled her life when she needed someone. Or they had until her mother and brother Mason had both married and found their own best friends in their mates. Dylan would probably be next to fall in love, and then where would she be? Isolated here. If the town turned on her, she could find herself in real trouble, alone and hated by everyone who had thought to get rich courtesy of Oxcart.

Rhett stirred next to her. It was way too soon to think he could be the one in her life if she found herself shunned. For now, though, it was good to have someone by her side. She ate slowly, barely tasting the food as she thought about what she needed to do.

Should she consider selling part of her land?

Not yet. Not until she heard from Dylan. Oxcart wasn't doing any of them any favors and obviously couldn't be trusted. Then there was still the problem of the barn fire. Who had set it? That was a desperate measure that surely none of the people she knew would try. But maybe she didn't know anyone as well as she thought she did.

Chapter Fourteen

Darrel woke up suddenly. His leg! Where the hell was that nurse? He punched the call button and waited. Then he realized what had really made him wake up. Not the sharp pain in his leg, that was bad enough. No, it was the squeal of that special ringtone on his phone. He'd given it to the number of that burner phone. No name, but the caller was always the same voice. It hurt him to reach for it, but at least someone had set it on the nightstand.

"Yeah?"

"I heard you had an accident."

"Busted my leg." He could tell this wasn't a sympathy call.

"Didn't I tell you to wait for instructions?" Oh, yeah, "mad as hell" was putting it mildly. "What were you thinking? Oh wait. I told you not to think at all. Remember that?"

"Listen here. I had it all worked out. My headlights were in her eyes. How was I to know she'd bring that new boyfriend of hers with her? It should have worked. If she'd fallen into that hole, it would have scared the shit out of her. Put her out for a good while too if *her* leg had been broken. That family of hers would have made her sell the ranch. Then your troubles would be over." Darrel was getting mad himself. Goddamn it, he'd put his life on the line. And now he was laid up and in pain. Not a bit of appreciation.

"Just how dumb are you?" The voice wasn't really asking. "Who the hell else could have dug that hole? Oh, yes. I've heard all about what went down out there. In case you haven't noticed, I have people everywhere. What was your half-assed plan to explain that away? And don't give me that bullshit about a utility pole. No one believes that." There was a long string of curses that Darrel would have admired if he wasn't starting to sweat.

"I figured everyone would be too upset, excited, you know, to think too much about it. Sierra would be taken off to Austin or Houston to fix her leg and that would give me time to fix the hole. She ordered me to bury them dead cattle. I could claim I tried to put them there but the ground was too hard."

"I don't know a single rancher who wouldn't have gone by and checked their property after ordering something buried. I'm sure Sierra knew exactly where you put her dead cattle. Didn't she?"

"Maybe, I don't know. What do you want me to do about it now?" Darrel couldn't catch his breath, sweat was running down his armpits and he figured that heart monitor thing had let off a shrill sound that made a nurse appear in the doorway. She frowned when she saw him on the phone.

"I want you to disappear, you fucking moron. If the sheriff comes by your room, you sure as hell better not be there. Your story doesn't hold water. Can't you see that?"

"I, uh, got to go. The nurse is here."

"Don't you hang up on me. Understand this. Don't talk to the sheriff. You get out of that hospital one way or another. Because if I catch you there, you'll be leaving in a body bag." The line went dead.

Darrel threw the phone on the bed. God. That was a death threat. Yeah, he knew he'd messed up, but not so bad that he was in line to be snuffed out.

"Mr. Lockhart, your blood pressure is up and your heart rate is fast." The nurse shook her head. "It's not a good idea to make phone calls. You need to relax and concentrate on healing. You're due for more pain medication in a few minutes. How do you feel now? From one to ten, ten being the worst."

"I hurt like hell. Eleven." He gripped the phone when she tried to take it away. "One more phone call. Then I'll set it back on the nightstand. I promise. I'm sure that pain pill or whatever will put me right to sleep, won't it?"

"Yes, it will. Make it brief, Mr. Lockhart." She smiled and started to leave the room.

"Wait! Where are my clothes?"

"They were ruined and the emergency room staff threw them away. Apparently when you broke your leg, you fell in the mud. Then they had to cut off your jeans. But your wallet and money are in the bedside table there. Your boots must still be in Muellerville where you were taken first." She held the door. "You'll need to get someone to bring you some things before you check out. But you'll be here a few days. There's plenty of time for that." She let the door close as she left.

Darrel frowned. At least he had his friends on speed dial. Because he sure as hell couldn't have remembered a phone number right now. Shit. How was he going to get out of here with this leg in a cast and stoned on painkillers? He sure wasn't going to turn those down.

He looked down the short list. Okay, who owed him a favor?

Chapter Fifteen

"I'm glad the heifer and her calf looked good." Rhett pulled Sierra down onto the couch.

"So am I. That means I don't have to call the vet." She smiled. "Thanks for going with me."

"I promised your brother I wouldn't let you out of my sight." It hadn't been a hardship. Except Rhett was certainly beginning to appreciate all the work Sierra had to do on a cattle ranch. How in the hell had she managed with the horses here too?

"At least the arson investigator was satisfied with taking our depositions over the phone. Much better than in an office somewhere." Sierra had her leg on the coffee table again. "Rachel left me a voicemail. Our dinner's in the oven. She had to leave to pick up Billy at school for Sally Ann." She turned to Rhett. "So we're alone."

"Really." Rhett knew an invitation when he heard it. He leaned in for a kiss. They were getting somewhere when the house phone rang. Of course. Either Sierra's cell or *that* damned thing had been blowing up all day. He pulled back. "Ignore it."

"Can't. It might finally be Dylan." She was still smiling, though, clearly as reluctant as he was to call a halt to making out on her couch.

"Let me grab it and look at the caller ID first. May I?" He was pushed to his feet as her answer. The answering machine kicked in, and they could hear the message as he crossed the room. It was Dylan.

"Sierra? If you're there, pick up the damned phone!"

Rhett grabbed it. "We're here. Just a minute, MacKenzie. Sierra's on the couch, resting her leg. We've been all over the pastures this afternoon getting the cattle settled to her satisfaction. Can you wait a minute?"

"Yeah, sure. I couldn't reach her on her cell so I was getting worried." Dylan still sounded impatient.

"Let me check her cell." Rhett saw it on the bar. "Looks like she's out of juice. I'll plug it in to charge while you talk to her. Here she is." He handed the cordless to Sierra then found the charging station next to the coffeemaker. He peeked into the oven and saw baked chicken and dressing with some vegetables that were probably fresh from Rachel's garden. His stomach growled as he headed for the hidden bar and selected a bottle of rosé from the cooler.

"You're kidding!" Her exclamation stopped him as he was pouring two glasses.

Maybe he'd better sit down and listen in. She was sitting up straight.

"You did all that today?" Her hand shook as she held it out for her glass. "Send me an email with the details. Do you have a list of names of the local investors?" She glanced at Rhett. "I'll take what you've got. I'm beginning to realize that all of these local people are going to suffer because of me, Dylan. Can we do something about that?" She sank against the sofa cushions.

Rhett put his arm around her. She'd asked a good question, one he'd been pondering himself. Those bastards in Dallas had put her in an impossible position. The little town of Muellerville was full of struggling entrepreneurs who had been given a glimpse of a financial future beyond their wildest dreams. Oxcart had cleverly dangled that future in front of them—a vision of hundreds of well-heeled seniors shopping in the town, using the local restaurants and stores on a daily basis, and bringing in their extended families for visits. Naturally the locals would resent anyone who stood in the way of making that brilliant dream come true.

The fact that Sierra hadn't jumped at the generous offer to buy her land had been a reminder that she wasn't like the rest of them. She could afford to thumb her nose at this once-in-a-lifetime opportunity. Not only had she been a rich girl, summering here so she could ride her horses in the local rodeo, but she had oil wells pumping liquid gold on her property. A quick internet search had shown Rhett that there were very few other properties with productive wells in the area. He didn't know why. It was something Dylan could probably explain to him. He noticed Sierra had hung up and dropped the phone next to her.

"You okay?" He kissed her cool cheek. "Talk to me."

"Dylan's investigator found some people he could talk to in Dallas. He even got copies of the contracts Oxcart used with the landholders here. Brubaker wasn't lying. There's a contingency clause in those contracts.

If I don't sell the company access to the highway, Oxcart can pull out of the deal and all the landowners will keep is the five hundred dollars of earnest money the company put down when they negotiated the price. Can you believe it?" Sierra reached across him for her wine. "That's so unfair, Rhett."

"Sounds like it. I'm not into real estate so I have no idea if that's the normal way to do business." He held her for a moment, savoring her soft body and sweet smell. He appreciated the fact that she cared so much for how the other ranchers were being treated. It was added pressure to sell out, but she shouldn't have been put in this position in the first place.

"Why can't they get to the development another way?" He had looked at a map and there were other roads, other routes.

"Every other ranch they've bought has limited access." She frowned. "I remember Dad bragged that he owned the only ranch that bordered on a state-maintained highway. Trust me, the dinky roads into the places Oxcart bought first will look as bad as my driveway as soon as they start construction and use heavy equipment. Then the county and city will fight over who has to pave them. Delays like that cost money. You ended up at my gate because you took a turn out of Austin, didn't you?"

"Yeah, it was pretty direct." He realized she was right. It wasn't a wide highway and not busy, but it was in excellent shape. "I see your point."

"Exactly. The highways from Houston and San Antonio connect not far from here. Like my brother said. The location is perfect. Daddy had friends all over Texas who would come enjoy our barbeques because of that." She sipped her wine. "Just my luck that an outfit like Oxcart took a notion to build in the vicinity."

"Right idea, wrong company." Rhett could see Sierra didn't want to hear that.

"Dylan says Brubaker is dodging his phone calls so he'll ambush him at Oxcart headquarters tomorrow. Or try to." She sighed. "I'm sick of this whole thing. What happened to my nice dream of rescuing and taking care of horses?"

"I don't know. What I do know is that you need another ranch hand if you're going to keep dealing with the cattle. Where are the two guys who were here working with the kids the day I arrived? I think their names were José and Pete, something like that."

"José and Brian. They actually volunteer their time once a month to help with the children who come for therapy. Great guys, but they have other jobs." She rubbed Rhett's leg.

A habit? As if it was her own leg that ached? Rhett didn't care why, he just knew he liked that she felt comfortable touching him. Earlier, they'd gone to separate bathrooms to shower. He'd had other ideas, but one look at Sierra's slumping shoulders as she'd limped into the house had told him she was too tired for the kind of shower shenanigans he had in mind. He hoped the wine would relax her and that lingering over dinner would give her time to get a second wind. Because later, he planned to sleep with her again. If she felt like it, he'd like to show her how much he admired the way she was handling things. And how sexy he found her toughness.

"You still plan to sell the cattle then?" He picked up her hand and kissed the back of it. Not a move, just affection.

"I'll call the guy tomorrow who can handle the sale for me." She rested her head on his shoulder. "Did I tell you how much I appreciated your support today? I would have hated to do any of this alone."

"Glad to be available." He rubbed the calluses on her hand. She had so much strength in every way. "It's time for you to tell me about your accident. All the details you can remember that will help me investigate it." Her grip on his hand tightened. "I know it's been a long time, Sierra, but see what you can recall. I need the names of people who were there at the time. Dates. Any little thing that might pop up as you think back to the day it happened. Before the race, then immediately after it." He let go and got up to get his laptop. "I'll be taking notes."

"I appreciate this. You sure you have time? I haven't seen you work on your book yet." She walked to the bar, glancing back to see if he needed a refill. He'd barely touched his wine so she just filled her glass.

"My deadline is months away. I turned in a book before I came to Texas. My editor will probably send me some notes, but I'll deal with those when they come. Right now I have time to give to you." He sat at her father's desk, opened the laptop and started hitting keys.

It gave Sierra a little chill to see him sitting at that desk, looking serious. Not that Daddy had done much work while they'd been at the ranch. No, what gave her a shivery feeling of dread was the idea of going through that awful day again. How many times had she relived it? Wondered if she'd missed something because of the haze of pain after the accident? Had she repressed the key to what had gone wrong? She took a quick drink then set the wine aside. That wouldn't help her think. Her leg ached. Good. It was a reminder of why this was so important.

"It was a big day for me. I got up really early to check on Destiny. My parents and I had spent the night at a hotel close to the arena. Destiny had a stall in the arena itself. I was in the stall at dawn, going over my horse to make her pretty because I was too wired to sleep. I'd taken my own car. Mama and Daddy knew I'd be like that and always came over a little later. I'd been racing all summer and it had become my routine." She paused behind Rhett to look over his shoulder. She gave him the date, the name of the arena, even the name of the hotel where they had been staying.

"Do you need to know what kind of car I was driving?" She rubbed his shoulders. Oh, she did love his shoulders, so broad, strong and solid. She was learning she could lean on them too.

"Not really, but who did know? Any of your competitors? They'd see your car at the arena and know when you were there and when you weren't." He was a fast typist. Of course, he was a writer.

"Sally Ann for sure. She hated the fact that Daddy had bought me a nice car for my junior year in high school. Nice, fast and red. Each of my brothers had gotten one at the same age and I nagged him to death until he caved. I don't know about Boston, but in Texas, we get a driver's license at sixteen if our parents can afford the insurance. Rachel claimed she couldn't unless Sally Ann got a summer job. They had big arguments about it. Sally Ann wanted to concentrate on her riding but finally took a part-time job at the Trading Post. She still didn't get a car, though. Rachel stalled her. We pay our housekeeper well, but they had Sally Ann's horse to board and racing expenses. You get the picture."

"Okay, that's interesting. Anyone besides Sally Ann have car envy?"

"Ellie and Marty. You met them both. Marty at the Wagon Wheel, then Ellie at the café. They were Sally Ann's best friends. Ellie had a truck, her big brother's hand-me-down. She'd give rides to the other girls, but it was a rusty heap they all hated. The three girls went to high school together. Ellie's dad owned the café before she took over. It's a Muellerville institution. When he died, she dropped out of college to help her mom run it. Her brother got to stay in college and get his degree. He left town years ago and works in Dallas now. I think Ellie wanted to finish school but then she and Mark got serious and the rest is history."

"Were all three of the girls at the race that day?" Rhett looked up from his keyboard.

"Actually, yes, they were. They were there to cheer for Sally Ann. I didn't blame them. I was always the outsider. But we did hang out together occasionally. I usually ended up driving and paying. I had a gas card and credit cards, a generous allowance too." Sierra frowned. "They used me. I didn't mind it. My best friends were in Houston so I was lonely when I was here in the summers. I loved my horse, but it's not the same as having girlfriends to talk to."

"What about boys?" Rhett turned around and put his hands on her hips. "You can't tell me you didn't date, a hot girl like you."

"Thanks, I think. I didn't date much but there was a guy I liked." Sierra thought back to that last summer. She and Sally Ann had been in competition for more than just barrel racing. "Joey Schlitzberger." She tugged on Rhett's ear when he grinned. "Don't laugh. He was the high school quarterback and cute as hell. He flirted with all of us but took me to the movies a couple of times. Then Sally Ann got hold of him." She shivered when Rhett's tongue touched her palm. "Stop it. I'm remembering my teenage angst."

"Oh, please go on. I'll kiss it and make it better later." He did manage to pull her in and press his mouth to the valley between her breasts. "Did Joey Shit-berger break your heart?"

"Schlitzberger. Yes, he did. Sally Ann put out. I wouldn't." She ran her hands through Rhett's thick hair.

"I'm glad that's changed." That got his hair pulled. "Ouch."

"Maybe it hasn't changed after that remark." She backed away from him. "Let me finish my story. Turn around and take notes."

"Was Joey there to watch the race? Can we make him the villain in this piece?" Rhett looked hopeful before he turned back to the keyboard.

"No, he was at football camp by then. Sally Ann was complaining about that. I think she was already pregnant. I heard later that's why they got married senior year and she dropped out of school. She eventually lost the baby. Joey turned out to be a jerk, telling everyone he had dodged a bullet. His daddy was a lawyer and got the marriage annulled. Sally Ann ran back to Rachel and got a GED instead of finishing high school." Sierra sighed.

"Too bad." Rhett stopped typing.

"I heard all this later, when I wasn't in a haze from painkillers. Marty and Ellie actually came to see me the next summer, full of gossip. They claimed Sally Ann was heartbroken and had to work full-time at the Trading Post to help pay back her mother for lawyer's fees. Sally Ann tried to get a big settlement from Joey's family, but no luck fighting the best lawyer in town. She had to sell her horse and her future looked pretty bleak."

"Drama for sure. That's really too bad." Rhett started typing.

"I wasn't around for any of that. I was going through my endless surgeries by then. Came here to recuperate." Sierra reached for her wine. She'd love to forget those painful times. "Sally Ann came out all right. She met Will Jackson working at that store. Story is, she sold him a pair of jeans, then helped him out of them in a back room. They've been together ever since."

She glanced at Rhett. What did he think of that? No sign he had even heard her. He was scrolling back over what he'd typed so far.

"Back to the day of the race. You got there early to groom Destiny. You sure you were careful to check all the tack? Harnesses, saddle, cinch, everything?"

"It's very important, Rhett. I can't imagine I wouldn't have. I had a new saddle." She sipped the wine. Very good vintage. Her brothers kept the place stocked for her. God knew what this bottle had cost. No, this wasn't the time to get distracted by her budget issues. She didn't want to, but she had to remember that day.

"Who else was around Destiny's stall?"

"My parents, of course, before the races started. Sally Ann's horse, Strider, was in the next stall so she and Rachel were around. Marty and Ellie came back, and a couple of other riders we knew from the circuit had horses in stalls nearby. I bet I have the lineup here somewhere." She moved closer to Rhett and rummaged in the file drawer built into the desk. She'd kept a file of her races and the printed programs. Because of her years of surgeries and hospital stays, her parents had let her run a little wild in college. Then she'd decided to come here, to the ranch, after her dad died. No one had tried to talk her out of it because she was still "poor Sierra." She'd surprised them all by becoming independent and doing a decent job rescuing her horses. Well, not so decent financially. After she sold the cattle, she was going to have to figure out her next move. Was she going to have to give in to Oxcart and their demands? She hated the thought.

"Hey, I'm waiting. You look miles and years away." Rhett looked over her shoulder. "That the program?"

"Yes, take a look. But it won't help. None of these girls had any reason to sabotage my gear." Sierra handed it to him. "They were a decent group of riders, but my closest competition was always Sally Ann."

"You think she had it in her to do something to your cinch?" Rhett looked serious now. "That's attempted murder, Sierra."

"I'm sure she didn't mean..." But who knew what Sally Ann had thought. If she had been pregnant then, her riding time should have already come to an end. No one in their right mind would continue barrel racing and risk a hard fall when pregnant. The fact that Sally Ann had, meant she might have been pretty desperate to finally win a race. "Rhett, she had the opportunity. In fact, Ellie and Marty asked me to walk outside with them for a few minutes right before my race. They swore a boy I liked—I'd moved on from Joey—had been asking for me. When we got outside, no one was around. They insisted he had come by in his new car and we were supposed to wait for him to pull into the parking lot. Finally, I had to go inside to get ready to race. But maybe..."

"Maybe Sally Ann had asked them to get you out of the way for a few minutes. So she could work on your cinch and saddle." Rhett stood and put his arms around her. "You look pale. Did you just remember that?"

"Yes. I think I've been afraid to think too hard about that day. I thought I rechecked Destiny's cinch, but they called for us to enter the arena as soon as I got back inside. All I had time to do was mount up and get behind Sally Ann in line. I didn't notice anything when I sat in the saddle, but I was so nervous I'm not sure I would have. This was a big race for me." Sierra laid her head on his chest. She could hear his heart beating as she thought back to that day.

"I was last to race. Sally Ann had a really good run, her fastest time ever. She was in the lead, holding first place. When they called my name, I took a deep breath, patted Destiny and waited for my signal." She looked up at Rhett.

"When you're waiting to start, you are full of adrenaline. You have no idea of the rush you feel, the nerves, as you wait for the judge to drop the flag. You're timed, so a quick start is everything. The flag fell and Destiny took off at my command. We were flying as we entered the arena and crossed the start line. I knew right away that this was going to be great, one of my best runs. We were in sync and the first turn was perfect. We hit our mark and then we were heading for the second." Sierra gripped Rhett's shoulders.

She was there again, seeing the barrel coming up and feeling the power of that incredible horse between her thighs. Destiny leaned as she took the turn and then it was all a horrible mistake. There had been the fall, the unreal feeling as she lost her seat and flew through the air. Desperate, numbing pain as she hit the dirt. Her poor horse had scrambled for purchase, trying not to fall, to land on her, but Destiny lost her balance, crushing Sierra's leg under her massive weight. Harsh breathing, screams, then...silence.

Chapter Sixteen

"Sierra! Talk to me!" Rhett shook her gently. "Baby, please. Come back here. Now."

"I—I'm here. It's just that remembering is so much harder than I thought. It's as if I relived it. My sweet Destiny. That horse wanted to win as much as I did."

"And you really, really wanted to win." He helped her to the couch then sat close beside her. "Damn the person who robbed you of that." He rubbed her hands.

She was glad. They felt like ice. In fact, her entire body was shaking, chilled.

"You want some more wine?"

"No, I want you to hold me."

"I can do that." He pulled her into his lap and wrapped his arms around her. "So brave." He took a deep breath. "It's clear to me that we need to confront Sally Ann. I wonder if her mother knows what she did."

"What if we're wrong? Think how that would hurt Rachel."

"You said her mother was near the stalls that day. Maybe Rachel saw something." Rhett's hold tightened.

"And didn't say anything?" Sierra jerked. "No, I don't believe that. Rachel would never have let her daughter hurt me. How could she work here after that and look at any of us if she knew?"

"Okay, that's an excellent point. Sally Ann could have sent her mother on an errand while she did her dirty deed. It's possible." Rhett wasn't giving up; he just held on to her.

Sierra soaked in his heat and the care he was giving her. He wanted to solve this mystery and he wanted to comfort her. Comfort. She had some ideas about how he could do that.

"I don't know, Sierra. I hope Rachel didn't know. But it's pretty clear to me that it had to be Sally Ann who tampered with your equipment. She had the most to gain; that's motive. And she was in the next stall with her horse; that's opportunity." He kissed the top of her head. "You could have been killed. As it was, the accident changed your life forever."

"Yes, it did. But I survived, even thrived, sort of. Of course I haven't forgotten all those surgeries and the pain I went through. My parents suffered too. If Sally Ann did it, just to win a damned race…" Sierra leaned against Rhett. "That's either incredibly sad or evil. Which is it?"

"I don't know. I guess it depends on what else she's done since then. Has she gone on to live an exemplary life? Or committed more bad acts?" Rhett smoothed her hair back from her face. "When I saw her at the Chevy dealership, she seemed to have a pretty decent life, married to a rich man, with a son. Of course, some people are really good at covering their tracks. She could be up to all kinds of shit under the radar." He sounded like he was thinking hard, working out a plot.

"Does she still run around with those two girls? Marty and Ellie? I wonder if she confided in them."

"I don't know or care. I am really tired of thinking about this right now." She gently pushed until she could look up at him. "I'd rather deal with the here and now." Sierra kissed his solemn mouth. He was obviously still determined to solve the mystery. She stroked his cheek. He'd shaved during the short break they'd taken to clean up, and she loved the feeling of his smooth skin under her fingertips.

"Thanks for being so understanding, Rhett. Now there's one thing I need from you."

"Anything. Ready for dinner? Good food always makes me feel better." He kissed those fingertips, sucking one into his mouth. He seemed to have a thing about her hands. She didn't mind it.

"Later." Men. Food. *Really?* Sierra smiled at him. "Right now I need you to take me to bed and make love to me. Reliving that day took a lot out of me. I think some up close and personal attention might just help me pull myself back together. What do you think? Can you do that for me? Comfort me?"

"Say no more." He jumped up so fast he made her dizzy. He held her in his arms as he walked down the hall. "You sure this is what you need? Not that I'm complaining or trying to change your mind."

"If you're not up to it…" She laughed when he did drop her on the bed this time. "I guess I have my answer." Snaps popped open and his jeans hit the floor. "Oh, my, I'd say you are definitely up to the task. Come here, Mr. Hall." Rhett climbed on top of her, kissing a path from her toes to her nose as he efficiently rid her of her clothes. Once she was naked, he stared at the scars on her leg.

"There's got to be some way we can make Sally Ann pay for these. You may think you're over it, but I am not. You still limp, Sierra, and are frequently in pain. I know you are. Then look at what you went through." He kissed his way along the proof of the damage that fall had done. The ugly evidence went from her ankle to her thigh.

"I really don't give a damn about that woman right now. You once said you'd kiss it and make it better. Forget my scars. I have an ache a little higher. Why don't you keep exploring and see if you can figure out where that might be?" Sierra sighed when he did work his way upward, then picked up both of her legs and draped them over his shoulders.

"Oh, my. I think you've found the spot." She stretched out her arms and closed her eyes. Whatever *had* happened all those years ago, she was definitely ready to let go of the past. When Rhett proved he was more than capable of making her forget even the here and now, she knew she was onto something.

She was finally relaxed and ready to think about dinner when Tramp went crazy. Most of the time the elderly dog slept in front of the fireplace. It was easy to forget he was even there. Now he was barking as if someone was trying to break into the house.

"What the hell?" Rhett sat up and opened the nightstand drawer on his side of the bed. He pulled out the handgun he'd put it there the night before. He was very serious about protecting her.

"Wait. We can check the cameras first." Sierra got up and grabbed her laptop from her dresser top. "Tramp, come here, boy." The dog just kept barking, but he did stop in front of her open bedroom door and jump around as if trying to get her to come investigate. "Good boy. Calm down. We'll see what's happening outside in a moment." The dog didn't care. He ran back to the kitchen, still barking. "Wow, he's really upset."

"Show me the outside camera feeds." Rhett kept the gun in his lap.

"I'm getting there. Move that gun. I don't want you to shoot off something important." She hit the keys to pull up the video feeds.

"The safety is on, but I'm glad you care." He leaned close so he could look at the screen, kissing her neck before he exclaimed, "Someone's out there. A strange truck, too."

"They must have had the gate code. We didn't get an alert that someone had come through without it." Sierra checked every angle, but it was obvious that the intruder had driven up the driveway and past the house. It was dark outside, but the security company had installed automatic lights with motion sensors and they were on now, showing her that two trucks were sitting side by side in front of the bunkhouse.

"Honey, the way we were going at it, I doubt a mere alert would have been enough to get my attention." He ran his hand over her bare back.

"True enough, but a car can't break in through the gate without the alarm going off. Look!" Sierra pointed to the screen. "There are two people. Someone is getting out and—"

"Getting into that other pickup. I recognize Darrel's truck from last night. The paramedic left it parked there." Rhett climbed out of bed and grabbed his jeans. "Maybe I should make sure this person is who he asked to get his truck for him. Ask for some ID."

"I don't recognize the vehicle and it's too dark to see who is getting into the truck. The paramedic probably left the keys in the ignition. The other one is just a generic Chevy truck. There are dozens like it in town. I think it's a woman driving." Sierra enlarged the picture. "Both of them are women. I didn't know Darrel had a girlfriend. But then he never talks about his personal life."

"You want me to go out there or not?" Rhett stayed next to the bed.

"They had the gate code. Only Darrel could have given it to them."

"Really? Didn't you give it to the paramedic last night? So he could deliver the truck here?" Rhett was playing devil's advocate.

"Come on, Rhett. If they got into my garage and tried to steal my new pickup, I'd say take your gun and stop them. Darrel drives an old beater. I doubt anyone would go to the trouble of breaking in here to steal it. I really don't think we need to get involved in this, do you?" Sierra saw the two trucks get in line, ready to leave the property.

"It's up to you." Rhett didn't move. "Maybe you should call Darrel and ask him if he had a woman coming for his truck."

"Last time I checked, he was pretty out of it on painkillers." Sierra watched the two trucks start around the back of the house toward the driveway. "They're leaving. I am surprised, though, that one of them didn't go into the bunkhouse and get a few things for Darrel to have at the hospital. Pajamas, razor, stuff like that."

"I'll go wave them down. Either they forgot or this isn't what it seems." Rhett stuck his gun into his waistband then ran out of the room. Tramp was on his heels.

Sierra watched the scene unfold on her computer screen. Rhett was definitely a mystery writer, seeing a plot everywhere. He emerged from the house with the dog beside him. They both positioned themselves in the center of the driveway so the trucks had to stop or run over them. For a moment it looked like the pickups were going to keep moving in a deadly game of chicken. Sierra sat up so quickly, her computer slid off her lap. *What the hell?*

Rhett pulled out his gun, and the truck in front stopped just inches from hitting him. He walked to the driver's side and leaned in to talk to whoever was behind the wheel.

Sierra grabbed her robe from the foot of the bed and ran through the house. Her rifle sat next to the back door where she'd left it. Gravel bit into the soles of her bare feet when she stepped outside and raised the rifle, taking aim. The second truck was trying to pass the first one, driving over the muddy mess next to her burned-out barn.

"Stop right now or I'll put a bullet through your windshield. And I won't be aiming at your sun visor." She was shouting, and the second truck jerked to a stop. She walked over to see who Rhett was talking to in truck number one.

* * * *

"Well, hello, Sally Ann. You're trespassing, you know." Rhett looked between the two women. Sierra held that rifle like she wanted to use it. Tired of thinking about the past? Apparently it had all come roaring back. He should try to defuse this situation, but this might be a chance to get some information from a smirking Sally Ann.

"Trespassing? I've been coming here with Mama since I was a kid, Sierra. So when Darrel asked me to pick up his truck, I said no problem. Marty drove me over to get it. You refusing to let me by?" Sally Ann looked too dressed up for driving a truck that had a pile of empty takeout coffee cups on the dash along with other litter. It was a wonder she could see over the trash.

"I didn't know you and Darrel were friends." Sierra swung her rifle over to aim it at the other truck like she meant business. "You dragged Marty out here for this? She usually works at night."

"It's her night off. She's doing me a favor." Sally Ann fluffed her hair. "Honestly, what's with all the gunplay? It's not as if this hunk of junk is worth stealing. I'm doing this for poor Darrel. He called me begging for it. Terrible accident right here on your property. You carry workmans' compensation insurance for him, Sierra?"

"You don't have to worry about that. But how do you know Darrel, Sally Ann?" Sierra had the rifle aimed at Sally Ann again. "He doesn't seem to be your type."

Sally Ann laughed. "You are so right. Never you mind about that. Just get out of my way." She batted her obviously fake eyelashes and focused on Rhett. "Hey, big guy, I saw you at the dealership. You rented that Tahoe from us, didn't you?"

"Yes, I did. I'm Sierra's houseguest, Rhett Hall." Rhett suddenly wished he'd flung on a shirt. This woman had a predatory look that made him feel like a piece of meat. "I'm wondering why you didn't let Sierra know you were coming. This *is* her ranch, you know. Seems like it would have been the polite thing to do." He saw her hands with their sharp red nails grip the cracked plastic steering wheel. Darrel's truck was old and in bad shape. The very sight of the polished and primped Sally Ann driving the hunk of junk, as Sierra had put it, made him wish for his camera. Another interesting piece of the puzzle.

Why would a woman like this do anything for a sometime handyman like Darrel Lockhart? Darrel was missing a couple of front teeth and smelled like cigarettes and infrequent bathing. Sally Ann Jackson wore expensive perfume and had capped teeth that had been freshly whitened.

"Rhett and I were talking about the bad luck I've been having." Sierra propped her rifle on the edge of the open window.

"Burned barn. Hurt ranch hand. I'd say it was a sign you should move on, Sierra. This ranch can be a dangerous place." Sally Ann looked Sierra up and down after she carefully pushed the rifle away.

"Funny that you should show up to get Darrel's truck. You know, the more I think about it, the more I realize he could be our number one suspect in the barn fire. And now here you are, helping him out after urging me to sell. You got a reason you want me gone, Sally Ann? You got a stake in this new Oxcart development deal?" Sierra kept her gun so close it almost nudged Sally Ann's shoulder. "You make it worth Darrel's while to torch my barn?"

"Get that damned gun away from me. What the hell, Sierra? You come up with this paranoid fantasy all by yourself? Or did the famous author write your script for you?" Sally Ann tried to roll up the window, but the glass stuck at an odd angle. "Fuck!"

"I can think for myself, Sally Ann. I've known you a long time. Sometimes, I think, too long." Sierra's finger twitched on the trigger.

"Put that fucking gun away! You're crazy. Where would I get money to invest in anything, much less in this new development that you're determined to ruin for everyone who lives here? Will keeps me on a budget ever since

I went wild at the Galleria in Houston last Christmas." She almost snarled, her red lipstick smeared on one perfect tooth.

"Yes, everyone in Muellerville heard about that shopping spree." Sierra actually laughed, but she didn't lower her rifle. "You do love your designer footwear."

Sally Ann's eyes sparkled with something like tears. "I swear to God, Sierra, you've always acted like an entitled bitch and you never change." She put the car in gear and it rolled forward. "Unless you've got something you plan to take to the sheriff, I think you'd better shut the hell up about conspiracy theories. You hear me?" She gunned the truck, gravel spewing out behind her as she drove on down the driveway.

"That bitch! I think she did have something to do with my barn burning." Sierra moved as if to go after her.

"Look out, here comes Marty." Rhett put his arms around Sierra and dragged her back out of the way.

"We should ask Marty about it. Maybe she knows—"

"Sierra, honey, she's still hopping to Sally Ann's tune. Why else would she be here on her night off to help Sally Ann get Darrel's truck? There's something fishy about that, I think. Neither of those women should be having any dealings with a hand like Darrel."

"What do you mean? I have dealings with him." Sierra pulled her robe tight. She called Tramp, who made a short run after the trucks then followed them into the house.

"He works for you. It seems strange to me that a woman like Sally Ann would come all the way out here to get his truck. Now what is she going to do, take it to the hospital in Austin for him? Why? She sure as hell wouldn't let him take her to bed."

"No, he's a good ranch hand, but I stay upwind of him." Sierra sniffed as she sat down to look at her feet. "Damned rocks. I'll really be limping now."

"Don't change the subject." Though Rhett did bring her a wet paper towel to clean her feet. "Sally Ann and Darrel. Does she owe him a favor? Seems unlikely. What could possibly be their connection? Unless you're right." He was thinking hard.

"Seriously? You think she could have paid him to burn down my barn? That was a wild guess." Sierra stood and moaned. "Never run barefoot on gravel. Lesson learned." She glanced at him. "You did it too. I guess I'm the tenderfoot here."

"I'm being stoic. It did hurt. But I'm sucking it up." He grinned. "Let's eat, then I'll tell you why you may be right about Darrel and Sally Ann's connection."

"I agree that Darrel is not Sally Ann's type. She goes for tall guys who are built like football players and have plenty of money." Sierra ran her hands over his chest. "I saw how she looked at you. She goes for guys like you."

"I think that was a compliment. But she's certainly not my type. Too cold. Too polished." Rhett pulled her in and peeled open her robe. "Now here's what I like. You were a badass out there. I was afraid I was going to have to bury a body."

"Speaking of that." She stepped back and tied her robe again. "Did you notice the shovel in the back of Darrel's pickup?"

"No! You should have said something. That's probably your shovel." Rhett opened the oven, found a towel and carefully pulled out their two plates. "This is still good and hot."

"It *is* my shovel. But my point is, that must be how that strange hole got next to the fence. The one Darrel fell into." Sierra disappeared into the den then reappeared with their wineglasses and the bottle.

"I don't know. If he dug it himself and kept the evidence, that makes him a dumbass. Doubly a dumbass if he made the hole, forgot it was there and broke his leg falling into it." Rhett grabbed silverware and napkins and looked at Sierra with a gesture. "Can we eat while we discuss this?"

"I get it. Crime solving makes you hungry." Sierra sat and put a napkin in her lap. "What if he dug that hole so *I* could fall into it?" Sierra stared at him. "Rhett, if Darrel was working for Oxcart or Sally Ann, it would be a good way to persuade me to give up and sell. A fall like that would put me down for a long time. This leg is still very vulnerable. It's held together with rods and pins. I'd end up in a hospital in Houston again and my family would have a fit if I tried to go it alone here after that."

"Darrel and Oxcart. Any other evidence of that connection?" Rhett tried to follow her logic. He had wondered about the placement of that fresh hole since he'd first seen it.

"The feed bags we used the night of the fire. You remember how Darrel grabbed them from right inside the barn door?" She stabbed a green bean.

"Yes, I was glad they were there."

"So was I. But that's not where I usually keep them. We put them in the back of the barn, in the tack room. Darrel must have moved them up there so they'd be handy. He wanted to save the horses. He's not a cold-blooded killer. At least not of horses. So I think he started the fire. There's a can of gasoline in the outbuilding where I keep the tractors. We can check to see if it's still full. I forgot to mention it to the sheriff. Darrel could have used it, then, when the alarm went off, called 9-1-1 and started bringing out the

horses. He was trying to make himself look innocent. Covering his butt."
Sierra ate the green bean then waited. "Make sense?"

"It does. Unfortunately." Rhett grabbed her hand. "Maybe we should call
the sheriff right now. Tell her your theory."

"I don't think Darrel is going anywhere. We can call Myra in the morning.
If she presses him, I'll bet he'll confess. She already has his fingerprints on
the fence posts that were down. Combined with the hole and maybe some
investigation into his cell phone records, I bet she can break him."

"Good work, detective." Rhett leaned across and kissed her. "You're
hired. Maybe you can help me with my next book."

"Maybe I can." She smiled and dug into the chicken on her plate. "I'm
still thinking about Sally Ann. You won't break her, not in a million years."

"I agree. She's tough. And, with food like this, I'd hate for you to risk
your relationship with her mother." Rhett was deep into the corn bread
dressing. "Delicious."

"Rachel is a treasure, but if she knew what Sally Ann did and kept quiet
about it, then she's gone." Sierra put down her fork. "I'd have to learn to cook."

"Don't be hasty. My gut tells me she had no idea." Rhett popped a green
bean into his mouth.

"Your gut is a selfish bastard." Sierra smiled and sipped wine.

"I'm not denying that. Eat. You'll feel better. And slip Tramp some chicken.
That boy was a better alarm system tonight than all of that expensive tech you
have here." Rhett dropped a piece of chicken too, but it never hit the floor.

"You're right. Good boy, Tramp. Your nose for skanks is still young and
unbeatable." Sierra sighed. "I said I was ready to forget the past but I'm a
freaking liar. When someone does a horrible thing like what was done to
me, they should be punished, Rhett."

He stopped eating and sat back. "You're right. We may not get Sally Ann
for that crime, but what if we get her for something else?" He paused when
he heard chimes from down the hall. "That's your phone and mine. I think
that brother of yours is sending us the information he's gathered. Let me
send it to my computer and we can print it out."

"Fine. Go get it and start the process. We can look at it after dinner."
Sierra kept eating. "Let me know if it's something else."

"You want to tell me where your printer is? It's not in the den."

"My real office is across from my bedroom. Let me know if you need
help figuring things out." She smiled as she refilled her wineglass.

Rhett hobbled down the hall. A real office. Sierra had a desktop computer
system, two printers and a filing cabinet. Some of it was clearly for ranch
work, but there was a full bookcase with an interesting variety of literature

that convinced him Sierra had depths he'd yet to plumb. Not the time for that, but he put it on his mental list, then got to work. Sure enough, there were attachments from Dylan labeled Investors and Contracts. Rhett sent them from his phone to his laptop and set up a printer connection. It didn't take long. Pages were printing by the time he joined Sierra at the table again.

"Your dinner was getting cold." She sat in front of her empty plate, sipping wine.

"I stopped to rinse off my feet." He dug into his meal. "Even cold, Rachel's food is delicious. We have to figure out a way to keep her here."

"I'd like that, but only if she isn't involved in her daughter's schemes." Sierra finished her wine. "I'm going after those printouts. Take your time."

"I like your office. Want to explain what exactly you do in there?" Rhett stopped her with a hand on her arm.

"This and that." She smiled mysteriously.

"And you just got more fascinating." He scooped up the last bite. "I'm done. I'll load the dishwasher while you get the papers." Rhett didn't want Rachel to be the only person Sierra kept when this was over. And wasn't that a kick in the pants? He mulled over that shocker while he scraped plates and rinsed everything before he got the kitchen in shape. He heard Sierra exclaim, then hurried to join her in the den.

"You won't believe this." She held out a page. "Look at this list of names. Most of them you won't recognize, though I certainly do. But fourth from the bottom. *Tres Amigas*. I know who that is."

"That's Spanish. It means—"

"Three friends. Girlfriends. What do you bet that's our three pals—Sally Ann, Marty and Ellie?" Sierra sat on the couch. "It has to be. They called themselves that in high school. Like they were a special little clique. They probably used it thinking no one would remember all these years later." She thumped herself on the thigh. "But I sure do. It pissed me off. I was always left out. I had a bad case of teenage jealousy when they called themselves that."

"So you think they invested as *tres amigas*?" Rhett studied the names on the list. Sierra was right; most of them meant nothing to him. "Then I have a theory."

Chapter Seventeen

"Oh, really? What's this theory?" Sierra dropped the rest of the papers on the coffee table then stuck her bad leg into Rhett's lap. "While you're telling it to me, would you mind rubbing my leg? I got a lot of exercise today."

"You did. You work too hard. Let me know if I'm doing it wrong." He began to stroke her calf gently.

"You can be a little more serious than that." She wiggled her toes. "Yes, my leg is vulnerable, but not delicate." She sighed as he massaged the sore muscles. "That feels good."

"You get physical therapy for it?"

"I used to. Not for a while now. This is as good as it gets." She put her other leg in his lap. "Don't think I'm getting distracted. I want to hear this theory you've come up with. Involving Sally Ann?"

"The connection between her and Darrel has been bugging me. Why would she drive over here and involve Marty to get his truck? In fact, how did she even hear about the accident?"

"That's easy. You've seen the small-town grapevine at work already. Wouldn't take five minutes for someone at the dealership to hear about it. In fact, the paramedic who drove Darrel's truck here works in the body shop at Will's place." Sierra dropped her feet to the floor. "Stop massaging. I can't think. You have great hands and I didn't ask you to massage *that*."

"Does Sally Ann talk to those guys? The body shop personnel?" Rhett got up to fetch his laptop.

"Sally Ann talks to any man with a muscular build." Sierra couldn't help admiring Rhett's when he stopped to open the computer and get it going. "Come back here."

"I am." He grinned at her. "I thought we were working."

"We are, but that doesn't mean we can't work side by side. You started something with that massage."

"I'll finish that something later." He set the laptop on the coffee table, then turned and kissed her, his mouth hot on hers in a way that had her leaning in, wanting more. Then he pulled back, ran his hand down her arm and opened the computer. "What about Darrel? You said he didn't have family here that you know of. Was he raised in this town? Go to high school with the girls?"

Sierra took a moment to catch her breath. Really? He could just do that and act like he hadn't... She rubbed her hands on her jeans, determined to stay just as cool as he seemed to be.

"Darrel isn't a hometown guy. I have his employment application in a file." She got up to get it. That kiss had moved her more than it should. She was way too vulnerable to Rhett Hall and his casual kisses. She concentrated on the business at hand as she pulled out the file.

"Not much in it. Ranch hands don't need many qualifications. He'd worked at another ranch for a man I knew. I had Dylan's guy in Houston run a background check for my own safety. Darrel had a bar fight on his record, a few speeding tickets and a DUI. I didn't let him drive a ranch truck for that reason. But there weren't any other red flags. You can't be too choosey when you hire someone for the kind of work I needed, especially since I couldn't afford to pay top dollar. Luckily I could offer benefits. I have a deal with Texas Star. Their group policy covers me and any of my employees. I took Darrel on three years ago and he's done a good job. I kept an eye out for drinking on the job but he told me the DUI got him sober and I believed him."

* * * *

Rhett pulled out the contents of the thin file. "Born in Oklahoma. High school dropout." He looked the application over. "Pretty bare bones. He left the next of kin blank."

"No surprise there for a thirty-eight-year-old man. He used Will Jackson as another reference. That was enough for me." Sierra sat with a sigh.

"Did you call Jackson?" Rhett raised an eyebrow.

"No need. I figured just putting down that name meant it would pan out. Everyone knows Will around here. I don't talk to Will unless I have to. You saw his attitude toward me." She made a face.

"He came on to you. Right in front of his mother-in-law. Proved to me he was a first-class jerk even before he acted that way about Billy. Wouldn't be surprised if he cheated on his wife." Rhett remembered how Will had touched Sierra familiarly. She'd reacted like a snake had crawled on her.

"He'd have to do it elsewhere. In this town, it would be impossible to keep it secret. I haven't heard news of it." Sierra was clearly thinking. "He'd risk a lot in a divorce. Though his family owned the dealership before they married. Not sure how much of their money she'd be entitled to, even though this is a community property state."

"You two have a history? Ever date before Sally Ann caught him?" Rhett got up to throw the file on the desk but not before he saw Sierra flinch. "You did, didn't you?"

"Remember the boy I told you I liked? The one who'd supposedly come by to see me at the arena?" Sierra leaned forward, not looking at him. "That was Will Jackson. We met at a barbeque my folks threw that summer. His dad owned the dealership then. Daddy invited him and his family over to meet some people in from Houston. Will came on to me and I was flattered. He was cute back then. And did drive a snappy car. You remember what teenagers are like?"

"A snappy car is a big draw." Rhett realized his fists were clenched. Sierra and Will. The man would have made moves. Sierra might have been dazzled.

"Hey, quit glaring. I didn't put out for him either, though he certainly expected it." Sierra got up to grab his fists. "We'd only gone out a couple of times when the accident happened."

"It wasn't an accident." Rhett opened his hands to hold on to hers. "I'm more sure of that than ever."

"Okay." She looked down to where he realized he was holding a little too tight. "You were telling me about your theory. Darrel might have started the barn fire. You think he could have done it because Sally Ann put him up to it?"

"Come sit and listen to what I'm thinking." Rhett guided her to the couch again. She needed to get off that leg. He still couldn't get over how scarred it was. How much pain she must have gone through. But that was her history. He needed to concentrate on the current situation. Whoever wanted her to sell out probably wasn't through trying to scare her into it.

"I just cannot believe Darrel would betray me like that." She shook her head.

"I hope you're right. Now here's what I'm thinking about the three *amigas*. Sally Ann is married to a man who has money. Does she? We just heard her say she's on a budget. So she probably doesn't have much she can call her own. What about Marty?"

"You heard her say her husband has an auto repair shop. It must not be doing well since she's still stuck in that waitressing job, working nights. She wants kids but they're still putting it off. I doubt she has much money of her own either." Sierra bit her lip.

"What about Ellie? Clearly she has an interest in that Oxcart deal going through. She didn't hide that when she went off at the café."

"Everyone knows she's working her butt off trying to keep her café running. Mark makes no secret of the fact that his pharmacy does a thriving business, but it doesn't make enough to see two kids through med school. You heard what her waitress said. Ellie's café isn't doing so well." Sierra looked thoughtful.

"Clearly, from the name they chose, these three women could have pooled what resources they had for a chance at a big return. This might be their one chance to make some decent money of their own. I don't know if Marty or Ellie are happy in their marriages, but I doubt Sally Ann is. The little I saw of her interactions with Jackson seemed volatile. She didn't hesitate to go off on him in front of a crowd, even accusing him of having an affair." Rhett waited for Sierra to react to that. She just nodded.

"That's Sally Ann all right. If Will does have someone on the side, he could be thinking of moving on. This fast-food franchise he's talking about could be part of a bigger plan he has. If Sally Ann's not bothering to placate Will, then she might have figured out her own exit strategy." Sierra gripped Rhett's leg. "But would she really hire Darrel to burn down my barn?"

"You never know, Sierra." Rhett put his hand over hers. "If the senior citizen development really takes off, returns on an investment could be huge. You're holding up the deal. They may be sick of waiting and Darrel obviously knows Sally Ann, at least."

"Exit strategies." Sierra's eyes were big as she turned to Rhett. "I guess they all might need one. Marty's husband is opinionated. She had dreams of becoming a fashion designer when we were teenagers. Maybe own a dress shop. Buddy laughed at that idea. She used to make her own clothes and they were great. I told her once I'd like her to design something for me—I had a special event in Houston to go to—even offered to pay well for it. Buddy told her I was mocking her. That no big-city 'broad' would wear anything with her name on it. Marty turned me down flat and never showed me her stuff again." Sierra frowned.

"There you go. Motive for Marty." Rhett picked up his laptop and began making notes again. "You already told me Ellie never got to finish college. She might feel trapped by that café and we've already heard she's desperate for money, with two kids dreaming of medical school. Just because her folks started the café, doesn't make it *her* dream. You told me her brother works in Dallas. Not involved in this Oxcart thing, is he?" Rhett saw Sierra bite her lip again. It was a sexy move that could distract him if he wasn't careful. "That would be way too easy."

"No, he's a sports analyst for a TV station there. It's the kind of glamorous job Ellie always dreamed of. You can see how pretty she is. She started in communications at Texas State University in San Marcos. She really wanted to go into TV or something with the media. In high school she made jokes about the café. She hated working there after school. She was always starring in their class plays and was the senior class president. She made great speeches to the student body. I saw video of them in the hospital." Sierra blinked, her eyes shining with unshed tears. "I missed my senior year, getting classes at the Texas Medical Center. I'd almost forgotten Ellie and Marty came to see me and brought those videos to show me."

"Hey, they *were* your friends. Sally Ann didn't come?" Rhett pulled her close. She was looking vulnerable, not like the tough woman who had chased cattle all day in a four-wheeler.

"No, she was working then and dating Will. He was in college and coming home weekends. The girls were full of gossip about it." She took a steadying breath. "It's good to remember that they did reach out back then. It makes me doubt this theory of yours."

"People and circumstances change, Sierra. But I hope you're right. Now, what were you saying about Ellie? Anything else?" Rhett rubbed her arms, warming her. She'd shivered, but then Sierra did that when she was upset.

"Just that she loves Mark, but her husband doesn't let people, Ellie included, forget that he has a couple of degrees from a prestigious college. If anyone asks, he says his wife is a cook, not a business owner. He's kind of a jerk about it."

"Motives all around." Rhett noted that in his laptop. "Let's call your brother again. He has got to get access to more than just a list of the local investors. I'd like to know how much they stand to lose if this deal goes south. The bigger the investment, the more frantic people will be to get you to sell your place. It may be you're right and the *Tres Amigas* have nothing to do with what's going on."

"Dylan said something about confidentiality agreements, but I know his private investigator can work around that." Sierra walked into the kitchen and came back with her cell phone. "When I tell him I almost fell into a hole, he'll put pressure on his guy to dig some more." She hit a button for speed dial.

"It's late, Sierra." Rhett sat on the fireplace hearth near the dog. "What's he going to do tonight?"

"Make a list of things he can do first thing tomorrow." She paced in front of him, pausing to rub Tramp's ears. "Dylan! Surely I didn't wake you." She put the phone on speaker.

"I fell asleep over a pile of paperwork. What do you want?"

"We have an idea. I'll let Rhett tell you." Sierra handed Rhett the phone then collapsed into the recliner.

"Hall, this had better be good." They heard water running.

"Just listen to him, Dylan." Sierra joined the conversation.

"I'm trying to wake up. Go on. Tell me your brilliant idea."

"Did you look at that list of investors? We think the *Tres Amigas* might have hired Sierra's ranch hand Darrel to burn down her barn. Then he tried to injure her last night by arranging a way for her to fall." Damn, when Rhett thought of how Sierra could have hurt her leg again... Well, it made him crazy.

"Tried to injure her?" Dylan's voice got louder. "What the fuck, Sierra? Are you all right?"

"I'm fine. Darrel is the one who ended up in the hospital. It's a conspiracy, bro. We've figured out who we think the *Amigas* are, but we'd like confirmation. Can you get more information for us? Clearly the people most hurt by my stubborn refusal to sell are those locals who invested the most in the development. If they put their life savings in it, they must be getting desperate to see it through." Sierra looked over at Rhett. "Really desperate."

"You're right about that. So who do you think the *Tres Amigas* are?"

Rhett told him the names.

"Shit, I dated one of them, know all three. You accuse them without solid proof and you'll have everyone in town mad at you, Sierra."

"That's why we're calling you. Plus, we're going to the sheriff in the morning. We think if she hits Darrel hard, questioning him while he's still in the hospital, he'll cave and tell her who was giving him orders. I can't imagine he did any of this on his own." Rhett heard Dylan curse.

"No, that guy doesn't strike me as the brightest bulb. They probably paid him to do it. We need to look for the money trail."

"I hope you can get your PI to look at bank accounts too. Someone on your list of investors should have records of payments to Darrel Lockhart if our theory holds water." Rhett itched to do a search for all of that, but he was no forensic accountant. If Sierra was right, her brother knew the right people for the job.

"Yes. I'm calling him as soon as we hang up. He's got a guy who can find just about anything to do with money. Don't worry. Someone comes after my sister and all bets are off."

"Check out Oxcart's financials too, Dylan. Maybe they paid Darrel." Sierra spoke loudly, and Rhett was sure her brother heard her.

"Way ahead of you. I don't care what time it is, I'm calling as soon as I hang up. First, tell me what Darrel did. How were you threatened, sis? When was this and where were you, Hall? You're supposed to be watching my sister."

"I was with her." Rhett got up and handed Sierra the phone. He couldn't sit still another minute. Yeah, he'd been with her and she'd almost fallen. *Shit.* What if it had been her in the bottom of that hole? He sat on the arm of the recliner. "I'll stay with her, too. Until this is settled."

"He's been great! Listen. Darrel had dug a trench, I guess you'd call it. This was last night. I was supposed to fall into it but Darrel stumbled into it instead. It would be funny if it wasn't so damned serious." Sierra waited while Dylan cursed. "Rhett grabbed me and saved me from falling in."

"I should hope so. You say Darrel's in the hospital? Anyone watching to make sure he doesn't make a run for it?"

"How could he? Darrel just had surgery for a complex fracture today, Dylan. When I talked to him, he was drugged up. I don't think he's capable of running anywhere." Sierra looked at Rhett.

"Listen to me. And I don't care if the Yankee hears me say this. I will never forget when you were hurt all those years ago. I can't go through anything like that again." Dylan cleared his throat. "I swore then I'd take care of my family. Whatever you do, wherever you go, I'm there for you. These people try to hurt you again? They can't run far enough, fast enough. Now take me off speaker and hand Hall the phone."

* * * *

Sierra's hand was shaking when she passed the phone to Rhett. God, her brother had never sounded so serious. She knew the family had been affected by the accident, but not how much. She wanted to have it out with Sally Ann. Somehow she needed the truth from the woman. It was way too late for justice, but she could at least get some closure. And if Sally Ann had been behind Darrel setting fire to her barn and then digging that hole? Well, this was just too much to take in right now. Just too much.

Rhett hung up and looked serious. "Your brother's right. We can't wait until tomorrow to call the sheriff. We have to call her now."

"Darrel isn't capable of going anywhere tonight, Rhett. I've been where he is. After a surgery like that, you're drugged and in pain. He may even be in intensive care." Sierra didn't look forward to laying this conspiracy theory out to Myra. In fact, she wouldn't be surprised if the sheriff herself wasn't an investor in the Oxcart venture. She reached for the list and looked it over again. No, Myra Watkins wasn't on it. Well, that was a relief. But there was another group name—Wranglers. That could be anyone in town. Just thinking about tracking down another list of suspects made her head hurt. She got to her feet, staggering a little when her leg gave out. Rhett caught her and pulled her close.

"You okay?" His eyes were full of concern.

"Just tired. Now tell me why we can't wait on this." She glanced at the clock and saw that it was almost midnight. Whoever they called wasn't going to be happy to hear from them.

"Sally Ann and Marty left here with Darrel's truck. They might take it straight to the hospital. To Darrel. Now that they know we've connected them to the ranch hand, they could also try to pay him off and get him to head out of town." Rhett guided her to the couch then pulled out his own phone. "I'm calling the sheriff, or I can call a Ranger I know in Austin. He can go by the hospital and check to make sure Darrel is down for the night."

"It's late. But I see your point. Still, even if we're right and Sally Ann or all three paid Darrel to do these dirty tricks to me, how could they possibly get him moving in the shape he's in?" Sierra remembered how hard it had been for *her* the days after her surgeries.

"I know why you don't want to have this conversation with Myra this late. It's opening a big can of 'What the hell?' I need to know Darrel's not skipping out on us and it *is* probably too late to call my Ranger friend. He helped my sister when she was in trouble, but I shouldn't take advantage of him now. Why don't we go check on Darrel ourselves?" Rhett sat beside her and looked up the hospital on an app. "I can drive and you can nap in the car. It's not that far to Austin. An hour and a half and we're there."

"You make it seem so simple." Sierra let him pull her to her feet. Simple. But nothing ever was. "First? I'd like to take a look in the bunkhouse. Maybe we'll get lucky and find some evidence that will help us."

"It's worth a try." Rhett followed her out. They left the dog inside, much to his disappointment. "I'll drive. Then we can take off for the hospital from there."

Sierra didn't argue. The idea of driving ninety miles after the day she'd had exhausted her. When the automatic lights came on as soon as they parked in front of the bunkhouse, everything looked normal. The large building was dark inside and locked. "No wonder Sally Ann didn't come inside to get Darrel a few things. She might not have had a key." Sierra unlocked the door and flipped on the light. "Jeez, if I'd known he lived like a pig, I would have thought twice about keeping him on." There was a row of beds but only one with linens. That mattress on the single bed was off the box springs and the bedding had hit the floor. Clothing was strewn about and drawers hung open.

"Honey, this isn't messy. This place has been tossed. Someone had a key and has been here looking for something." Rhett walked over to the kitchenette and picked up a fork from where the silverware drawer had been dumped. He then used it to lift up pieces of clothing to look under them. "I'd say they did a pretty thorough search."

"I don't think Sally Ann and Marty had time to do this. Tramp started barking as soon as they drove in." Sierra guessed the fork technique was to keep from leaving fingerprints. Now she had something else to tell the sheriff. Unless the sheriff had ordered the search. Unlikely. As far as Myra knew, Darrel wasn't yet considered a suspect in the barn fire. The sheriff would have told Sierra if the police had searched a building on her property.

"Do you know of any good hiding places in here?" Rhett had made a quick circuit of the room. "You practically grew up on this ranch. Ever explore the bunkhouse as a kid?"

"Actually, when we had the chance, my brothers and I played out here." Sierra walked over to the closet and stomped around until she found it. "There's a loose board where we used to hide treasures. I'm sure the ranch hands knew about it." She bent over and wiggled it free. "Look, there are some papers here." She pulled them out. "Oh, boy. I think we've found something." She glanced through the envelopes. "Darrel has a bank account in Ada, Oklahoma. That's interesting. He set it up under his initials, not his first name."

"Let me see that." Rhett frowned. "He also has a post office box in town here. So he isn't getting his mail at the ranch."

"Not all of it, apparently." Sierra pulled out her phone. "I'm calling Dylan. I'm sure he's still up anyway."

"Give him the account number. The latest bank statement isn't here. If Dylan can find a large deposit right before the barn fire, we've got Darrel dead to rights. Let him know when your fence was pulled down, too." Rhett hugged her when she shivered again. "I'm sorry, Sierra."

She took a shaky breath before she hit speed dial. "So am I. I trusted that son of a bitch."

Chapter Eighteen

They were pulling into the well-lit parking lot when the truck hit a speed bump that jolted Sierra awake.

"Oh, we're here." She looked around but didn't see Darrel's battered pickup. Of course, the hospital near downtown had a couple of lots. The truck could be anywhere. Rhett found a spot not far from the emergency room entrance, the only one open at this late hour, and turned off the engine.

"Do you have a plan?" She hated asking him that. *She* should have a plan.

"We need to find out what room he's in. Then I can wander by. Just do a casual bed check. I'm calling the hospital now. Want to pretend to be a distraught girlfriend? Checking on his condition?"

Sierra took the phone. "Sure. Listen and learn." It was already ringing. When a woman answered, she was ready.

"Oh, my gosh! Oh, my gosh! I just found out my boyfriend was hurt in an accident and they took him to your hospital." She fake-sobbed. "Can you tell me if he's okay?"

"Honey, calm down now. What's your fella's name?"

"Darrel Lockhart. He fell on the job over in Muellerville. That's a long way from Austin. It must have been bad for them to carry him to such a big hospital." More fake sobs. "Is he gonna die? And us with a baby on the way. What will I do?" She managed a long, drawn-out "do."

"Now don't you worry. I guess you count as a relative. I'm looking him up right now. Yes, I see his name. It's just a broken leg, sugar. A serious break, though. They did surgery today."

"Surgery!" Sob, sob. "He said he has good insurance. Is that covered? We don't have a lot of money."

"Yes, looks like he has good insurance, but I'm not supposed to say anything about that."

"I need to see him. What room is he in? Can I come now?"

"It's too late for visitors tonight, honey. But you come in the morning. He seems to have made it through that surgery just fine and I'm sure he'll be glad to see you. They moved him to a room after he left recovery. Should be in room nine fifteen. You got that?"

"Nine fifteen? Is that on the ninth floor?"

"Sure is. He'll be in a lot of pain, of course. I'm sure they'll be taking care of that with sedatives so he should sleep through the night. Don't you worry about a thing."

"That's great. I sure do appreciate you telling me this. You are so kind. Have a good night now." Sierra hung up and looked at Rhett. With the phone on speaker, he'd heard the whole thing. "How did I do?"

"You were perfect. You convinced me." He touched her chin and looked her over. "I almost expected tears."

"I wouldn't waste waterworks on a phone call." She grinned at him, pumped that she'd managed to pull that off. "What's next?"

"Now I need to take a trip up to nine and make sure Darrel is sleeping like she promised."

"I'd feel better if we saw his truck here." Sierra realized Rhett hadn't moved yet. "Wait a minute. You said 'I,' not 'we.' I'm going with you. Don't even think you're leaving me here."

"One person could sneak in unnoticed." He stuck his phone in his pocket.

"Save your breath. I want to see for myself that Darrel is there. I've been in this hospital before. Know it too well."

"All right. Your knowing the hospital just won me over. Careful, it's starting to rain." He jumped out of the car and ran around to open her door. "I've learned from a few previous adventures that walking in like you belong is the best way to get into places where you don't."

"Oh, really? I want to hear about those previous adventures sometime." She clung to his arm as they walked toward the emergency entrance. The arrival of an ambulance helped them slip inside unnoticed. Busy doctors and nurses were taking care of the patient who had been in a car wreck. Sierra looked away from the sight of blood as she let Rhett lead her toward stairs instead of a bank of elevators.

"Sorry about the stairs. Are they going to be a problem?" He shut them inside the stairwell.

"Only if we have to do nine flights." Sierra hated to admit that. Too bad it was the truth. She didn't do stairs easily in the best of circumstances, and today had already been a hard day.

"No, we'll come out on the next floor and take the elevator. Like I said, we'll act like we have a legitimate purpose for being in the hospital at this time of night." He started up then stopped. "Want me to carry you?"

"Don't be insane. I can make one flight of stairs. Call it physical therapy. Probably overdue." Sierra took her time. "Go ahead, please. Don't watch. I'm slow and awkward. You can check the exit door at the top and make sure the coast is clear."

"You're amazing, you know that?" He stopped and came back down to kiss her. "Take your time. Hopefully Darrel is in a morphine haze and we made this trip for nothing."

"Hopefully." Sierra grinned at him. "Keep kissing me like that and I'll think you like me."

"Oh, I do, Sierra MacKenzie. I'm liking you a lot." He brushed her cheek with a fingertip then bounded up the stairs.

She watched him go, so athletic, so…everything. Why would a man like that want *her*? She was clumsy as she lurched up the stairs. Her leg hurt like hell, and she had to sit on the top step of the landing and breathe through the pain. She was surer than ever that her accident was on Sally Ann. She wanted to pound the woman. No one else had had the means and motive to do this to her. And now it looked like Sally Ann might have had a hand in this latest attack on her property and her life. Oh, but that bitch was going down.

Sierra looked up. Ten more steps to go. She could practically feel Rhett's impatience as he waited at the top. But he didn't say a word. She used the handrail to drag herself to her feet. She wasn't about to disappoint him by letting a tear fall, but she felt perilously close to it. She was not a victim, damn it. She was a survivor. And she was going to make Sally Ann or whoever had started this pay and pay big.

They came out on two and were waiting for the elevator when a nurse stopped them.

"Excuse me, but it's past visiting hours. May I ask your reason for being here?" She looked them over.

"Baby, I'm not sure I can make it." Sierra collapsed against Rhett. On cue, he swung her into his arms. "Isn't X-ray on four?" She put an arm around Rhett's neck. "I fell at the ranch and my doctor ordered me to come in. I've had multiple surgeries on this leg." She gestured at it.

"Maybe you remember me. Terrible fall from my horse at the arena here a dozen years ago."

"No, honey, I just got hired here last year. Are you in terrible pain?" The nurse reached past them to punch the up button again, even though it was already lit.

"God, yes. I've got a rod and pins in it and any fall is worrisome." Sierra buried her head in Rhett's shoulder when the elevator doors opened. "At last. I don't know what we were thinking, getting off on two."

"Good luck. Hope everything comes out all right." The nurse looked concerned as the door shut in her face.

"Punch four. In case she watches to make sure we get there."

Rhett did then hit nine. "You really are quite the actress." He kept his arms around her.

"You can put me down now." She smiled up at him.

"Now why would I do that? I kind of like where you are now." He put on a frown when the doors opened on four but they didn't see anyone. "Okay, nine coming up. I'll put you down, but only because we don't want to draw attention. If we get caught again, I expect you to save us."

"Nine isn't as easy, just patient rooms, but I'll do my best." Sierra slid down his body. When the doors opened again, she was relieved to see the floor deserted.

Nine fifteen. A right turn and then a left. They could see a nurses' station down the hall. When they got near Darrel's room, two nurses stood in front of his door, arguing in quiet voices.

"I told you, I didn't take him anywhere. He's not scheduled for tests at this time of night." The tall nurse held a chart.

"Darrel Lockhart had his medication two hours ago. He should be sleeping soundly. So where the hell is he?" Nurse two, a short redhead, looked over her shoulder. "May I help you?"

"Are we lost? My doctor sent us for X-rays." Sierra clutched Rhett's arm. "I'm in so much pain I can't remember what he said."

"Sorry, honey. It's on four. Down and to the left. Someone in the emergency room should have escorted you." The nurse turned back to the one with the chart. "We've stalled long enough. We either find him or call the supervising nurse and security."

Rhett picked up Sierra again and strode back to the elevators. "Don't say a word."

"Don't worry, I'm speechless." She waited until they were in the elevator and on the way down before she pushed and he let her go.

"What now, Rhett?" Sierra was clearly pissed. "Where could he be? How did he leave?"

"I'd say he had help. No way could he be in any shape right now to leave on his own." Rhett stared at the numbers flashing on the board in front of him. Before they reached the lobby, he held her shoulders. "We'll find him. I swear it."

"You can't promise that." She kissed his cheek. "But thanks for trying. Maybe it's time to call in the authorities."

"At two in the morning?" Rhett took her hand and pulled her into the hall. "Let's look for his truck first. Drive around the hospital. He might have passed out somewhere close by. We still only have conjecture that he's done anything wrong. Maybe he dug that hole. But you didn't get hurt; he did. Maybe he started the fire, but so far the sheriff hasn't found proof of it."

"Stop sounding so logical." Sierra wobbled. "I want to *do* something. Doesn't the fact that Darrel ran prove he's guilty?"

"It is the act of a desperate man." Rhett stopped talking when a doctor walked quickly past them toward the emergency entrance. "Guess they had another ambulance come in."

"It *was* raining. This late, drunks are hitting the road after the bars close. It's a recipe for disaster." Sierra grabbed Rhett's arm and held him back as several hospital workers rushed past them. "This must be a bad one." They heard the siren shut off abruptly as it arrived at the emergency room doors. Soon a gurney was shoved inside.

The EMT was talking rapid-fire as he handed the patient off to a doctor. "Looked like a high-speed chase, the cops said. This guy was in the first truck. It went through a guardrail and hit a tree. No seat belt." He shook his head. "Look at his wrist, Doc. He's a patient here. See the hospital bracelet and gown? I called it in. Patient is post-op named Darrel Lockhart. Records confirm he's carrying a shitload of morphine in his system. Don't know how he managed to get out of the hospital, much less drive a truck on one leg and stoned out of his mind. You save this one and you're going to get a medal."

Sierra gasped, and Rhett helped her get through the emergency room. They'd almost made it when another ambulance arrived.

A female EMT pushed inside with a doctor listening intently to statistics. This time it was a crying woman on the stretcher. "Vic in second truck spun out when the first one went airborne. Her truck lost control then flipped. This one was luckier. Had on a seat belt. Trauma to abdomen, possible internal bleeding. Possible concussion." The woman on the gurney held on to her stomach and moaned loudly. Blood ran down a cut on her forehead and partially obscured her face.

"Marty!" Sierra ran toward her. "What the hell happened?"

"Ma'am? Do you know this person?" A policeman stopped her before she could get close enough to touch the gurney that was pushed past them into a cubicle.

"Yes, it's Marty Lewis. She's from Muellerville." Sierra put her hand to her mouth. "Is she okay? Was anyone else in the truck with her?"

"Paramedic said she'll live, even though she was clearly driving recklessly. Far as we know, she was by herself." The cop held Marty's driver's license. "You happen to know her next of kin?"

"That would be her husband. I have his phone number." Sierra pulled out her phone. "He's my mechanic." She fumbled with it.

* * * *

Rhett eased over to where the medical team was working on Darrel while Sierra kept talking to the cop. What he heard before he hurried back to Sierra's side wasn't reassuring. She'd finally found Marty's home number and passed it on.

"Everything okay?" Rhett grabbed her arm when she swayed.

The cop noticed him. "A little late to be here. May I ask your business?"

"A friend just had surgery. We were waiting to see if he came out all right. Finally got word a few minutes ago." Rhett tugged Sierra toward the exit. "We were just leaving. Hell of a thing, seeing a friend come in like that."

"Strange situation." The cop turned toward the emergency bays where they were working on the patients. "This was a two-car pileup. What about the other guy just brought in? Do you know him?" He focused on them again. "I'll have to check with the other patrolman for a name. He ran the license plate."

"Uh. I can't imagine…" Sierra managed to sway again, as if about to faint. Clearly she wasn't going to admit a connection to Darrel. "I don't feel well, honey. Can we go home now?"

"Sure. Sorry we can't help you, Officer. The sight of blood makes her queasy." Rhett nodded and hustled Sierra out of there, relieved when the cop didn't try to stop them. Outside, it was still raining as they hurried to the car and climbed inside. He started the engine. "You're shivering. I'll turn on the seat warmers."

"Thanks. It's just..." Sierra wiped rainwater off her face. "I wanted answers but I didn't want anyone to get hurt. Poor Darrel. Why did he think he had to run?"

"If he burned down your barn, he knew he was facing jail, Sierra. We need to call the sheriff right now." He stared at Sierra in the dim interior. "You realize Darrel may die?"

"What? I knew it sounded serious, but where did you get that?" Sierra's face was white.

"While you were giving the cop Marty's husband's number, I managed to hear a little of what the doctors working on Darrel were saying. He was thrown through the truck windshield when it hit that tree. He's critical and hanging on by a thread." He glanced at the two highway patrol cars parked near the ambulances. "Cops said it looked to them like Marty was pursuing Darrel in her truck. Can you imagine why?"

"Wait. It wasn't the other way around?" Sierra frowned. "Marty was behind Darrel?"

"That's what the other cop said." Rhett picked up her hand. "Could Marty have been trying to stop Darrel from taking off?"

"That doesn't make sense. She helped Sally Ann get his truck. So where's Sally Ann now? I don't think she had time to take Sally Ann home then come back to the hospital." Sierra tugged on Rhett's hand.

Rhett turned on the windshield wipers. "I didn't want to get too inquisitive, raise questions with the highway patrol. But one of them did say there were still people there, measuring skid marks and figuring out exactly what had happened. If Marty had a passenger, they would have found her." He put his hands on the wheel. "We can't stall any longer. We have to call the sheriff. The highway patrol will talk to Myra. Once she's involved, hopefully we can get some of the answers we want."

"Maybe. Or we can get some answers we don't want." Sierra looked down at her phone. "You realize it's almost three in the morning? Myra won't be happy to hear from me. She'll want to know why we're here in the first place."

"Maybe she won't mind, Sierra. We were being careful, making sure Darrel hadn't taken off. Then look what we found." Rhett pulled out his own phone. "Let me call. Darrel making a run for it looks suspicious. This may mean things are coming together. Maybe not in a good way, but coming together. Marty is now trapped in that hospital too. She's going to have to answer some important questions."

"Right. How did Darrel get out of the hospital? Was Marty the one helping him? Why was she chasing him? And where the hell is Sally Ann?" Sierra shook her head.

"I can tell you are exhausted, and you're rubbing your leg again. Those stairs were too much for you." Rhett felt like hell. They should have called the sheriff from home. Had her send someone to the hospital. Damn it, he'd dragged Sierra into this and she looked like she was either going to cry or fall over.

"Stop it!" Sierra glared at him. "I don't need taking care of, Rhett. I can tell that's what you're thinking. Call the sheriff. Yes, that'll mean we'll be here forever, waiting for her and answering her questions. But I can handle it." She reached across the console and grabbed his hand. "Do it now. Darrel ran. What if Marty gets the bright idea to bolt as soon as she has the chance?"

"Determined to be tough, aren't you?" He leaned over and kissed her, savoring her taste, her spirit. "Okay. I'm calling."

"I *am* tough. And it was a good guess that the sight of blood makes me queasy. That's another reason I need to get out of the cattle business." She sighed and ran her other hand over his cheek. "I wonder…"

"What?" Rhett had learned to listen to Sierra. If she had an idea, he wanted to hear it.

"If Darrel dies, I wonder if Marty will be considered responsible?" Her grip on Rhett's hand tightened. "A sharp lawyer might be able to get her to spill all her secrets if it meant saving her butt from a murder charge."

Chapter Nineteen

"What were you thinking?" Sheriff Myra Watkins paced in front of them. "You're damned lucky Darrel Lockhart wasn't here when you got to the hospital. You should have told me your so-called theory and let me handle it."

"We were planning to, Sheriff." Rhett could see that Sierra was beyond exhausted. He wanted to get her home and into her own bed. She'd let him call the sheriff, then had taken the phone, and the heat, when the connection had been made.

"I couldn't believe this man who'd been a loyal employee of mine for three years would have done something so horrible to me. I could swear he liked me." Sierra had her bad leg propped on a chair.

"Sierra, loyalty can be bought. Darrel might like you but need money more." Rhett hated to say that, but he'd studied crime for too long not to believe that.

"He's right, Sierra. Tell me more about this theory of yours." Myra sat down and waited, but she wasn't happy.

"My brother is in Dallas, working right now to find proof that Oxcart is behind the fire and the accident on my ranch. He's looking for a money trail. When we came to the conclusion that Darrel had to be involved, Dylan got concerned that my ranch hand might make a run for it. We decided to see if Darrel's condition was such that he *could* take off. That's all. Clearly he shouldn't have been able to leave the hospital so recently after surgery. Not without help."

"And you think Marty Lewis provided that help? I find that unlikely. As far as I know, they have only a passing acquaintance, if that." Myra had her notebook out and wrote something. She'd managed to commandeer a conference room in the hospital. The highway patrol was glad for her help since they'd had a busy night. There had been four more serious accidents in the area, two with fatalities.

"I think Marty and Sally Ann Jackson both helped Darrel." Sierra put her foot on the floor with a wince, then leaned forward. "It took both of them to come get Darrel's truck. Marty was there when Darrel had his wreck, but where is Sally Ann? Where was she when Darrel flew the coop? I'd like to ask Marty a few questions. Will you let me?"

"No." Myra got up. "She's having tests and not going anywhere. Her truck was totaled and I talked to her husband. He's already here and not a bit happy that she was out driving crazy in the rain somewhere she wasn't supposed to be. Buddy thought she and Sally Ann were having a girls' night in San Antonio. Next thing he knows, he's getting a call from the highway patrol that she's been in a wreck outside of Austin heading north. That's not the direction toward San Antonio, now is it? Buddy is pissed. Though, to give him credit, he's also worried sick."

"See? Marty was supposed to be with Sally Ann. Have you tracked *her* down yet?" Sierra obviously really wanted to have it out with the woman again.

"I'm looking for her. You leave her to me, Sierra. So far she's not answering her phone and Will tells the same story as Buddy. Sally Ann was supposed to be in San Antonio with Marty. Girls' night. Will didn't seem worried. He said she always shows up eventually." Myra flipped through her notebook. "How do you like that attitude from a loving husband?"

"It's not one I would have." Rhett glanced at Sierra. "You *are* going to question Marty, though, aren't you? She helped Sally Ann get Darrel's truck. We were there when they drove away in it. We find it strange that the women were doing a favor for a man we didn't know they considered a friend. If Darrel did set the barn fire, maybe Sally Ann and Marty know something about it and the latest problem on the ranch."

"That hole Darrel fell into. You really think it was intended for you, Sierra?" Myra focused on her. "No other reason there would be such a hazard on your property?"

"I've been asking myself that. Darrel had to bury some dead cattle recently. But I know where he put those bodies. He tried to blame the utility company, didn't he, Rhett?"

"Yes, he did, but that didn't make sense. There were no signs of recent utility work along the highway and the dig was fresh and on the wrong side of the fence line." Rhett sat beside Sierra. "Darrel had a shovel in the back of his truck, too, Myra. It had fresh dirt on it. Put that together with him calling us to go out there, making sure Sierra walked toward the trench, and I'd say he wanted her to fall into the thing."

"That's a serious allegation." Myra made a note. "You saw the shovel? The cattle had to be buried a few days ago. Not close to the fence line?"

"No, he put them in the back pasture, well away from where the cattle grazed. That's where I told him to bury them. I checked to make sure he did it right."

Myra put down her notebook. "Then this sounds like a vicious trick that could have put you in the hospital in much more serious condition than a mere broken leg." She nodded toward where Sierra sat with her foot propped again. "With your history, it's almost attempted murder."

"Thanks for believing us, Myra." Rhett put his arm around Sierra as her face went white. "That's exactly what I think. When Darrel wakes up, I hope you throw the book at him."

"He'll certainly have a lot to answer for. I'm getting a story from the highway patrol that Marty needs to explain as well. Appears she was chasing Darrel when the accidents happened. If she helped him escape the hospital, as you two think, then why would she be chasing him down in her truck? Doesn't make sense."

"Maybe she had a change of heart. If this was all Sally Ann's idea, I can see how Marty would want to back out of it. Darrel wasn't fit to drive. That was clear from the little we heard in the emergency room when they brought him in." Rhett saw this news didn't sit well with the sheriff.

"My, you two were busy bees. Hanging around the emergency room?" Myra waved her ballpoint pen in Rhett's face. "Let me make myself clear. No more amateur sleuthing from either one of you. Let the police do their jobs."

"We didn't mean to step on your toes, Myra, but people are out to get me." Sierra stopped short of saying she'd never do it again.

"I get that this is very important to you, Sierra. And traumatic." Myra sighed. "Honey, you walk with the reminder of what you just told me you think Sally Ann did to you all those years ago. How in the hell could you forget any of that? I can assure you, there is no statute of limitations on attempted murder in Texas or any state in the Union. If we can get proof she tampered with your tack, I will see that she's punished. But let me find the proof. You can't be involved. Do you understand?"

"Yes." Sierra's eyes were bright with unshed tears.

Rhett kept his arm around Sierra. "Thanks, Sheriff. I'm afraid the only way you can get anything on that earlier crime is to get Sally Ann to confess or to get one of her girlfriends to testify that she admitted it to them."

"For now, let's concentrate on what we've got going in the here and now. We've got arson, a suspicious accident on your place, Sierra, and that wreck." Myra stuck her notebook in her back pocket. "I'm going to interview Marty now. Darrel is off limits. He's in intensive care in a coma. Not sure he's going to make it. You want to do something? Pray he pulls through. He'll probably be eager to say if he was paid to burn down the barn and by whom so he can cut a deal for a lighter sentence." She turned toward the door.

"Uh, Sheriff." Rhett knew they had to tell her. "We did look in the bunkhouse, where Darrel stays, before we came here."

"Damn it! More amateur detective work." Myra stomped her foot. "What the hell did you do there?"

"The place had been tossed. Someone else beat us to it." Sierra laid her hand on Rhett's arm. "We did find some bank statements hidden under a floorboard. Don't you think that's suspicious?"

"What did you do with them?" Myra obviously didn't trust them to figure out the right procedure.

"They're safe at home. I'll bring them to your office, first chance I get." Rhett didn't add that Dylan was running down that account for them.

"You'd better." Myra looked them up and down. "Go home. Get some sleep. You both look like you were put through a hay baler backwards."

"Thanks, Myra." Sierra followed her to the hallway. Rhett was right behind her. "I appreciate you taking me seriously."

"How could I not? Darrel Lockhart ran out of the hospital in his gown and almost killed himself. That says guilty of something to me. We're looking for his cell phone. Maybe we can figure out if he got a call or something that set him off. So far, no luck. But they tell me they're combing the crash site." Myra looked past her to Rhett. "Hall, get this woman home. She looks like she's about to fall down. Are *you* okay to drive?"

"Of course. We napped in the car while we were waiting for you." Rhett held Sierra's hand. "Please keep us informed."

"Sierra, if that brother of yours comes up with pertinent information on Oxcart, you tell him to send it to me. Proof that Darrel was paid to torch your barn is an important part of this cluster. You hear me?" Myra stuck her pen in her breast pocket. "I swear she's asleep on her feet."

"I'm awake. Just resting my eyes. Dylan will send copies of anything he gets to you." Sierra sighed. "Don't worry."

"Ha! Don't worry? After what you two tried to pull, I can't help but worry." Myra stalked off, her gun belt slapping against her hip.

"Do I need to carry you?" Rhett didn't like how Sierra was swaying.

"No, I just wanted to get rid of her. I want to see if Rachel knows anything about where Sally Ann is." Sierra tugged him toward the elevators. "You didn't really think I was going to give up, did you?"

"I guess not." Rhett punched the down button. "You're getting some rest. The sheriff was right. You look exhausted."

"So do you. I'm not saying we track down Sally Ann ourselves, just see if Rachel's had word. Let the sheriff know what we find out, then hit the hay." Sierra bumped against him.

"Of course. But we're eating first." Rhett pulled her to his side as the elevator stopped and began to fill.

* * * *

They ate at an IHOP. Sierra devoured everything on her plate and drank three cups of coffee. It was almost enough to make her feel alive again. Almost. But the past day's marathon had taken its toll, and she was really glad to finally see her gate and house.

"Rachel's car is here. That's good. I need a tactful way to ask her about Sally Ann and her whereabouts." Sierra almost fell into Rhett's arms when he opened the car door.

"You sure you want to do that? She's been a faithful employee. You might alienate her if you start interrogating her about her daughter." Rhett kept a hand under her elbow as they walked to the back door.

"I hear voices. Maybe Sally Ann is here!" Sierra pulled open the screen door. "Hello! We're home. Spent the night in Austin. I hope you weren't worried about us, Rachel." She stopped when she saw who was rolling out dough on the counter.

"Hope you don't mind, Sierra, but I'm keeping Billy today. He didn't have school. It was a teacher in-service day."

"No, of course not. Hi, Billy." Sierra smiled at the boy. He didn't smile back, just kept working on the dough. "What are you making?"

"Cookies." That was all he said before he picked up a round cookie cutter.

"Can't wait for that." Rhett steered Sierra through the kitchen. "We're going to take a nap. Had lunch on the road. Is Sally Ann coming to pick up Billy later?" He threw out the question casually.

"No, I'll take him home with me when I get off. He's not any trouble." Rachel wiped her hands on her apron. "You sure you don't want anything to eat?"

"No, thanks." Sierra really wanted to stop and ask questions, but knew Rhett was right to push her along down the hall. "See you later."

Once they were in the bedroom with the door closed, she sat on the bed. "Well, we didn't get anything there."

"Of course not. With Billy listening? Rachel looked worried. She probably got a call from Will to come get the boy. For all we know Sally Ann still hasn't shown up." Rhett pulled off his boots.

She fell against him. "I'm so exhausted I'm afraid I might fall down in the shower. Can I get you to help me out in there?"

His eyes gleamed as he ripped open his new snap shirt. "I think I can manage that." He gently peeled down her jeans, careful of her leg. "Maybe you'd rather soak in a tub for a while."

"If I lie down in a tub, I'll fall asleep. I'd rather take a quick shower, with some handy help, then get comfy in my bed." Sierra looked over at the bed. "I have this wonderful housekeeper who put on fresh sheets today. I can't wait to cuddle naked with a sexy man next to me."

"Hmm. That's quite an agenda. Handy help." He unclipped her bra and showed her how handy he could be. "Then that sexy, comfy cuddle." He threw off his own clothes then stood to pick her up. "Ah, did I tell you I love the way you feel next to me when I hold you?"

"No, you didn't." Sierra looked into his eyes. He threw the love word around fairly easily. He loved chicken-fried steak. At lunch he'd loved the hash browns and pancakes. Hell, he even loved how that big Tahoe hugged the curves on the road near the ranch. But the way he was staring at her as he headed into the bathroom... Well, there was something there, something real. Then he sat her tenderly on the closed toilet and adjusted the temperature in the shower. When it was perfect, he picked her up again and protected her from getting water in her face.

She knew then that this man was hers. He'd won a place in her heart. He soaped his hands and ran them over her. His smile, his playful ways, were so endearing she had to blink back tears and force herself to match his light tone.

"I may never bathe myself again, mister, with this kind of handy help." She grabbed the soap and gave him the same treatment. She couldn't let herself worry about the future. He was temporary. Neither of them had thoughts of forever. But wouldn't it be... *No, live in the moment.* Who knew better than she that the future couldn't be controlled? Everything could change in a heartbeat. Could go to hell. He kissed her and touched her in that way he had. Or could go to heaven. She let her mind drift to focus on the feelings. Yes, that was better. Enjoy what she had. That was the only way to live. Take what was in hand and...

Tomorrow would take care of itself.

* * * *

The ringing phone woke her. A glance told her they'd slept the day away. Rachel would be gone, so there was no chance to find out if Sally Ann had arrived back home. Sierra answered when she saw who was calling.

"Sheriff, what's the word?"

"I finally talked to Marty and got her story. I'm not sure I believe what she's saying, but I'll let you decide. She wants to talk to you."

"Really?" Sierra felt Rhett move behind her. "When can I come?"

"They're keeping her overnight. Seems like it's a mild concussion and some cracked ribs. No internal bleeding. She was lucky there. They'll be releasing her tomorrow. If I were you, I'd get there tonight. That husband of hers didn't want her to say a word to anybody, but he's gone home so the coast is clear."

"Thanks, Myra. Is she facing charges?" Sierra didn't know how she felt about that. Marty had been a friend for years, but if she'd had a hand in the attacks on her or her barn...

"The wreck appears to be an accident. No witnesses can verify that she was speeding, and the roads were slick. Lockhart is still unconscious so I have no idea what his story will be. For now, all I've got is your say-so that this is a conspiracy against you. I need proof, Sierra. I couldn't get a thing out of Marty incriminating Sally Ann. I don't like it, but maybe you can do better."

"I'll try." Sierra didn't like the sound of this. Seemed like the three *amigas* were sticking together. If Dylan could find a payment from one of them to Darrel, though, the women were screwed.

"Did your brother find anything? Is there a paper trail that can help with my investigation?"

"Just a list of investors. I'm not sure it will help but I'll send it to your office. I'll let you know if I find out anything useful from Marty."

"You do that." The sheriff ended the call.

Rhett pulled Sierra against him. "Any good news?"

"Marty wants to talk to me. Don't know if that's good or not." Sierra started looking through her phone. "I got a text from Dylan. He's got his man working on those financial records and he'll be back here tomorrow morning. He says he has news he wants to share in person." She pulled away from Rhett and climbed out of bed. "We need to get going. I assume you want to be with me when I talk to Marty."

"Of course." He was out of bed and by her side fast. "Bring that list of investors. Read it to me while I drive. See if it helps us figure things out. Funny that there's another anonymous group—the Wranglers. Maybe we can use process of elimination to decide who the Wranglers are."

"True. You aren't helping me calm down, Rhett. I'm finally realizing that I've been lucky I only lost a barn and a ranch hand so far. When it comes to people and their money, obviously sometimes they're willing to do crazy, desperate things." Sierra hurried into the bathroom, eager to get to Austin. She was glad to have Rhett's help. Glad to have someone by her side when she felt surrounded by hate.

"I'm sorry you have to confront Marty. You have any idea what she could want?" Rhett stood in the bathroom doorway.

"I hope she's going to explain why she was chasing Darrel. Or where Sally Ann is now. Since she just had a near miss, rolling her truck, maybe she's ready to clear her conscience. Almost losing your life can help get your priorities straight." Sierra knew where her own priorities were right now. Rhett came up behind her as she was spitting out toothpaste. His hands were warm on her skin as he slid them around her waist then up to touch her breasts. It was too tempting, and she turned in his arms.

"I don't have time for this." She pressed against him and kissed his whiskery chin.

"Neither do I. But I couldn't resist at least a little taste before we leave." He kissed her with a depth that made her bare toes curl. "Mmm. Later I'm going to want more of that." He aimed her toward the bedroom. "I want answers just as badly as you do. The sooner we can get this settled, the sooner we can think about the future."

The future. Her heart was still pounding from that kiss. Sierra hadn't dared think too far ahead. Apparently Rhett liked to plan. What did he have in mind? She juggled all the possibilities while she found clean underwear and a fresh outfit. A future with a man like Rhett Hall? She couldn't picture it. Or was afraid to try. She'd had dreams once, and they'd shattered on a hard dirt floor in an arena. That had taught her a lesson she'd never forgotten. Work hard and never let down your guard. Or count too much on tomorrow.

She pulled on boots and reminded herself that trusting Rhett was becoming a habit that could be dangerous. He had no ties here. He could be amusing himself by trying to help her solve her personal mysteries. When they were done? Well, then he might well be done with her.

She looked up and saw him in the bathroom door, staring at her. "I'll
check the kitchen. I bet Rachel left us something for dinner. It'll beat
hospital cafeteria food." She headed for the hall.

"Whoa!" He snagged her by the waist. "You're practically running.
What's got you spooked?"

"Nothing. Everything. You know how I feel about hospitals." She gently
took his hands off her. "I want to get to the truth. Will I? Finally? Allow
me to freak out. Okay?"

"Okay." He backed up and grabbed his jeans. "Just remember, I'll be
with you every step of the way."

"And you remember,"—she forced herself to face him—"this is my fight,
not yours. Feel free to bail anytime you get sick of me and my problems."

He looked a little stormy as she left him with that and walked down the
hall. Sure enough, Rachel had provided a meal that would be easy to heat
and eat. Her note on the table explained that she'd taken Billy home and
would be back tomorrow. No mention of Sally Ann. Of course not.

Sierra stuck the food in the microwave and sat at the table. What did
Rachel know now and what had she known all those years ago? That question
was going to drive her crazy if she didn't ask it soon and get answers.

Rhett walked in with her laptop. "We need to check your video
surveillance around the bunkhouse. Clearly the sheriff's office didn't search
the building, so maybe we can see who did." He pushed it in front of her.

Sierra accessed the video feed and started scanning back until she got to
the day of the barn fire. "Okay, I see Darrel going in and out. No visitors.
Here's the morning after. He let a few firemen inside." She paused the
picture. "I guess he let them use the restroom." She started the feed again.
"That's funny, the insurance adjuster and Fred Meadows are walking
around there. The fire didn't reach the bunkhouse."

"Probably making sure you didn't try to pad your claim. People do that.
Say there was smoke damage on outbuildings that didn't have any." Rhett
leaned over. "Look, they're taking pictures."

"I guess you're right." She kept going. "Fred again. He was being a dick
about my claim. He came a couple of times, trying to make sure I didn't
start the fire myself. Even asked Rachel for keys to the outbuildings."

"He's arranged for you to be paid now, though, hasn't he?" Rhett realized
they'd gotten to the day he and Sierra had gone inside. The view wasn't
good because he'd parked the Tahoe in front of the door. "Damn. You can't
see the door if there's a car parked in the way."

"That's the way the ranch hands wanted it. Privacy concerns." She backtracked. "See? Someone could have gone in there when Darrel's truck was still parked and we have no view of it."

"Then someone with a key or good lock-picking skills may have done the search before Sally Ann got the truck." Rhett punched a button. "Once it's gone? Clear view of the door. Shoot!"

"Okay, now we know. That we've got nothing." Sierra hated the feeling of insecurity that had blossomed in her stomach. Someone had been in the bunkhouse, someone who was in on the conspiracy to run her off her ranch. Would she ever feel safe again?

Chapter Twenty

"I've read this list of investors until I'm carsick and I still can't figure out who the Wranglers could be." Sierra pushed the papers into the glove compartment then slammed it shut. "We need to know who they are and how much they have at stake in the success of the Oxcart venture."

"You're right. I'm sure Dylan will have that for us tomorrow. At least the names behind those two consortiums." Rhett kept his eyes on the road. More rain. Yes, this was a state highway into Austin, but it wasn't *the* state highway. There was a better way to get to the city, wider and with less construction. He had to pay close attention to his driving as night fell.

"Calling anyone from little Muellerville part of a consortium seems a stretch." Sierra patted his shoulder. "Sorry it's turning out to be such a miserable evening. I could have driven, you know. The one blessing in my fall from my horse is that the bad leg is my left one. I'm a decent driver."

"I know. Call me a control freak, but I like to be in the driver's seat." He glanced at her to see how she took that confession.

"I'll consider that a red flag, Hall." She smiled at him. "However, so far that's the only one I'm aware of."

"Wow. I'm stunned. But then you haven't known me that long." He reached for her hand.

"We've been through a lot in a short time. I don't know how I would have made it without you." She looked at the side mirror when bright lights flashed inside the car. "Someone is on our tail. Way too close. Are we being followed?"

"I was hoping it was my imagination." Rhett had been aware for a while that they were on a lonely stretch of road. No gas stations, not even a ranch house with lights on that they could turn toward if trouble found them. He slowed down below the generous speed limit to let the vehicle pass. Didn't happen. It was a truck and it matched their speed.

What the hell? If he punched his brakes, the other vehicle would surely hit them. The road was lined with water-filled ditches and empty fields that seemed to stretch for miles in either direction. It was absolutely dark. Who knew there were still places like this in America, with no signs of life?

"Rhett, they're passing us." Sierra let go of his hand. "Put both hands on the wheel. I don't like how close they are."

"Shit, I think they're trying to run us off the road. Hold on!" Rhett gunned it, leaving what he now saw was a black or dark blue pickup behind. He hit eighty and pulled away. The truck swerved back behind them, then accelerated and tried to pass again. Rhett put his foot down and they got up to ninety miles per hour. The big car could handle it, but so could that truck.

Without warning, it slammed into their rear bumper, making the Tahoe rock and Rhett temporarily lose control. He wrestled with the steering wheel and barely managed to keep them out of a ditch on their right side. Thank God he'd rented a heavy-duty SUV.

"Hang on! You okay, Sierra?" Rhett didn't dare glance toward her to see how she was taking this. He concentrated on holding the car on the road.

"Don't worry about me. Just outrun that moron."

"Yeah." Thank God for good tires and a hefty vehicle. There was no doubt in his mind that someone wanted them to crash, or at least to scare them shitless. This time when the truck started to nose up beside them, trying to push them into the ditch, Rhett jerked the steering wheel, slamming the rear of the Tahoe into the truck.

Bang! The other vehicle swerved with a screech of tires, then fell back behind them. Just in time, too. Lights flashed as another car came straight at them from the other direction. Rhett laid on his horn. Maybe they'd get lucky and the driver passing them would call 9-1-1 to report reckless drivers on the road. The other car honked too before it drove out of sight.

"My God, Rhett. That was close. Good driving." Sierra sounded excited.

"I took a professional driving course once. But we were lucky that time. Better to outrun them." Rhett hit the button on his steering wheel for phone service. *Of course.* He didn't have any. "Hang on, Sierra. This asshole isn't giving up." Rhett sped up again. The truck driver kept coming. The Tahoe jerked as they were rammed again. "Shit!"

"Look! I see lights ahead. They're going to have to give up, Rhett, if you can pull in there."

"I will. I hope those aren't just lights, but people too. My gun is in the console. Get it out in case they shoot at us." He hated to say that and scare her even more, but someone as reckless as this guy could be capable of anything.

"Got it!"

"Brace yourself, they're coming up again. I'm going to give them one more love tap. I'm sure as hell not waiting for them to make their move this time." Rhett swung the wheel hard and they hit, jarring the Tahoe and sending the truck skidding toward a ditch on the other side of the road. "There, that should give us time to pull into whatever is ahead. Then I'm calling for help if I have to find a pay phone."

Sierra blew out a breath that was loud enough for him to hear, and he risked a glance at her as he pushed the car up to ninety-five. Her face was pale, and she was hanging on with white knuckles to the grab bar above the passenger window. The gun was in her lap, and she just stared at him, eyes wide.

"That was amazing. It must have been some driving course."

"We're not out of this yet." A glance in the rearview mirror showed the truck had managed to stay out of the ditch and was speeding toward them again. Too late. Rhett said a silent prayer of thanks as a well-lit strip center came into view. He moved his foot to the brake, gradually slowing until he could wheel past a gas station to a lot in front of Katie's Kolaches, whatever that was. There was a pawnshop on the other side of it. The pawnshop was closed, but the kolache shop apparently served food and had attracted a small crowd.

Rhett pulled in between a battered truck and a Camry, then took his gun from Sierra. He opened the driver's door, stood behind it and waited, watching the road. The dark truck slowed but went past. It had a long scrape on the passenger side. The front quarter panel was caved in where it had hit them. The front bumpers weren't chrome, but a dark color. The windows had a dark tint and he couldn't tell how many people were inside the late-model four-door truck. No license plate. When whoever was driving realized Rhett was out of the Tahoe and watching for them with a gun aimed at the road, he or she accelerated and roared on down the highway.

"Should we chase them? Did you see a license number?" Sierra had hopped out of the car and stood by his side. "I couldn't see a thing. I did notice it was another damned Chevy truck. I told you there are dozens of them in Muellerville alone."

"I didn't get anything that would help identify it except it was black or dark blue, a recent model and had damage from what just happened." Rhett pulled her close. "Come here, out of the rain." He guided her to the overhang in front of the pawnshop. "Were you scared to death?"

"You won't believe me, but I was kind of excited. It was like barrel racing. An adrenaline rush." She looked up at him, her eyes shining. "Do you like roller coasters?"

"What? Yeah, I do." He knew exactly what she meant. Of course, he'd been scared, for her more than anything. But during the chase he'd kept thinking he needed to remember every detail of the chase for a book. Foolish, but Sierra was onto something. Were they both nuts?

"I knew I liked you. Still,"—her voice lost the excitement—"I have a feeling whoever was in that truck just made one more attempt to scare me off my land. What do you think?"

"Scare you off or kill us both. High-speed chases like that are nothing to play with. Look what happened to Darrel." Well, that got them both back down to earth. "Now I have to find a phone so I can call the sheriff. She needs to know about this, and to tell the highway patrol to be on the lookout for that truck. You know I never have a signal out here."

"Let me." She had her phone in her hand. "If you're going to stick around for a while, you'd better get a satellite phone." She hit speed dial and began talking.

Rhett left the reporting to her and put his gun back in the car. Stick around for a while. Yes, he wanted to do that. He didn't bother to analyze why. Just knew it would take more than a car chase to peel him away from Sierra's side.

"Tell Myra we'll hang here until someone shows up to get our statement. I don't want to head into Austin until I'm sure that truck driver knows we reported it. The driver could be waiting, lurking around farther down the road until we move on so he or she can try again."

Sierra did as he said. When she hung up, she slid her arms around his waist. "You really do see plots everywhere, don't you?"

"You and the sheriff think I'm wrong?" He kept his eyes on the highway running past them as a customer came out and left. Every once in a while a new one arrived. There was a delicious smell coming from the kolache shop.

"No, Myra thought it was a good idea. She's contacting the highway patrol. Someone should be here soon." Sierra pinched his middle lightly. "You ever eat a kolache?"

"I don't even know what one is. If they have them in Boston, I never noticed." He saw a patrol car pull in and waved it over.

"A kolache is a pastry with either a fruit filling or sausage inside. Can you handle the cop while I get us each one?" She eased away from him. "I smell coffee too."

"Why don't you stay and help me tell him what happened?" Rhett was surprised that she seemed to be eager to get away as the patrol officer pulled into the parking space behind them and climbed out of his car.

"You were driving, and I recognize this guy. His name was on our list. He invested in Oxcart."

"You're kidding me." Rhett stared at her. "What are the odds?"

"Higher than you think. Rhett, he lives in Muellerville. The Texas Highway Patrol has people everywhere and this is probably the territory he regularly patrols." Sierra eased toward the kolache-shop doors. "If Ray wants to talk to me, I'll come out, but quick, what kind of fruit do you like? They'll have just about everything."

"Apple, cherry, I don't care." He watched her go. He'd have called her chicken or teased her about this, but he knew she'd had her fill of being blamed for holding up the Oxcart deal. A sturdy-looking man in uniform had put on his cowboy hat and approached them. He noticed Sierra enter the glass doors of the shop.

"That's Sierra MacKenzie."

"Yes, she was my passenger in the incident we just reported." Rhett introduced himself and pulled out his driver's license and registration.

"Ray Paulson." The patrolman shook hands, examined Rhett's papers and took some notes. Then he pulled out his flashlight and walked around the car. "Looks like most of the damage is to the rear and driver's side rear quarter panel here." The man bent down and looked closely. "You see what color the other vehicle was? These paint scrapes along the side look black or navy blue."

"In the dark, it was impossible to tell for sure. No license plates. Might have been a new truck." Rhett stayed beside him. At least the rain had let up and was now barely a drizzle. He was impressed with the officer's thoroughness as he asked for details about the high-speed chase.

"Good thing he didn't knock you into a ditch, or roll you over. You cut him off, do something to inspire road rage?" The officer scraped some paint samples into a plastic bag and labeled them.

"No, not a thing. Sierra and I noticed we were being tailgated after we left her ranch. We're on our way to Austin to visit a friend in the hospital." Rhett glanced back at the kolache shop. "In my mind, this was just another attempt to scare Sierra into selling her land."

"I hope you're wrong, but we'll follow up on that. Sheriff Watkins is taking this seriously." He wrote something then put his notebook away. "I hear her ranch hand, Darrel Lockhart, is in serious condition in Austin. That's too bad."

"Yes, you can imagine Sierra's upset about that. There's been one thing after another since Oxcart started trying to buy her land. First her fences were torn down, cattle poisoned, then her barn burned. Darrel fell into a hole we think was meant for Sierra. That kind of accident could have been serious for a woman with Sierra's history. You know she has a bad leg." Rhett didn't correct the impression that Darrel was who they were on their way to see. "Do you need to interview Sierra now?"

"No, I imagine this shook her up. Tell her I'm sorry about this. I married a woman from Muellerville. It's a nice little town but everyone there is stirred up about that senior living thing. I went along with it, but no land deal is worth a person's life." The officer took several pictures with his phone. "Here's my card. If you see that truck again, don't do anything yourself, just give us a call. That's what we're here for."

"Thanks, Officer." Rhett shook his hand. "What you just said. About the land deal. We have a list of local Muellerville investors and you're on it. How do you feel about Sierra holding out on Oxcart?"

"Well, I'll be damned." He looked toward the shop. "So that's why Sierra's hiding in the kolache shop. That list of investors is supposed to be confidential."

"I know. But you should realize that in the age of the internet, confidentiality is almost impossible." Rhett was very aware of how dark the parking lot was and that he'd put his gun back in the console. The patrolman had a big gun on his hip. Now Rhett was being paranoid. So far the man had been sympathetic and reasonable.

"Let me tell you what I think. Call me Ray." He leaned against the Tahoe.

"Okay, Ray. I'm Rhett. I'll tell you this: we have no idea how much you invested or what happens to your money if this deal falls through."

"It's like this. My wife Annie runs the local beauty shop, the Twist and Curl. Sierra goes there. That's why she recognized me and took off. Anyway, in a small town like Muellerville, the beauty shop is a hub of gossip." He laughed. "I come home and get an earful. Brother, I just tune it out. Though I have heard of a crime or two and passed it on to the bosses."

"Interesting." Rhett was fascinated, but he really wanted Ray to get to the point.

"Those Oxcart people came to town and started buying up land. They set up an office with Joey Schlitzberger—he and his dad are lawyers, though the old man is retired now. Joey claimed you could buy in to this senior development for a small amount and earn big bucks once it was finished. Well, you can imagine it was a hot topic in the beauty shop. My woman was determined to get in on that investment opportunity. I'd been saving

for a new bass boat and had a nice chunk of change put away toward it."
He frowned. "You fish?"

"I have a time or two." Rhett hadn't, but he wasn't about to discourage
this story. "I imagine there's good fishing around here."

"You bet. Anyway, she wore me down. I finally agreed to invest my bass
boat money in this Oxcart deal. The contract, and there was a contract,
said we'd put in our money and we would own a certain percentage of the
profits. Oxcart even promised to buy back our shares if the development
hadn't broken ground within a certain time frame." Ray looked around as
if noticing the light rain had stopped. He took off his hat and hit it on his
khaki pants. "Practically risk-free, don't you think?"

"What's the time frame?" Rhett hadn't heard anything about this. No
wonder the threats were escalating.

"It's about to run out. I'd say we have less than a month or Oxcart
is going to have to return our money, with interest." Ray put on his hat
again. "Now, the interest rate is pitiful, less than two percent, but then it
is everywhere these days. I'm not too worried about it. Even if the deal
falls through, which it seems like it's going to with Sierra refusing to sell
her land, I'm still looking at buying that boat. The wife can just give up
her dream of living rich and having her own string of beauty shops. Annie
doesn't know squat about running a big business anyway." Ray chuckled,
sure he had it all figured out.

"Thanks, Ray. You've been a big help. I don't want to worry you, but—"
Rhett didn't like what he was thinking. "What do you know about Oxcart?
Does it make sense that they could just walk away from this great deal
and then return your money with interest? How could a company afford
to do that?"

"Joey said it'll be all right." Ray rubbed his forehead. "Annie went to
high school with him. I know he put some money in it himself. He must
think this is a good deal."

Rhett nodded. "That was probably when everyone thought Sierra would
just roll over and sell her land. But unfortunately that's not happening. I'll
just put this idea out there. Don't be surprised if Oxcart starts making noise
about Chapter 11 or some other bankruptcy dodge to get out of paying
creditors."

"Well, shit!" Ray put his hand on his gun. "Joey said it would make us
all rich. He pushed it hard. Some people even took out loans so they could
invest." He narrowed his gaze toward the glass doors. "Sierra's dead set
against selling?"

"We've been doing our own investigating. Oxcart is a shady company. Even if she sold, you have no guarantee those people would do what they said with your money. They've let down investors in New Mexico and Arizona before, regular people like you. You should check into that." Rhett stepped back toward the shop as if to put himself between Ray and Sierra. Foolish. Surely the officer wouldn't go after her with his gun. But then this land deal had clearly made people desperate.

"I'm going to see Joey Schlitzberger in the morning. He'd better have something to say about this. He was right there with the Oxcart people, urging us on, saying we could trust them. They had slick brochures, maps. Well, I'll be damned!" Ray kicked the wet gravel then straightened. "I stand by what I said, though. No land deal is worth what's going on with Sierra now. I'll be watching for that truck. Wish I had a license number, but that damage won't be easy to hide." He scanned the highway but there was still little traffic. "Land deals. What the hell was I thinking?" He took one more look back at the kolache shop. "I could use a coffee but don't want to make Sierra uncomfortable. You tell her no hard feelings here. Okay?"

"Sure. I hope it all shakes out all right." Rhett shook the man's hand.

"You be careful, you hear?" The officer's radio squawked. "Got to go."

"I hear. Good luck, Ray." Rhett watched the officer stalk to his patrol car then peel out of the lot. The man was pissed. He felt sorry for whoever broke the law in Ray's vicinity in the next few hours.

"He's gone?" Sierra approached with coffee in a Styrofoam cup and a white paper bag.

"Yep. And he just got a reality check. Wait till you hear what I learned about an old boyfriend of yours." Rhett opened the bag. Apple something, kind of like a danish. He took a bite and smiled. "Kolache. Who knew? From now on, I'm stopping at every place with a kolache sign. And I've seen a lot of them around Austin."

"Yes, they're Czech. Czechs and Germans settled around Austin a long time ago." She walked around the car and climbed in. "Let's go. I want to hear all about what Ray said. Am I going to be able to get my hair cut in Muellerville ever again?"

Rhett chewed and swallowed then got behind the wheel. "Doubt it." He leaned over and kissed her. Mmm. She'd had strawberry. "But I like long hair anyway." He got hit on his arm for that one. Didn't matter, he was smiling. They had more information and the highway patrol was on the job.

Chapter Twenty-One

It was a relief to finally get to the hospital. Sierra stopped Rhett in the lobby after they got Marty's room number.

"I need to check on Darrel first."

"Even after it seems apparent that he burned down your barn?" Rhett stood in front of the bank of elevators. "But then I'm not surprised. You're a caring person."

"How do you know I'm not going to cover his face with a pillow?" Sierra quickly looked around. She shouldn't have said that quite so loudly. "I think he also poisoned my cattle and tried to get me to fall into a hole."

"When you put it like that, what floor is the bastard on?" Rhett slid his arm around her. "I'll watch the door for you."

Sierra patted his hand. "Except the sheriff insists we don't have any real proof that Darrel did any of that. I'm holding off judgment until Dylan finds out if significant payments show up in Darrel's Oklahoma account." The elevator had arrived. "Let's go. I know the floor for intensive care. And, yes, I'm worried about Darrel. He did work for me for three years."

By the time they made it to intensive care, Sierra had a bad case of déjà vu. Oh, yes, she knew this floor. The memories made her stomach churn and even the sounds were like a waking nightmare. They'd hit the right time for visiting. Things had relaxed since the days when only family could see a patient. They walked into the open area and stopped at the nurses' station.

"We're here to check on Darrel Lockhart. Is he up to seeing visitors?" Sierra was using Rhett's philosophy of "act like you belong here."

The nurse looked grim as she consulted a chart. "He's still unconscious. I hope you're next of kin. We haven't been able to locate any family."

"No, as far as we know, Darrel doesn't have any family. I'm his employer." Sierra swallowed a rising nausea. Still unconscious. That could mean anything. "How is he doing?"

"He's over here." The nurse walked them to a curtained cubicle. "He looks pretty bad but he's better now than when he came in." She smiled. "You can talk to him. We feel that unconscious patients can hear us. Still, don't stay long. He's scheduled for more tests soon. We're monitoring his brain activity."

"But he has some?" Rhett asked that.

"Yes, yes he does." The nurse pulled back the curtain.

Sierra gasped. Poor Darrel looked like a mummy. His head was so wrapped only his eyes and a slit for his mouth showed. There were tubes everywhere. He was on a ventilator. She glanced at his heart monitor, and it looked erratic to her. But then what did she know? Her daddy always said she'd just upset herself when she'd been on one and tried to figure out those blips and beeps.

"Is he going to live?" She forced out the question. "He looks bad."

"Like I said, he seems to be improving slightly. Holding his own." The nurse left them when an alarm sounded from the nurses' station. "Just a few minutes, please."

"You okay?" Rhett had his hand under her elbow. "Do you need to sit down?" He seemed to be looking for a chair. But the room, if you could call it that, was crowded with medical equipment.

"I can't breathe. I have to get out of here." Sierra hated herself for that. She jerked away from Rhett and almost ran to the double doors to the hall, looking frantically for the restroom. *Thank God!* It was close and she bolted for it. Inside, she sat on the toilet and put her head between her knees.

"Here." Rhett came in and wet a paper towel at the sink. "Put this on your face. You're pale as paper."

"Thanks. You shouldn't be in the ladies' room." Sierra slapped the towel over her eyes and leaned over again. It did help.

"This restroom is unisex. Plus, I'd like to see someone keep me out when you look like that. What happened?" He knelt in front of her.

"I don't know. Hospital anxiety. Seeing Darrel like that. Our near miss a little while ago. It all hit me at once." She raised her head and thought how she must look—hair wet around the edges and makeup long gone. Why did Rhett bother with her? Most men would have hit the road by now.

"I'm going to ask the nurse for a cup of cold water. Stay here and breathe." He took off.

Sierra did just that. In and out, calming down. She had dropped her purse next to her feet. But she didn't have the energy to root around for a brush or lipstick. Looking sickly in a hospital was almost right and proper. *Hah!* She was going to have to pull herself together.

The door opened, and Rhett handed her a plastic cup of water. "Drink this. I explained to the nurse that you were overcome with emotion, seeing your good friend so helpless. I'm sure that was part of your reaction."

Sierra drank, and the cold water felt good going down. "Yes, you're probably right. Now let's go see Marty. That is why we came." She took his hand and wobbled to her feet. "I'll be fine. Just needed a little meltdown. Hospitals. What can I say?"

"Say you're okay." He brushed her hair back from her face. He still looked concerned.

"I'm okay." She pressed him toward the door. "Thank you. Most men wouldn't have handled this so well."

"I hope you've put me in the category of not-most-men by now." He kissed her cheek then pulled her into the hall.

Sierra held on to his hand. Oh, yes, she'd definitely done that. She didn't even mind letting him take the lead as they headed downstairs.

Marty looked like hell. She had puffy eyes with a bruise and stitches on her forehead. When they pushed open the door, she flinched, as if afraid of whoever might come in next.

Sierra hoped that reaction didn't include her. She was relieved when she got a smile from someone she'd always considered a friend.

"Sierra! Oh, the writer is still with you?" Marty held out her hands.

Sierra gripped them for a moment. "Yes, you remember Rhett Hall. He drove me here and is staying in this room while we talk. I hope you don't mind." Sierra could see Marty jumping to her own conclusions. "He's been helping me, since it seems people will stop at nothing to persuade me to sell my land."

"Oh." Marty clutched her bedding. "I guess you're talking about your barn being burned down. Terrible. Myra was here and told me they suspect arson."

"That's not all that's happened. You asked to see me. Is it to talk about your car wreck and chasing Darrel? Or did the sheriff bring up my accident all those years ago when I was barrel racing?" Sierra stood close to the bed. She watched Marty's face closely for any sign that she was hiding something. The little wrinkle that appeared between her brows could mean anything.

"Yes, she brought it up. Which I tell you shocked the hell out of me. I couldn't believe you wanted to ask me about that. After all these years and what I just went through?" Marty gestured at her forehead. "I've got a killer headache and now I'm supposed to remember what happened then? I couldn't believe Myra even cares about that with everything else going on."

"I unloaded on her, Marty. It's important to me. You can imagine why." Sierra wondered if Marty was really that surprised or if she was avoiding a straight answer. "But you asked to see me, so you must have something to say."

"Yes! To leave it alone. It *was* a horrible accident. Ages ago. I don't know where you got your crazy theory. Do you actually think Sally Ann would tamper with your saddle?" Marty frowned. "Come on, Sierra. That's outrageous. Everyone knew she was dying to beat you in those races, but to do something like that to win? She'd have to be insane." She shook her head. "I sure as hell wouldn't know anything about it if she did do something so crazy."

"Why did you and Ellie pull me outside that day? Looking back, the timing seems suspicious."

"Oh, come on!" Those puffy eyes flashed. "Neither Ellie nor I were ever into horses. We were there to watch you two race. Then we helped you out because of your crush on Will. He was all you could talk about. Remember?"

"Yes, we'd had a couple of dates." Sierra could almost hear Rhett growl.

"Exactly. So when someone told us he was looking for you outside—I honestly don't remember who—we figured we'd drag you out there. How the hell did we know it was almost race time? You were free to say you couldn't come with us." Marty flushed. "Truth be told, either Ellie or I would have been happy to ride around with Will in his new Camaro. He was hot and rich, dream boyfriend material. We should have just gone out to meet him by ourselves."

Sierra heard Rhett snort at that dream boyfriend comment. "I get it, Marty. So Sally Ann didn't ask you to get me out of the way?"

"No, not that I remember. Have you ever confronted her about this? Do it. Because no one was more upset about your accident than Sally Ann and her mother. You should have seen them. Sally Ann was so broken up she could hardly accept her winning trophy that day. Then she and her mother made sure your horse got back to the ranch and checked out by your vet. They also collected all your stuff at the arena and took it back to your place." Marty looked very earnest.

Sierra had no doubt Marty was telling the truth as she knew it. "Rachel and Sally Ann took charge of my tack?"

"Yes! Someone had to do it. Your family was at the hospital and in no condition to worry about details like that. I thought it was really great that Rachel and Sally Ann took care of everything. It wasn't easy to get your horse calmed down and into a trailer. You had a lot of crap in your stall, even little things like your lucky stuffed horse. You remember that?"

Sierra blinked. Lucky. The poor ragged thing had slept with her until she'd started riding in competitions. Then he'd gone with her to the races. It was the only thing Daddy hadn't burned. Someone, probably Rachel, had put it in her room after that race. The weight of Rhett's hand on hers felt reassuring and helped her hold it together.

"Go on, Marty. Anything else you remember about that day? Naturally Sierra was out of it. The fall is the last thing she's clear about." Rhett's hand slid up to her neck. "She needs to have as many details as you can supply."

"We helped Sally Ann get it all together. She just couldn't stop crying. I think seeing you fall like that made a big impression on her. She quit racing not long after that." Marty kept her eyes on Rhett. "We found out a month or two later that she was pregnant. That could account for how emotional she was. You know she's usually tough as nails, like she was at the ranch when Sierra had that gun aimed at her. If she'd fallen back then, she would have lost her baby even sooner. That was a terrible year for Sally Ann."

"Sierra told me the story. It had to be traumatic for her. Sounds like Joey Schlitzberger wasn't such a great catch." Rhett moved closer.

"No kidding. We all thought he was hot stuff, but I guess Sierra told you how that turned out for Sally Ann. Water under the bridge now. He grew up, went to law school and is doing fine. Even talks about running for office. State legislature or higher." Marty looked down at her hands, twisting in the covers.

"We just heard he's involved in this senior living thing." Sierra was ready to try for the truth. "We got a list of investors, Marty. *Tres Amigas* ring a bell?"

"How do you know about that?" Marty looked startled.

"You think I wouldn't remember your little clique's nickname?" Sierra pulled up a chair. "I can't believe Sally Ann would have anything to do with Joey Schlitzberger. Apparently he's ramrodding this deal with Oxcart."

"Like I said, Joey's changed. And Sally Ann isn't dealing with him directly. That's why we chose a group name for our investment." Marty was picking at the cotton bedding. "We let Ellie do the negotiating and handle the paperwork. You have no idea how important this is to us."

"Not too important, I hope. Not so important you hired someone to burn down my barn or try to make me fall into a hole—all to scare me into selling." Sierra sat and leaned her elbows on the bed. "I want the truth, Marty, and I want it now. Did one of you hire Darrel to burn down my barn?"

"No! Hell, no!" She gaped at them. "Why would you think that? We were your friends. Don't you remember how Ellie and I came to visit you when you were going through those surgeries? I know Sally Ann didn't come with us, but she said it hurt her too much to see you like that."

"Really? Or did she feel guilty? I think she damaged my cinch and that's why I fell that day." Sierra jumped when Rhett squeezed her shoulder.

"Sierra, Marty already said she doesn't know anything about that. What she does know about is this Oxcart deal." He sounded serious. "Ask about that. You can confront Sally Ann when you see her, like Marty suggested."

Sierra took a breath, fighting that overwhelmed feeling again. God, but she hated hospital smells. It took her right back to some of the worst days of her life. Rhett was right, much as she hated to admit it. Marty winced as she moved restlessly. Yes, broken ribs could be a bitch. *Concentrate.*

"I'm sorry, Marty. You're right. You have been a friend." Sierra touched Rhett's hand. "We've learned some things about Oxcart that are going to make you wish you hadn't trusted Joey. I'm wondering why you risked money with him in the first place."

"Sally Ann is always going on about how you're rich and don't understand how it is to need money. I guess she's right." Marty shook her head. "Yes, your family is rich but what have you got? A lonely life on a ranch with only the hired help for company. That and a bunch of sad, abused horses to care for. I don't see you happy, with a husband or family."

"That's not necessary, Marty." Rhett's rebuke was sharp. "Get to the point. The investment. Why? Investors seem to be getting anxious for Sierra to sell. Her life has been threatened more than once. We were almost run off the road on the way here. Is your group so hard up that you'd try something like that?"

"That's terrible! You can't blame one of us for that." Marty reached for a cup of water and drew on the straw. "I'm stuck here and I left Sally Ann in a hotel close by with no means of transportation. I'm sure Ellie is working at the café. She spends most of her life there."

"Answer Rhett. Sally Ann must be desperate, to invest in anything Joey Schlitzberger is promoting." Sierra appreciated Rhett's solid presence behind her and his support. She needed it, because that sad summary of her life by Marty had cut deep.

"She *is* desperate. We all are. You know Will. Our onetime dream guy is a bully who is hell to live with. He's a controlling bastard. Sally Ann wants to get away from him, but she signed a prenup that gives her very little if she leaves him. I'm still childless because Buddy thinks we can't afford kids yet. So I work my fingers to the bone at that restaurant, come home late and then have to listen to him gripe about his own business." Marty's eyes filled with tears. "You remember when I used to design clothes?"

"Of course. I even told Rhett how talented you are." Sierra realized she'd been on target with her theory.

"Thanks. Well, I've never given up my dream of opening my own shop. Not that I'd let Buddy see any of my designs with his attitude. But Sally Ann came up with this scheme." Marty leaned forward, then grabbed her middle. "Damned ribs. Anyway, Sally Ann buys way too many expensive clothes and shoes. She says shopping fills a hole inside her or some such shit. It's got her in trouble with Will and he put her on a budget. That really pissed her off and she found a place where she can sell what she's tired of wearing. She gets good prices for the stuff. Sally Ann took the money and opened a secret account here in Austin. Calls it her getaway money."

"No kidding!" Sierra had to admit that was clever.

"Sally Ann introduced me to the shop owner. I showed her some of my dresses and she loved them, even agreed to take some on consignment. I get a good commission every time she sells one. Now I've started a getaway fund too." Marty's eyes were shining. Then she sank back. "But it's going so slowly. I want to move to Austin, eventually open my own shop. But the cost of living in Austin is so high."

"What about Ellie? There are three *amigas*." Sierra had to admire the way the women had figured out how to make their escapes.

"Ellie has always wanted to get away from that stinking café. Her brother in Dallas thinks he can get her on at his TV station. You remember those videos we showed you back in the day? She's been making some and putting them up on YouTube to advertise the café. They've gone viral. She has a funny one about her chicken pot pie that'll make you laugh your ass off. Her brother showed them to someone at the station and she's got interest there. But she's worried about those twins of hers. College and med school. Did you hear about that? Those kids are brilliant."

"Yes, we heard." Sierra wondered what it would be like to have her own children and dream about their future. "So what did Ellie do to get money to invest?"

"We warned her not to risk it, but she decided it was worth it. Joey made this Oxcart deal sound like a sure thing. The amount she had put away was growing too slowly." Marty froze. "Are you saying Oxcart isn't a good deal?"

"Even if I sell them my land, Marty, the Oxcart company is not to be trusted. They may have fooled Joey, I don't know. But they don't have a record of success." Sierra wished she didn't have to say that. The look on Marty's face was pure devastation.

"Oh, God! Don't tell me that! Ellie can't afford..." Marty grabbed a tissue from the nightstand.

"What did Ellie do, Marty?" Sierra grabbed her hand. "Tell me."

"She invested her kids' college fund. Every dime of it." Marty buried her face in her blanket and sobbed.

Chapter Twenty-Two

Sierra knew she should leave then. But she had more to learn. She did give Marty a few moments alone, taking Rhett out into the hall.

"This is worse than I thought." He put his arms around her. "I guess she told the sheriff this."

"I don't know. I'll pass this along after I ask Marty about Darrel. You know I'm not letting that go." Sierra rubbed her leg then pushed back into the room. "Marty, we have more questions."

"More? Sierra, please. I'm hurting and exhausted. I think I'm due for a painkiller; then I just want to sleep." She glanced at the door. "If Buddy comes back, you shouldn't be here. He told me not to talk to anyone."

"We'll leave in a minute." Sierra sat again.

"You'd better. Buddy sure doesn't know about the investment and I don't want him to find out. Don't you think there's still a possibility that it'll work out?"

"No promises, but my brother has some ideas." Sierra had to throw out that hope. Marty looked so worried.

"Dylan? We all had a crush on him and your brother Mason as teenagers. I heard Mason got married last year. Lucky woman." Marty sighed.

"I love both my brothers. But I'm not getting sidetracked. Why don't you tell me about Darrel and why you and Sally Ann came to the ranch for his truck? We went by to see him before we saw you. He looks bad."

Marty sighed. "You won't believe me, but Darrel and Sally Ann are friends."

"Really?" Sierra realized she'd been rubbing her thigh and stopped. "How on earth did those two get to be pals?"

"You know Darrel used to work for Will at the dealership. Odd jobs. Will would send Darrel over for Sally Ann to use around the house. Will worked all the time, or so he claimed. Sally Ann would get lonely, especially once Billy started preschool. She and Darrel would sit and drink beer and talk once he finished whatever little jobs she gave him. Sally Ann says Darrel has done some interesting things—rodeo work, even did a stint as a clown. Then he'd listen to Sally Ann for hours when she was on one of her rants about Will."

"I'd forgotten he'd done some rodeoing." Sierra glanced at Rhett.

"Anyway, I think Darrel had a crush on Sally Ann. Not that she encouraged him. Her type of man is way different from good old Darrel. He accepted that, but seemed eager to be her hero, I guess you'd call it. He even got into a bar fight and ended up arrested when someone called her a bitch down at the Rusty Bucket." Marty rubbed her forehead. "You know Sally Ann can be one. Especially at that dealership, pushing her weight around as the owner's wife. But Darrel wouldn't hear it. He knocked some fella into next week over that."

"No kidding. I saw that arrest on his record, but didn't know it was about Sally Ann." Sierra squeezed Rhett's hand, which had landed in hers. "He really was crushing on her."

"Yes, but the biggest thing he did for her was one evening when she was driving him back to his truck at the dealership. They'd had a few too many beers and she did something stupid like run a red light. A patrol car pulled them over. Before she could stop him, Darrel insisted on changing places with her. Climbed right over and put himself in the driver's seat. That move got him a DUI. He had to do community service for two years." Marty frowned. "That's a deep dark secret I wasn't supposed to tell. I sure didn't share it with Myra."

"I guess not. We won't tell her." Sierra couldn't believe it. That was beyond a crush, to risk losing his license. "Sally Ann must have hired a lawyer for him to just get community service."

Marty nodded. "Yep, and Sally Ann never forgot what Darrel did. She'd told him how close she was to losing her license." Marty blew her nose. "So when he called her and said he needed his truck at the hospital today, there was nothing for it but we had to get it right then. Didn't matter that it messed up my plans."

"So you picked her up and drove to the bunkhouse." Rhett finally spoke. "You didn't go inside, did you?"

"No, we didn't have a key. Sally Ann could have gotten one from Rachel. It would have been a nice thing to do. Darrel needed clothes. His were bound to be torn and muddy from falling into that hole. But Sally Ann was in a tearing hurry. Then you came at her with a gun, Sierra. I don't know what had your panties in a wad." Marty glared then seemed to remember something. "Oh, yeah, the barn. And the accident. Sorry."

"When you got to the hospital, what happened?" Rhett took over the questioning. Sierra was quiet, thinking about what she'd just heard.

"Darrel had come out of recovery and looked bad, but was on his phone. He was obviously upset. When he hung up, he asked us to put his keys on the nightstand. Sally Ann gave him a hug and was ready to go." Marty opened her own nightstand drawer. "I have my phone here. I can call Sally Ann if you want her side of this."

"That's okay. Finish your story." Rhett clearly wanted to get to the car wrecks.

"Well, she decided it was too late to go on to San Antonio like we'd told our husbands. That pissed me off, but I knew she was right. I had a phone call to make so I left Sally Ann at the hotel. I was too wired to just hit the hotel bar anyway. That's Sally Ann's routine. I thought Darrel should have a few things here in the hospital. I stopped at a Walmart and bought a pair of pajamas with loose pants he could get on over a cast, some shaving stuff and clean underwear. He's about Buddy's size."

"That was nice of you, Marty." Sierra smiled at her friend. Marty had always been the heart of the *Tres Amigas,* the one who remembered birthdays and had kind words when the others didn't.

"I felt sorry for him. You should have seen him, Sierra. He looked scared and in pain. I wouldn't leave a dog in that shape." Marty rubbed her forehead again. "Shit, where is that pain pill?" She picked up the call button. "I'm calling the nurse."

"Won't do any good. Been there, done that. She'll bring it when it's time." Sierra could use one herself—her leg was killing her.

"She'd better." Marty gave up and dropped it. "Sally Ann is Sally Ann. She's all about herself and she keeps score. As far as she was concerned, she and Darrel were even now. She didn't seem to give him another thought once we left the hospital. She even complained about driving Darrel's junker, said the brakes were bad." Marty's eyes widened. "No wonder Darrel couldn't stop!" She looked at Rhett. "Why didn't I remember that before?"

"A lot has happened since then. Take me through it. How you ended up chasing him down the road." Rhett was determined to get to the crash.

"God!" Marty closed her eyes. "If I'd only known…" She took a breath. "Anyway, when I got up to his room, I saw nurses outside. They were trying to hide it, but they were upset, trying to figure out where Darrel Lockhart could be. They kept checking his chart for orders. I asked if I could put the bag of clothes in his room. They let me because they weren't about to admit he was gone. But I knew, as soon as I saw his phone and car keys weren't on that nightstand, that he'd managed to get out of the hospital." Her eyes filled with tears. "Can you imagine how hard that had to have been? I feel like shit and all I have are some broken ribs. How did he get out with his leg in a cast and half-drunk on painkillers?"

"We don't know, Marty." Sierra handed her a tissue.

"I did hear the nurse say a walker was missing from a supply room. I guess he found that, but he didn't have any clothes!" Marty blew her nose. "I kept thinking about how upset and scared he'd looked when he was on the phone. Whoever he'd talked to must have threatened him. I knew Darrel had made a run for it. So I went back downstairs, got in my truck and drove around looking for him."

"It was raining, wasn't it?" Rhett got up. "Mind if I look at your phone?"

"What? Why?" She snatched it from the nightstand.

"Come on, Marty, you've got nothing to hide." Rhett held out his hand. "Prove you weren't the one who threatened Darrel or got a call from someone who told you to run him off the road. Maybe a Dallas area code? Unlock it first."

"No problem. Remember, I almost got killed in that wreck, too. Jeez, Sierra, where did you find this guy?" Marty punched in a code then practically threw the phone at Rhett. "Poor Darrel. I hope you do find whoever scared him so bad he risked everything to get out of here."

"Thanks, Marty. So do I." Sierra took a watery breath. "The only reason I'm not lying in intensive care myself right now is because Rhett has saved me twice. He's a hell of a driver for one thing. It's a miracle whoever rammed us on the highway when we were coming here didn't push us into a ditch or flip us over."

"My God!" Marty stared at him.

Rhett scrolled through her phone. "I see Buddy, Sally Ann, Ellie, Mom and the Wagon Wheel. There's one number here without a name next to it. Who does that belong to, Marty?" He showed her the number with a different area code from the rest.

"That's a burner phone." Marty flushed. "I've been seeing a guy I met at the Wagon Wheel. Nothing serious."

Sierra raised an eyebrow but didn't say anything.

"Well, it's probably over now. I was supposed to meet him in San Antonio tonight. I had to call it off." She held out her hand. "Now you know my deep dark secret. If this gets out to Buddy, Sierra, you'll have someone else gunning for you."

"Don't even joke about it." Rhett pulled out his own phone. "I've been recording this conversation. If there are any more attempts on Sierra's life, I'd hate to use that comment to add you to the suspect list."

"Holy crap. Give me my phone." Marty hit the bedspread.

"You sure this guy who called you isn't connected to Oxcart?"

"Give me a break. He's just a nice guy I've hooked up with a time or two, not some evil investor out to get Darrel or Sierra. He thinks I'm pretty. I needed to hear that." She flushed. "We do not talk about investments when we're together, you can trust me on that. Now give me my phone."

"Sure. Now tell us about the rest of your night." Rhett tossed her the phone.

"You were looking for Darrel's truck, Marty. Then what happened?" Sierra had to ask the question.

"Isn't it obvious? I saw him driving out of the parking lot!" Marty's hands were shaking. "I couldn't believe he was behind the wheel in his condition. He ran over the curb just exiting the lot."

"So you followed him." Rhett stood closer to the bed.

"Of course. He noticed and took off, getting on the freeway right away." She winced. "I tried to pass, to wave him down, but he wouldn't look at me. He was weaving through traffic and kept going faster. Finally he came to an exit and took off. He was driving crazy and almost hit a car before he cleared the ramp. Then he turned onto a two-lane road that wound away from the freeway. It was dark, no streetlights, and creepy as hell. I guess he hoped to lose me."

"Highway patrol said you were going fast when the accident happened." Sierra leaned in, picturing it.

"I was trying to keep up with him! I was so worried. He couldn't stay in a lane and was speeding like crazy. I honked, blinked my lights, tried to get him to stop. I wanted to offer to take him somewhere. If he was scared of someone then he obviously didn't want to stay in the hospital, though that's where he should have been in his condition." Marty's eyes filled. "But instead of stopping he just kept going faster and faster. My truck isn't new and could use better tires. I sure heard about that from Buddy. I had told him I bought new Michelins but instead put the money in my getaway fund." She sobbed.

"Marty, you've got to know the wreck was Darrel's fault, not yours." Sierra put her arm around her friend and looked at Rhett. "He wasn't fit to drive in the first place. He made that decision."

"But by chasing him I made it worse." Marty pushed Sierra away. "It started raining harder and I don't think he even remembered how to turn on his windshield wipers. He just sped up. When he spun out I thought my heart would stop. He flew right in front of me and over the guardrail. When he hit that tree there was such a crash! I'll never forget it. Glass and bumper everywhere. I swear a piece of his bumper came right at me! I hit my brakes, but the pavement was wet and I lost control. Then I was up and down and up and hanging by my seat belt from what felt like the ceiling. I hurt so damned bad."

"Marty!" Sierra stared at her.

"That seat belt saved me. That man, my new friend. He works as an EMT. He told me once that he never takes a dead one out of a seat belt. That sure stuck with me." Marty's hand was shaking as she grabbed a tissue and wiped her eyes. "What if Darrel dies? Is it my fault?"

"What the hell is going on here?" The voice boomed from the doorway.

"Buddy! I didn't think you were coming back tonight." Marty blew her nose.

"Martina, I told you not to talk to anyone. Who is this man? What's he doing here with Sierra MacKenzie? Sounded to me like you were talking about that wreck again." The big man stalked over to the bedside. He was wearing dark blue coveralls with his name stitched over the breast pocket. He carried a black box with a bag on top. "I brought you a lawyer. You don't speak until he tells you to, hear me? You may be in trouble, baby. There's talk of a charge of reckless driving."

"They were just leaving." Marty smiled at her husband. "What did you bring me, Buddy?"

He scowled. "That can wait." He glared at Rhett. "Who is this?"

* * * *

"I'm Rhett Hall, Sierra's houseguest." Rhett held out his hand.

"Houseguest?" Buddy ignored the gesture. "I heard you and Sierra asking my wife questions. What the hell is going on here?"

"Buddy!" Marty lost her smile.

Rhett understood his surly attitude. His wife had had a near miss and he was worried.

"Relax, Buddy. Can't I come visit an old friend?" Sierra got up to touch his sleeve.

"What about those questions? Sheriff Watkins already came by. That's why I went back to Muellerville to get a lawyer. Marty needs legal advice and clothes for tomorrow. Maybe I shouldn't have left her alone." Buddy turned back to hit the door. "Come on in here."

"Excuse me. Joey Schlitzberger." The tall man with wavy black hair wore a gray suit and blue tie like it was his uniform. He walked into the room, murmured a greeting to Sierra then kissed Marty's cheek before he gripped Rhett's hand. "I'm Mrs. Lewis's attorney. She is clearly in no shape for any kind of interrogation if that is what we interrupted. She won't be answering any more questions about her accident unless I am present as her counsel. I'm sure you understand." He swept his manicured hand toward the door. "Sierra, I know your ranch hand was involved, but let the law handle this. Now I'd appreciate it if you two would leave so her husband can visit her for a few minutes. Then I'm sure Mrs. Lewis is ready for a well-deserved rest."

"On our way out." Rhett gripped Sierra's elbow as they headed for the door.

"Sierra, wait!" Marty gripped her husband's hand. "Thanks for coming by. We have always been friends." She nodded. "I hope we understand each other better now."

"Sure, Marty. What did you bring her, Buddy?" Sierra smiled. She'd keep Marty's secret.

Buddy flushed. "I figured she might get bored here. I brought the DVD player and found a box set of that show you like at Walmart, Martina."

Marty looked into the bag he'd dropped in her lap. "*Project Runway*? You remembered!"

"Of course I did. I remember everything you like, baby." He walked over to the TV, setting the player on the dresser under it. "Hope I can get this hooked up."

"Buddy, come here." Marty's eyes filled. "I'm sorry. About the truck. I should have bought those tires."

"Yes." He walked over and kissed her carefully on the lips. "You should have. You—you could have been killed. Then where would I be?" He sniffed and went back to the door. "You folks were just leaving."

Rhett nodded and held Sierra's arm as they stepped to the door. He could feel the tension in her body when he stopped next to the lawyer. "Mr. Schlitzberger, would it be possible for us to meet with you tomorrow?"

"Regarding?" The lawyer followed them out into the hall.

"Oxcart." Rhett put on a smile. He and Sierra had talked about setting up this meeting in the car. He couldn't believe this opportunity had fallen into their laps.

"Really?" Schlitzberger turned to Sierra. "You're finally ready to discuss the best thing to come to the community of Muellerville in a century?" He beamed and extended his hand to shake hers, but Sierra scooted out of reach. "I can't tell you how relieved and happy the investors will be if you are going to be reasonable about this at last. Let me check my schedule."

He pulled out his phone and consulted his calendar. "Ah, yes, tomorrow at two? How is that for you, Sierra?" He ignored Rhett. "I'm sure we can hammer out an agreement that will make us both happy and allow this project to proceed."

"Joey, I'd like to hammer something, but it wouldn't be an agreement. We'll see you at two." Sierra's smile was decidedly chilly. "Rhett, I'm pretty sure I could eat another kolache if that place is still open."

"Sounds good. Let's go." Rhett looked back at Joey, who'd lost his smile. "I'll alert the sheriff that we're on our way back to the ranch. I'll bet Officer Paulson is still on duty. Maybe he'd like to meet us for coffee and escort us the rest of the way home. There are some reckless drivers on that road to Muellerville."

"Yes, there are." Sierra limped toward the elevators. "I wonder if he's found that dark blue pickup yet. Hey, Joey, what do you drive?"

Rhett wanted to kiss her then and there. This woman had nerves of steel. Too bad Joey just turned on his heel and walked back into Marty's hospital room. No confession from Joey tonight. That would be too easy.

Once they were out of the hospital he tucked Sierra into the Tahoe and pulled out his phone.

"Did you really record our conversation with Marty?" Sierra looked beautiful in the dim light from the dashboard.

"You bet I did. I also noticed something helpful in her call log." He finished his internet search, then pulled Sierra close so he could kiss her. "Will you be disappointed if we wait a while for those kolaches?"

"What do you have in mind?" She kept her hands on his shoulders. Her eyes were at half-mast from that kiss he'd let go past casual to serious, despite his best intentions. There was something about this woman that made him always want more.

"I just found the closest Marriott, on Lady Bird Lake. The number matches another one on Marty's list."

"I assume we're tracking down Sally Ann and not checking in for a wild night for ourselves." She licked her lips.

That did it. He had to kiss her again. When he finally pulled back, they were both breathing hard. "Is there any reason why we can't do both?"

"Well, without a ranch hand, I'm thinking I'd have a very unhappy dog shut inside. We didn't even let him out before we left." She ran her hand over his cheek. "But hold that thought. Some future night I can arrange something with Rachel."

"Unless we find out she's involved in a cover-up with her daughter." Rhett hated to mention that. He might as well have thrown cold water on their fire for each other. Sierra stiffened and moved over to stare out at the wet parking lot.

"I refuse to believe she knew a thing."

"She helped Sally Ann get all of your things out of the arena. It's a good way to cover up evidence." Rhett had to say it.

"And a natural reaction from our longtime housekeeper. Just shut up about it. Please?" She buckled her seat belt. "Now let's go. I want to get on with the confrontation. I've waited long enough. Too long. I just hope Sally Ann isn't too drunk to make sense. But I won't be sorry if she's had just enough alcohol to be ready to open up about that day."

"I'll record what she says." Rhett buckled his seat belt too. Not only was there a seat belt law, but Marty had said something that had made an impression on him. Yes, Darrel had hit a tree head-on, but maybe a seat belt would have kept him from death's door. Marty was clearly going to live without sustaining lasting damage. He had to admit that seeing Darrel like that had upset him as well. He wouldn't be surprised if the man didn't pull through. No matter what the ranch hand had done, hitting a tree headfirst was a horrible way to end his life.

He started the car and drove out of the parking lot. Sierra was silent, the only noise in the car the soothing voice of the woman in his GPS giving them directions.

He didn't think they were followed this time, but could he really be sure? Austin's streets were crowded and the hotel was close. Vehicles had been all around them and many were trucks. None of them looked like the one that had tried to run them off the road earlier, though. By the time they arrived at their destination, he knew he needed to say something.

"Sierra, look at me." He turned off the motor and waited for her to unlatch her seat belt and turn toward him.

"Do we have a plan?" She was solemn. Worried, of course. This was a big deal to her.

"I'm on your side. Never forget that. *You* are calling the shots. This happened to you. Handle it any way you want. And you decide who we tell about what we find out." He reached for her hands, relieved when she let him take them. "Understand?"

"Yes. Thank you." She sniffed. "It's finally hitting me. That I could actually know the truth. At last. I honestly don't know what I will do if Rachel knew and did nothing, said nothing." She pulled her hands away and wiped off a tear. "Damn it, I'm not crying about this. If Sally Ann tells me she deliberately caused me to fall, I'm not sure what I'll do, but I should be mad, damn it. Not hurt, mad."

"That's right. Keep an open mind. Let's see what she has to say. I know I was prepared to meet Marty's husband and think he was an asshole. Instead, he turned out to be a nice guy, just worried about his wife."

"Yes, everyone likes Buddy. I admit I was shocked to hear she'd cheated on him. I know she loves him. Maybe he's finally coming around to the designing thing. He brought her a DVD of a design show. That's big." Sierra took a deep breath. "I guess she forgot why she loved him in the first place."

"Maybe they can save their marriage, with counseling." Rhett unlocked the car doors. "Ready?" He climbed out of the car at her nod. Hell, he was nervous for her. He scanned the parking lot. A high-end hotel like this, clearly one of their fancier ones, should have better outdoor lighting. The rain had stopped, and a sliver of a moon appeared through the clouds. The gleaming lake was just feet away. Walkways lined the water, and he could imagine this as a romantic getaway. Will Jackson's credit card was probably getting a workout. Sally Ann must not care if her husband noticed she was at a Marriott here instead of on the River Walk in San Antonio.

"We should come back here." He helped Sierra out of the truck. "When all of this is settled."

"Will it ever be?" She looked up at the night sky and shivered. "Don't listen to me. I feel like someone just walked over my grave. Ever hear that expression?"

"Yes, and I don't like that you're feeling that way." He slung his arm around her and guided her to the entrance. More lights. Good. A dark SUV drove into the lot, and he hustled Sierra to the sidewalk. Was it coming at them? No, but it had been going fast before it pulled in near where he'd parked. Hell, he was getting paranoid. Still, he was glad to get inside the spacious lobby. The bar was off to one side. It was dark and featured cozy seating and a piano player.

"There she is." Sierra had found new energy and moved away from him to head straight for the woman who had settled into a leather stool facing the bartender. "Sally Ann! We need to talk."

Chapter Twenty-Three

"I don't think so." Sally Ann turned her back on them.

"We're talking whether you feel like it or not." Sierra sat on the barstool next to her. "We can do it here, where everyone can hear us, or in your room. Your choice."

"I have nothing to hide." Sally Ann looked Rhett up and down. "I see you still have your man hanging around. That's the first in a long time."

"Don't try to change the subject. I'm here to get the truth about the day I got hurt barrel racing." Sierra grabbed Sally Ann's arm. "I will get it, once and for all, if I have to bring the sheriff into it. I told her my suspicions."

"You talked to Myra about that day?" Sally Ann dropped her glass on the bar. "Suspicions? What did you say to her? It was an accident. That's all I know about it."

"I'm not calling it an accident. I had a new saddle. There's no way my cinch could have broken without help from someone." Sierra saw something in Sally Ann's face. Guilt? The way her eyes suddenly shifted and she seemed furtive. "What did you do while I was outside with Ellie and Marty?"

"What do you think I did? I was getting ready to race. Nervous as hell. It was a big deal to both of us. The biggest race of our lives." She slid off her barstool and looked around the dark room. "You're right. I don't want everyone hearing our business. Let's get out of here." She signed her bar tab and walked out of the room.

For a moment Sierra thought she was going to the elevators, but then Sally Ann darted toward the door to the outside. Rhett seemed to have anticipated that. He stepped in front of Sally Ann and blocked the exit.

"You're not going anywhere until Sierra gets the answers she needs. It'll be either here or in the sheriff's office." He had on a stern look that obviously convinced Sally Ann she'd better not try to get past him.

"Leave me alone. I've told you I don't know anything. That should be enough for you." Sally Ann stalked to the bank of elevators.

"If you have nothing to hide, you won't mind telling us all about how that day went. Step by step. You can imagine that my memory is a little hazy." Sierra stood beside her. Rhett had planted himself at Sally Ann's back.

"Why do you have to dredge that up now? You have bigger things to worry about." Sally Ann stepped inside when the elevator doors opened and she punched a button.

"It doesn't bother you that if I sell and move, your mother will be out of a job?" Sierra faced her.

"I'll always take care of my mother. You don't need to worry about her." She bumped Sierra as the elevator lurched into motion. "You have no idea how important that new development is for a lot of people, and you're ruining it." She pushed against her again. "You always were a selfish bitch."

"That's enough, Sally Ann." Rhett tried to step between them.

"Let her vent. Apparently she's hated me for a long time. Did being the daughter of our housekeeper do that, Sally Ann? Is that why you hate me?" The doors opened, and Sierra followed Sally Ann down the hall. They waited for her to use her key card and throw open the door.

It was a simple room with two queen beds. Sally Ann had dumped her suitcase and purse on one of them. There was a table and two chairs in front of a window with a view of the parking lot and the lake beyond. Sierra headed for one of the chairs. She had to get off her leg.

"My mother is the hired help. She has no education, no future, but that doesn't seem to bother her. Me? I wanted more. Always did. My daddy took off when I was six. You didn't know that, did you?" She laughed. "Of course not. No one cared about why Mama was stuck cleaning up after other people."

"Your mother is a proud woman. She works hard and always made sure you had a decent life, Sally Ann." Sierra fell into the chair, ignoring Rhett's look of concern when he took the other one. "You know I admire your mother. My entire family does. Will you get to the point?"

"Don't rush me. You want to hear my version of that race day or not?" Sally Ann went to the minibar and pulled out a small bottle of tequila.

Sierra waved a hand. "Fine. Proceed at your own pace."

"I certainly will. You've always had everything handed to you, Sierra. New clothes, fancy house, great horse and riding lessons from the best teacher. Hell, that huge ranch was your weekend home, vacation retreat, whatever the hell your family called it. Me and my friends were stuck in that dinky town all year long, going to the crap schools and entertaining ourselves at church bake sales while we'd hear you talking about cotillions and shit."

"I never went to a cotillion in my life. By the time I was old enough, I was spending my life in hospitals, trying to save my leg." Sierra almost jumped up, but Rhett's hand on her knee stopped her. No, not now. She needed to hear Sally Ann's rant.

"Oh, sorry. Those were the older sisters of your 'real' friends. Your besties. Every fall you'd go home to Houston and those girls. Me, Marty and Ellie, we were just your summer friends." Sally Ann roamed the room, stopping to open her designer bag. She smiled knowingly as she looked inside. "You know why we called ourselves the *Tres Amigas*?"

"You all spoke Spanish. Marty is Latina. Ellie's mom was Latina too. I assume you learned Spanish so you could talk with them about me behind my back. It was common knowledge I couldn't speak a word of it. Or at least you didn't think I could. It was your way of making me feel like an outsider." Sierra frowned, remembering how that had hurt. "I took Spanish in high school. I never told you that, did I?"

"Of course not." Sally Ann opened the bottle and drank. "Did you understand what we said about you?"

"Not really. You talked too fast for me." Sierra hated to admit it. She'd tried so hard to learn their secrets but had no talent for languages. "I did learn *puta* meant whore. That was a favorite of yours."

Sally Ann laughed. "Ironic. You were a prude, a good little virgin. Which left Joey and Will for me." That was said with a malicious grin.

"How did that turn out for you?" Sierra couldn't help herself.

"Why you—" Sally Ann ran toward Sierra, but Rhett jumped up between them.

"Stop it. You're not teenagers anymore. Go back to the day of Sierra's accident." Rhett stood there until Sally Ann stepped back and sat on the end of the bed, near her purse.

"Yes, that day. Did you do something to my saddle while I was outside looking for Will? You were desperate to beat me in that race, Sally Ann. It was your last one for a while because you were already pregnant with Joey's child." Sierra leaned forward.

"Ah, one of the major mistakes of my life, hooking up with Joey. I sure lived to regret it." Sally Ann finished her little bottle of tequila.

"You wanted to win that last race."

"I wanted to win every race. But I didn't have a chance!" She threw the bottle toward the metal trash can and missed. "My gear was threadbare and Mama sure couldn't afford a new saddle for me. She was already griping about the cost of boarding my horse and the racing fees. You had Destiny, the best horse in the competition. I needed something to give me an edge. Anything to help me win that last time."

"What did you do, Sally Ann? How did you get that edge?" Sierra had a sick feeling in the pit of her stomach. Suddenly she knew. God, she knew. "You switched saddles, didn't you?"

"Sierra, wouldn't you have noticed if you had the wrong saddle on your horse?" Rhett asked.

"Not if she put my old saddle on Destiny. Remember, I came back inside at the last minute. All I had time to do was jump on Destiny and ride. I'd used that old saddle so many times, it felt right. My new saddle was identical. It sat the same way, looked the same. I'd had them both custom-made. When the first one got worn, I had the new one ready to go."

"Do you hear her?" Sally Ann's eyes filled with tears. "Custom-made saddles. *Two* of them. 'Oh, dear, this saddle's a little worn, better order a new one, just like the old one. Write a big fat check, Daddy.' Fuck!" Sally Ann hit the bedspread. "She gave her old one to me. *Charity.* Told Mama all it needed was a good repair job and I'd be set. You know how much even that costs? Of course not. And never mind the finger-pointing. 'Look at that, Sally Ann's using Sierra MacKenzie's hand-me-downs.' I'd be a laughingstock!" She sniffed and dug into the minibar again. Her hand shook as she twisted off the cap of another bottle of tequila.

"I'm sorry. I didn't know how you felt." Sierra just stared at her.

"Of course not." Sally Ann waved the bottle. "What I want to know is, why now? Why are you bringing this up now?"

"I never forgot it. I still hurt all the time. Worse lately." Sierra rubbed her leg. "Now this Oxcart shit has raised a lot of questions. I decided there was one part of my life where I needed an answer." She took a deep breath and gripped Rhett's hand.

"Answer me. Did you switch my saddles, Sally Ann?" Sierra asked quietly.

"I didn't think it would matter!" Sally Ann jumped up. "They looked the same! How was I to know your cinch was that frayed?" She turned her back and put her fist in her mouth, her shoulders heaving.

"Why did you think I needed a new one? Not just for vanity, but because the old one was completely worn out. It was dangerous." Sierra got up.

"You had the ride of your life on my new saddle, didn't you?" She grabbed Sally Ann's shoulders and shook her. "Didn't you?"

Sally Ann jerked loose and faced her. "Yes! Yes, I did. I was leading in the standings. So I sat there, waiting for the last rider and the final results. Your results. I watched when you started your run. You came out as fast as I'd ever seen you. I thought then that it was over and I'd lost. You and Destiny, such a fine horse. You couldn't be beat. You know what I thought when you fell?" She wiped her eyes. "I won! Yeah, I finally did it. I won!"

"Because you cheated!" Sierra slapped her. Right across her face. Her hand stung. *God.* Brought down to Sally Ann's level. Suddenly Rhett was between them again. He must have sensed that Sally Ann Jackson didn't let anyone hit her without swinging back. He caught Sally Ann's fist before it could land a blow.

"That's it. What we came for. You and your mother cleaned out Sierra's stall and got all the saddles back where they belonged before anyone noticed, didn't you? Marty told us that." Rhett stayed between the women while Sierra sank back into the chair. "Did your mother know what you did?"

"No, of course not. I put the saddles back while Mama was still hovering around the MacKenzies. She was in shock, just like your family was." Sally Ann seemed to realize he had a reason for asking that. She was smart enough to want to keep her mother out of it.

"Poor Sierra. Mama was putting you first. I'd won the fucking trophy and she was crying over you!" She staggered over to the bed and reached in her purse. She pulled out a pistol and aimed it at Sierra. "God, I wonder what she would have done if I'd killed you? Would she have taken my side? Realized you'd pushed me to it? Because I'm sick of you, Sierra MacKenzie. You and your rich-bitch ways. Now you won't even sell your fucking ranch and make things right."

"Settle down, Sally Ann. You don't have to do this." Sierra saw that gun weaving from her to Rhett. It was as if Sally Ann didn't care which one of them she shot first.

"Don't I? I just confessed to what I'm sure the sheriff will call attempted murder. I've had a long time to think about this, you know. A long, long time." She aimed at Rhett when he took a step toward her. "Stay back, hot stuff. Yeah, of course Sierra gets a good-looking man, too. Mama says you're a rich author, polite and kind." Sally Ann moved back between the two beds so Rhett couldn't reach her. "Take another step and I'll shoot you in the leg. Or maybe in between them. Wouldn't that break Sierra's heart?" She sobbed. "I'm sick of everything I wanted turning to shit."

"Sally Ann..." Sierra needed to calm her down.

"Shut up. Do you have any idea how guilty I feel every time I see you limping? It *kills* me." Sally Ann wiped her eyes with her free hand, tequila splashing her wrist. "I know you don't care, but I'm sorry. I never meant to hurt you. When I lost my baby I knew then that God was punishing me." She sobbed again and the gun barrel aimed at the floor. Rhett moved and she raised it again. "No, stay back. Maybe I'll plead insanity. I was pregnant. Hormones raging. Something like that."

"Sally Ann, calm down and listen to me." Sierra felt drained. She now knew the truth, or as much of the truth as Sally Ann was willing to share, but it didn't make her feel better. It didn't heal her leg or her resentment. "Give Rhett or me the gun and we'll forget this happened. I won't tell Rachel about this."

"You won't?" Sally Ann looked at the gun as if wondering how it got in her hand. "What about the sheriff?"

"It won't do anyone any good to relive this. It would certainly hurt your mother." Sierra held on to the table. "I just realized that I'm done with it. I needed to know the truth. You're the one who has to live with the fact that your actions crippled me for life."

Crippled. God, Sierra hated that word. She never used it. She was fine. So she had a little limp and pain—oh, the pain. She dealt with it every day and managed better than most people did. Sierra faced Sally Ann. She wanted to scream at her, tell her that she hadn't managed to ruin anything for her with her dirty trick. That she could take her barrel racing trophy and stick it... But the one punishment she could leave with this selfish bitch was guilt. If she was telling the truth and really capable of feeling it. Let her wallow in it, a life sentence.

"Give me the gun and we're done." Sierra took Rhett's arm. "I'm going to do what I can to forget the past. Can you?" She held out her hand, surprised it wasn't shaking.

"I—I'm sorry Sierra. Believe me, please. I didn't mean for that to happen. It really was an accident." Sally Ann threw the gun on the foot of the bed. "The safety's on. I can't shoot people, or even a rabbit or deer." She fell onto the bed. "If I could, Will would have been dead a long time ago."

Rhett scooped up the gun and checked. "Yes, the safety is on."

Sally Ann stayed where she was as Rhett opened the door. "I was horrified after I realized how bad that fall was, how it affected you. Truly."

"I hope you mean that." Sierra stopped in the doorway. "You married Will so you could be rich. Have you found that money buys you happiness, Sally Ann? Is it everything you thought it could be?"

Tears rolled down Sally Ann's cheeks. "You know Will. What do you think?"

"Then consider this: everyone is after me to sell my land for this big investment, even you. But I like my place as it is. Why would I change things just for a few more dollars?" Sierra put her hand on the doorknob.

Sally Ann took a shuddering breath. "Maybe because it would help other people?" She looked away. "But then you have no reason to listen to me, do you?"

* * * *

Rhett pushed Sierra outside before either woman could say more.

"Hey, come here." He pulled Sierra into his arms as soon as the door shut behind them. "How are you?" He could feel her shaking.

"How do you think?" She pushed away from him and headed for the elevators. "Sorry, but I need to get out of here."

"Okay. I get it." He hurried to punch the down button and stuck Sally Ann's gun behind his back, then pulled his shirt over it. "That didn't turn out like I thought it would. You were amazing." He looked into Sierra's face. She was too calm, too controlled. He had a feeling she was a dam about to burst. "It really was an accident."

"You're not defending her, are you?" She whirled to face him, her eyes suddenly blazing. "Tell me that's not what you're doing."

"No, of course not. What she did was inexcusable." Rhett was relieved when the elevator doors opened. Too bad there were people inside. A couple snuggled close and talked about going out for dinner. Dinner. He knew better than to suggest that right now.

"We need to tell the sheriff what Sally Ann did." He started to guide Sierra into the elevator, but she stepped away from him.

"I promised we wouldn't. I keep my promises."

Shit, was she mad at him now? They rode down in silence after that, the small distance between them yawning like a canyon. The elevator doors opened onto the lobby.

The other couple hurried toward the exit. "Look, honey, the rain has stopped. We're definitely trying that new steak place on Sixth Street."

"Sierra, say something." Rhett pulled Sierra to a halt before she could step outside. "You want a drink? I know I could use one." He nodded toward the bar. The piano player was having a moment with "Send in the Clowns."

"After what we just heard? What she just did?" She shook her head. "I decided long ago not to turn to alcohol to dull my pain, emotional or otherwise. I've known people who did that. I wasn't about to go down that road."

"I didn't mean..." Rhett followed her outside. "Is there anything I can say to make you feel better? Anything I can do?" He stopped her again before she stepped off the curb. "Wait. I'm still not sure you're safe. It hasn't been that long since we were almost run off the road."

She took a deep breath and turned to him. "I'm sorry. Of course you aren't the bad guy here. I think I'm still in shock." She put her face against his chest then held on to him. "Thanks for being there with me. You've been a rock and I just treated you like dirt instead." She managed a chuckle. "How do you like my metaphors, writer guy?"

"You're amazing." He wrapped his arms around her. "I'm here for whatever you need."

"Pity party of one. No help needed for that." She smiled up at him. "No, I won't subject either of us to that. Let's go home. I'm actually feeling relieved. I finally know what happened that day. I believe her when she said she didn't intend for me to fall. She wasn't thinking when she switched the saddles. She did it in a hurry, I wasn't outside that long. So it's entirely possible she didn't notice how frayed that cinch was when she tightened it on Destiny, especially if she thought I was just being vain when I said it was worn out." Sierra pulled away.

"Home. You're sure? It's a long drive and you look exhausted." Rhett kept checking the parking lot around them. He still had that itchy feeling on the back of his neck, like they were being watched. No signs of moving cars though, as he finally got her to the Tahoe. The dent on the back bumper was a grim reminder that they wouldn't be entirely safe even while on the road.

"What about you? Are you too tired to drive?" She waited next to the passenger door. "Do I need to call Rachel to go let out Tramp for me? We can check into a hotel here for the night." She looked back at the lights from the lobby. "Not here, of course. Not with the chance of running into Sally Ann. There are other nice hotels in Austin."

"I can make it to the ranch. Your bed is where you'll feel comfortable and safe." He unlocked the car and helped her climb in. "I hope asking for that meeting with Schlitzberger will stop the attempts to scare you."

"You think he's been behind all of this?" Sierra stopped Rhett before he could close the door. "That's my gut feeling too. But then I haven't liked him since he treated Sally Ann so horribly in high school." She held up her hand. "I know. Sally Ann's not my best bud, but I heard plenty about him from Rachel years ago. I don't care how he's supposedly changed. Once a bastard, always a bastard."

"I think you could be right. Or maybe he's a victim of the Oxcart flimflam." Rhett kind of liked the idea. "Right now he seems the most likely suspect. He ramrodded the deal here and pulled in the local investors. Probably got pressure from Oxcart to get the deal done when you balked." Rhett leaned in and kissed her. "If he's not, he knows who is pulling the strings. So I'm hoping we're in the clear for now with that appointment on his books for tomorrow. Unless your hammer comment made him think you're still determined to hold out."

She held on to his shirt before he could draw back. "Me and my big mouth."

"I love your big mouth." He kissed it again. "Let's go. The sooner we get home, the sooner we can get to bed."

"Have plans, do you?" She pulled him down to her. "So do I." She whispered a naughty one in his ear.

"You expect me to calmly drive ninety miles after hearing that?" He leaned in and took her mouth hungrily. God, but he did love her mouth, her body and much, much more. He finally left her breathless and slammed the door. Just in time. A car pulled into the parking spot next to them and a laughing couple got out. They walked hand in hand toward the hotel. Damn it, he wished he could drag Sierra in there right now. Then he noticed a man sitting in the dark SUV that had arrived when he and Sierra had. Was the man there when they'd come out of the hotel? Had he been watching them?

Rhett hurried around the car. He stuck Sally Ann's gun in the console then started the car and buckled up. He didn't need to remind Sierra to do so. When he drove out of the parking lot, he turned onto the freeway and merged into traffic. It was getting late, and he couldn't tell if the dark SUV was back there.

He didn't say a thing to Sierra, just kept driving. When he took the turn toward Muellerville, he realized the other car wasn't behind them. Okay, then. Maybe he'd been right about Schlitzberger and he'd called off his dogs. All he had to worry about tonight was pleasing this woman whose hand was creeping up his thigh.

Chapter Twenty-Four

"I'm calling the sheriff." Sierra shifted in her seat. "You think I didn't notice you looking in your rearview mirror every five seconds? Are we being followed?"

"It's okay. I've checked and double-checked. No one is behind us." Rhett glanced at her. "If it'll make you feel better, call. I'm sure she's been informed about our earlier incident on the road, but better safe than sorry."

"You've got that right." Sierra pulled out her phone and hit some numbers. "It's a sad thing when I've got the local sheriff on speed dial. It's ringing."

"Sierra? I hope you aren't in trouble again." Myra sounded out of sorts.

"I thought I'd let you know we're on the road home." Sierra couldn't resist looking behind them again. The road was deserted. That was good and bad. If they did run into trouble, there would be no help for them.

"Yes, I got a call from the highway patrol. You two okay? I swear I'm checking out any lead that comes my way. If Darrel Lockhart would wake up, I think I could squeeze him, make him talk. Running like that, he's guilty. No doubt in my mind."

"Rhett and I stopped by intensive care." Sierra blinked back sudden tears. "I'm afraid he's not going to make it."

"Wouldn't surprise me." Myra could hardly be heard over the squawk of her radio. "Listen, I've got a call coming in. You just got away from the hospital now?"

"Yes, we did. We don't think anyone is following us this time, but if there's a patrol car in the area, you might alert them to watch for us."

"Will do. How did your talk with Marty come out? Anything I need to know?"

Sierra cleared her throat. "She suggested I confront Sally Ann about my accident. We tracked her down at a hotel in Austin and had it out." She could feel Rhett's eyes on her, urging her to unload on the sheriff. She shook her head and looked out at the passing scenery. "We talked and cleared up what happened when I fell off my horse."

"Fell off your horse? Accident? Honey, how could you just clear that up?" Myra shouted at someone with her. "Damn it, I want to hear what happened but we just got a call I need to handle."

"Then you'd better take off. I'm not going to dig into what happened again. Talking to Sally Ann made me realize that it was just an accident. I let my imagination turn it into something more. Sorry I bothered you with it, Sheriff. I want to let it go. Please do the same." Sierra hung up and dropped her phone in her lap.

"Will she?" Rhett reached for her hand.

"I hope so. I'm not going to tell her squat about what we said in that hotel room and I'm sure Sally Ann won't. If you recorded it, please delete it." Sierra finally looked at him. "I can tell you aren't happy about my decision."

"You're damn right I'm not. She threatened to shoot both of us. We have her damned gun to prove it." Rhett squeezed her fingers. "She admitted she put a bad saddle on your horse. You could have been killed, Sierra."

"Sally Ann did something stupid to win a race when she was sixteen and pregnant. Yes, the accident, and it was one, left me with permanent issues, but I wouldn't trade my life for hers. No way in hell."

"It's one thing to feel sorry for her, another for her to be allowed to get away with attempted murder." Rhett dropped her hand. "But you warned me this was your problem, your decision. So I'll learn to live with it. Maybe I should give her gun to her husband when I take this car in for bodywork."

"And tell him what?" Sierra hoped he didn't think stirring up Will would be a good punishment for Sally Ann.

"Relax. I'm not going to tell Jackson something that will send him after Sally Ann in a jealous rage. I'll make up something. I do tell stories for a living." He nodded at lights ahead of them. "Still in the mood for kolaches?"

"Not this time. We can come back when I'm not so bone tired." Sierra rubbed Rhett's leg. "Do you mind?"

"Of course not." Rhett smiled.

"Thanks. I'm going to put Sally Ann and her confession behind me for now. We still have plenty of things to deal with—insurance claim, the meeting with Joey, and of course my brother. He's coming back with whatever he found on Oxcart and a mysterious plan he has cooking. If I know Dylan, it's going to be very interesting. He'll be here before noon. I need to arrange my cattle sale too."

"All right then. Tomorrow will be soon enough to work on that to-do list you just produced. Do you always make lists?"

"Of course. Don't you?" Just one more thing Sierra didn't know about this man.

"Nope. I'm not a structured kind of guy. But I admire people who are that organized." He reacted when her phone rang. "Now who's calling you?"

"Sheriff again." Sierra's stomach twisted. "What now?"

"Sierra, that call I got was from the highway patrol. They found the truck that must have tried to run you two off the road earlier. Dark blue pickup with dark bumpers and damage that matched what Rhett described to the patrolman."

"Really? Where did they find it?" Sierra put the phone on speaker.

"It was left sitting in front of the service bay at Will Jackson's Chevy dealership. He'd reported a stolen pickup with that description last night. Whoever took it joyriding or whatever, brought it back with damage. Of course Will's hot under the collar."

"I imagine. Any fingerprints? Can you figure out who did it?" Sierra held the phone toward Rhett in case he had any other questions.

"It appears to have been wiped clean. But the boys from the highway patrol want to go over it more thoroughly in the morning." The sheriff shouted at someone with her. "Will has surveillance cameras but the perp wore a ball cap and kept his head aimed away from them. No clear view of his face."

"So he might be familiar with the dealership." Rhett said that into the phone.

"Everyone in town is familiar with Will's dealership, Hall. But I'll make a note of that and pass it on. The attack on you two was across county lines so we're cooperating with the highway patrol on this. Since no one was hurt it's not high on their priority list, but this is the third vehicle stolen from the dealership here in the last month. First one to be brought back, though." She chuckled. "Oh, shut up, Will. I know it's serious." She lowered her voice. "Someone was in a bad mood when he got here. He has insurance. I mean, what's it to him?"

"Thanks for the update. I hope whoever tried to run us off the road is done with that." Sierra realized Myra had ended the call. She dropped the phone in her lap.

"Interesting. I'd say whoever did pursue us in that truck has Muellerville ties. Why else give the truck back to the dealership?" Rhett glanced at Sierra.

"And we think the motivation is obvious. Scare me into selling my land." She sighed and closed her eyes. "I'm about ready to do it, if you want to know the truth. They've worn me down. I want to be able to just relax and live in peace."

"Now, Sierra. That doesn't sound like the strong woman I've come to know." Rhett patted her leg. "Try to sleep and I'll get us home in no time. The rain has stopped and there's hardly any traffic on the road. I'm taking it as a good sign that since the bad actor turned in the truck, he's through chasing us."

"At least in that vehicle." Sierra said it but didn't open her eyes. She was just too damned tired. She should have been on edge after all that had happened to them. Instead, she fell into a bottomless pit.

* * * *

The next morning the smell of coffee woke them both up early. Rhett turned to Sierra and pulled her to him. He was beginning to think waking up with this woman was a habit he didn't want to break. He'd had trouble unwinding when they finally arrived at the ranch. Sierra had been so deeply asleep that he'd carried her inside and put her to bed without waking her. She'd needed the rest. He took care of the dog, set the alarm and finally crawled in naked beside her. The emotion that had filled him at the sight of her sleeping had taken him off guard.

God, standing by while she'd gone at it with Sally Ann Jackson had been almost more than he could take. But he'd known he couldn't interfere. This had been a long time coming. The look on Sierra's face when she'd admitted how that accident had crippled her... If Rhett had held a gun just then, he wasn't sure he wouldn't have pulled the trigger himself to make Sally Ann pay.

What kind of person just walked away after a confrontation like that? Sierra had. He knew she thought it was because she didn't want to keep reliving the accident over and over again. But he knew better. She was protecting Rachel. That was the kind of woman Sierra was—strong, forgiving. Not only that, she put others first. Hell, she was still worried about that loser Darrel Lockhart, and Rhett didn't doubt the ranch hand had started the barn fire.

He reached out to brush her hair back from her face, and her eyes opened.

"Good morning." She smiled and touched his cheek. "You need a shave before you do more than kiss me. I hate beard burn."

"Oh, is that an invitation?"

"Sure is." She stretched, and he saw she must have gotten up in the middle of the night and undressed. Oh, yeah, definitely an invitation when her pink-tipped breasts peeked above the sheet.

He threw back the sheet. "Shave and tooth brushing, coming up."

"Hurry." She smiled. "I brushed my teeth about five."

"Planning ahead. Is there a list?" He stood in the bathroom doorway, water running in the sink.

"Of course. But I know you like surprises, so I'll keep it to myself." She inhaled. "I could go get us coffee."

"Don't you dare. Rachel must be here. That might delay the start of what promises to be an exceptional beginning to my day." Rhett grabbed his razor and shave cream then did a quick job of smoothing his face. A speedy tooth brushing and he hit the bed at a run. Yes, he was still careful of her, but he was always going to be. She had damage. Not that she wanted to be coddled, but it was only fair that she be treated with care, damn it.

"Now let's see if I can guess the first thing on your list." He ripped away the sheet and settled on top of her. "Good morning." He kissed her until he had to come up for air. "How was that?"

"Perfect." She wiggled under him. "Now work your way down."

"I can do that." He was circling a nipple with his tongue when there was a loud and persistent knocking on the door.

"Obviously you don't keep ranch hours anymore, sis, but we need to talk. If that Yankee is in there with you, kick him out. Breakfast in five minutes. Rachel made my favorite waffles."

"Go away, Dylan!" Sierra shouted.

"You've had plenty of time alone. This is business and it's important. We need to move fast. You can go back to pleasure when I'm not here." Dylan smacked the door this time. "For God's sake, make sure I can't hear."

"I'm sure you love your brother, but he's something of an asshole." Rhett rolled off her.

"At a time like this, I agree. He obviously has important news, though. He must have taken a really early flight from Dallas to get here in time for breakfast. Let's humor him and put this on hold." She leaned over him, her soft breasts pressing against his chest. "I promise. We'll get back to this later."

"Oh, yes, we will." Rhett held her close for a moment, his hand drifting down to smooth over her rounded butt. "Did I tell you how much I admire the way you handled Sally Ann last night?"

"I thought you were disappointed I wouldn't turn her over to the sheriff." Sierra stayed where she was, a softly feminine pleasure.

"You were wonderful. You slapped the shit out of her. Even when she aimed a gun at you, you didn't fall down in a heap." He kissed her again. "I have never known a woman like you. I am in over my head on this one, lady."

"I know what you mean. This has moved fast." She smiled and laid her head on his shoulder. "Intense. Maybe some of it is because of the dangerous things that have happened. I don't know." She sat up and looked down at him. "What I do know is that I'm not done with you, Rhett Hall. No matter what happens with this Oxcart thing."

"Good. Because I'm not done with you either, Sierra MacKenzie." Rhett smiled and shoved her out of bed. "Get dressed. I wouldn't put it past your brother to barge in here if we keep him waiting much longer."

Chapter Twenty-Five

"So what do you think?" Dylan pushed the pile of papers at her, but Sierra was a little too overwhelmed to even look at them. Rachel had tactfully gone out to tend her chickens as soon as they'd finished breakfast. Then Dylan had explained his plans. For half an hour.

"Let me get this straight. You're proposing that the MacKenzie family go into the senior living business." She glanced at Rhett. He took the papers and started going through the stack since it was obvious she wasn't even going to touch them.

"That's right. Mama and Harvey are all for it. She's always wanted a place for them here." Dylan focused on Rhett. "What do you think?"

"I'd like to get in on this, if there's room for another investor. The minute Sierra explained about the advantages of the location, I was intrigued. I have parents who aren't all that far from retirement. They would enjoy wintering here. You can keep your summers." He nudged Sierra with an elbow. "I haven't lived through one yet, but I've heard it can get up to a hundred in the shade around here."

"Yes, yes it can. But don't distract me." She glared at her brother. "You called Mama in London about this? Without talking to me first?"

"We're on a time crunch. Oxcart has been pressuring you because they have promissory notes coming due. It's all about to hit the fan for them. We can take this project over at a bargain price. And you heard my plan. We can cut that road through, use a section for Mama and Harvey as a kind of buffer zone near your pond, and you won't be inconvenienced at all." Dylan pulled out a map. "Look at this."

"Hold up." Sierra threw her hands in the air. "Mama will always be welcome here. Doesn't she understand that?"

"Of course she does. But she's married to Harvey now and wants them to have a separate place. If you want, you could give her a plot of land to build on." Dylan poked a finger at the map. "Right there would be a good spot."

"I would, I totally would." Sierra knew all eyes were on her. This was just like the pressure she'd been under from Oxcart. *Sell the land, Sierra. Let strangers come in and settle all around you.* Mama and Harvey weren't strangers, but that was the bottom line here.

"Sierra, take a breath." Rhett put his arm around her. "Look at the map. Can you see the riding trails? You already decided to get out of the cattle business. Wouldn't it be great to rent horses to people for the day? Or you could offer boarding for the people living in the community who have their own horses. It would be a moneymaker. You can hire help to take care of the animals. And, look, there's still plenty of pasture left for you." Rhett stabbed the map with his finger. "Dylan's got the houses for the seniors and their amenities way over on the property Oxcart had already starting acquiring with those down payments."

"I don't have extra money to invest for my part of this." Sierra hated to admit that. Of course she liked the idea of her horses being ridden regularly, and of having a steady income. But she'd have to build a new, better barn than the one she'd had before if she went for this. She was already sweating trying to figure out how she was going to manage to replace her barn. She had that giant deductible, and the insurance claim could take forever to pay out.

"You could use the value of your land as your investment. Brubaker told me what they've been offering you for your property. It's more than enough to make you a serious investor." Dylan eyed Rhett's arm around her.

"It'll take millions to build the houses and provide the infrastructure. You'll need roads, electricity, water and gas. Plus you'll have marketing and those fancy amenities to build." Sierra finally picked up the prospectus that Dylan had managed to print in what was an amazingly short amount of time. The fact that it was so complete meant he was seriously motivated to do this.

Rhett was back to studying that map. "Yes, those impressed me, Dylan. The pool, tennis courts, even a health club. My dad is a serious tennis player. If he decides to buy into this, he'll talk his doubles partner into it too. Since it looks like my sister is settling in Texas now, I'm sure my parents will be coming here regularly. You could market the hell out of this in the Boston, New York area. There are great direct flights into any one of the three major cities nearby."

"There you go. The more options we provide, the wider our market. But I'm pretty sure we could fill up just from our tri-city area. You have any idea how many seniors are in Houston alone?" Dylan grinned. "This is a potential gold mine. Sierra, you know how the oil business has been, up and down. Mason liked this too. We all need to diversify our holdings and senior living is the next big thing."

Sierra wanted to hit someone. "Spare me. I've heard all this from Oxcart. Remember, I've been called, inundated with paper, even texted about it for months." Now even her family was pressuring her.

"You slamming the door on this?" Dylan didn't bother to hide his disappointment.

"No, of course not. I can see you're carried away with the whole idea." She hated to stop the rising tide of enthusiasm, but there was something they hadn't talked about yet.

"Sorry. What's on your mind?" Dylan settled back and crossed his arms over his chest. His body language said it all. He dared her to throw a wet blanket on his plans.

"Are you kidding me? Have you forgotten that my barn was burned down, I almost took a header into a booby trap and just yesterday Rhett and I were nearly run off the road?" Sierra jumped out of her chair. It fell back and hit the tile floor with a crash. Tramp ran into the room and started barking. "Not only that, but my ranch hand may still die. What are we going to do about that, Dylan?"

Both men were on their feet. Dylan grabbed one of her arms, Rhett the other. If she'd been a wishbone, she wasn't sure which one of them would have managed to get the bigger side of her. Didn't matter. She threw off both of them and stomped into the den.

"Wait! I'm sorry. I got carried away. I didn't forget what you've been going through, sis. I swear it. Look." Dylan grabbed more papers out of his briefcase before pursuing her into the den. "I did get the details on those investors. Sit. Let's figure out who is targeting you."

"Listen to him, Sierra." Rhett stayed right beside her, trying to touch her, soothe her.

Sierra wasn't having it. She dropped down on the couch. Dylan had ambushed her with his proposal and Rhett was talking about investing in property right next to her. For his parents! What did that mean? She couldn't think about that now. It was only a few hours until they were supposed to meet with Joey Schlitzberger, and she was a bundle of nerves.

If Rhett thought she'd forgotten that confrontation with Sally Ann last night, he'd be wrong. It was still haunting her. Who said the truth will set you free? It was rolling round and round in her head until she wanted to scream. Unfair! Selfish bitch Sally Ann had done the unforgivable. Could she really let it go like she'd claimed?

"Sierra, what's wrong?" Dylan sat next to her and handed her a paper. "You were miles away just now."

"I have a lot on my mind, that's all. Let me look at this." She forced herself to focus. "Who has the most to lose if the deal with Oxcart goes south?"

"That's easy. The Wranglers put in a cool million. That was the biggest local investment. The minimum Oxcart would take was five thousand. The way the contract was written, the poor saps would wait a hell of a long time for what would amount to peanuts. The company could deduct all kinds of expenses before they would show a profit—net, not gross."

"You're kidding!" Rhett glanced at Sierra. "We talked to some of the investors. They were counting on a big return."

"I'd never screw over people like Oxcart planned to do." Dylan shuffled papers. "Involving local investors was a ploy to get the townsfolk behind the project. Only the big investors would see a dime on the back end." Dylan nodded toward Rhett. "The real winners are the local business owners. I'd say they had the most to lose if the deal collapsed. Them and Oxcart itself."

"Who were the Wranglers? Did you figure that out?" Sierra looked down the list. "Oh, here it is—Joey Schlitzberger, I'd thought so. And Fred Meadows."

"Meadows. Why is that name familiar, Sierra?" Rhett sat on her other side, reading over her shoulder.

"He's my insurance agent. No wonder he kept me stirred up, threatening not to pay if I was involved in the arson. Then he kept putting off paying my claim. He told me to increase my deductible a while back too. Now I'm hurting to come up with that."

"Son of a bitch. The Wranglers." Dylan jumped up. "No wonder you've felt pressured. If we could just tie one of those two to the payment to Lockhart..." He pulled out another paper. "I'm sorry, Sierra, but I did get proof that your guy Darrel Lockhart received a money transfer right before your barn went up in flames. He was definitely involved."

Rhett touched her hand. "Can you tie one of the Wranglers to that payoff?"

"Still working on it. The wire transfer came from an account in a name we didn't see on that investor list, but my guy is running it down." Dylan sat again. "You know a Fred Hawkins?"

Rhett slapped his hand over his phone when it vibrated on the coffee table. "I'd better take this." He left them and headed into the kitchen.

"What?" Sierra tried to steady the paper shaking in her hand. Darrel had taken money to burn down her barn. She'd been afraid it was true but now they had proof. Obviously his loyalty had a price. That shouldn't hurt so much, but it did.

"Fred Hawkins." Dylan watched her. "He made the transfer from a local account. He deposited a money order for a large amount then sent ten thousand dollars the next day to Darrel's Oklahoma account right before the barn fire. Same thing happened again the day after Darrel broke his leg. The time line is right." He picked up his phone. "I'm calling him now to see if he's found out anything else. Like where Hawkins got his money."

Rhett stood in the doorway from the kitchen.. "Hawkins. I know that name. Rancher. We didn't like the look or smell of his barn and moved Charley out of there."

"Yes, that was Fred Hawkins." Sierra was thinking hard. She was surprised when Rhett walked over to sit beside her. He put his arm around her. "Hey, everything okay?"

"No." He pulled her closer. "I've got some bad news." He locked eyes with Dylan. "Tell your guy you'll call him back."

"Sure thing." Dylan murmured into his phone and set it on the coffee table. "What the hell, Rhett?"

"Sierra, Darrel's dead." Rhett kept his eyes on hers.

She tried to take it in. This wasn't exactly a surprise. Darrel had looked bad when they'd seen him. All those injuries. Her eyes filled with tears and she pressed her face into Rhett's shoulder. She should hate Darrel. He'd thrown his loyalty out the window for money. But she couldn't forget all the times he'd helped her with horses in such horrific shape that she'd prayed they'd make it through the night. Darrel had loved horses. Many times, he'd cleaned up after sick ones, a dirty job that had turned her stomach. He'd done the jobs cheerfully too, calling her Miss Sierra with a respect that had made her feel competent and, yes, in charge.

A sob caught her off guard. Another hand landed on her back. Dylan was there with her, adding his own sympathy. She was so lucky. Darrel hadn't had anyone. No family. His friends had been the kind who kept score. Like Sally Ann. Obviously he'd had a rough life, so rough he'd done the unthinkable, just to make a few bucks. Of course, thousands of dollars wasn't a few bucks to a man like Darrel Lockhart. She sniffed and sat back.

"You okay now?" Her brother was ready to move on.

Sierra saw Rhett give him a hard look.

"I'm getting there. I had to remind myself that Darrel took money to make my life miserable."

"Damn straight." Dylan reached over and picked up his cell phone. "Now tell me what you know about Hawkins."

"There's a connection between Fred Hawkins and Fred Meadows." She sighed. Rhett brought her a glass of water and a box of tissues. "Thanks."

"That's great, Sierra. Tell us when you're ready." Rhett still wasn't happy with Dylan's eagerness to move on. That was obvious.

"I'm ready." Though she blew her nose first. "Fred Hawkins is Meadows's brother-in-law. Well, used to be. Fred the insurance guy is a widower. His wife died a few years ago of cancer. He hasn't remarried, though the single ladies have been after him."

"Get to the point, Sierra." Dylan hit his speed dial. "Hey, we've got a connection. Meadows and Hawkins are related. Check to see if there are any money ties between those two accounts." He nodded at Sierra. "Anything else?"

"Meadows doesn't have much to do with Hawkins but Hawkins has obviously fallen on hard times. We saw that when we were at his ranch a few days ago. He offered to take one of my horses after the fire. But the place was run-down. I wouldn't let my horse board there. When we moved Charley, Fred was disappointed. I had offered to pay for feed."

"She's right. It was clear that Hawkins needed money. What didn't track with me was that he had more horses than space. What do you think, Sierra? Maybe he thought he could rent riding horses for the new development when it opened." Rhett kept her close, still looking concerned.

"I noticed that too. Fred—Hawkins, not Meadows—does love horses. He might dream of running a stable. If Meadows offered him some easy money, he wouldn't ask too many questions, he'd just do it." Sierra rubbed her forehead. "I wonder who tried to run us off the road, though. Now we have three candidates."

"Yes, Schlitzberger, Meadows and their hired guy Hawkins." Rhett pulled out his cell phone. "Maybe we should let the sheriff in on this."

"I'd like to talk to Schlitzberger first. We have that meeting you set up at two, right?" Dylan answered when his cell phone chirped. "Yeah?" He listened then smiled, but it wasn't pleasant. "Okay, that tracks with what we're thinking. Thanks, keep digging." He ended his call.

"Okay, you have that look that says you're about to close a case in your favor." Sierra rubbed her leg. Damn it, why did it hurt today? She'd done nothing but rest and sit on a comfortable couch.

"Seems that a chatty clerk at the bank told my guy about a deal Hawkins and Meadows have cooking." Dylan tapped his phone. "I didn't tell you, but Leroy has been in Muellerville since this started, his ear to the ground."

"No kidding!" Rhett actually smiled at Dylan. "Great idea."

"What kind of deal?" Sierra patted Rhett's knee. "My brother isn't one of the best lawyers in Houston for nothing."

"*The* best." Dylan grinned. "Anyway, she told Leroy about the new riding stables Hawkins is going to build, with brother-in-law Meadows backing him. They've been keeping it on the down low because they didn't want anyone else stealing their brilliant idea."

"I'm sure Hawkins would do a lot to make sure that deal didn't go south." Rhett held up his phone. "The sheriff needs to hear about this."

"Okay. Maybe we can go in to this meeting with Schlitzberger with one of us wearing a wire. I want a plan in place." Dylan was serious. "I have a question for you, Hall. Did the sheriff say if Darrel died from his previous injuries? Or was it murder?"

"What?" Sierra stared at her brother. "Murder?" She couldn't believe he'd thrown that word out so casually. "Darrel had a serious accident, Dylan." She blinked back tears. "No one really expected him to survive that."

"She's right. But they're doing an autopsy anyway." Rhett squeezed her hand then took the paper. "Obviously the Wranglers are our number one suspects to hire Darrel. We met Joey Schlitzberger and I didn't like his looks."

"Forget his looks. With a cool million on the line, that's motivation to put the screws to Sierra." Dylan frowned.

Sierra nodded. "I had no idea either of these men had that much money squirreled away."

"They didn't and they don't. Both of them took out loans to supplement their savings." Dylan leaned forward. "More motivation to do whatever it takes to get this project off the ground. We need proof, though, to nail them to the wall."

Sierra looked at Rhett. "Someone threatened Darrel. That's why he ran out of the hospital. If we could find out who did it, that would tie this all together with a bow."

"What's this?" Dylan focused on her. "Last I heard Darrel had a broken leg. That shouldn't have killed him."

"He got a phone call, then panicked and left the hospital, tried to drive when he was high on painkillers and totaled his truck. He was in intensive care in a coma when he died." Rhett kept his arm around Sierra.

"Damn. If one of the Wranglers paid him off then figured he was a liability, they might have told him to get out of town. Anybody check his cell phone?" Dylan looked through his contact list. "I've got a guy who can do all kinds of shit with a cell phone."

"They haven't found his phone yet. You need his number?" Sierra wondered if it could be that simple. Why hadn't the sheriff's office or highway patrol followed that lead? Of course they had many cases and the night Darrel had crashed had been an especially busy one.

Dylan was on his phone. "This is a long shot, but tell me his number."

Sierra recited it. She'd been calling that number for three years every time a cow got out or a horse needed help. Why had the man who'd been so eager to help her turned on her?

"Okay, he's working on it. If it's on somewhere, he might be able to find it. Don't ask me how, that kind of technology is above my pay grade." Dylan hit another number. "Checking again on that wire transfer."

Sierra scanned that investor list again. There were the *Tres Amigas*. Yes, Ellie, Marty and Sally Ann. They'd managed to pool forty-five thousand dollars. Astonishing. Ray's bass boat money was another twenty thousand. So many local people were hoping to cash in on the senior living project. Compared to the millions it would take to build the development, it was peanuts, but those peanuts would seem like a banquet to the people who had invested their life savings in a hope for a better future. Could she really hold out for her own selfish reasons? Right now she was having a hard time remembering what those were.

Chapter Twenty-Six

"Are you sure you're ready for this?" Rhett didn't like the way Sierra was walking. Her limp was worse than usual.

"I want to get it over with." She held on to his arm.

"Leave everything to me, sis. I can't wait to nail this bastard to the wall." Dylan wore his lawyer suit and his lawyer face. He'd insisted on being the one to wear the wire as well.

"Settle down, people. If I had more evidence on these people, I'd refuse to let you go in there." The sheriff had listened to Dylan's information about the wire transfers to Darrel. "I admit you've got a good case for the arson payoff. I can take it to the DA. But everything else is just speculation. Lockhart's condition was bad to begin with. They're doing an autopsy but proving anyone sped him to his grave, well, that's another matter."

"Myra, my private detective talked to the nurses. They said there was no way Darrel could have pulled that IV out of his own vein. He was comatose. You don't see anything suspicious about that?" Dylan had already argued his point.

"Without witnesses, you've got nothing. People were going in and out of that ICU all the time in masks and gowns. His condition was critical and declining. We'll have to wait for the autopsy." Myra frowned. "Get me a confession and I'll be happy to slap handcuffs on both men. But Meadows and Schlitzberger as partners in crime? I just can't see it."

"When I called and told Joey I wanted both Wranglers there, because they are the biggest local investors, he seemed pleased. " Sierra finally spoke. "I think he's dreaming that I'm coming to make a deal with Oxcart."

Rhett gave her an encouraging smile. "We'd better go." They were in Sierra's kitchen. Rachel had left them alone, doing laundry in another part of the house. The sheriff would be monitoring the meeting from her car parked down the street from Joey's office.

"I still think we're wasting our time. Neither man is stupid enough to confess to anything." Sierra got up from the table then staggered. "I don't know what's wrong with my leg today."

"Do you need to see a doctor?" Her brother frowned. "Maybe you've been overdoing it."

"I can take it easy when this is settled. I'm selling my cattle, Dylan. Did I tell you that?" She explained her plans to Dylan as they walked out to the cars.

"Hold up, Sheriff." Rhett waited until Sierra and Dylan were outside.

"What is it, Hall?" Myra frowned. "This has been hard on Sierra."

"Yes, it has. I have a permit to carry and I plan to take my gun into this meeting. Sierra seems to think these men aren't dangerous. So far they've hired people to do their dirty work, but who knows what they'll do when confronted with the evidence Dylan has found." Rhett figured Myra was the kind of lawman who wouldn't like surprises like his handgun.

She held out her hand. "I noticed you were packing the minute I walked in. I tried to talk Sierra into letting me bring Joey and Fred in, but she was dead set on having it out with them."

"Yes. I don't blame her, and I will do my best to protect her if there's a problem." Rhett pulled his gun from behind his back. Myra went over the weapon.

"So will I." She handed it back.

Rhett slid the gun back to nestle against his spine. "We'll be three against two, but that's two snakes against three people who…"

"I get it. Sierra's tough, but she's been through too much lately and it's showing. Dylan is hell in the courtroom, but I have no idea if he can throw a punch." Myra looked Rhett over. "Be careful. Don't you pull a gun unless someone draws on you first. I'll be listening and close by. Snakes. Yes, Schlitzberger always struck me as the cottonmouth variety. Big talker but can strike at any time. Meadows? Well, he's been hiding in the grass. Fooled me. But not anymore. I'll come running if I hear it's going south in there."

"Thanks, Sheriff." Rhett shook her hand. "I want to end this. Sierra deserves peace."

"Damn straight." Myra led the way out of the house.

The ride over in the Tahoe was silent except for Dylan on his phone. Rhett could almost hear Sierra grinding her teeth. They were parking in front of the brick building that housed Schlitzberger and Son Lawyers when she spoke.

"I can handle this. Don't try throwing your weight around, either of you." She turned around to stare at her brother who'd finally finished his call. "I know you're the hotshot lawyer, but it's my land. Let me say my piece before you get into your new plan."

"Fine. Do your thing." Dylan reached up and thumped her on the head. "Bossy bitch."

"Asshole." She smoothed her hair. "If you messed up my hairdo, I'll sue."

"Try it." He opened the car door.

"Nice. Sibling rivalry, now?" Rhett got out of the car and walked around to take her hand. She stumbled and leaned against him for a moment. "You're worrying me. Will you go to see a doctor about your leg?"

"When this is over." She took a steadying breath. "At least he's on the ground floor."

"Right. Because if there were stairs, I'd definitely carry you." Rhett glanced at Dylan, waiting by the front door. "Your brother would hate that."

"Then maybe you should do it." Sierra grinned and limped away. "Kidding!"

Rhett just shook his head. He loved the way she made light of what had to be worrying her sick. She was going in to confront the men who had paid Darrel to torch her barn. God, he loved her.

That stopped him in his tracks. Yes, he did.

"Hey, you coming?" She looked over her shoulder, her smile tight but just for him.

"Of course. Wait for me." He hurried, ignoring Dylan's probing looks. Yeah, her brother was catching on. Rhett didn't care. He was sticking around as long as Sierra would have him. Now he hoped it was forever. Damn, that felt good, thinking it. He'd find time to say it as soon as all this shit was shoveled out of the way.

A secretary greeted them. She was someone Sierra knew. "Joey and Fred are waiting for you. Sierra, I heard about your barn. Anything I can do to help?"

"No, but thanks for asking, Mandy." Sierra smiled.

"Too bad they don't have those old-fashioned barn raisings like they used to. We could have a picnic and all the men could throw a new barn together." The woman eyed Dylan and Rhett. "I was watching an old movie the other day...lots of fun, and the guys aren't allowed to wear shirts."

Sierra laughed. "Mandy, love that idea. If I didn't have to put up a steel structure, I'd be all over it. I'll see you in church. Maybe next Sunday?" She glanced at Rhett.

"Yes, then out to lunch afterwards." Mandy grinned. "Paul and I found a cute place over in Smithville."

"I'll call you." Sierra held Rhett's arm as they walked into the big office behind Mandy's desk. "Bet you didn't know I went to church."

"We still have a lot to learn about each other." Rhett couldn't wait. He got a shove between his shoulder blades.

"Can we get with the program here?" Dylan looked ready to explode.

"Relax, bro, I'm finally realizing I have the power seat at this table." Sierra smiled. "Isn't that right, Joey?" She settled into a chair in front of a massive desk. "My, you have a big desk. Trying to prove something?"

"Sierra, you're in a good mood. I'm surprised, after all you've been through." Joey had stood when they walked through the door. Now he sat in his leather swivel chair. "I got Fred here, as you asked. Fred, do you know Dylan MacKenzie, Sierra's brother? This is Rhett Hall, her houseguest." His emphasis on houseguest made it an innuendo.

The men shook hands. Rhett sized up Meadows as a man who was full of himself. He wore a serious look and one of those suits that cost a lot but strained over his expansive middle. Even his collar was tight. His red power tie fell short over his belly.

"We just got word that your ranch hand Darrel Lockhart died. My condolences," Meadows said solemnly.

Sierra looked directly at him. "Since you paid him to set my barn on fire, I'm sure his death is a big relief. He can't testify against you now, can he?"

Meadows fell back like he'd been hit. "What the hell? I didn't pay him a dime!"

"Here's the proof." Dylan threw two papers on Joey's desk. "Wire transfer to Lockhart from your bank, Meadows. First, a big withdrawal from your account to buy a money order that went straight to Fred Hawkins, your brother-in-law. Hawkins deposited it then made a wire transfer—"

"All that proves is Hawkins—" Meadows's face now matched his tie.

"As your counsel I'd advise you not to say another word, Fred." Joey picked up the papers and examined them with a scowl. "Not another word."

"As his coconspirator, be sure to note the second payment, the day the accident landed Lockhart in the hospital with a shattered leg." Dylan nodded toward the papers. "It certainly disappointed Sierra to learn that a man she'd trusted for three years could be bought, but there's your proof. When she still wouldn't sell, Darrel was paid again. This time he set a trap, a hole in her path. If she'd fallen into it, Sierra's leg would have been the one shattered. With her history, she could very well have lost her leg this time, or worse." He glared at Meadows. "That's conspiracy."

"That fool. He came up with that on his own. I would never—" Meadows stomped around his chair.

"Shut the fuck up, Fred, and sit down." Joey was furious. "What proof do you have my client ever spoke to Lockhart?"

"It's interesting you should ask that. My private investigator helped the highway patrol recover Lockhart's cell phone this morning. It had a weak signal, but was finally discovered in a tree near the crash site. Calls and texts were traced back to a burner phone purchased in a local Quik Stop." Dylan must have just received the report. "They're checking surveillance photos at the store now to see who bought that burner. Of course, Muellerville is a small town. Someone might even remember the purchaser."

Meadows had finally sat down and gave Joey a desperate look.

"Say nothing," Joey commanded.

"No need. We'll know the truth soon enough." Dylan settled back. "Sierra, want to tell Joey and Fred your decision about Oxcart?"

"Yes, that's why we came, after all." She sighed. "I've had a lot of time to think about the impact of the senior living project on our town."

"Thank God!" Joey ignored Meadows, who had pulled out his phone and started texting.

"I think I can live with it. If done right." She reached out for Dylan's file folder. "There's a problem with Oxcart though, Joey."

"A problem? Sierra, Oxcart had a brilliant idea. I couldn't believe no one had thought of it before. We are perfectly located to take advantage of the booming senior citizen market." Joey leaned across his desk, selling.

"You went all in on this investment opportunity, didn't you, Joey?" She pulled out the investor list. "You and Fred. To the tune of a million dollars."

That got Fred's attention. "Yes, we did. And you wouldn't cooperate."

"I told you to shut your piehole." Joey hit the desk with his fist.

"You denying it? Holding out so long she put us on the verge of bankruptcy." Fred hit his side of the desk. "You think I'm taking the fall for this by myself? Hell, no." He focused on Dylan. "Joey was with me every step of the way. Who do you think found Darrel Lockhart? Joey represented Lockhart for a DUI."

"Goddamn it, Fred." Joey raced around the desk and grabbed Fred's tie, jerking it until the man's face went purple. "Not another word."

"I'm sure you'd like that." Sierra scooted her chair away from the fight as Meadows flailed his arms, hitting Joey with his fists.

"Calm down." Rhett was ready to jump into the fray if it looked like Sierra was in danger.

"Let's be reasonable. Nothing has to leave this room." Joey whispered something in Fred's ear, shook him one last time, then they both took a breath. Joey walked back to his chair, running his hand over his hair. Fred smoothed his tie. "Sierra is coming around to the senior living project. Right?"

"Right. But did you do research on Oxcart before you invested, Joey?" Sierra shook her head. "Did you know they've tried this before and failed? They have a poor track record and usually drop out before it's finished. Then they leave investors holding the bag."

"I'm not stupid. Of course I checked them out. This time is different. We can't miss. Location is everything. Brubaker explained it to me." Joey aimed a warning look at Fred, who groaned.

"I agree. He didn't lie about that. But Oxcart can't be trusted." Dylan handed Joey another paper. "So I bought them out."

"What?" Joey snatched it. "The MacKenzies took over the project?" He laughed. "Praise the Lord! Right, Fred?"

"Don't celebrate yet, Joey." Sierra obviously wanted the last word. "Do you really think I'd let the men who tried to run me off my ranch get one damned dime from this project?"

"Now, Sierra, you can't prove *I* tried to do that." Joey ignored Fred's gasp at what was clearly Joey's attempt to throw him under the bus. "Besides, we invested in good faith. We had a contract with Oxcart. Surely your lawyer brother explained that he has to honor that contract. Fred and I borrowed money so we could get in on the ground floor."

Rhett wanted to knock Joey's smile off his face. He desperately wanted to do something, say something. But he'd promised Sierra this was her show. Hers and Dylan's. He was ready to act, though. Joey was not going to like what he heard next.

"Ordinarily you'd be right, Joey. Except you were so excited about Oxcart's get rich quick scheme, you didn't read your contract. Or maybe you slept through contracts at that law school you went to in—where was it—Padre Island?" Dylan couldn't hide his smile. "I hear their class in how to make a perfect margarita is dynamite."

"It was a perfectly respectable..." Joey shut up, obviously figuring out he was on shaky ground.

"Here's the deal. I bought out Oxcart for pennies on the dollar. I will make the small local investors whole and rewrite the terms of their contracts to give them a decent return on their investments." Dylan had another paper, but he didn't pass it over. "But you and Fred are shit out of luck. The original contract that Oxcart wrote has plenty of traps guaranteeing investors little or no return. Loopholes, real lawyers call them. Sound familiar? You broke several of the terms when you tried to force Sierra off her land with your dirty tricks."

"That's ridiculous." Joey looked offended.

"I have a notarized statement from Alfred Brubaker admitting you assured him you'd do whatever it took to make Sierra sell. He said deadlines were approaching that would have put all of you out of business. I'm sure we can prove paying off Lockhart to burn down Sierra's barn was just one of your strategies. Then there was attempted murder. She and Hall were almost run off the highway."

"You were in the hospital visiting Marty. Did you take a trip up to intensive care, Joey, so you could finish off Darrel? He was a loose end, wasn't he?" Sierra bit her lip and Rhett reached for her hand.

"Goddamn it. Sierra MacKenzie, this is all your fault. Interfering bitch." Joey dragged a gun out of his desk drawer. "And Fred. You used your brother-in-law? I thought you were smarter than that."

"Put the gun away, Joey. What are you going to do with it?" Sierra said it first. She had pulled her own gun out of her purse and aimed it at him. "You can't kill all of us."

"She's right." Rhett trained his gun on Fred. Of course Fred also had a gun in his hand.

"Good God, am I the only one in this room who isn't armed?" Dylan stood. "This is crazy. Joey, you're caught. I'm wearing a wire. This is all recorded and the sheriff heard everything."

"I sure did." Myra walked in the door, two deputies behind her and all of them with their weapons drawn. "Every one of you put the guns down. Joey, stop that."

Joey had his gun aimed at his head. "I can't go to jail, Myra!"

"A fast-talking lawyer like you can surely make a deal and not do serious time." Sierra put her gun away.

"Ask yourself what proof they've got? Don't let your emotions take over." Rhett slid his gun behind his back and stepped in front of Sierra.

"Shooting yourself is the coward's way out. You can stall things for years with a good defense and you know it." Dylan grabbed Sierra's arm and eased toward the door, behind the deputies.

"Go ahead, blow your worthless brains out. You got me into this." Fred gave his gun to a deputy and put his hands on his head. He was crying. "I'm not a criminal. Joey made me do it. It was all his idea. Get rid of that bitch, he said, if she won't sell. He even told me to try to run them off the road."

"Fuck that." Joey aimed at his partner. Then there was a shot, and he fell back into his chair. "Ah! I'm hit! You shot me." He sounded surprised.

"Sure did." Myra rounded the desk and took his gun from his useless right hand. She'd wounded him in the shoulder. "You'll stand trial. We're working on a nice list of charges. Attempted murder for starters. Aimed your gun at a roomful of people and peace officers. Quit struggling!" She chuckled. "Resisting arrest. Yep, you just made my day."

* * * *

"Fred is singing like a mockingbird, trying to cut a deal with the county attorney. Joey wants to go to Austin to the hospital. No way in hell. Local doc took care of him. It was a flesh wound." Myra waved Sierra, Rhett and Dylan out of her office after they finished their statements. "I got everything on tape. If the attorney needs more, we know where to find you."

Rhett didn't waste time getting Sierra out of there. Dylan jumped in the backseat and got on his phone again. Rhett tuned out Sierra's brother. He didn't like how pale Sierra was.

"I've got business in Houston. I'll be in your office on the phone if you need me, Sierra." Dylan headed down the hall as soon as they got back to the ranch house.

"We need to talk," Rhett said as he pulled Sierra to her bedroom.

"I know." Sierra fell back on the bed. "I have to tell you something first."

"What?" He sat beside her. He could tell there was something wrong.

"I'm scared, Rhett."

"Now? Everything's over. The bad guys are in jail." He pulled her into his arms. "What's the matter, baby?"

Tears flooded her eyes. "There's something seriously wrong with my leg. I need to see the specialist in Houston."

Chapter Twenty-Seven

"I swore I'd never have surgery again." Sierra threw another nightgown into her bag. She never wore nightgowns. These were ancient. Left from the days when she'd been through this before. Another reminder of hospital stays. A cast on her leg. Physical therapy.

"Come here." Rhett pulled her to him. "You should be excited. You told me the doctor is optimistic. That technology has made great strides in the years since your accident."

"I know. But…" Sierra hugged him. How had she gotten so lucky? She'd called him her rock once. He was so strong, so steady. More than a rock, a living, breathing, and very warm presence who insisted on being there for her.

"No buts." He moved the suitcase over and sat, then eased her into his lap. "When we get back to Houston we'll be surrounded by your family. I know that. So let me say this now. I don't care if you always walk with a limp. I love you just the way you are."

"Rhett." She touched his face. "How can this happen so fast?"

"I have no idea. Cupid's arrow?" He laughed and kissed her. When he drew back he was serious. "I never thought I'd say it, but maybe it was meant to be. Like that song I heard on the radio coming here."

"I know what you mean. Just when I needed someone most, you were there. Every minute." She kissed him this time. "I hope you don't come to regret this, but I love you too." She looked around the room. "I saw you packed your laptop. Starting a new book?"

"That was a quick subject change." He stood and carried her down the hall to her office. "No. I finally got what my editor calls 'suggestions' for the manuscript I sent in before I headed to Texas." He set Sierra in her desk chair. "I came in here to print out her notes when I spotted this." He pulled out her Lucky folder. "Care to explain?"

Sierra flushed. "It's nothing." She never showed her stories to anyone, and she sure hadn't planned to show them to a *New York Times* best-selling author. "Really, Rhett. I hope you didn't look inside."

"Are you kidding? I peeked and there was a manuscript. By Sierra MacKenzie. How could I not read every word?" He pulled up a chair and faced her. "It's great, Sierra. A kid's book, Lucky the horse and his owner. I can see a series here." He picked up the folder and paged through it. "There are some wonderful lines I wish I'd written myself."

"Stop it. You're embarrassing me. I wrote it for fun. Nights get lonely on a ranch. I work with those special kids, you know, and I found myself making up stories for them. It's a way to reach the quiet ones." Sierra snatched the folder. "We need to get ready to go."

"Maybe. But I'm not forgetting about this." He pushed her wheeled desk chair to the hall. "My publisher does children's stuff. Can I send it to my editor? She'll know who to pass it to."

"Don't be ridiculous. I haven't looked at it in months. It needs revising." She looked at him suspiciously. "You're pulling my leg."

"I wouldn't dare. Work on it if you want to, while you're recovering. And I'll work on my book." He grinned. "Doesn't that sound cozy?"

"Like a partnership." Sierra held up her hand. "Stop rolling me. This feels too much like a wheelchair."

He stopped instantly. "Sorry."

"No, don't be. Come here." She stood, a little wobbly. Not because her leg was killing her even more than usual because of all the tests in Houston the week before, but because her heart was full and she was fighting tears. "Rhett, you've got to stop paying me rent."

"Really? Not kicking me out, are you?" He brushed a tear off her cheek.

"No, of course not. I mean…" She smiled. "Oh, you know what I mean."

"Then what can I do to make it up to you? If I stay here for free." He ran his hands down her sides. "Rachel does the cooking and cleaning. Cattle are gone but I would love to ride a tractor. Can I mow your pastures? Help supervise the barn building when we get back?"

"Sure. I'd love to see you on a tractor. Shirtless, of course." She wasn't going to cry, refused to do it. But she could see a future with this man. Children someday and evenings with them in front of the fire working on books, then off to bed where the fire would still be blazing.

Rachel cleared her throat. "I hate to interrupt, but I found another nightgown for you, Sierra." She had a small stack of laundry in her arms.

"Thanks." Sierra took it. "I'm not sure how long we're going to be gone. Rachel, take a vacation. Rhett will be at my mother's and we decided Tramp could come with us."

"I'd like that." Rachel's face crumpled, and she pulled a tissue out of her pocket. "Sally Ann needs me."

"What's the matter?" Sierra dropped the clothes on the bed and pulled Rachel into her arms. Had Sally Ann told her mother about her confession? Sierra had been trying to put it behind her these last weeks since the confrontation. She'd had plenty of other things to think about—like doctor appointments, depositions in what Muellerville residents were calling the Oxcart scandal, and coming to terms with the fact that she was going under the knife again.

Rachel stepped back and wiped her eyes. "She's finally divorcing Will. It will be hard. He made her sign a prenuptial agreement that was supposed to leave her with next to nothing." Rachel cleared her throat. "But Sally Ann will do all right. She found a sharp lawyer in Austin. Seems there's plenty of community property she can claim. Of course she'll get Billy."

"That's good." Sierra sat on the bed.

"They've been staying with me and I can already see a difference in the boy." Rachel glanced at Rhett. "I know Billy acted out when you helped with the horse therapy. But Will was always too hard on him. We're getting Billy into therapy, the talk kind, and he's going to that horse camp you told me about, Rhett." She smiled. "Thank you for that."

"I'm glad I could help." Rhett patted her back. "Will is one angry man."

"Yes, he is. But then his daddy was rough on him too. Guess it goes on down the line unless something stops it." Rachel wiped her eyes again. "I wish…" She walked to the door. "What do they say? If wishes were horses, beggars would ride. Don't do any good to dream. I learned that the hard way."

"Aw, Rachel. I'm sorry." Sierra was glad now that Rachel knew nothing about Sally Ann's saddle switch.

"I'm just praying your surgery makes you whole again. Or at least helps ease your pain." Rachel ran back and gave her a big hug. "I love you, Sierra. Just like a daughter." She shook her head. "Sally Ann doesn't always do what's right, I know that. Please forgive her." She sobbed and left the room.

"Oh, God. She does know." Sierra locked eyes with Rhett.

"Apparently." Rhett sat beside Sierra on the bed and put his arms around her. "You can't blame her for any of this."

"No, of course not. She's always done the best she could." Sierra wiped away a tear. "Makes you wonder what Rachel's husband was like."

"He might not have run away. Rachel might have kicked him to the curb." Rhett held her tight. "But those early years must have done damage, making Sally Ann the way she is."

"Selfish? Mean?" Sierra sighed. "Forget her. I'm through dredging up the past. It's the future I want to focus on now. You sure you want to go to Houston with me? Not only will you be surrounded by MacKenzies, but you'll have to deal with me in my pissy 'I hate hospitals' moods."

"I think I can handle it." He kissed her until she pushed at his chest.

"Then let's get moving. Let's see how many kolache shops there are between here and Houston." She laughed at his look of surprise.

"Woman, I sure am glad I killed Bambi in front of your gate that day." He pulled her back into his arms. "Even if you did almost shoot off my foot."

She kissed his smile. "It was a reckless shot that could have gone very wrong."

"I love reckless women. It's a story to tell our kids one day." Rhett laughed at her look of surprise. He'd save the proposal for later. But it was coming. Because Texas had his heart now. Texas and Sierra MacKenzie.

ABOUT THE AUTHOR

A nationally best-selling author, Gerry Bartlett is a native Texan who lives halfway between Houston and Galveston. She freely admits to a shopping addiction, which is why she has an antiques business on the historic Strand on Galveston Island. She used to be a gourmet cook but has decided it's more fun to indulge in gourmet eating instead. You can visit Gerry on Facebook, Twitter or Instagram. You can also check out her latest releases on her website at http://gerrybartlett.com where you can sign up for her newsletter or read her articles with advice for aspiring writers, The Perils of Publishing.

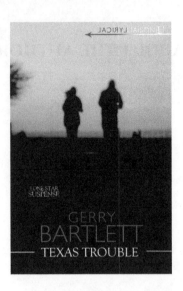

She was starting a new life in Texas—until old trouble turned up...

Scarlett Hall followed a job and a friend to Texas, but that cost her more than she'd bargained for. Now, wounded but determined to get past one of the worst days of her life, she decides she has to pull herself together. First step: cover up the physical scars left from her ordeal. That's easy. But the emotional scars are proving harder to handle...

Then she meets Ethan Calhoun. This bad boy seems ready to make his own changes and might be just what she needs to start a new chapter in her life. When he offers her a job as manager of his new bar, she decides to go for it. A change of pace and a hot guy who makes her forget her troubles while she's in his arms are a great cure. But it soon becomes clear that danger will be in Scarlett's life no matter how many changes she makes. As Scarlett comes face to face with her worst nightmare, it seems happiness was just an illusion. Maybe Texas is just too much trouble . .

A million-dollar idea. A city girl in the country. And a man who brings out her wild side…

Anna Delaney is thrilled to leave Boston for Austin, Texas, when her small tech company is bought out by a conglomerate. Born into a family of overprotective brothers, this is her chance at true independence—and a name-making professional breakthrough.

Even when gorgeous billionaire rancher King Sanders forms a one-man welcoming committee, Anna insists that she doesn't need a tour guide—or another bodyguard. But after she narrowly escapes a kidnapping attempt, she can't say no to King spiriting her away to someplace safe…and very private.

Someone wants the valuable software Anna's developing, and King is determined to keep her safe until the culprit is caught. The hunky cowboy lights her up brighter than the Lone Star sky at night, but neither one of them is prepared for just how wild Texas can get—and just how hard they're willing to fight to stay together…

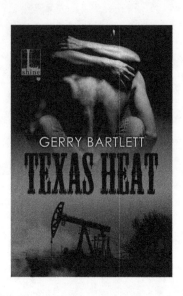

A surprise inheritance. A family of strangers. And a man she can't avoid...

Cassidy Calhoun can't believe she's the secret daughter of an oil billionaire. This small-town Texas girl with student loans by the barrel has never gotten a thing she didn't earn for herself.

The terms of her late father's will say Cassidy—and her newfound spoiled half siblings—must work a year at the family's floundering business before they inherit a dime. Too bad the only thing Cass knows about oil is that it makes the junker she drives go.

Mason MacKenzie, the evaluator for their test, will help her get up to speed. Or will he? Mason is a boot-wearing, truck-driving Houston hottie who runs Calhoun Petroleum's biggest rival. The sparks between him and Cassidy could combust any minute. But the closer they get, the more strange near accidents Cassidy seems to be having. And Mason has plenty of reasons to play up their attraction for his own benefit.

If she can trust him, the two of them working together might save a crumbling dynasty. But if she can't, Cass might just lose both her fortune and her heart...

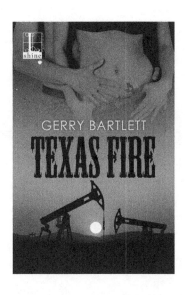

Her father's dream. Her crossroads. And a man who sees just her...

Megan Calhoun doesn't stick with anything long. She's the daughter of a billionaire—why pretend to be somebody else?

Until she finds out her father's will says she has to. She has to last a year in the oil patch, in the dust and heat of west Texas, working for her daddy's company. Otherwise she's cut off without a cent—and no way to earn one.

The only upside is her new pal Rowdy Baker, ex–football star, Calhoun engineer, and grade-A stud. If she has to live in a trailer, his doesn't sound so bad.

Rowdy knows the roughnecks running the rigs won't take kindly to a smartass blond rookie whose last name matches their paychecks. He can't control his attraction to her. And with everyone from the foremen to the stockholders spitting mad at the Calhouns, he expects trouble ahead.

But Megan has never been scared in her life. And with Rowdy to help her plot, she has the chance of a lifetime: to find her calling, to fix her company, and, if she doesn't screw it up—to capture a heart...

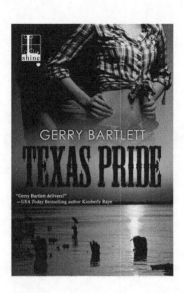

GERRY BARTLETT

TEXAS PRIDE

"Gerry Bartlett delivers!"
—*USA Today* Bestselling author Kimberly Raye

A fight for her rights. A job she can't quit. And a man who makes her burn...

It's not Shannon Calhoun's first rodeo. She's supposed to be running the show. But since her father's will landed her in a wretched cubicle, typing out press releases for her own family's company, she's been trapped in a job with no prospects, no control—and barely any cash.

When her old flame Billy Pagan turns up with a hundred rude questions and a thousand-dollar suit, Shannon isn't sure if the heat she feels is from humiliation, fury, or desire. But whatever else has happened, the chemistry between them has only intensified.

Long before he became Houston's best defense attorney, Billy had a thing for the spoiled rich girl who got away. But now that Shannon is hustling to save the family business, she's more irresistible than ever. Too bad about the murder investigation and the fraud that's going to bring the company crashing down around her.

Unless, of course, his Texas princess actually pulls off the save of a lifetime. With Billy's negotiating skills and Shannon's determination, the hardest part might be keeping the business away from the pleasure ...

Printed in the United States
by Baker & Taylor Publisher Services